# THE FAMILY

# THE FAMILY

P.R. Black

First published in the United Kingdom in 2019 by Aria, an imprint of Head of Zeus Ltd

Copyright © P.R. Black, 2019

The moral right of P.R. Black to be identified as the author of this work has been asserted in accordance with the Copyright, Designs and Patents Act of 1988.

All rights reserved. No part of this publication may be reproduced, stored in a retrieval system, or transmitted, in any form or by any means, electronic, mechanical, photocopying, recording, or otherwise, without the prior permission of both the copyright owner and the above publisher of this book.

This is a work of fiction. All characters, organizations, and events portrayed in this novel are either products of the author's imagination or are used fictitiously.

A CIP catalogue record for this book is available from the British Library.

ISBN 9781789543070

**Aria**
c/o Head of Zeus
First Floor East
5–8 Hardwick Street
London EC1R 4RG

www.ariafiction.com

*For Claire*

# I

Then

The night before they died, the two girls and their little brother shared the biggest room in the cottage.

Pillow fighting had long since given way to tired contemplation over cocoa as the candlelight flickered.

Becky Morgan lay back, one hand behind her head, the coconut smell of the sun cream lingering on her wrist. On the first night of their holiday, this was the best kind of tiredness. It made you impatient to be asleep, greedy for another day of fishing for sticklebacks with their nets, stone-skimming competitions, trailing their fingers in the water by the side of the boat, and considering ladybirds ambling across the backs of their hands and butterflies drifting just out of reach. It was the kind of tiredness that stopped short of exhaustion, but promised deep sleep.

Her younger brother Howie read the comic their dad had bought him on the ferry, his blanket pressed against his mouth – a gesture from infanthood he'd carried into his fifth year. He looked very seriously at Becky, and said, 'Is the man outside staying with us?'

'What man?' Becky said.

'The man who was hiding at the bins.'

'There's no man,' Becky said, suddenly alarmed.

Clara sighed. At 13, she was the eldest of the Morgan children, and, in her opinion, the cleverest and best-looking. 'He sees bogey men everywhere, don't you Howie?' she said. 'The other week there was a skeleton in the freezer.'

Becky raised an eyebrow. 'And was there?'

'Oh yes. We pretended it was ice cream. Dad ate the lot. He was none the wiser.'

'Could just be a ghost,' Becky said, a wicked gleam in her eye.

'Ghost? Where's the ghost?' Howie said.

The bedroom door opened slowly, startling them.

'Goodness me,' their father said, chuckling. 'You all look like you've seen a ghost!'

'Is there a ghost?' Howie asked.

''Course there isn't.' Their father wore an open dressing gown over striped blue and white pyjama bottoms, knotted at the front, and a T-shirt that struggled to contain his paunch. 'There's no such thing as ghosts. And if there was, I'd give it a bloody fright and a half.' He ruffled the boy's hair. 'I hope your sisters haven't been telling you silly stories.'

'It was the Middle Child's fault,' Clara sniffed. 'Pure and simple. She'll give that boy a complex.'

'I suspect the Elder Child might have a little something to do with it, too,' said their mother. She stood behind their father in the hallway. She was dressed for bed, and her long chestnut hair flowed over the shoulders of her nightgown. She reminded Becky of a vampire in a creaky old Hammer horror movie she'd stayed up to watch one night – lovely, but uncanny. She might smile and give them all a fright. 'Come on, now. Lights out. We've got another big day tomorrow.'

A hand touched Becky's shoulder in the middle of the night, startling her awake. She sat upright, disorientated for a moment in the unfamiliar room. It was lit only by a sliver of moonlight, keen as a razor through a crack in the curtains.

Howie stood by the side of her bed.

'What's up?' Becky said, rubbing her eyes.

The little boy spoke in a whisper, and his face was stricken in the moonlight. 'Becky… There's the man.'

'Don't be daft. Go on back to bed, now.'

'For god's sake…' mumbled Clara from the other side of the room, shifting beneath the sheets.

'Becky… There is. There *is* a man,' Howie insisted, his voice louder.

Becky sighed. 'Shut up, Howie. There are no ghosts. Come on – back to bed. You're not getting in here with me, if that's your game.'

'But there is a ghost. He's beside the wardrobe. I *see* him. Look!'

The little boy pointed.

And there, beside the wardrobe, breathing deeply through his mask, knife glinting, stood the man.

# 2

### Now

The man let himself into Becky's room, etched against the door, all in black. It was a tall, slim figure, without no definition other than the rudiments of the human shape. It seemed somehow less than shadow – a kind of anti-light, an anomaly.

In her bed, Becky wheezed at this apparition, fists clenched in the dark.

As before, the figure only ever gazed at her. Faceless, hands by its sides, it gazed down upon her.

Becky gave a low, mournful cry.

When the black hole in the face began to resolve itself into a mask, Becky finally screamed, and woke up.

The figure dissolved, absorbed into the gloom. There was only her room, in the dark, and her pounding heart. She groped for the nightlight switch, but her fingers were not quite awake yet, either, and the lamp slithered from her fingers and rolled across the floor. She kicked off the covers and stood, tense, her breath whining at the back of her throat. She felt the room spin in the darkness and had to catch her balance against the back wall, palms braced. Finally, she found the light switch.

Empty room. Nobody there. As ever.

She started her routine by checking her pulse, then her breathing, counting slowly. In, then out. She imagined the tension leaching from her shoulders, melting down her arms and dripping off her fingertips. Slow, steady breaths, and then the world settled back onto its axis, turning at the right speed, in the right direction. Her heartbeat became less erratic, more settled. Becky felt the sweat cooling on her back.

Then it was into the bathroom for a glass of water. The low-pitched light was perfect for these moments, less of a slap in the face with the click of the cord. She drew a glass of water and dared to look herself in the face, as if she might see cuts and bruises suffered as she slept. This was part of the process, staring herself in the eye. It was then that she saw the tears on her cheeks. She went with it, sobbing as quietly as she could, allowing the feelings to bleed out along with the tension.

She sat on the edge of the bed, occasionally wiping away the tears and blowing her nose. Her phone showed 03:32.

Becky sipped at the glass of water, then muttered, 'There goes sleep. Thanks again, mate. Thanks a lot.'

She settled down under the covers, knowing that there was no man – nor ghost, for that matter – in this flat, not here, not now. Just to be sure, she felt underneath the mattress for the knife handle.


Dr Fullerton was a compact, bearded man, his face still constrained by the one chin and his waist unusually trim and tight for someone in their late fifties. 'Three times a week at the gym,' he was fond of telling his patients. 'There's some good mental health – your starter for ten.'

He smiled kindly at Becky, sat opposite him. His consulting room was small, but not uncomfortably so, and the soft leather armchair swaddled her. 'How's your week been, first of all?' he asked.

'Not so bad. Just the one dream.'

'Last night, I take it?'

'Yes. Are you now a fully qualified mind reader?'

'Not quite. But you've yawned four times already.'

'What can I say? It's very cosy in here.'

'Tell me about your dream. Anything new?'

Becky clasped her hands. 'Nothing to report. Night terror. Sleep paralysis, the usual deal. The door opens. The guy comes in. He stands and watches me. I wake up gasping and thrashing like a landed fish. I feel for my knife. Then I lie awake with the light on and my eyes on the door, like a 6-year-old.'

Dr Fullerton nodded. 'What you're experiencing might be a typical night terror, in typical circumstances. But your experiences haven't been typical.'

Becky shrugged. 'That's why I'm here, I suppose. Lucky old you.'

'Has anything happened during the week to stress you out?'

'Not really.' She sighed. 'I guess there's one guy at work. He started a couple of months ago. A rising star. Tipped for the top. And by that I mean, an arsehole. Younger than me, annoyingly. Well spoken, but rude. Expensive suit. Seems like he drifted into journalism for larks, while he waits for his inheritance.'

'Yes, I think you mentioned something along those lines last time.'

'Do you remember that I told you he seemed nice enough, but had the potential to be a pillock?'

Fullerton studied his notes. 'This was the lad from Scotland?'

'That's him, yes. Well, he went for the "pillock" option. Started throwing his weight around in a matter of days. Picked on the weak point, which was clearly the woman. He gave me a dressing down in front of the office this week for a report I filed on a bus drivers' strike. "Not enough flavour," he said. "I know you can do better." He might as well have sent me away with a slap on the arse and told me to make the tea.'

Fullerton frowned. 'That doesn't sound very professional to me.'

'It isn't. But everyone looked the other way. When you get a new big dog on the floor, everyone falls into line. I asked for a meeting to discuss what happened.'

'Good. How did it go?'

'He keeps pulling out. I've half a mind to collar him in front of the office. But it was a couple of days ago. You know that way? I froze. The moment's gone.'

'How did you react to what he said? Once you got home?'

Becky gave a wan smile and swirled a plastic cup of water. Her hands were steady. 'Not by drinking, you'll be pleased to hear.'

'I am pleased to hear it. Are you ready to talk about the reconstruction?'

Becky took a sip. 'Sure. Why wouldn't I be?'

'It's bound to bring back a lot of feelings. Bad ones. Trigger points, and worse. How do you feel about being on television?'

'I see it as an ambition achieved. My friends always said I'd appear on *Crimewatch* one day. Though strictly speaking, I won't actually be on television. I'll be pixelated, like I'm behind frosted glass. And someone will be saying my lines for me – an actor. Hopefully Stephen Fry, or Patrick Stewart. Someone rrrich, and fruity.' She rolled her 'r's for effect.

Fullerton snorted. 'Mariella Frostrup for you, surely?'

'You old flirt. Really? I'm almost flattered. But yeah, I won't really be on TV. It's not like I'll be front and centre of the broadcast. Though I had considered it.'

'What good would that have done?'

'It might bring him out of cover.'

Fullerton gazed at her. 'What makes you think he would do that?'

'I'm unfinished business. No one forgets the one that got away. It's the same for killers as it is for the rest of us.'

'Don't you think that might be dangerous?'

She shrugged. 'I'm only doing it because it might lead to a positive result. I hope so. You do get these breaks in cases, years later. You hear about it. That kid who was snatched in Lincolnshire… Those two potholers in the Lake District… The killers don't stay ghosts. Not with forensic science, these days. Sometimes, the people who do these things get caught.'

'And if they don't?'

'I accept its unlikely, in my case. If they catch my guy, it'll probably be from a random positive result from a DNA test. Something that sets off an alarm on a database, after his second cousin twice removed gets pulled over for bald tyres. But I'm confident I'll see him in a courtroom one day.'

Fullerton considered his next question carefully. 'Have you thought about how you might feel if you see him again, if they do catch him?'

'Relieved, for a start. Goes without saying that he's dangerous.'

'Anything else?'

'Yeah. A little bit disappointed.'

'How so?'

Becky bit the inside of her mouth. 'Well, if they catch him, he'll end up in a nice cell. Maybe he lives in a hovel right now. Maybe he lives under a bridge. He's getting old, that's for sure. If he gets caught, he'll get to be comfortable. Might end up in a nice jail in the Netherlands. With a view of a canal, or an art gallery. People would be safe, though. That's something.'

'Have you thought about revenge?'

She sat forward. 'Asking me if I've thought about revenge is a bit like asking Godzilla if he ever thinks about Tokyo. Yeah. I've thought about revenge. Wouldn't be human otherwise, would I?'

'Violence?'

'Humane violence. A nice orderly lynching, they used to call it. A bullet to the head. Something clean. Not violence like... like what he did. That wouldn't be justice. He'd deserve it, that's for sure. But it's not something I could do.

Not many people are capable of that. There aren't many people on that shelf. So no, I don't think about killing him.'

'I'm not sure I believe you.'

She made no response to that.

He glanced at his watch. 'We're almost out of time.'

'Said the working girl to the parson.'

'Nice imagery.' He smiled, kindly. 'I'll be on call tonight, Becky, if you need me. Out-of-hours, for one night only. No payment necessary. Any issues resulting from that programme, you let me know about them.'

'You're never usually this worried about me.'

'Your problems are never usually aired on national television, when you've spent twenty years trying to deal with them. It's bringing what happened very close to the surface.'

'I'll be fine.'

'Have you got company tonight? Friends... work colleagues?'

Becky shook her head.

'It might be an idea to spend the evening with someone. Especially if you insist on watching the show.'

'It's nothing I haven't seen before.'

'Quite. Just making sure you know. Any other questions today?'

'Yeah. What shoe size are you?'

He raised his feet, displaying a heavy pair of deep-tread shoes, with large heels. She wondered at the psychology of a therapist's need to wear thick-soled shoes to appear taller, and smiled.

'I'm a ten,' he said. 'What makes you ask that?'

'Just curious. You've got kinda big feet.'

# 3

Becky drained her gin and tonic, fished out the lime and sucked on it. The bar was chrome-plated and poorly lit; everything shone, but without any real brilliance. It reminded her of a dingy public toilet. It was Monday-night-quiet, and the big screen in the corner was turned over from a football match, at her request. There were no complaints from the sparse clientele. Becky braced her elbows on the bar's uncomfortably clinical surface, waiting for her part of the show.

On screen, the presenter perched on the end of the desk, clipboard held loosely in his hand.

'Now,' he said, 'we have a special report on the twentieth anniversary of one of the most notorious unsolved crimes in the modern era. We take you back to a fine May day, in the South of France. A family of five have just arrived at a holiday cottage in the picturesque Grange aux la Croix valley. An idyllic spot… but one which would bear witness to unspeakable horror.'

Becky gestured with her glass towards the barman. He frowned and reached for a fresh tumbler.

Back on the big screen, the image dissolved into a long shot of deep green pasture with a white cottage at the bottom right.

'11th May 1999. And the Morgan family have arrived for a holiday in the south of France at the picturesque cottage, *Les Deux Chevaliers*.'

Becky smiled at the parade of figures on-screen. It was them, but not them. A boy with fashionably unkempt hair and modern trainers, young, but still much too old to be Howie. He was followed by a tall poppy of a goth – Clara. This girl had a stud through her nose, red streaks in her hair and thick black eyeshadow, which Clara never had. But the vintage Mötley Crüe T-shirt – *Shout at the Devil*, with pentagram, slashed above the navel – was correct and proportionate.

The man representing her father was way too stout, while the woman playing her mother was too plain, although the hair colouring was a perfect fit.

The on-screen Becky looked a little too young.

'I guess I *was* 11,' she muttered, handing the barman some cash and sipping a fresh G&T.

Then Becky – the real Becky – appeared in silhouette, with her face pixelated out. The text at the bottom of the screen read, 'Actor's voice'.

'It was a beautiful day,' said the actor. 'We'd been out on a boat, and it seemed like we had the whole world to ourselves. But... we didn't.'

The next shot established that it was night time. The cottage was brightly lit, as seen from a distance. Then a dark figure stepped in front of the camera, blocking out the light.

Becky nearly spilled her drink.

At that moment, someone sat down on the stool next to her, his face a beige smudge on the brushed chrome bar. Becky ignored him, watching the ersatz Morgan children saying goodnight to their mother and father.

'Artistic licence,' she muttered. 'Mum didn't wear pyjamas.'.

The man next to her scratched his chin and said, 'Oh, strewth. I remember that case. Horrible. Family that got done in France, wasn't it?'

Becky glanced at him. He was in his late thirties, chubby, with a fringe combed down at both sides to disguise the slow retreat of his hairline. He still had today's work clothes on – a battered jacket, his tie loose, top button undone.

'Yeah,' she said. 'Nasty one, wasn't it?'

He supped at a pint of beer. 'Hell of a case. Ritual thing, they reckon.'

'Spoilers!' She gripped his forearm. 'Wait and see.'

On the TV, blue light flooded the children's bedroom. The music swelled, as the same dark figure blotted out the light. The young Becky woke up to Howie tugging at the sleeve of her pyjama top. 'Becky... there's a man,' the boy said.

On-screen Becky looked up. Her eyes widened in shock.

The real Becky looked down at her drink, focusing on the surging bubbles. She had made a pact with herself earlier not to look at the mask and had no intention of breaking it.

The man on the stool next to her sucked in breath through his teeth. 'God almighty. Imagine waking up to *that*. Terrifying.'

Becky looked up. They had cut to another long-shot of the house, with all the lights down. A muffled scream echoed out across the moonlit fields.

'It doesn't look like much fun,' Becky said, then swallowed the G&T in one gulp. She turned to the man. 'If you were thinking of asking, I'll have a gin and tonic. If you weren't... then shut up.'

The man blinked for a few seconds, then grinned. To her surprise, he ordered two G&Ts.

On-screen, it was daytime, and a young girl was seen running from the trees into a clearing. She was still wearing her pyjamas, which was another example of artistic licence, though Becky had to give the director credit for the blood spatters.

There, in the clearing, was a teenage boy, walking a dog. The dog barked at the young Becky's approach.

'Help!' the girl cried. 'Somebody help me!'

The presenter's voice returned, as images of Becky's real family were shown, culled from family albums. Smiling photos, happy photos. One of her mother and father taken at a wedding they had attended a few years before Howie was born, the clothes, hairstyles and make-up jarringly old-fashioned. The reds, yellows, oranges, blacks and browns in the analogue photos were bleached out, the fine grain lost. All that remained was blue.

'Four members of the Morgan family were murdered the next morning, after an ordeal that lasted hours,' the presenter said. 'Eleven-year-old Becky Morgan was able to escape and find help, despite being pursued through the forest by her attacker – a situation that almost doesn't bear thinking about.

'The rest of the family were sexually assaulted, tortured and finally stabbed to death in an attack which was described by local police as ritualistic. Despite a Europe-wide manhunt that lasted years, the killer was never caught.'

The camera returned to the present-day, pixelated Becky. 'I still dream of the night it happened,' the actress said. 'I'll never forget that man standing over the bed, and the things he did to us. There are times when I wished he'd killed me too.'

The man on the bar stool beside her placed down a G&T. 'Here you go, smile-a-while.'

'"Smile-a-while", did you say?'

'Yes.' The man grinned. 'Don't take it so hard. It was a joke, love.'

'Well, your joke's not very funny, "love",' she said. 'You might need a new scriptwriter.' She snatched up the fresh drink, spilling a good deal of it down her chin.

'Oops, missed the target. Here.' The man offered her a napkin from the bar.

Becky dabbed it against her chin. 'Thanks,' she mumbled.

'Long night, eh?'

She held up her hand. 'Just a minute, please.'

On-screen, the presenter spoke to a big-boned, cherry-cheeked man in a mismatching suit jacket and trousers, all flesh and girth and clearly uncomfortable under the studio lights.

'We join Inspector Thomas Hanlon now. Inspector, you're in charge of the cold case review. Clearly this is a horrifying incident that's ruined so many lives.'

'Yes indeed,' Hanlon said, gravely. 'And I'd just like to say thank you to the brave young lady who survived the incident for agreeing to talk about what happened. A lot of the details are too upsetting to describe, even at this time of night, and we can only imagine what she went through as a girl of just 11.'

'Let's turn to the perpetrator – who is it we're looking for?'

'I'm afraid that clues are few and far between, which is why it's taken so long to find him. He never showed his face, but what we can say is that the man we're looking for was around six feet tall or more, well-built, and probably aged between 25 and 40 – certainly a young, fit man. That means he'd be between 45 and 60 today, of course. He had a strong accent – not English, and, we think, not French, but perhaps Eastern European.'

The presenter faced the camera. 'I apologise to viewers in advance, as this is a particularly distressing detail. But we have to talk about the mask.'

Becky looked away.

'Yes,' said Inspector Hanlon. 'As far as we can tell, it was *this* mask.'

'We should stress, this is an artist's interpretation,' the presenter added.

'Yes. This object seems to have been created by the killer himself. We believe it's made of real bone, attached to some dark cloth. It's nothing that was available in fancy dress shops, but it is just possible that someone, somewhere, might remember a man buying this mask from a specialist shop.'

'It's difficult to imagine what that poor girl must have gone through.'

Becky toasted the TV screen. 'Don't have nightmares,' she said, remembering the final words uttered by the presenter who hosted an earlier series of Crimewatch.

On-screen, the presenter said, 'Inspector, what more can you tell us about what the killer was wearing?'

'When he arrived at the cottage, he wore all-black clothing. The only other clue we have is that he had size-fourteen feet, going by footprints left at the scene. He was wearing these shoes...'

The man beside Becky said, 'I bet he wasn't wearing all-black clothing when he got going. He might have kept his shoes on, though, for a quick getaway.'

She glanced at him for a moment – and then *he* was wearing her G&T.

Rivulets meandered down his jowls like tears, and a sliver of lemon clung to his chin like a slug on a bannister losing its fight with gravity.

'What do you think you're doing?' he spluttered.

'Hey.' The barman pointed at her. 'You've had enough, love. Out.'

'I was just going. *Love.*' Becky lurched to her feet, clinging to the counter until her shoes found purchase, and then strode out the door.

The bar was set in the basement of a refurbished tenement block, and Becky had got halfway up the stairs to street level when the man who'd sat beside her gripped her shoulder. She gasped and clung onto the railings to avoid falling backwards.

The man's hair was still plastered to his forehead with her gin. He looked like a young boy grotesquely groomed by his mother for church.

'I dunno who you think you are, freak,' he snarled, 'but you're lucky I don't kick you up and down this street.'

Becky jerked her shoulder clear of his grasp and hurried up the rest of the stairs. The man followed. On the even ground, she spun to face him. He did not stop.

'Don't touch me,' she said.

'Touch you? I wouldn't dream of touching you. Miserable cow.' Still, he came forward, teeth gritted. Something glinted in his hand. When she realised that it was his own half-finished G&T, primed and ready to throw, fear gave way to rage. Becky lunged.

The heel of her hand smacked into the centre of his face with a flat, ugly crunch. His glass of G&T tinkled back down the stairs as he gaped in stupefaction, blood gushing from his nose.

Becky gripped him by his dog-eared lapels, spun on her heels and hurled him against the railings.

The man clattered into the ironwork then pitched backwards, flat-out on the pavement. After a second or two he sat up, blinking, blood glossing his lower jaw and drenching his shirtfront. The railings were still reverberating.

Across the street, someone shouted, 'Hey!'

Becky turned, and began to run.

# 4

Becky rose as a scuba diver might, in order not to pop her lungs. She had a cotton wool mouth and a cattle tongue, and her brain suppurated with that slow-pulsing pain that signalled a hangover – a good one.

The white, sparse walls of her own bedroom surrounded her, so that was something. She was alone, and that was something else.

A sound had woken her; low, steady peals, muffled like everything else in her universe. Her alarm? Surely it was way too early for that, barely even full light beyond the gauzy curtains. As she groped for her phone, pain jolted her wrist, and with it came familiar feelings of dread and shame. That kind of pain usually meant there had been a fall, or perhaps a push – with a fist attached. She checked her knuckles; they were unscabbed, and so was her face, although there was a slight twinge at the uppermost arch of her right eyebrow.

She found her phone under her pillow. It was silent, but the pealing sound continued. Not from her phone, then.

Abruptly, the tones shut off. Then the floorboards creaked outside her door.

After a knock, a figure stepped inside, indistinct in the morning's gloom, as if filtered through a smokescreen.

Becky's cry choked in her throat. She was not asleep, nor was she paralysed. She sat up as if on a spring, and the edge of her fingers found the knife handle in a well-practised move. She tore the blade from underneath the mattress.

Lights flared in her head as she leapt from the bed. The quilt clutched at her ankles and she stumbled, giving the shadow face enough time to resolve itself – not into a mask, but a face she knew.

'Christ almighty! Becky, it's me!'

Becky stumbled, dropping the machete.

'Aaron!'

'You off bushwhacking, Becky?' the man spluttered, indicating the machete. 'What the hell have you got that for?'

Her head spun, and throbbed. 'It goes with my pyjamas. Never bloody mind! What are you doing here?'

'Take it easy, it's okay.' Aaron raised his hands. 'I stayed over.'

'What for, exactly?' Becky wore a long nightshirt with a big-eyed cartoon pig stencilled on the front. She still had her underwear on. This, too, was a good thing, although it pointed towards someone other than herself undressing her for bed. She grabbed a dressing gown from the back of a chair and threw it over her shoulders.

Although she was decent, Aaron Stilwell averted his eyes anyway. He was dressed for work and seemed to have had a shave and a shower. His forehead was a little too big for his hair and his cheeks had filled out in the six years they'd known each other. A cute little pot belly, which he was absurdly touchy about, hugged the waistline of his working trousers.

'I take it you don't recall last night's fun and games, then?' he asked.

'Do I want to?'

But she did. The ugly collision between the heel of her hand and someone's face. She could have sworn she felt his flesh ripple with the impact. Jesus. *Jesus*. She covered her face with her hands.

'Come on,' Aaron said. 'I've got some coffee. See how we go.'


Aaron had made himself busy in her kitchen. While not quite going so far as to break out the bleach, he'd certainly tidied away the dishes that inhabited a vicious cycle of table-sink-draining board. The overflowing bin had been emptied, too.

Best of all, he'd drained the swamp of ancient grounds in the coffee machine and made a fresh pot. Becky poured a cup, took a sip, sighed, and said, 'Aaron Stilwell: the house invader who tidies up for you.'

'You asked me to stay over, Becky. Not like that,' he added, quickly.

'Like what, then?'

'Seriously? You don't remember *any* of it?'

'Humour me. Take it from the top.'

'All right. We'll start with the drunken phone call. Something about "mincing some guy through the railings". You remember that?'

'Yeah, that bit I understand.' She massaged the joint of her wrist and hand. What if he was dead? Had he hit his head on the way down? Becky must have read dozens of horribly similar police releases over years and years of Sunday morning shifts. One punch, then down and out. Head, meet pavement. Game over. You threw a punch after a night on the pop, all of a sudden, you were a murderer. She literally writhed in her seat with dread and shame, clutching her stomach.

'Okay. So I came out to The Flutterby, where you said you'd be. You weren't there, but the bartender frowned when I described you and mentioned that the chap on the doors had escorted you out. I noticed a potted plant near the ladies' had been split in half. There were some footprints in the loose soil which may have matched your own. It felt like *Cinderella*, just in an evil parallel universe.'

Becky shrugged and sipped her coffee.

'From there, the tale gets more interesting. You had mentioned McGlashan's, and that it was lame. This is when I followed a hunch, guessing correctly that you'd already transferred from there into Bingo across the road.'

'Bingo? What the hell is that?'

'You know it, or you must have gone past it a few times. Bell Street. Pink neon. Eighties retro style, or trying to be. Most of the bar staff weren't even born then.'

'I think I've got you.'

'Now picture the scene. You're talking to two guys at the bar just as I walk in. They're playing Duran Duran. "The Reflex". One of the two guys with you is singing it at the top of his voice. His eyes are all pupils, no whites that I can see.'

'I get the feeling you're building up to some kind of grand finale.'

'And here it comes. You spot me coming across the bar, and you say something to one of the two guys. These guys have that look of two people who had just landed after being stuck on an oil rig for a fortnight. Or maybe they'd just got out of jail. Anyway, before I can even open my mouth to say hello, the smaller one comes over to me and says, "I've heard all about you. Get stuffed, or you'll get your head to play with."'

Becky's stomach roiled. It wasn't just the coffee. 'Colourful phrasing.'

'Fortunately you could still run, by this point, and proceeded to the nearest convenient exit. I decided this was a superb idea and followed you, double-time.'

Becky frowned, and pointed to her eyebrow. 'So how did I get this bruise, then?'

'Oh, I haven't finished the story yet. So finally I get you back to the car. You've taken your shoes off, and insist on throwing them in the back of the car before getting in. So I humour you, and then you click open the boot. You start rummaging around in there, trying to open my bag... and you smack your head on the edge of the boot. You're not unconscious... well, not quite, but your head is in the boot, and your backside is stuck in the air like a bloody peacock. It's at this point, while I'm trying to lift you out by the legs, that the police take an interest in our adventures.'

'Oh god. Aaron... I don't remember any of this. I'm sorry, it was an unusual night for me. There was stuff going on in the background.'

'You kept saying something about a mask. And you shouted at the policeman, something about taking twenty years to sort out something so simple. You're lucky you didn't get jailed. I talked them out of it. They seemed amused, more than annoyed. It's just as well they hadn't spoken to anyone in Flutterby. So finally, I got you back here. And for the record, you got yourself undressed. Well, you paraded around in your knickers until I dug your nightshirt out, truth be told.'

'Nothing you haven't seen before,' she mumbled.

'By the time you calmed down and got to sleep, it was 2 a.m. So I crashed out on the couch. Luckily, I know to bring an overnight bag when you call me up in the middle of a lapse.'

'"Lapse". I don't like that word.'

'It's an excellent chapter title for last night's farce. As good as I can think of.' A high colour had crept into his normally pallid cheeks, and he fiddled savagely with his cufflinks. 'Look, I'm not going to lecture you. But I think you should come back to meetings with me.'

'I'm fine, Aaron. Honestly. I feel better already. I had a bad night. I should probably have gone home after work, but I came off the rails. Part of me wanted to come off the rails. I started and couldn't stop. You know the drill.'

Aaron drained his coffee and threw on his suit jacket. He fished around in his pocket. 'Here. They've got a new number. In case you decide to go back without me.'

'I told you – I'm not into the praying and spiritual stuff. Does nothing for me. Plus... I'm in control.'

'Not from where I was standing. Are you joking?'

She let that stand.

'Anyway,' he said. 'You got work today?'

'I do. I've got to give the boss the good news.'.

'Are you sure this is the right thing for you? All that dead time?'

'Without a doubt,' she said coldly. 'And it won't be dead time, I can assure you. I'll be busy.' She checked her watch. 'Why are you up so early, anyway?'

'So I could make sure I'd got you into some sort of fit state. This is old territory for me, remember.'

Becky bit the side of her mouth. 'Thanks, Aaron.'

He smiled and patted her on the shoulder. 'De nada. Take care. Give me a call. Think about coming to the next meeting. You're always welcome. And good luck with the boss.'

As soon as he was gone, she switched on her laptop and checked her work emails for something from the police. She knew how it would be worded, its banal rhythms:

*A 45-year-old male was found unresponsive in the street at approximately 10.30 p.m. He is believed to have suffered an assault, and was taken to hospital where he was pronounced dead. Officers are looking for a woman aged in her late twenties to early thirties, five foot eight, with long shoulder-length dark hair...*

But there was nothing. He'd got up. He'd let it bleed. He'd gone home. Perhaps he'd had some explaining to do to his wife. And perhaps, if there was some grand plan in the universe, no harm had truly been done.

'But that is that,' she whispered to herself. She spread her fingers and watched them shake. 'That is definitely that, for now. That's you and me finished, Mr Gin.'

With a little bit of time to kill and a pressing need to think about something other than what had happened the previous night, she crossed to the back room. There was no bed in there, just a table and chairs and an extendable lamp bent out of shape. Dominating one wall was a map of Europe. On the desk lay a folder filled with printouts from the international news wires and even newspaper cuttings. She had circled one printout, taken from the AP wire two days before.

### Russian police draw blank over Gursky family disappearance.

MOSCOW: Mystery surrounded the disappearance of the Russian oligarch Maxim Gursky and his wife and daughter as they drove to an airport 150 miles outside Moscow. Gursky, a controversial figure who made his fortune in steel and other commodities before expanding into pro-Russian media channels, had been driving with his family a short distance from his rural retreat to an airfield where his private plane was ready to take him to a media awards dinner in Stockholm. But Gursky, 51, his wife, Emelda, 34, and daughter Bella, 12, never arrived, and no trace has been found of the high-spec Mercedes they were travelling in. Rumours abound that Gursky had Russian mafia connections. Other commentators have theorised that Gursky had become overly critical of the Russian government of late, with some wondering if the media baron was pushing for a regime change, culminating in a possible tilt at the presidency himself. However, police have said that there are some indications that Gursky had been suffering from depression, and notes that were left at the family home hinted at a possible tragedy.

Next to this was a scanned copy of an old newspaper cutting. The scan was so good that the ingrained texture of the yellowed newsprint had been faithfully represented in the printout. It was only a short news-in-brief paragraph.

**Family horror in Orkneys**

Police have ruled out foul play in the case of a family found dead at their remote home in the Orkney Islands. Officers said they are not looking for anyone else in connection with the case.

She double-checked a locator graphic on her phone, then turned to the map of Europe. She took a coloured pin and stuck it in the rough location of the Russian disappearance.

There were several of these, now, dotted around Europe. Becky studied the map for a moment more, then gathered her things for work.

Him

The girl refused to take her hands away from her eyes. Covering her face was the first thing she had done when he had taken the bonds off. She had made no attempt to escape from the room – only to escape the sight of him.

They were in a portable builder's cabin. He had lit some candles, eschewing the brutal strip-lighting.

Outside the window, torchlight flickered, lending the dark trees a febrile animation. Worse than that was the sound; a suggestion of music or singing.

He drew up a seat and sat in front of the girl. 'Are you thirsty?' he said.

'Where's Mama?'

'Mama's safe, now,' he said. 'She is in good hands.'

She pressed her hands tighter against her eyes and shook her head. 'Are you going to hurt me?'

'I'm not sure. That depends on how you answer my next question.'

Slowly, the girl peeled her hands away from her eyes. Then she flinched.

The mask leered at her from the gloom, its rotten yellow surfaces burnished by the candlelight. 'How would you like to go on an adventure?'

# 5

Becky had expected a day of general calamity while her hangover remained on life support, but the Skype connection on her computer at work was pixel-perfect.

Andrei from the wire service in Moscow was younger than Becky supposed, with short spiky hair, glasses and a thick-lipped smile. He might have looked perfect as a student in the mid-eighties; she could see him on a bicycle, trailing a scarf.

'Becky! How nice to see you!' He waved. 'Always nice to put a face to an email address!'

'Ah, likewise. I'm not bad, Andrei. Nice of you to agree to this.'

'Not a problem. You want to know a little more about Mr Gursky?'

'Colourful character, I take it?'

'That would be correct. Well, he has always been involved in the steel trade, so he has always been linked to unsavoury people. Mafia, in particular. But he enjoys the spotlight. Many feel he would have a natural home in politics. Always presentable. A confident man, that's what we would say.'

'Lots of enemies, then?'

'Oh, for sure. It would be odd to get to that position in life and not upset anyone.'

'The police don't seem to have any leads or clues.'

'No, and that does seem odd. It's as if they want Mr Gursky to go away.'

Becky tapped her notepad with her pen. 'This is why I wanted to talk to you about him. I always hear rumours of allegations that he was involved in criminal activity – but there's never been anything concrete. Can you say what some of these were? I promise it's off the record.'

'Well...' Andrei looked uncertain. 'Mr Gursky is... or maybe was, we should say... extremely litigious. So no stories made it out either at home or abroad. But Mr Gursky was apparently linked to human trafficking, prostitution... there were hints that he was into darker things, still.'

Becky sat up. 'Darker things?'

'Again, I must say, this is the stuff of gossip in a bar. There were rumours that he had very odd tastes. That he was involved in some sort of sex ring, very dark things, murders, even. He is a very rich, very media-conscious, very charismatic white man, so as you can imagine this opened up many opportunities for exploitation over the years, were he to be involved in anything like that.'

'Yeah, we've had a few of those sorts in our country.'

'There was nothing to link him to any of the rumours, and something mentioned in silliness has a way of turning into a full-blown rumour by word of mouth, even in the digital age. There was a story about a pay-off for a girl from Volgograd, but it disappeared quickly enough. I have to say we never found anything of a sinister nature whenever we investigated him. That's not surprising, as any inquiries about Mr Gursky tended to hit a brick wall. There is very little about him in any public records – tax offices, employment invoices, things of that nature. When you have billions in the bank, it's quite simple to click your fingers and make anything awkward or unsavoury disappear.'

'Strange that his family vanished along with him. Any chance they've simply tried to escape? Maybe there were financial problems he had to get away from, legal issues…?'

Andrei shook his head. 'None that we know of. He was flirting with political ambitions, but making him disappear would have been an outrageous move – too much even for our current government. They would have engineered something they could easily deny, like a plane crash, if that was the motive. A disappearance is a big question mark no one wants to have hanging over them.

'Also, we think that if Gursky and his family were going to vanish, they would probably have taken the private plane that was fuelled up and waiting for them – there would have been nothing to stop them. Once they were out of Russia it would have been a simple matter to disappear from there. But they didn't. It seems a strange way of going to ground. Surely the first priority would be to leave the country. I think they were abducted, Becky, and we probably won't see them again. As to why – who knows?'

'One other question for you, Andrei, and it may seem a little strange – are there any monuments in the area where Gursky disappeared?'

'Monuments? What do you mean?'

'Ancient things – like cairns, stone age settlements, or standing stones?'

'Not that I know of. There's a lot of forest though. Unspoiled forest, apart from the road. Going back thousands of years.'


Becky carefully punched in the number she'd taken from the book of general contacts in the library section.

A calm, sober voice with a very heavy accent answered on the second ring. 'Five-three-two-one.'

'Hi there, would I be speaking to Chief Inspector Colin Raeside?'

'Retired, yes. Who am I speaking to?'

'Ah, hello, just the man I am looking for. You don't know me, but my name's Becky Hughes. I'm a journalist, and I'm researching a story that took place on the island.'

'Oh. I see.'

'Yes. It relates to the Sloan family. Would that case be familiar to you? It was way back in 1984.'

'Sloan?' There was a slight faltering in the voice, the first sign that Becky was talking to an old man. 'Sloan, you said, is that right?'

'That's right.'

There was a deep sigh. 'Listen, there's not much to be said about the Sloan family. I get these calls, now and again, and I've never appreciated one of them.'

'You were the senior investigating officer on the case at the initial stage, is that right?'

'That's correct.'

'So you knew the island well, and a lot of the people on it?'

'I'm an Orcadian. Born and bred,' Raeside said, stoutly.

'As they died on your patch, you must have known about the Sloans, then?'

'Not much. I think Mr Sloan might have contacted us once about the young dafties tearing up and down the road on moto-cross bikes, and we put a stop to it. That was all.'

'You didn't meet them socially, maybe at church, or a community event?'

'No. The islands are funny that way. Some people come here so they can be cut off. That's the goal. And you get people going the other way – teenagers who've grown up here, desperate to leave, to get to the mainland, to start a life where there's more people. The Sloans didn't just come to Orkney for peace and quiet. They wanted to get away from *everything* – down to their neighbours. I gathered that Mr Sloan was some kind of survivalist. Thought a nuclear war was coming, and he could ride it out up here with us. Growing his own food, keeping his own livestock. Only it didn't work out.'

'Do you know what happened?'

'Just what you read from the inquest, no doubt,' Raeside said, tartly. 'Something went badly wrong. What was left of their four walls would tell you if they could, nobody else. Maybe Mrs Sloan decided that life wasn't for her, and she wanted out. Maybe the kids weren't adjusting. Or maybe it was this great big time bomb that had always been ticking away in his head. We'll never know for sure. What we do know is that he murdered his family, then killed himself.'

'No sign it might have been any outside agency? Made to look like murder-suicide?'

'Oh, love, the amount of times I've heard that one. You think we'd have missed that? You reckon we're still to discover forensics up here, or something? It was open-and-shut. There was no one else around. Sloan lost the plot, that's all there is to it. I'm tired of people trying to link it to something it wasn't. It's happened before, up here. I hope to Christ it never happens again.'

'There wasn't any suggestion of wife-swapping, something going wrong there? Murky, organised stuff among the islanders? That's the rumours I heard.'

'Fairy stories. People making something out of nothing. They see an island, they meet islanders, they imagine things. There's no truth to that at all.'

'Officers from the mainland took over the investigation quite soon afterwards, didn't they?'

'Yes,' he said, as if from behind the teeth. 'And our conclusions were identical.'

'It's been very difficult to get hold of the final report from the fatal accident inquiry.'

'Well...' Raeside coughed. 'It's true there were elements that people didn't want to get out. That was on the grounds of taste and decency. The sheriff at the time made an order not to release certain details, but there's nothing unusual in itself about that.'

'What details exactly?'

'The sheriff ordered them sealed, so they're sealed. Now, there were some politicians who would rather have kept the whole thing quiet. No use upsetting people, giving the islands a bad rep, that kind of thing.'

'Who were they?'

'It doesn't matter. They didn't succeed. The inquiry's conclusions were correct. They tallied in with ours. Whatever you're trying to find here, it simply isn't there.'

Becky wrote 'politicians' on her pad, in longhand. Then she said, 'Another question… It's hard to tell from the maps that are online, but didn't there used to be a stone circle near the Sloans' farm?'

'Yeah. Not much of a stone circle, mind. There's a theory that some lunatic made it themselves in the fifties, rather than cavemen or whatever. Most of it's been vandalised or fallen over by now. Overgrown.'

'And would this have been close to the Sloans' farm? Like, walking distance?'

'You're the journalist. Come up here and investigate.' The line went dead.

Jarrod had turned his corner of the office into a cosy little nook that Becky secretly envied. He lived in the IT station, a bank of desks that had once been staffed mainly by men in their twenties, always vaguely grubby, always vaguely threatening. On Saturdays during the football, it had turned into a total zoo, grown men shrieking and clutching themselves before the big screens. Any time she'd had to venture over there to speak to someone directly, Becky had felt uneasy. Thanks to the general direction of the newspaper industry and the wider economy, the IT station was something of a ghost ship, now. One or two heads were dotted round the desks, but now it was a lonely place.

Jarrod's corner had a few band pictures up, though he was surely closer to 30 than his teenage years. Cacti spiked the top of his desk, on either side of a framed black-and-white picture of a girl with a deep dimple in her chin and her fringe cut square across her forehead. Jarrod was tall and very good-looking, with a clear brow and long, unruly dark blond curls that reminded Becky of wheat. He had the look and demeanour of a rock star, and many people thought him aloof. But Becky knew for a fact that he was simply shy, a face badly out of sync with the personality behind it.

'Hey,' she said, startling him. 'I want to say thanks for that copy you ran off for me – works like a dream.'

He turned sharply, pulling off a set of headphones and pausing what he'd been watching on his computer. 'No worries... Yeah, good material, that.'

'No security alert, no online scan prompt, no flashing lights and alarms... nothing. Foolproof. Only your friendly neighbourhood pirate knows for sure.'

'Well, yeah. I think I said we should keep it on the QT, though?'

'Oh sure, mum's the word. Something I wanted to pick your brains about, though...' She wheeled a chair towards him and sat down. Their knees almost touched, and he visibly recoiled. 'I guess you know your way round certain things. You're just about the best in here.'

'I wouldn't go that far.'

'Ah, don't be coy, Jarrod. You're the only person who seems to actually care and get stuff fixed.'

He shrugged, struggling to make eye contact. 'It's a job.'

'I wonder if you could help out with one or two things I need to check.'

'Is this for you, or for something in here?'

'Something for me.'

'And what kind of thing do you want to check?'

'See, I've got this thing about politicians. Not a "thing", god, that's not the right way to put it. I am a little bit suspicious about some public officials, and there's one or two little checks I want carried out.'

He sipped what was left of a coffee. 'Freedom of Information is your friend.'

'It's not open public information I'm looking for. It's something dirtier than that.'

'Oh.'

'A long inquiry. Using some information that wouldn't come up on a Google search. By someone who would like to see what public officials do brought into the light. You'd like that, wouldn't you Jarrod? Or you know people who like that kind of thing?' Jarrod's green army-style jacket was draped over the back of his chair. Becky traced an 'Anarchy' symbol decal stitched into one of the shoulders.

'That'll be difficult.'

'But you maybe know someone who could help?'

He shrugged. 'I could ask.'

'That'd be good. Could you ask them soon?'

'I could maybe do that.'

'Could you maybe give me a number to call?'

'No, they'll call you.'

'I'd best give you a number then.' She did so, using a burner phone she'd bought the other day.

37

'It'll cost,' he said. 'I'll say that upfront. A bit more than a knock-off version of Office.'

'That's absolutely fine. So long as I get what I pay for.'

'Leave it with me.' He replaced his headphones. 'I'll do it as a favour. But I'll deny I ever spoke to you. I'd advise you to do the same for me.'

'Of course.'

'There'll be some code words, when they get in touch. You've got two things to remember. Number one, you're Jessica Rabbit.'

'I'm not sure how I feel about that, but okay.'

Jarrod waved his hand, irritably. 'This is important. The second thing to remember is the position of the mouse. Which is in the grandfather clock, in his house.'

'This is great!'

'Don't write it down. Seriously – just remember it. No records. All right?'

'Sure. Thanks. Ah, you're a love, Jarrod. By the way, fascinating blog you wrote. The one about Jesus coming from Tahiti?'

He frowned and turned towards the screen. 'I'm a bit busy, Becky. Speak soon.'

'Not to worry Jarrod. I've got a meeting, as it happens.'

Apart from a persistent tic at the corner of her good eye, Becky had just about annulled the pain and most of the shame by the time she caught up with the Human Resources lady at one of the country's last remaining mid-market tabloids, The Mortar. The woman, whose name was

Rose, hefted a folder full of material like a battleaxe, but she seemed a little embarrassed to be there.

'Devin will be along in a minute,' Rose said, as she unlocked the conference room.

'Doing his "I'm late" routine, I guess. He usually saves that for the university kids he takes for interview.'

'I don't think you should mention that, Becky.'

'Best we sit in awkward silence, then.'

Rose did not smile at this.

Becky studied a sheet outlining the formal procedures, the only blemish on top of a long table buffed to a high sheen. She could remember when this room was full during the daily conference, when news editors and senior reporters would go through the agenda of the day. That had been less than seven years ago, but now only a handful of people were involved, and the vast empty spaces throughout The Mortar building told a sad story of an industry in denial.

Rose coughed occasionally to break the absolute silence.

The door burst open a few minutes later, and Devin McCance squeezed his bulk inside. He was still in his twenties, a tall, thick-set man with spiky blond hair and startling blue eyes which lent him the look of a truculent child. A survivor of bad skin in his teens, his cheeks looked corrugated in a certain light, but this didn't spoil his looks. What came out of his mouth did that instead.

'Sorry I'm late,' he mumbled, pulling out a seat opposite Becky and Rose.

Rose cleared her throat and squared her paperwork. 'If we could just get started?'

Becky said, 'Well, in a nutshell – why can't I go on sabbatical, Devin?'

'Because deep breath, his gaze unwavering. "erwork up for the fifth or sixth time. "eens, but he didn'd himall, thick-set man wit I've got a paper to run, Becky. You're our chief reporter – you're a trusted member of staff. I could get some 21-year-old in to cover you while you go off on your great big holiday. But I'd rather not. We need you, and that's the truth of the matter.'

'I understand that, Devin, but I've also got a life to lead. Technically I've been here since school, and I've asked for nothing. My first year, in fact, they had to beg me to take some time off. I've asked you for one period of unpaid leave. It's all perfectly valid under regulations. Right, Rose?'

Rose's eyes did not leave the table. 'That is correct, Becky, but as you know, operational issues can sometimes take precedence.'

'Isn't that only in an emergency, though? Like if there's a major incident or some sort of crisis?'

'It's at my discretion,' Devin said, squaring his shoulders.

'I don't think that's the case. I've looked at the company regulations, and I am entitled to take an unpaid sabbatical if it's reasonable and appropriate to do so – which it is.'

He grinned. 'Well sunshine, there's company regulations, and there's reality.'

Becky folded her hands. 'I think the union might want to help out with your idea of reality. Or I could cut out the middle man and just go with some lawyers.'

'What? Are you actually *threatening* me?'

'You can take it any way you like, Devin.'

'Well,' Rose said, blinking rapidly, 'I'm sure there's no need for that. We can have a sensible discussion here.'

There was a quick tap at the door. Before anyone could answer, a tall, thick-necked man with long whiskers, a knee-length dark overcoat and broad-brimmed hat entered the room. The coat and hat were beaded with rain, and the big man took his time removing both garments and hanging them up on a stand. He seemed to lose nothing in girth by taking off the big coat, and a white shirt clung to his monumental paunch as he pulled up a chair and sat down.

Jack Tullington was in his late fifties, but might have been younger or older by a differential of about ten years, with more grey than black in his thinning hair.

'Blowy out there,' Jack said, brightly. 'Sorry I'm late, Devin.'

'No problem Jack,' Devin said, neutrally. 'I didn't realise you were coming along.'

'Thought I'd sit in. I hope that's all right.' There was a hint of Scots in Jack's voice, buried after years of enunciating for English ears. There was a hint of it in his face, too, Becky thought – something in the whiskers, the small, tight-packed eyes and the flinty hair that struck her as peculiarly Caledonian. One of the lads on the sports desk had referred to him as 'Willie Miller', although that name had no meaning for Becky.

'Well,' Rose said, squaring and re-squaring her paperwork, 'I didn't expect to see you in here today, Mr Tullington.'

'I won't take up a lot of your time.' Jack turned to Becky: 'You sent in your paperwork for your sabbatical as outlined in the Human Resources policy document?'

'Yes, Jack.'

He turned to Rose. 'And was it all in order?'

'Well, yes. Pending review.'

'It's reviewed.' Jack beamed. 'Consider your request granted, Becky. Don't be doing anything silly like running off and getting married now, will you?'

Devin's cheeks flushed much as a cuttlefish might change colour after a fright. He raised a hand. 'Just hold on a second, Jack. We haven't scratched the surface of this.'

'There's no need. I'm calling it in. Becky's one of the best we've got. And her leave's unpaid. We can hire someone on secondment for... how long you off for?'

'Three months.'

'There you go. We can get some housekeeping done. Save a bit of cash in the short term. Pay less than the going rate for a chief reporter. Helen on accounts will be cheering you to the rafters for that.'

Devin set his jaw. 'I didn't agree to this, and to be honest, Jack, I'm not happy.'

'Duly noted,' Jack drawled.

Devin stood up and strode towards the door. 'We'll talk about this in a bit,' he said to her, thickly.

Jack stabbed a finger at him, and the kindness disappeared from his eyes. '*We* will. And we'll do it in my office, in twenty minutes' time. Got it?'

The door crashed shut behind Devin.

'Well,' Jack said, relaxing, 'that was quick and painless. What do you say, Rose? Can we get the paperwork signed off today?'

Rose looked drained. 'I suppose I can get that seen to.'

'Great. Becky and I were just going to step out for a bite to eat. Roughly lunchtime, is it not?'

Becky grinned. 'Only if you're buying.'

# 6

The atrium at The Mortar had been intended as an oasis in the midst of a glass and brushed chrome structure which, to Becky, had always looked unfinished. The reception desk and the revolving doors dominated the space below them, but up here you could sit down in soft leather set amid broad green palm fronds. There was even a water feature – a gentle accompaniment to the pattering rain above.

Jack Tullington spread himself thickly across the sofa. 'Did you know, we once had Sean Connery up here?'

'Everyone's had Sean Connery up here. Who hasn't had Sean Connery up here?'

'It was a drinks reception. He was in town for an award or something. Excellent big guy. Sort of intimidating, in a strange way. It's like a mountain range moving towards you. Then speaking.'

'In a shtrange accshent.'

'Of courshe.'

'Thanks for today, Jack.'

Jack sat forward and swirled his coffee. 'It was a pleasure. Perk of the job. What is my job, again?'

'Being McCance's boss. As you so nicely illustrated.'

Jack frowned. 'You know what he calls me? In his bitchy emails to folk? "Editor *emeticus*." The cheek of it! I was 22 the last time I spewed on a night out. And that includes my stag do.'

'You read people's emails? Didn't think that was your style, Jack. I'll have to watch what I say in future when I'm bitching about you.'

He chuckled. 'What can I tell you? I'm a hack. I was born that way. I don't usually snoop… but if anyone tells me I *can't* snoop… things get problematic. This time, I was snooping in an official capacity. We had a bit of a leak in the office. You might recall *The Bolt* had an annoying habit of running with our scoops on the same day?'

'I thought that was the same Whitehall creep, briefing different papers separately?'

'Nope. Someone in here was leaking our splashes. Big ones, too – like when Brian Louvens was caught with rent boys, or when that old lady turned out to have been a Soviet spy back in the 1950s. We never found out who it was, but it did turn up some interesting stuff in Devin's deleted mails file.'

'I guess you can't cheat a thief, as they say.'

Jack chuckled. 'So, kiddo… did you see the telly last night?'

'I did.'

'How are you feeling about that?'

'I want to say "mixed feelings", but that doesn't cover it.'

Jack indicated Becky's eye. 'I hope your mixed feelings didn't extend to nutting somebody.'

'Nah, I shut a car door on myself.'

'My brother used to be a copper. Know how many times he's heard that one?' He sipped his coffee. 'Anyway, I'll keep it brief. You know where I am if you need anything. The police been in touch to update you? Anything new from the show? Sometimes they turn up a new lead.'

She shook her head. 'I'm not expecting much. They've dug up as much as they can. I can't see someone sitting in front of the telly watching the show, thinking, "You know, that rings a bell. I think I do remember something about a mass ritual murder from round about that time. Completely slipped my mind."'

'Don't rule anything out. You do get results. The smallest details can trigger memories, it can happen. Lots of cases have been solved from these shows…'

'Never underestimate the value of a nosey old bugger.'

'Loyalties can change, too. The guy who did it might have had a wife who suspects something. It's a fair bet that he's been abusive. A guy like that surely can't be normal behind closed doors. Say they're getting divorced. That's all it would take – for her to see the show, connect the dots, lift the phone.'

'I'm not holding out much hope, Jack. If something shows up, it might nail him. But most of it will probably be a distraction. Kooks and loonies giving false information, which they'll then have to follow up. It might even be well-intentioned people, just desperate to help. People who make things up but hardly realise they've done it.'

He sighed. 'Yeah. That's the truth.'

'Did you watch, Jack? I know it will have been hard for you, as well.'

His shoulders flinched. 'It's hardly on the same scale, Becky.'

'Technically, you knew Mum and Dad longer than I did. Stands to reason.'

'Reason doesn't come into it, really. "I'm fine" is my formal answer.' Jack smiled kindly. 'Whatever happens, you know where I am. Anything you need, lift the phone. I'll be there. And if that toilet-brush-headed twat gives you any nonsense when you come back, let me know, and I'll straighten him out.'

'Appreciated.'

'Where are you off to on this sabbatical, anyway? Don't tell me you're going to "find yourself". When people say they're going to find themselves, they mean "I'm off to Thailand to smoke doobies and shag surfers". Is that your plan?'

'I'm going to do a spot of travelling, that's true. Take a proper holiday. I'll do Europe. Minus the beaches. Do you know, I realised that I'd never been to Budapest before?'

'One of my favourite cities, that. To say, I mean. To pronounce. Just sounds exotic. Budapest.'

'My favourite city to say is Caracas.'

He burst out laughing, and that's when he hugged her.

After the usual promises to call – or at least exchange Christmas cards – she watched him plod down the spiral staircase.

As Jack started to flirt with the lady on the front desk, her phone rang. The number was withheld.

Instinctively, she turned away from the staircase, her face to the wall. She took two deep breaths before pressing 'answer'. She knew. This was it.

The young man on the end of the line said: 'Hello there. Can I speak to Jessica Rabbit?'

Becky's heart picked up the pace. 'This is Jessica Rabbit.'

'Is the mouse in its house?'

'The mouse is in the grandfather clock.'

'Okay. Tomorrow night, Masquerade. Bewley Street. Just you, no one else. The corner booth, opposite the DJ box, stage left. That means on the right-hand side.'

Becky bit her tongue.

'Two minutes to midnight,' the man said. 'Midnight minus two. Got it?'

'That's a little past my bedtime. But I'll be there.'

'One more thing to remember – so listen very carefully. You'll be sent a text message with a code. You'll need this in order to proceed. Got it?'

'Got it.'

He hung up.

# 7

Him

He woke up moments before the alarm, as usual. He knew precisely where his phone was in the dark, reaching over without looking to silence it upon the first pip.

His exercise regime had changed over time. For many years, his mornings had begun with painful stomach crunches, press-ups and stretches, before the tyranny of dumbbells and bench presses. One or two pulled muscles and an alarming tendency for his back to seize up whenever he dead-lifted weights had put paid to this early-morning violence. Now, he preferred to stretch slowly, his body resisting gravity rather than sparring with it.

The light underneath his bedroom door cast his body in a thin effulgence, and he made sure to admire his ghostly outline as he passed the mirror. His face was utterly motionless as he flexed and preened. The stomach was not what it once was; there was no disguising that. Perhaps there was nothing to be done about it, at his age.

'All things must pass,' he whispered to himself, and smiled.

He put on a dressing gown and joined his family.

His wife was always awake, showered and dressed for work well before him, and usually had breakfast ready for the three of them. Making breakfast was a task she preferred doing, part of a long-established routine. If he was home, he cooked the evening meal, and he was far more fastidious about household chores and keeping their house clean and in good order.

'What time do you fly out tonight?' she asked, buttering a slice of toast.

'About eight o'clock.'

'Will you be in a fit state to go out with Mats and Verena on Saturday?'

He shrugged. 'So long as the flight's not late, I can't see it being a problem.'

'I don't want you falling asleep on their couch again. You did that last time.'

He bit the corner off a slice of toast. 'That was different. I was jet-lagged. I won't be going so far this time.'

She smirked. 'It was funny, though. You fell asleep clutching your dick. You looked so peaceful. Like a baby sucking its thumb.'

He brushed a crumb from his lips and fashioned a smile.

Their daughter loped downstairs, a thin, dark 14-year-old. She had inherited her height from her father's side and kept her hair long and black. It sometimes pained him to see her in this guise. The girl was willowy, lissom, and would have suited delicate things. But she was in the midst of a gothic phase: dark make-up, purple fingernails, black T-shirts, bands with incomprehensible names glowering from her walls.

'I don't like it when I see you two smiling,' the girl mumbled. 'Makes me think you're up to something.' She pulled out a seat and slumped down at the table.

'Did you finish your physics problems last night?' he asked.

'Yes,' she said, part-reply, part-exhalation, as she spooned raspberry preserves onto her toast. 'I even showed Mum, before dinner.'

'Good.'

Two weeks earlier she had been caught copying a friend's homework. Classic folly – they had made the same mistakes. A letter had been sent from school. The teachers were thorough, and he had been pleased with the action they had taken. He had been brutal when he confronted his daughter about it. His anger at her had surprised both wife and daughter. Sloppiness was something he did not tolerate but even so, his bellowing had frightened them both.

He'd had things on his mind.

Once his wife had set off with their daughter on the school run, he entered his stark white-walled office and booted up the desktop computer, checking out the news. An application alerted him to the presence of news stories which might be of particular interest to him. According to a red-bordered number on his starting menu, twenty-four news stories awaited his attention. This was an unusually high number, but it had to be expected the day after the *Crimewatch Special*.

He read these without any sense of unease.

Afterwards, he took off for a run, already formulating plans, calculating angles of approach.

In truth, the logistical part of his activities was a big part of the thrill, nowadays. With modern technology being what it was, he had to plan very carefully.

But then he'd always been a cautious man. It was the reason he had never been caught.

Once he was down the hill from the front gate, he pounded the cycle path and pavement past ranks of pines, head down, teeth gritted, his hood over his head. He was a capable runner, injuries permitting, though he would readily concede that he wasn't as fast or as strong as he had been even three years ago.

He passed only one person on the journey, a dog-walker whom he saw most days on the road, but never said hello to. The dog was a mongrel, a happy imbecile which cocked its head and unfurled its tongue whenever he passed.

Not for the first time, he fantasised about killing it right there and then, jumping on it with both feet in front of its astonished master, and then continuing on his way.

After a sharp left through the path, the road became steep, hard and stony, and he took a brief rest. The route diverted into an old logging trail, less well paved and almost never used. The ground grew boggy very quickly. One had to know where best to run in order to avoid getting too muddy, or more specifically to avoid leaving identifiable footprints which might set quickly in drier conditions.

Another turn took him through dense woodland, and he had to squeeze through the trees at some points in order to continue travelling. There was something about the grey skies visible through the black, jagged forest canopy that moved something within him. He especially loved this view on clear nights, when the shadows were thicker in contrast with the moonlight.

This was when he felt closer to his true nature than at any other point, except one.

He soon came upon the pit. There was always an element of danger, here. Supposing one day he should come upon it and find the pit empty?

But there were no such worries today. He took off his backpack, put on some gloves and then, of course, the mask.

He cleared away some of the bushes, delved into the muck, found the chains, and heaved.

A thick wooden trapdoor opened up from the swampy ground, heavily camouflaged with a thick covering of branches and other arboreal detritus – and there she was, just as he had left her. He saw no horror in her eyes, and no hope.

He tossed her some food which he had brought in his backpack and sat on his haunches to watch while she ate. Something startled the crows in the trees above, and the girl's head shot up, only the one eye showing through her matted fringe.

Entirely confident that there was no one around to disturb them, he smiled beneath the mask.

After he was sure she had eaten every scrap – even things which had fallen into the slick mud – he cleared his throat and said, 'Morning!'

# 8

Masquerade was in an unexpectedly smart part of town. Becky strode past Georgian architecture, high windows and Greek columns; For Sale signs harried the streets like angry mobs in a Hammer movie.

She spotted some basement bars and restaurants, none of them looking more than a couple of years old to judge by the décor and the signs. Masquerade was situated down a stairway in the midst of these establishments.

Any information Becky had turned up on what to wear to the club was worryingly vague. She decided that indigo jeans and an open-necked black blouse underneath a dark jacket would do. At the last minute before leaving the house, she swapped a pair of black, patent leather heels for her well-worn ass-kicking boots, which reduced her height but boosted her confidence. After double-checking that she had the right address, she was delighted to see that a regular pub was positioned across the road, somewhere with a square bar, brass taps and a cadre of ruddy-faced older men. The kind of place where boozers came to die. Perfect.

She took a position at one of the outside tables and nursed a near-as-damn-it zero-alcohol beer. When she'd ordered it, the barman had pretended to blow dust off the bottle. She'd nearly smiled.

She watched people arrive at Masquerade in ones, twos and threes, most of them double-checking their phones before trooping downstairs. Many of the men wore tuxedos and smart suits, with several of the women in evening dresses. One or two of the better-dressed couples in the pub also headed across the road, hand in hand. One of the women giggled excitedly, tossing her blonde hair over her shoulder. Disregarding the glad rags and wedding suits, they might have been going to a Bryan Adams concert, she thought.

Becky waited until the trickle of bodies became a steady stream before heading across the road. At the bottom of a stairway that sagged at an angle like an old mattress, a bullet-headed man scanned in codes on phones proffered by the punters.

She double-checked her own phone, making sure the text message with the code attached was ready to open with a single swipe.

A man and a woman in their late thirties were in the queue ahead of her. They looked as if they'd stepped out of one of those headache-inducing Christmas perfume adverts. The woman wore a backless, fairy-princess blue dress, which displayed shoulder muscles that had done serious time on a rowing machine. Her physique complemented her partner's jawline, a geometrically-perfect construction from a superhero comic. They turned round to glance at Becky as the queue shuffled down from step-to-step. The man's eyes were keen, but his partner's appraisal was cold, tracing Becky from head to toe and back, slow and deliberate. The woman paid particular attention to Becky's boots.

She leaned over and said to Becky, her lip curling, 'Are you the half-time entertainment?'

The man laughed.

Becky grinned. 'Wait and see.' She took out a packet of chewing gum, put a stick in her mouth, then offered the pack to the couple. The woman in the blue dress grimaced, shook her head, then whispered something else in the man's ear. They both turned to the front.

The queue reached a booth, where they were handing out masks. They were Viennese style – some white, some embossed with gold or faux diamonds, and some bearing obscenely long noses.

Becky hesitated, shoulders tense. As well as handing out the masks, the pair inside the booth took coats and jackets. The black woman in the booth was strikingly beautiful even beneath a white lace-fringed mask, with an elegant chin, perfect teeth and a black evening gown that represented an entire month's salary to Becky. The man beside her was similarly handsome, and in a tuxedo like most of the patrons. He had a notable lack of body fat and clean lines round the brow and jaw. The pair could have been models hired for the evening, and probably were.

The man wore a simple highwayman's mask, which left plenty of space for a frown to become apparent when he spotted Becky.

'You come to the right place?' he said, in a gruff accent.

'Had my ticket stamped, haven't I?'

The man shrugged. He turned to a rack of masks, but before his hand could alight on a plain white cowl, she said, 'No – the harlequin pattern one, please.'

'That one's for men,' the woman told her.

Becky chuckled. 'I thought you people were kinky?'


The harlequin mask amplified Becky's breathing as she filtered through to the main room. A doorman in a fox mask ushered her in through dark drapes, allowing his hand to trail across her back. Becky chose to ignore this.

The room was lit in ultra-violet, the kind that showed up dandruff and outlined dilated pupils to the more diligent bouncer. To the credit of the men in tuxedos milling around, white flakes could only be discerned whenever Becky got close to one of them. The room was fitted with booths along both sides; many couples were sat at them.

Some of the clientele queued up at the bar. Thanks to some pounding trance, it could have been a nightclub anywhere in any city, if you ignored the headgear. Becky noticed that some of the couples were shaking hands and sitting down, with others getting up and moving on to the next table.

Becky clocked the DJ booth – the person on the decks wore a zebra head mask – then found the corner booth she'd been told to sit at. It was empty, with a 'reserved' sign on the table.

Becky sat with her back to the wall. She did not have long to wait.

A man wearing what seemed to be a white linen suit with an open-collared shirt strode through the purplish glow, dappled by light from a lazy mirror ball poised above. He raised a hand to a bouncer who had moved to intercept him, and the bouncer returned to his post, frowning in Becky's direction.

The newcomer wore a black and gold jaguar mask. It was too tight and gave him a chubby-cheeked appearance he almost certainly hadn't intended. He appeared to have bright blue eyes beneath the cowl, and was perhaps the youngest person in the room.

Becky cleared her throat and leaned close in order to make herself heard. 'So, here we are. Speed dating for swingers. What do you call it? Speed shagging?'

The man remained very still and stared at Becky. Probably he imagined this would intimidate her.

His voice was deeper than she expected. 'You forgetting something?'

'Whippoorwill,' Becky said.

The man nodded and relaxed a little, resting his arms on the table. 'To answer your question about this place – you're right. This is quite an exclusive gathering of what we like to call broad-minded couples.

'Strange venue. Couldn't we just have met in the pub across the road?'

'I chose this venue for a good reason. I prefer to do my business somewhere people actively avoid being recognised and don't take kindly to surveillance. This is a strictly private party.'

'It's different, I'll say that for you. We could have done this at Mickey Ds.'

He sighed. 'Shall we just get down to business?'

'Okay. Let's see the goods, then.'

The man passed her an envelope. Becky did not open it but tucked it into her jacket pocket. Her fingertips told her a memory stick was lodged inside.

'Any instructions to go with it?' she asked.

'You use it at midnight tonight, on the nose. Apart from that, we only ask that you treat it with the utmost caution. You are moving into a dangerous world, here. It's no game. I would say, "don't pass this onto anyone," but to be frank, if you try to do that, we'll know, and we'll delete every connection and all the information in the stick. After that, we'll get angry with you.'

'I don't want to share it with anyone. It's very important that the connection is as secure as possible and I'm the only one who can use it. I was quite specific about that.'

'Good, then we have an understanding. Now, to be clear… if we should have to come looking for Miss Elizabeth Hounslow, of 61 Maxwell Terrace, flat 3/1, drives a Kia Cee'd, 2014 plate, has a Samsung mobile phone, works at the National Portrait Gallery… then it won't be anything dramatic. Not right away. You might notice the odd withdrawal from your bank account, or a few units added to your utility bills, or an unusually high insurance premium. Things like that. Nothing severe. But you will notice them. And you will be given to understand that it can get a lot worse. Because if you cross us, we can and will destroy you. It's very easy to do if you know how. And we know how.'

Becky tried hard to suppress a smirk. He had taken the bait. She had worried that the fake ID she's cooked up looked amateurish; evidently not.

He had practised his lines. They were curiously devoid of threat, the polished spiel of the telesales operator he probably was in his day-to-day life. Becky nodded, and in a similarly businesslike tone, said: 'That's right, Mark. You've got me bang to rights. Elizabeth Hounslow, that's me. I expected no less. You are the best at what you do, is that right?'

To his credit, he gave no indication that her use of his name had unsettled him. She'd managed to get the name of the contact out of Jarrod, quite by accident, when she took him for a coffee. She hoped he wouldn't get in trouble for it.

'And I hope we do understand each other,' Becky continued. 'Because if my personal data should go anywhere I don't want it to, then I might come after you – personally. It won't be anything dramatic. Nothing severe. Maybe just a quick call to the police. Or your employer.'

He grinned. The babyish gap in his teeth was a surprise. 'Touché, Miss Hounslow,' he said, applauding ironically. 'Now, if you don't mind…?'

'Of course.' Becky handed over an envelope. The man pocketed it without opening it, then got up and left without another word.

'Miss Elizabeth Hounslow… I wouldn't want to be in your shoes,' she whispered to herself. She chewed her gum for a while, checking and double checking the envelope was secure in her inside pocket. She paid close attention not to the masks, but to the evening gowns, the black shoes and the beer bellies.

It hadn't taken long for things to warm up. One couple were kissing openly, lasciviously, in the booth opposite. Another couple watched from the seat opposite.

Finally, she found what she was looking for; a pale blue strappy dress, twirling under the mirror ball, a study in grace amid the throng on the dance floor.

Becky strode past this baby blue dervish.

Quick as a stiletto strike, she spat her gum into the folds of the sheer blue material. Then she headed for the door.

# 9

Despite the hooded top obscuring most of her face, Becky felt like she was going on a date. She was in the spare room but had angled the camera away from her map and other jottings on the pinboard. The map in her spare room had grown threads now – strands of wool stretching between murder sites pinpointed on the map, criss-crossing each other like a Tube map in an off-kilter dimension. Once Becky had tried to find a pattern in these criss-crossings. There appeared to be none, though the idea that she might have missed some component that would complete a symbol or a message of some kind haunted her.

She checked the time, dimmed the lights at her back and turned the laptop on.

Becky fully expected something chaotic to happen when she put the USB stick into the port

She had certainly prepared well for this, using an ancient, but souped-up Toshiba laptop, requisitioned from a dodgy garage outlet situated under a railway bridge more used to dealing pirated copies of Office and video games.

Becky knew she had to be more than careful. She thought of her activities now as though they were a live court case. Restrictions applied; rules were in place; details had to be checked, logged and checked again; infinite care and accuracy had to be taken from now on.

A plain white box opened in the centre of her screen. One word appeared, with a blocky cursor tapping its foot at the end.

*Password?*

She typed without hesitating: 'Whippoorwill.' Cap W, two Ps, two numerical zeroes, two Ls.

The cursor paused, then a video screen opened up. A man with long red curly hair appeared. He wore a black T-shirt, and from the doughy quality of his forearms beneath the cuffs, just visible at the bottom of the screen, Becky guessed he didn't lift. Like her, he was sat in the dark, the electric blue glare of his own screen the only illumination. An untidy space was just about discernible over his shoulders, boxes and books crammed into shelves amid the oil slick sheen of stacked CDs.

His face was distorted. At first Becky thought that it was some corruption in the video feed, a bulge of magnified purplish pixels, circles and squares. She trailed the cursor round the face, hoping the digital interference would clear. Oddly, she could still see the man's brown eyes in the midst of the maelstrom, but the digital muddle remained.

'Ah, I wouldn't bother with that, Elizabeth,' the man said, in excellent English, but with a heavy accent. 'It's not your connection. This is my mask. You will understand my need for anonymity.'

She smiled and nodded. 'Of course. That makes two of us. Do you have a name I can use?'

'You can call me Rupert.' Scandinavian accent, Becky thought; perhaps northern Germany, at a stretch. It was difficult to tell, and a waste of time asking.

'Rupert? As in the bear?'

The shoulders on-screen shrugged. 'As in anyone you like. Maybe your uncle Rupert?'

'Uncle Rupert it is.'

'I'm not seeing very much of you, Elizabeth.'

'Good.'

'Okay. You're shy. I follow. That makes two of us. So, what can I do for you?'

'I have a number of jobs I need looking into. This could be spread out over a long period of time.'

'If you've got the money, we've got the time.'

'It's going to involve the police, and maybe one or two politicians.'

He chuckled. 'Politicians? Man, that's a piece of cake. Police might be a bit more difficult.'

'But not impossible?'

Rupert drummed his fingers on his desk, as if typing. 'If it's online, nothing is impossible.'

'Okay.

'What's first?' Becky took a breath. 'Let's take it from the top. I'm investigating a very serious crime, which I think was hushed up at a fairly high level. It's a hunch, but it adds up. I need hard evidence. My idea is that there is a well-connected conspiracy involving crimes committed right across Europe which have never been solved. That sort of conspiracy means highly-connected people. In particular, I want to know about… people of influence in politics. The police and politicians. The higher up the chain, the better. I want to find people who could cover things up.'

It was difficult to read anything into the bubbling mass in the centre of the face, but she imagined two eyebrows raised in the centre. 'Whoa there! I'll need a little bit more information, Elizabeth. Did you say "across Europe"?'

'I did. Don't worry. I'll go into specifics.'

He began to write on a notepad. 'What kind of crimes do you mean?'

'I'm looking for something that you can only find under the radar. Dark net stuff.'

'Again… you'll have to be specific. If you want an idea of how much data this involves, type the word "sex" into Google.'

'I'm aware of that. That's why I hired you.'

'When you say "dark net stuff" …?'

'I'm talking about murder. Ritual abuse. Teenage girls. Families.'

He grunted. 'You a paedo hunter?'

'I don't think our arrangement entitles you to ask me personal questions.'

'I'm just curious. We've had a few of those before. A couple of our previous clients worked for the British press.'

She barely paused. 'I want to find out if there is a ring of people interested in that sort of activity. Any group, however loosely organised. If you can cross-check it with dark net searches or people who regularly watch videos featuring that kind of material, fact or fiction, it would be a starting point. If they exist.'

'Oh, they exist, all right. If you've thought about it, someone's into it.'

'Then you have something to go on.'

'Well, the thing about these establishments – like drug dealing, or weapons, or anything else on the dark net – the organisers aren't ignorant about the risks they run by advertising themselves online. That's why they don't do it openly. Things are still word of mouth, usually, localised industries. And if they do have an online presence, it'll be vanilla. Something respectable-seeming. Nothing you could ever stumble upon. You would have to know precisely what you were looking for.'

'I understand that. This is just a starting point. It's worth a try. See what turns up. Anything at all, based anywhere – I want to know about it. I'm particularly interested in anything linked to the South of France, as well as Eastern Europe and Russia.'

'Okay.'

'And after that, I want you to take a sidestep. People who are into wife-swapping, hook-ups, sex clubs – kinky, but nothing illegal. So long as it's organised. Then I want you to cross-reference it with anyone who is, or has been, a serving politician.'

Rupert burst out laughing. 'Again, we could be talking about a wide field here. I understand your Houses of Parliament have some interesting characters.'

'"Interesting" is a loaded term there.'

'This will take some time. And it's dangerous. There may be an extra payment required.'

'You've been paid plenty. Hacking is dangerous, full stop.'

'That's cool. We can discuss it nearer the time.'

She let this pass. 'I'm looking for anyone at all – but anyone based in Brussels would be a close fit. Someone who might be able to shut something down before it spreads across Europe. A person of influence who can make investigations disappear. Someone who can set up a dead end.'

Rupert scratched where his skin met the stretched neck of his bleached-out black T-shirt. 'You know, at the expense of mansplaining… when it comes to that kind of stuff, you'd be surprised how much of it goes on. I'm bound to turn up a few results.'

'I'm not looking for a big, obvious thing. I'm not even looking for a particularly big fish. I want a starting point. I'm looking for a guy who might know a guy.'

'Someone you can blackmail easily, you mean?'

She frowned. 'I'm trying not to make any assumptions about you, Rupert. Try to do the same for me.'

'Noted. You mentioned police, too?'

Becky nodded. 'Anyone involved on a personal level would be a start. Later, I'll be looking for criminal records. Names of detectives, signatures. Photos.'

'Any specific investigation?'

Becky paused. 'We can come to that later. Let's start at the top. Ritual murders. Families. Go from there.'

'Timeframe?'

'Go back thirty years, but focus on the last twenty.'

'Okay. I'll see what turns up for now.'

'When's the soonest you can get back to me?'

'Let's give it a week. I'm busy at the moment.'

'A week's ideal. That'll let me make some arrangements. Shall I use the same password?'

Rupert's pixelated face shook from side to side. 'Absolutely not. Check your mobile. I'm going to assume it's a burner phone?'

'I'm not a complete amateur.'

'Great. We'll instruct you from there.'

Becky nodded. 'See you around.'

'With a face like this, you couldn't mistake me for anyone else.' She got the impression he smiled. 'Nice to meet you, Elizabeth.'

# 10

Becky stared into the maelstrom.

It was her term, not Dr Fullerton's; in reality, it was just a flat laminated disc comprising concentric circles, black, then white. The curves were treacherous to the eye, blending into one another in exactly the wrong places. It was an optical illusion, like something posted onto social media that made you feel uneasy the longer you tried to focus on it.

The disc was set up on a vertical stand on Dr Fullerton's desk, with the lights turned low all round them. Becky sank into his armchair. Many times, she had wanted to ask him where he got the seat. It seemed to want to swallow her, but the feeling was not unpleasant. She could see herself curling up in its lap for a sleep on lazy afternoons.

Fullerton's voice had a slightly camp air to it at these points. Becky thought he sounded a little bit like a Glaswegian Vincent Price. 'Just look at the centre of the circles, Becky. Clear your mind. There is nothing here that can harm you, nothing to cause you alarm. Your fears are locked out, barred, and they can't make a sound.'

Eventually she became drowsy, thanks mainly to Fullarton's soothing drone, allied to the lights, the world-class chair, and the circles. She had no idea if she actually was 'an ideal subject', as he had claimed, or if her trance state was simply a cumulative effect of soft tones, sound and ambience.

Presently, her eyes wanted to cross over; the circles wanted to converge.

He droned on: 'You know what it means; beans means Heinz, or cleans means beans' dream.'

Nonsense phrases, of course, a means of lulling you into the dream zone, that slightly giddy place where nothing made sense except the poetry, or maybe just the cadence.

'And I'm going to count back. With every number you hear, you are growing more and more relaxed... five... you feel like you could just close your eyes and drift off, so let's do that, Becky... eyes closed... four... your head feels very heavy, just let it relax back into the chair... three...'

On 'one' he allowed a few seconds of quiet, filled only with her deep, calm breathing.

'Now, Becky. Let's go back to the day with the crooked tree.'

'... Crooked tree...'

'The crooked tree, flat enough to lie down on...'

Then

Howie clambered over an immense fallen tree trunk, shrieking to himself, lost in his own daydreams of war and heroism. The dead tree's husked bark, bleached in the sunlight, reminded Becky of an elephant's skin. She lay against an ash tree, head resting against its smoother surface. A knot pressed against the back of her head, but the feeling was not unpleasant, like the trance sensation she sometimes got by touching the space at the crossroads of eyes and nose. She closed her eyes, visualising the bee that murmured through her auditory field from right to left.

'That thing will be a haven for mini-beasts,' Clara said. She was closer than Becky had supposed, startling her younger sister.

'What? The tree?'

'That, and everything else round here. The ground you're sitting on, for example.'

Becky opened her eyes. Clara was scratching at her arm. For no reason she could articulate, the older girl's tiny twist of bellybutton, poking out above her stonewashed jeans beneath the cut-off Mötley Crüe T-shirt, offended her.

'I'm thinking Howie's more likely to fall off than be attacked by insects,' Becky said.

As if in direct response, Howie leapt off the trunk, crouching low on the ground as though to avoid gunfire, then hurled an imaginary grenade into the air. After supplying his own explosive sound effects, he sprinted back to the far end of the trunk, scampered on top of it, and returned fire at the top of his voice.

'No... he's annoyingly robust,' Clara said. 'Besides, he'll be fine if he falls off – so long as he lands on his head.' She pulled something shiny from her pocket and jabbed it into the tree where Becky lay. The younger girl cocked an eyebrow at her sister as she blocked out the light.

'What are you doing?'

Clara flicked a splinter from the blade on her penknife and hacked at the bark again. 'Have you heard of patrins?'

'No. I've heard of vandalism, though.'

Clara sniffed, disdainfully. 'Patrins are signs left for people to follow. Gypsies use them all the time.'

'Who are you leaving a sign for?'

'Monsieur Fabrice, of course.'

'Who?'

'Fabrice. My pen-pal. Goodness, do you mean to say you *haven't* been reading my diary?'

Becky shrugged.

'Keep up with current events, dear sister. Fabrice is going to be my boyfriend.'

'How did you meet Fabrice?' Becky said the name in a silly accent she'd heard on *Monty Python*.

'Pen-pals' column, in a quality newspaper. Not the type of thing *you'd* read, I imagine.' Clara jabbed the penknife hard into the bark, gritting her teeth as it met resistance. 'We've been corresponding for months, Fabrice and I. His English is perfect.'

'What about the boy at school? The guitar player?'

'He's just for now. Fabrice could be for life. He plays rugby, you know. Says he is more than six feet tall already. He wants to captain the French national side.'

'Rugby? Ugh, rugby players are horrible.' Becky mimicked thrusting two fingers down her throat. 'All hairy legs and muddy shorts. Their ears look like cabbage and they brag about having noses turned ninety degrees.'

'Only on the field of play,' Clara replied, after some thought. 'Off it, they're perfect gentlemen. Besides, Fabrice is handsome. French men are just so damned *sophisticated*.'

The blade stuck fast. Clara braced one hand against the bark, then pulled hard on the silver handle with another. Becky felt the tree shiver as the knife jerked free.

'There.'

On the bark, she had gouged out a rough pentagram, like the one printed on Clara's T-shirt.

'Great. Fabrice is a devil freak.' Becky began to giggle.

'You wouldn't understand,' Clara said, clasping the knife and returning it to her pocket. 'It's not about devil worship. It's actually an ancient symbol. It can ward off evil.'

'Why do all your silly devil bands have it on their album covers, then?'

'It also looks cool.'

Becky smiled mischievously. 'And Fabrice is all the way out here, is he? Coming to meet you? And you're using that tiny little sign, in the middle of the forest, to communicate?'

'That's right.'

Becky clapped her hands. 'This is brilliant! You actually think it's going to happen. Are you going to wait here all day for him to show up? Maybe the whole week?'

Clara rubbed her chin, suppressing a smile of her own. As ever, it was difficult to tell if she was making it all up or not. 'If Fabrice says he'll be here, he'll be here.'

It was then that Becky noticed the break in hostilities. She wouldn't have called it a silence. The forest was always full of sounds, if one listened carefully. Birds, trees, running water... the absence of these noises frightened her.

'Hey... where's Howie?'

They called out, checking round and underneath the fallen tree. They split up, shouting, calling out into the forest, but only the birds answered them.

'We're going to have to go get Dad,' Becky said, querulously.

'Nonsense. He's hiding somewhere. He's done this before.' But Clara didn't look too sure. Her face was pale.

'What if he went back to the lake? What if he fell in?'

Clara swallowed. 'He wouldn't have.'

'I'm going back,' Becky said.

And in that moment, the boy sprung from the long grass, levelling his imaginary rifle.

'Ha ha! You got a fright! Got you, got you, got you!'

'You little bugger!' Clara yelled. She ran after the boy, and he shrieked, sprinting off into the trees, delighted. Reluctantly, Becky trotted after them.

Once they were gone, a dark figure emerged from his hiding place in the bushes, not quite twelve feet from where the boy had lain in the scrub.

His fingertips traced the edges of the pentagram on the tree, its edges oozing sap.

Now

'And let's count back now, from twenty... nineteen... eighteen... you can feel yourself slowly coming back to normal... seventeen... you're very close to the surface...'

*Was I out, or not?* Becky thought. She was never totally sure. Perhaps that deep sense of relaxation was enough. Maybe that was all a trance was, a step or two up from being asleep.

One way of proving the trance state existed at all would be to simply get up and walk out of the door in the middle of a session. She wondered if she was in fact stuck to the chair, as Fullerton had insisted she was, earlier.

What if he dropped dead? What if the fire alarm went? Would he have to talk her back out of it, with his Lancaster bomber-burr voice, even as smoke seeped through the crack in the door?

'Five... four... coming fully alert now, eyes open... eyes open, Becky... three, two, and one, and you're back.'

She blinked, perhaps for form's sake.

'Welcome back. How do you feel?'

'Not bad. Relaxed.'

'I'm glad. You're such a good subject.'

'And you're a little bit cheaper than a spa day.'

'How do you feel about reliving these memories?'

'Same as before. No difference. It's no better or worse. What's happened is what happened. I'm beyond trying to change my responses to that.'

Fullerton got up, laid the disc flat and dimmed the desk lamp. 'I used to worry that you'd react badly to hypnosis.'

'I'm paying the bills though, right?'

He grunted. 'Quite. It's your call. I'm doing what you've asked. Even so, I wouldn't recommend that treatment to someone like you, right away. Not for any fear something bad will happen, or get dislodged. I just think in your case that the therapy should be about moving forward, not back.'

Becky scratched her chin. 'If I was the psychologist, and you were the patient... I'd say you were worried about what we just did.'

'Not worried,' he said, carefully. 'Curious, if I'm being honest. Why do you want to retrace your steps?'

'Practical reasons.'

He raised his eyebrows. 'Now I'm even more curious.'

'I'm looking for details, in a nutshell.' Becky yawned and stretched. 'The fine grain. Something that might have been missed.'

'A detail... about the case?'

'That's right.'

'Like the crooked tree? You keep mentioning it.'

'The tiniest thing could be relevant. You never know.'

'It seems that every conceivable angle has been explored there, Becky.'

'I would disagree.'

'Why's that?'

'They haven't fucking caught him, have they?' She exhaled, the truth of her anger appearing for only a moment, before she stowed it away again. 'Sorry.'

'You never have to apologise to me.'

'I know. But it was unfair and uncalled for. Listen, thanks for being around. I don't think I'll see you for a few weeks.'

'Oh?' He sat back down in his seat, resting the notepad on his lap.

'Yes. I'm going away for a bit.'

'Ah... I had hoped we'd have another few sessions, to guide you through the TV show. And how you might react to the case being in the public eye again.'

'We can pick that up when I get back.' Becky stood up and began to gather her things.

'Where are you off to?'

'On holiday, Dr Fullerton. You'd be the first to say that R'n'R is important.'

# 11

Becky grinned at herself in the hotel room mirror. She didn't quite recognise the person she saw. Her hair was different – restyled that morning, before she took the Eurostar; she'd asked for something to 'impress at an interview' – and she wore far more make-up than she was used to. She was unsure of how she looked, but had that fugitive feeling that she was in disguise.

A five-minute trip on a tram took her into the centre of Brussels, and after a quick security check to verify that she was, indeed, Marion Clifford, a freelance journalist, she was soon through into the main parliament building.

She waited a while in a shiny leather sofa that looked and smelled new. More than anywhere she'd ever been, including Westminster, this place was epic; despite the bustle of activity round her, human endeavour of any sort seemed muted in such an enormous space, perhaps even up to and including explosions. It was a cathedral of peace and light.

The man she had come to meet was precisely on time.

'Miss Clifford?' She nodded and rose to meet him.

Edwin Galbraith, reluctant MEP, enthusiastic right-wing upstart, sometimes in Strasbourg but today in Brussels, smiled disarmingly and thrust out his hand. His handshake was firm, but brisk. His sober blue suit, slight paunch and rounded spectacles made him look older than he was, while his long chin and the high, tight cropping on a good head of fair hair reminded Becky of a technical drawing teacher she hadn't thought of in years. He would particularly suit a V-neck pullover that hadn't been changed in a while, she decided, and perhaps a pencil perched behind his ear.

'What do you think of the seat of power of our European oppressors?'

'I was just thinking it was like the biggest cathedral I'd ever seen.'

'I've always thought it was like that spaceport in *Star Wars*. Though the music's not nearly so catchy.'

'Mos Eisley? So long as there's no ray guns, I think we'll be fine.' Becky smiled, hoping she hadn't stained her teeth with lipstick.

'So... Miss Clifford...'

'That's me.'

'Come into my parlour.'

Galbraith's 'parlour' was a beautifully-appointed canteen, occupied by well-dressed, important-looking people. Becky kicked herself for being unable able to identify them. Galbraith chose a secluded table in a corner, and decided to order coffee on her behalf, which threw her to an almost absurd degree.

'I must admit,' Galbraith said, sniffing at the strong, thick brew, 'it's not often we get volunteers of your calibre, Miss Clifford.'

'Please call me Marion.'

He nodded gracefully. 'The people I usually get approaching me are, to be blunt, not particularly subtle when it comes to the world of politics. How can I put it? They might be better suited to... our security team.'

'That's very sad,' she said, allowing him to pour milk into her cup to his own specification. 'I mean, enthusiasm for our cause is a good thing. But in my opinion, we need fewer bald heads and thick necks to get our point across. Those are precisely the type of people that have stifled the debate on the right wing.'

He leaned forward, eyes keen. 'Sad, but all too true. That's why meeting people like you gives me such hope.'

His accent was perfectly British, perfectly refined, and utterly reasonable. Edwin Galbraith was seen as the great white hope of the extreme right, a polished, considered performer who was rarely flustered no matter what invective was aimed at him. He hadn't quite made it to Westminster, but he'd made Brussels his home and the source of his extremely comfortable lifestyle for a decade – a sublime irony.

One of Becky's colleagues had sparked envy and admiration among his fellow hacks when he perfectly described Galbraith as having the unnerving habit of becoming acceptable background noise: 'When he speaks, we're like babies lulled to sleep by a washing machine.'

'I'm all clear for the next couple of weeks,' Becky said. 'My core skills are in public relations, so if I could attach myself to your office, that'd be terrific.'

'I'm sure we could find a role – you'd be amazed at the amount of work we get through on a daily basis. The media, Marion – it never sleeps. It's an unkillable beast. Now, more than ever before, even with the newspapers in their death throes.'

'That's true. Everything's spread online, now. Everything.'

'Indeed. But TV's still a must, arguably more important than the internet for getting a message across. We've had one or two good people in the past, but... it takes a thick skin to work in politics, Marion. Bulletproof, in fact. And to work on our PR team, I have to tell you – you'll need an especially thick skin.'

'I think my skin's thick enough,' she said, dropping a sugar lump in her cup.

'I don't doubt it.' Galbraith smiled, diffidently, then suddenly brightened. 'This is silly. We're in the middle of Brussels and we're stuck in the factory canteen. Why don't we head out and get some proper lunch?'

She blinked, rapidly, and lowered her eyes, throwing herself into the role. 'Oh... only if you're *sure*. I was surprised you even had time on your schedule for a coffee.'

'I've always got time for a first-rate CV,' he said, smiling broadly – and revealing why he rarely did so in his publicity shots. English teeth was the phrase; more claw than enamel. 'Let's get out of here, come on. My treat.'

And so they went off-campus, and soon found themselves in a bustling lane. Waiters threaded their way through the brisk lunchtime crowd; tourists mingled easily with people in businesswear. Despite the perilous scenario, Becky felt a treacherous tug in her breast. There was the smell of fresh bread, the tang of seafood and garlic butter – and there, a mellow gold in the light, was a tall, clear glass of Pilsner laid down in front of a portly tourist. Everywhere she looked offered the promise of alcohol and laughter – and all that followed. She felt younger than she was.

Incredibly, Galbraith ordered for her again. 'Seafood platter okay? Not allergic, are you? This is the best in the city.'

'Absolutely, seafood's fine for me.'

'And you'll have a beer? It has to be beer in Brussels, you know.'

She hesitated, but only for a moment. 'Why not? I'll have the peach beer, in fact.'

'Excellent choice. I'm more of a raspberry man, myself.' He ordered Friuli, and watched with a kind of reverence as the waiter poured half of it into a glass shaped like a tulip bulb. The deep red brew kindled in the light.

Becky sipped at her drink, and felt its treacherous cool fingers tickle her stomach. 'So, do you have much close contact with our friends from the Netherlands and France in parliament?'

He nodded. 'Quite a lot, in fact. They want the same things, that's no secret. Despite dear Albion's imminent exit, there's broad consensus between us on many matters, as you might suppose.'

'Immigration being one of them.'

'Naturally.' He palmed away froth from his upper lip. 'But their methods leave much to be desired. The key thing about our kind of politics is that we must calm people's fears. We must appeal to rational, educated people. We have to show we're civilised and reasonable. That there's nothing wrong with our views and our goals.' He chuckled.

'I can't tell you the problems I've had, trying to make sure our voice is rational, consistent, logical.'

'I totally agree. So many people I speak to make the assumption that "right wing" equals "some kind of nut". It's so frustrating.'

He laid a hand on her arm so gently she might not have known it was there, had she not seen him move. 'I sympathise, totally.'

*How easy this is. A smile, a skirt, some lipstick, high fucking heels. What a simple matter it is to reel them in.*

'I want to redress the balance,' she said, earnestly. 'And I think I'm the person who can do that for you. If you want me, that is.'

'I'm flattered, Marion. It's a great offer.' He had liquid brown eyes that captured the light, but they weren't quite those of a puppy; they were too small. They belonged on another creature.

'So,' she said, 'seeing as this is my first day on the job – what's on the agenda for me today?'

He laughed and sat back. 'Well, for a start, you can tell me where you're hiding it.'

'Hiding...?'

'The camera. Is it in one of your earrings? That buttonhole on your jacket? The handbag on the table is a classic, you know. But you seem smarter than the average blagger.'

Her heart lurched. 'I'm sorry?'

'Oh, come on.' He folded his arms. ''Can I be your intern?' You expect to just walk in and start work in this party just like that?'

'I don't understand. I thought we had an agreement? That this was a job interview?'

'Yes. A job interview for someone who doesn't appear to exist.' He raised a hand to cut off her protest. 'Oh, don't bother, I'm sure you've got ID. It probably looks legitimate. But we're not entirely stupid. We carried out some research on Marion Clifford. There wasn't much in the way of bylines to be found.'

'I've mostly worked in an editorial capacity,' she stammered. 'My CV is quite clear about this.' Did the colour rising on her cheeks complement her lipstick, she wondered?

'I took the liberty of calling one or two hacks of my acquaintance. Birds of a feather, you might call them. Not many of them had heard of a Marion Clifford. And not on the *Gauntlet* or Shockwave FM, either. So… if you don't mind… who are you, and why are you here?'

She felt like she was at school, all of a sudden. Singled out, with a raptor-eyed teacher freezing her with one single pointed finger. She felt faint; for an absurd second, tears prickled the corner of her eyes.

Becky collected herself, pulling her sleeves tight. She considered leaving, just cutting her losses and getting out of there. She'd been careful to plant the odd byline here and there in the past few months; 'Marion Clifford' had in fact been a fake ID she'd used in her early days in journalism, one of a host of fake names. She had wanted to reel Galbraith in before addressing what she really wanted. In her arrogance she had wondered if she might even have dug a little extra dirt on him by then – political dirt, that is.

Becky decided to get to the point. Only just concealing the tremor in her voice, she said: 'It's not usually my style to ruin someone's day like this. Please bear with me, Mr Galbraith.'

'I beg your pardon?'

'First of all, I want to assure you that I'm not recording this in any way. No pinhole cameras, no hidden microphones, and, I can assure the audience, nothing up either sleeve.' She showed him her wrists, theatrically.

He snorted. 'Short of running you through a metal detector, or having you searched, that hardly proves anything.'

'I don't know why you're so shy, Mr Galbraith. Surely a seasoned, front-line politician like you wouldn't have anything to hide?'

He grinned, but not pleasantly. His posture had completely changed; he was sat upright, with his hands clenched before him. 'Oh. This is good. Now you sound like a proper journalist. Now it sounds like we're down to business.'

'I can also say at this point that I'm not interested in catching you out or recording you covertly... if you were to make some offhand racist comments, say, or if you offered some unpleasant commentary about letting refugees drown. Or if you said something to do with your party's policies and core beliefs, for example. I think they're well enough known by now. They're not news.'

'I resent what you're implying, and I would urge you to be extremely cautious, miss.'

'Snap. That's why I have to say, if *you* happen to be recording this conversation, say, with a pinhole camera in that lovely tiepin you have there, or in your cufflinks, I think you should stop. Right now.'

He frowned. 'Out with it. What is it you want? Money? You think you've got something to bribe me with? I've heard it all before. I've had tabloid cretins like you crawling through my *bins*. Grubbing round like rats. They've spent days on end trying to put my shredded files together with sticky-tape. And you know what they've found? Nothing. No extra-marital affairs, no drug-taking... nothing. You know why? Because there *is* nothing.' He held up his Friuli. 'The odd one of these, sure. When I'm out for lunch, or the odd one on a Friday night when I'm back home with my wife. But that's all. And frankly, the way you people take to the stuff, you've got a bloody nerve writing anything about it.' He slammed the beer bottle down.

One of the waiters glanced in their direction, frowning.

Her wires thrumming with adrenaline, Becky's natural inclination was to bite back. But she kept her voice low, and her expression neutral. 'I am not after your money. Frankly, I'm not even interested in your politics. Your stock has dropped in the past six months. Or hadn't you noticed? Your party's had its day.'

Galbraith got to his feet. 'I think that's about all I have time for, Miss Clifford. Do enjoy your stay in Brussels.'

'Please sit down, Mr Galbraith. What I want is information. That's all.'

He hesitated. 'What kind of information?'

'If I mentioned the Billy Goats Gruff... would that phrase mean anything to you?'

You could fake a lot of things, Becky thought. Surprise was an easy one. Confusion was another. But that split second of realisation – that instant of time where you understand someone has hit the target, dead centre – that reaction was in fact hard to feign, and near-impossible to conceal.

'I don't know what you're talking about.'

'You do. Billy Goats Gruff. Hertfordshire. Early nineties. Does any of that seem familiar?'

His lips trembled. 'You'll be hearing from my solicitors. And I'll make sure any editor worth his salt never has anything to do with you.'

'Take it easy. I'm not threatening you, and I don't intend to. Sit down, Mr Galbraith. Let's talk it over. We do have a seafood platter to enjoy after all.'

He sat back down, his face the colour of putty. It seemed impossible that hair could grow on that chin, or ever had before. 'There's nothing to talk about.'

'We both know that there is. I won't go into any details. I won't tell you what I have. I will only say that it makes it abundantly clear that you know all about the Billy Goats Gruff.'

Galbraith's eyes narrowed. *He's going to fight*, Becky thought. What a marvel. 'You know,' he whispered, 'I could make things more uncomfortable for you than you realise. Extremely uncomfortable.'

'You could – I don't doubt it. My research has shown that the Billy Goats Gruff was a serious club, for extremely serious gentlemen, committing extremely serious offences. Well, one of the three of you did, anyway. The one who was all set to go to court, before he had that unfortunate business on the east coast main line.'

'I have no idea what you're talking about. None whatsoever. It sounds like pie in the sky.'

Becky ignored him. 'Here's some rules. First of all: if anything at all should happen to me, then the Billy Goats Gruff will become public knowledge. Even if the papers won't touch it – and they will, believe me – then I'll spread it across the internet. It's a very easy thing to do these days, especially when it comes to politicians and… well, the kind of things the Billy Goats Gruff did.'

Galbraith checked his watch. He affected boredom, now; he'd had time to think. 'You've got one minute, Miss Clifford. I have things to do this afternoon.'

'Finish your beer, Mr Galbraith. Just listen. I won't be a minute more. The second thing I want you to understand is that I don't want *you*. I don't even want the Billy Goats Gruff. But I do want you to do some digging for me. I want information. I want to know about similar clubs to the Billy Goats Gruff you may have encountered in your travels. Based in Europe. And not ones who just like tying up schoolgirls. I want to know about ones who take things a bit further than that.'

He leaned back in his seat and shook his head. 'You've gone cosmic on me. Really, I have not the slightest inkling of what you're talking about.'

'Murder is what I'm talking about,' Becky said. 'I want any names you can find among your contacts who might be into that sort of thing. Use the old school tie, if you must. The harder stuff is just a hop, skip and a jump away from the Billy Goats Gruff. I assume you're still in touch with the other member, whoever he is? Last meeting you held was… whoa… 2006? That's not in the too-distant past, really.'

'Time's up,' Galbraith said. He drained his beer and counted off some banknotes. 'I'll get the bill. Don't be making off with this cash, will you? This is a reputable place. I suppose I can't stop you claiming it on expenses, though.'

Becky dropped a business card on top of the money. 'Do some digging. Ask some questions. You're a clever man. You can do it without attracting attention. You might even do it on… what's the name of that forum you use? On the dark web? Pink Candles? Something like that?'

Galbraith said nothing. His eyes watered. His hands clenched, tight enough to bleach the knuckles.

'Get back to me sooner rather than later, if you would, Mr Galbraith. I want to know some names. Europe. Early nineties onwards. Groups of people or individuals who are into making young women and girls disappear. Trafficked women, kidnapped women. Ones who vanish. Ones who end up dead. Men who are into that kind of stuff.'

He turned to leave; jaw clenching. At the last instant, he took the card. Then he was gone.

Becky placed her hands flat on the table, willing them to stop shaking. They obeyed, insofar as she did not spill any peach beer as she drained it in two long gulps.

A waiter appeared with an immense silver platter piled high with seafood, a bouquet of red and pink still life. The claw of a lobster seemed to reach out for her. 'Miss?' he said in French. 'Is everything well?'

'Everything is marvellous,' Becky replied. 'It's been an excellent day.'

## 12

Fresh from the shower in her hotel room, Becky wrapped her hair in a towel. Then, as an afterthought, she allowed it to drape on each side of her head, part-concealing her face.

She checked her watch. Precisely on schedule, her laptop's messenger programme bleeped.

Rupert's own mask of choice for today was either a moving bank of clouds, or an approximation of a sheep. She could still discern the mirth in his eyes.

'Nice get-up,' he said. 'Are you going through a Jedi phase?'

'It was either that or a dead president's mask.'

'I like it. It's very... *you*.'

'Did you find any cold case material? Specifically in Europe?'

'Got one interesting hit. A very big one. A murder case from about twenty years ago.'

Becky kept her voice level. 'Oh yes?'

'Yes. Family was butchered. Absolutely twisted stuff. They were kidnapped from a holiday home. British. Seems like it's a notorious case. Strange, though – I hadn't heard of it, but it was a big deal in the UK. Not much official information online, either. It's kinda suspicious that it was so quiet across Europe. No one was caught. People remember the case in the UK, though. Surely you've come across it before? It's near the top of Google rankings, there was an appeal on the TV recently. You must know something of this?'

'I know about that case, yes.'

'There was one little spike in the past couple of weeks. An anniversary passed. Doesn't seem like the police expect much from the inquiry, though. Guy who did it just dropped out of existence. Like a ghost.'

Becky swallowed. 'That case is of interest to me. It may be connected to what I'm looking for.'

'I see.' Rupert leaned forward. 'This case… is it what you wanted to check out with the police? Any signs of a cover-up? Links to other cases? And that message you sent me about checking pen-pals' listings, and Monsieur Fabrice?'

'It'd be a good starting point.'

'How much do you want to know?'

'As much as you can tell me. I want access to all the case files, investigating officers, and above all, suspects. Every avenue they followed. Details of the case. Things which might have been hidden from the media. Tip-offs. Lines of inquiry they dropped. The stuff they might have hidden to discourage kooks coming forward and claiming responsibility.'

Rupert scribbled things down. A cartoon smile spread across the cloudy face; the effect was similar to a man's mouth suddenly breaching a layer of shaving foam. 'Great! I love the Nancy Drew stuff. It'll take me a while to breach Interpol and Europol. From there I can access the regional stuff. Such a shame – I used to have a man on the inside, but he's moved on to other things.'

'Do what you can – anything at all is valuable. Redacted notes, weird dead ends – that's what I'm most interested in.'

'You thinking that there's been a cover-up? Related to this case, the British family?'

She was wary about how much she should tell Rupert. 'It wouldn't shock me. In that case and others, there are too many cold trails and false starts. And lines of inquiry that start off promising but seem to go nowhere. Plus there are a few cases I think are linked, but police have never made the connection.'

The white face grinned again. 'Hence the focus on police and politicians. Who better to sweep stuff under the carpet?'

'Exactly.'

'How did Mr Edwin Galbraith MEP take the information we dug up?'

'You know, I think he was a little bit emotional about it all. He'll need some time to think about it.'

The cloud-face grinned. 'That's what I like to hear.'

'Your information was golden. What else have you turned up on the politicians?'

On-screen, Rupert flipped through a shorthand notebook. 'Regarding organised, ritual killings, and the like… I found a few things here and there. Not much of it was pretty.'

'The uglier, the better. What have you got?'

'There doesn't seem to be anything organised outwith the usual lone perverts and the odd snuff video which sneaks through. But murder and such... that's a niche interest. Tends to be done by people who like to keep themselves to themselves. They're not really part of the sharing generation.'

Becky drummed her fingertips on the dresser. 'Any names?'

'No. It'll require more work, or a more refined search. I've snagged a few guys who accessed or uploaded snuff, but it looks like they didn't create it. Sourced from the usual tourist hotspots – Iraq, Syria, Haiti, Mexico, Colombia, West Africa. Where the real crazies live. Machetes, heads on sticks, you know? Nothing particularly European. As I said, anything like that which exists online is probably a closed shop. It'll be set up to look like a fashion website or, I don't know... a textiles enthusiasts' blog. The board game association's list of rules and regulations, fully annotated. Something which isn't what it appears to be. It'll be especially hard to link it to police and politicians if they're involved – you'd think they're too smart for that. That's why you need to give me more data.'

'I might be able to help you with that shortly.'

Rupert took a deep breath. 'Okay. I have to tell you... if you want me to help you... you're going to have to be little more upfront. I get the impression you're hiding something, Elizabeth.'

Becky didn't like the way he laboured *Elizabeth*. 'I'll want you to work with the information I'm giving you, nothing more. Understand?'

Rupert raised a hand. 'Not a problem. If you're worried about legality – let me put your mind at rest. This is *totally* illegal. We're both committing a crime. But don't worry, you're as safe as you can be online, when you're doing something very illegal.'

She smiled. '"Safe as you can be," says the man with the cloudy face. Look, when it comes to hacking, I don't think anything's safe, and I'd prefer us to be as neutral as we can. Fair enough?'

'That's cool.'

'How about the classified ads and pen-pals' pages in France?'

'Ah, your mysterious Fabrice. This one I particularly enjoyed.' His fingers danced a tarantella on an unseen keyboard, and documents appeared on-screen. 'There were three possible hits in the timeframe you mentioned. One of them appeared in a school magazine that was sent out nationwide, on creative writing.'

Rupert enlarged one of two entries on a single column of text, underneath a 'pen-pals' header'. It was decorated with sketches of the Coliseum, the Eiffel tower and – Becky almost burst out laughing – a pair of clogs underneath stripy tights. The first one was from Erich, who lived in Hamburg, whose hobbies were go-karting and moto-cross. Below that, was Fabrice, from Provence. His hobbies were 'all sports, particularly rugby union'.

'Oh, Fabrice. There you are. In a school magazine. "Quality newspaper" my sainted arse, Clara.' Becky took note of the details. 'Excellent work. Have you found out where his address was?'

'It'll take some digging. This is all pre-internet, remember. There may not have been accurate records taken; anything relevant on him might be handwritten, shoved into a box file somewhere. And that's only if you're lucky. But that looks good for your mystery man.'

'It does indeed. Very interesting. Hello, Monsieur Fabrice.' Becky tapped the screen with the tip of her fingernail.

Rupert asked, 'So, are you expecting anything more from Galbraith?'

'He called me this afternoon – we've got a lunch date set up in the Atomium.'

'Sounds good. Well, as soon as you've got something, get back to me, and I'll get looking.'

'Thanks. And... good work.'

Rupert raised his index finger. 'But be careful now, you hear? Politicians never were a trustworthy lot, even if you do have this one by the balls.'

'I'm a very careful girl. Don't you worry.'

'Dope,' he said, simply, then the screen went blank save for the bubbly face. Stripped of its living eyes and mouth, only a white mask remained, which discomfited Becky so much she slammed the screen down flat.

# 13

The Atomium had the look of something that might have been dreamed up in 1989, rather than thirty years earlier, designed by someone with a geometrically precise haircut whose favourite musician was Jean Michel Jarre. That wasn't to say Becky disliked it.

Her rendezvous point was on the upper sphere, nearly 300ft above Brussels. Although Becky was sure it wasn't holiday time, the place was swarming with schoolchildren, delighted with the spaceship windows, angles and contours. This riotous activity reassured Becky, but not to the point where she let her guard down and ignored the men who were tailing her.

The two lumpy no-necks in long black coats had stuck out like the sore thumbs they so closely resembled, all the way up the escalators, from sphere to sphere. They had failed some of the most basic tests when it came to tailing someone by matching her movements as she retraced her steps up and down the escalators.

That was when she was sure she was dealing with people connected to Edwin Galbraith – amateurs, in other words. She wondered what northern English town they lived in; whether they'd have stuck it out forever in nightclub doorways with earpieces embedded in their coarse sandy heads had they not discovered that old-time religion Galbraith preached: barracking Muslims.

Pausing by one window, she gazed out towards the Basilica in the distance, keeping one eye on the two shadowy smudges growing on either side of her shoulders.

'Quite a view,' the man on her right said, in soft East Anglian tones. A plague upon my prejudices, Becky thought.

She turned to him and beamed, aware that his colleague was now flanking her on the left. 'It's amazing. We're quite a way up. I was just wondering what I might think about if I was to jump off.'

'You'd have lots of time to think, I suppose. You might even have time to change your mind.' He chuckled, and his face was transformed; that of a butterbean at a roadside Hungry Horse, someone with a brood of kids and a plump momma for a wife. Her heart kicked hard, and she began to doubt herself.

But she pressed on: 'Is Ed not with us today? I cancelled some important business to be here.'

'He's here,' the man on her left said. 'We're here to give you a little message first.' Now, his accent was more like it: north of England, possibly Leeds, or further east into the wilderness gouged out of the coastline towards Hull. He was younger, keener-eyed, than his colleague. The hairline dotting his scalp showed that he had no real need to skin it, and a movie star jawline was hidden beneath clotted muscle cladding. If it weren't for 'roids and an addiction to lifting heavy things, he would have been a strikingly handsome man.

'Go on then. What's the message? Bear in mind, I can scream. Really loudly.'

'You won't, though,' the bigger man said, amiably. 'There's no need. We're only having a conversation, aren't we?'

'Freedom of speech,' his younger colleague agreed. He scratched stubble that was more pound shop than designer. 'Journalists know all about that, eh? Just speaking our minds.'

'The message is, we can find you for a chat,' the big man said. He, too, was strangely distracted, reaching out a forefinger and picking at some speck on the window pane. 'Any time we like. We like having chats with people who have really interesting ideas.'

Becky played with her hair and affected a girlish laugh. She used the gesture to peer into a corner. Yes; the red winking light of a security camera. 'Oh, I understand perfectly. Hey, did you get that coat out of Matalan?' She touched the older man's lapels. 'I've been thinking of getting one for my dad.'

The older man stared at her hand for a moment as she rubbed the material, and then she traced her fingertips over his chest underneath. He shook his head for a moment, astonished. 'You've got some balls on you, I'll tell you that for nothing.'

'Balls being the operative word.'

The younger man spotted what her other hand was doing and reached out for her. But he was too late. 'Hey!'

'Back off,' Becky spat, teeth bared. She turned towards the older man. 'Tell him, Butterbean.'

'Patch it for now,' the older man said to his colleague, levelly. His back was rigid. He smiled at Becky, but all the warmth was gone.

She jammed what she held in her left hand tight against the crotch of his black trousers, and he grunted, quietly. 'Now, a man in your line of work will know all about what a stun gun can do to sensitive parts of the body, don't you? It's a bit like the stuff they don't tell you about baton rounds and rubber bullets, when they're aimed at the same place. Did you used to be a policeman, Butterbean?'

'No. But if you've got an offensive weapon on your person, then I'll be introducing you to one shortly.'

'Excellent. You can explain why you were following me around, while you're at it. We'll both go, in fact – you and me, down the escalator. Your sidekick here can stay and look at the scenery, because you're going to tell him to do that. Then when we're downstairs we'll speak to security, and then they can call the police. Sound fair?'

She hadn't raised her voice; indeed, she angled her hips and parted her legs slightly so as to make her position seemingly flirtatious, even brazen. In fact, it gave her more leverage to knee him in the groin, as hard as she needed to.

'Fair enough,' the big man said. 'You should know that accidents can happen on escalators.'

'Accidents can happen when your finger is on a trigger, too.' She jammed the barrel hard against him. She watched his Adam's apple bob.

Six or seven children cascaded past them in a shrieking throng. Becky ignored the interruption. She only took her eyes away from Butterbean's to glance at their reflections in the window, to be sure the younger man was still there, but a safe distance away.

At this point, another figure joined this blurry procession, a scarecrow's shadow materialising between Becky and the big man.

'That's enough, lads,' Edwin Galbraith said, brightly. 'I think the point has been made.'

'You reckon?' Becky kept her left hand where it was, until Butterbean slowly backed away, both hands raised. She slid what she held in her hand back into her bag, gunfighter-quick.

'Absolutely,' Galbraith said, joining her at the railing as the two sullen blobs melted away in the glass. 'Granted, these boys were a little slapdash, but I hardly wanted to put my best men on the job. This is merely a demonstration. One I hope you have taken note of.'

'Yeah. I think it went really well for you. Next time, bring your big brother.' She stood a good distance from him – still close enough to kick him in the throat, if the occasion demanded.

'I'll be brief, Miss Clifford – my schedule is chock-a-block these days.'

'Yeah, you're rushed off your feet. Just like the other day. You could have taken me back to the restaurant, you know. Picked some other things for me to eat. No reason why we can't spin things out into a nice lunch.'

Galbraith gripped a handrail. 'It's been a very trying week. I've had to speak to some old acquaintances I'd rather not have had occasion to think about ever again, far less contact.'

'It gets that way with old mates, doesn't it? They just know too much about you. Skeletons in the cupboard. Where the bodies are buried. It's sometimes much easier to step away, isn't it? Keep them restricted to Christmas cards. Maybe the odd round-robin letter.'

'Maybe. But in any case, I found what I think you're looking for, Miss Clifford. After today, I don't expect to see you or hear from you ever again. If I do, well... there'll be consequences.'

'You don't have to speak in tongues, Edwin. I'm not recording you.'

'Shut up!' he said, with sudden venom. He did not turn his head to look at her, his mouth compressed into a livid white line. She noted the dark patches underneath his eyes, the sloppy angle of his tie and the wayward parting in his hair. 'Just... stop talking.' He sighed, then looked down at the floor. 'Terrible mess they leave in these places, isn't there? Maybe they cut the cleaning budget.'

Galbraith turned sharply and strode towards the escalators, falling in behind a young couple, their broad smiles and flushed faces a jarring contrast to his bent posture. She watched Galbraith's high mop of hair sink out of sight, then scanned the floor.

At her feet was a crumpled piece of paper she hadn't noticed before. She picked it up and smoothed it out. Inside, in thin capitals sloped right-to-left, two words were scrawled in what looked like felt tip:

JANUARY ORCHESTRA.

She put the paper into her jeans pocket.

Still gripping the barrel with her left hand, she pulled the object she'd held on Butterbean from her handbag, placed it under her chin, and pulled the trigger.

Then she sprayed both her wrists, dabbed them together and smiled to herself, before making her way to the escalator.

# 14

Becky zipped her holdall and heaved it onto the hotel room bed. She was somewhat obsessive about leaving these places in good order, as blank and sterile as her home; the bed as hard-pressed as when she'd first peeled the sheets back, the damp towels folded neatly into a corner of the bathroom floor.

She was about to double-check the train tickets when one of her phones grumbled.

Becky had to paw through an inside compartment of the holdall before she reached the right pay-as-you-go. The number was withheld.

'Hello?'

'Hey, Elizabeth. It's Rupert.'

'Hey... I thought we were restricted to video chat, Rupert?'

'I tried to get a hold of you there, but you were offline. It's important. I think I've got a fix on your Fabrice.'

'Okay. I've got five minutes.'

She set up the laptop and was soon connected. Rupert was in the same shadowy spot as before, but he had forgotten to cover his face. He was thin-featured and bright-eyed, with a long, sharp chin. He somehow suited his long straggly ginger curls where a million other faces would have struggled. If she was being unkind, Becky thought he resembled a witch from a long-forgotten childhood TV show.

'Hey. There you are,' he said. 'Nice to see a pretty face, for once!'

She smiled. 'Touché. Your mask has slipped, Rupert.'

'Oh!' His hand flew to his mouth. Then he grinned. 'I forgot. I'm meant to be in disguise. Ah, never mind. You'll need to be some kind of tech Jedi to crack this encryption.'

'What if I'm recording you?'

'You're not recording me.' He waggled a finger. 'I'd know if you were.'

'I've got a train to catch; let's hear it.'

'I found Fabrice – it turns out there was a computer record of him kept at one school… the head of computing there was very keen on electronic records. He was still there when Windows appeared; he transferred every single file. I had to reinstall old versions of Word, but I got there in the end. Apparently a girl there made contact with the mysterious Fabrice through the inter-schools' magazine. Does the name Clara Morgan mean anything to you?'

She paused. Her chin quivered before she spoke. This was absurd, that she could be so close to tears, at the mere mention of the name. She swallowed hard then said, 'Yes. She's one of the murder victims in France, isn't she? Twenty years ago?'

'Yes. The ritual thing you wanted me to check out with the police. Direct hit, right?'

Becky scratched at her neck and nodded.

'Anyway, this Clara got in contact with Fabrice. There's a postal address connected to the PO box for the student exchange service. I had a quick look at census data and local councils; there's no Fabrice listed there, at the time, or now.'

Becky leaned forward. 'What was that address?'

He gave it to her; she wrote it down, longhand, in the hotel's headed notepaper.

'The other thing was, the house hasn't changed hands in, like, forever… It's a family home, former farmhouse kind of thing. Same family passes it on, generation to generation.'

'Who lives there now?'

'You want a name?'

'Yes. Come on, man!'

He told her. She leaned back and pinched the bridge of her nose.

'What's the matter? You know the dude?'

'Not exactly. I expected this. Or I suspected it, anyway. He's the man I'm going to speak to next.'

'You okay? You don't look okay.' Rupert bit his lip. 'This guy giving you trouble?'

'No. Nothing like it. I was just hoping it would be someone else.'

It was a chocolate-box village that might have been somewhere slow-paced in England. A place where lorries wouldn't fit on the roads. There were one or two thatched roofs and white walls on the older periphery of the town where, so the guidebook said, some Roman settlements remained. But most of the houses were toasty red brick, set among cobbled lanes. An old slate-grey church stuck right in the centre had survived the war, although the saints and angels lining its ancient corners and stretching out their arms in blessing or welcome had lost their heads. This would have been thanks to hammer and chisel rather than the guillotine, but probably happened round about the time *Madame* carried out her bloody work.

The day was clouded over but not cold, with a hint of summer in the air. Snowdrops curtseyed demurely beneath the shade of trees; greedy starlings hopped along the top of the higher walls. A few tourists roamed here and there, grinning impalements on the end of selfie sticks near the entrance of a walled garden. Water tinkled somewhere, but Becky couldn't be sure which garden hid the feature.

She waited on a bench on some flat parkland, near a play area where a boy terrorised his younger brother, pushing him ever higher on the swings. Their mother sat with her head bent low into a paperback book, oblivious to the screams.

Sometimes, in the quieter moments, the sadness returned to haunt Becky. It was here that she felt the echoes of things which could not be, and had never been – scenes of families out in the park – even when siblings bickered, or parents grew tetchy. It was a subtle blow, but a telling one.

Becky fixed the pink carnation in her lapel and waited.

She kept her eye on the dog-walkers who appeared on a playing field throughout the afternoon. If she were in his shoes, she would take her time to stake the place out, and dog-walking was a decent cover story if you wanted to do that. One woman walked past with two Cairn terriers; a younger woman struggled to contain an immense Irish setter; later, a tall man was seemingly borne aloft on a billowing cloud of small yappy dogs – clearly a walking service of some kind – with admirable cool.

She wondered how she should play it when she finally met him. Friendliness? Cool reserve? Cold professionalism? She felt none of these things. Becky tried to focus on her breathing, to calm her heart, and to dab the moisture that prickled her palms.

She spotted the man she had come to see from a long way off. By the colouring and its wiry frame, she made out the details of his dog first – a farmer's mutt, an English sheepdog. She took care to keep her chin tilted upwards and her shoulders back as he approached, and kept her breathing slow, deep and steady; in through the nose, out through the mouth.

She wondered if sheepdogs were vicious. Should he turn tail on her, she fully intended to keep step with him.

Becky shuddered as the face grew more distinct. It was him. The pink carnation pinned to his coat confirmed it.

As he grew closer, Becky realised that he had barely changed; his close-shaved face suited a few more lines, and his fine head of longish wind-whipped hair was mostly dark, though spiked with the white cat's whisker spines. The mullet had long gone, naturally, but he still had the look of a rock star, and a French one, at that. Becky didn't feel nearly as nauseous as she'd imagined she would. Perhaps that would come later, when they spoke.

He squinted, rather than frowned, as he approached. The dog strained at the leash once or twice, but came to heel with a single command. Perhaps it was a descendant of the dog she remembered in the woods.

His thin, black eyebrows arched as he approached. He was slightly shorter than she remembered. If he'd played rugby he'd have been a fly half; certainly his ears hadn't negotiated too many scrums, but he was still in good shape. He had a longish nose but thin cheeks and high, well-defined cheekbones. He might have made a good Musketeer.

He checked himself; possibly he recognised her at some level, but didn't put it together immediately. 'Hello,' he said, diffidently. 'Are you Monique?'

'I am,' Becky said, standing. She held out her hand, and he switched the dog lead to his left hand in order to shake it.

'I'm Roger,' he said. Becky always had loved the French pronunciation, the trailing consonants soft and tactile. 'I know this sounds like a corny thing to say, but... have we met before?'

'We have. It was a long time ago, though. A good distance away from this place. Near your house.'

She studied his reaction closely. The slight tug at one corner of the mouth. The startled look. Then the wide oases of realisation spreading in his eyes. 'You sound as if you are from England.'

'I am. And I know your name isn't Roger. It isn't Fabrice, either. Is it, Leif?'

He opened his mouth to speak, then thought better of it. He turned sharply and stalked away. The dog yelped, astonished, as he dragged it alongside.

Becky caught up with him in two or three long strides. The dog tried to sniff her, but its owner yanked the lead savagely, and growled a command either too low or too guttural to be understood on a human level.

'It's all right, Leif. You're not in any kind of trouble.'

'I do not want to talk to you. Why are you here?'

'I have to speak to you about what happened.'

'I have nothing more to say about that, to anyone. Do you understand? I had to speak to the police again two weeks ago. *Again.* I cannot remember one single detail I haven't already described, over and over again. I cannot help you.'

Leif would not look at her, drawing his chin down towards his chest, as if he was bent into heavy rain.

Becky swallowed an angry response and softened her tone. 'I'm sorry I had to contact you the way I did, it wasn't a nice thing to do. But if I'd gone to your house you might have just shut the door on me. I have to speak to you. It's important. Leif, if you have any understanding of the situation, please stop, and at least talk to me for two minutes. Please.' Her French wasn't used to being harried in such a way; usually Becky had the luxury of time taken to construct the phrases. Perhaps something in the desperate delivery made him stop.

His eyes were bloodshot. She resisted an urge to put a hand on his arm.

'I will give you two minutes. Becky.'

# 15

Then

Leif took up the stick and examined it for weight and heft. He pulled out stray twigs and stripped off sharp edges along the bark. Finally, he stared along its tenderised length, then made as if to throw it.

By his side, Petra waited, sat on her haunches, patient and composed.

He frowned at her, then grinned. His hair and eyebrows were wild, but his face was too open and handsome to be intimidating. The boy resembled a matinee idol trying to play the tough guy.

'You know me too well, old girl. No suspense? No drama?'

Petra licked her chops and panted. It was as close to a shrug as an animal could get, Leif supposed.

'Go on then – show me what you can do!'

He hurled the stick as far as it would go. It sailed overhead before crashing into the line of trees, where the path began.

Birds shot out of the uppermost branches, startled into shrieking motion. Petra shot off after it, barking loudly.

Leif checked his watch. He was far too early, but it paid to be cautious. He believed in preparation.

It was a fine day today – still chilly at first light, but otherwise there were signs that summer was nearby. Leif had the luxury of a few days off from college, and chose, as ever, to spend it in the valley with his dog. La Grange aux la Croix was alive, and with its prime yet to come. In the morning, in the little bedroom opposite the oak tree, he woke each day with the skylarks' clamouring. Petra – not as enthused over early starts as she once was – grunted as he threw back the bedclothes, but would still pad over the scrubbed floorboards to join him by the window, in anticipation of a walk. Leif would gaze at the early morning skies, elbows resting on the windowsill, the same way he had as a boy. A lonely child grown into a shy young man, Leif loved the emptiness and stillness of the house at these times. Then, as now, his father, who had long given up on him, was out working on the farmland he had retained. Most of the livestock had long been sold off, but the old man could not quite let the lifestyle go, even though his wife's insurance policies had long afforded him the luxury of retirement.

The solitude and the mystery of the woodland in the valley was something Leif could never forgo, whatever the time of year. Even if the rain slicked the trees and the wind clutched their branches, Leif felt safe beneath the swaying canopies. The shadows thrown during the brightest parts of the day were places of refuge for him, and the ditches, dells, rotten brown pine needle carpets and thin creeping fingers of the young birches brought a feral thrill to his heart.

*Perhaps I am a predator at heart.*

Although there were *gîtes* and even a hotel nearby, there were never any people to be seen on this path, unless he should meet his father. Today, Leif followed the familiar pathway, a whitened groove winding its way through the trees.

Petra returned, expertly manipulating the fetched stick so that its weight was perfectly counterbalanced at each side of her jaws. Leif scratched behind her ears, and one of her back legs twitched with delight. It was a gesture that never failed to please the dog. He had missed her while he was at college – missed everything. Although his father was an old hand with animals, particularly dogs, he was of necessity unsentimental about them. His son was different.

Leif knew his dog would not live forever. As a boy he had been through the unique, exquisite agony of losing a pet, when Petra's sister Katrina had to be put down after being hit by a Land Rover. His fear was not simply that Petra would die, but that she would die while he was away from home, and that when he returned, there might not even be a grave to visit.

'You're a clever one, still,' he told the dog. When he reached for the stick, she let go of it immediately, with no dissent. 'You should be out herding sheep somewhere hilly, my dear. You're quite wasted out here with me.'

As if revelling in the praise, Petra panted, tongue drooping. Leif took up a strong stance, then braced his shoulders to throw the stick like a javelin. Petra tensed, ready to run. And then something caused both of them to snap their heads up.

Petra stood up, back tense, and barked. Her ears wavered.

'You heard it too, I bet,' Leif whispered. 'That means I'm not imagining it. Easy, girl.'

He kept hold of the stick, and they moved forward. Leif was given to daydreaming and wandered thoughts, but he was never quite superstitious. Although the dog-eared paperbacks his mother had battened upon contained many horror stories, and he had thrilled to these by torchlight after dark, the woods had never been a place of dark fancies and creeping terrors. They were not haunted, for him. Had god given him the same abilities as the fox or the wolf, he might even have walked through the woods at night, enjoying the play of the moonlight in silvery puddles on the forest floor. He loved the mystery, the jagged outline against the skies, the ancient forces that had led to the forest springing up and flourishing, the unknowable geometry and algebra which governed the course of its life far from the hands of men. But he never allowed that wonderment to turn towards any idea of spirituality. As for more earthly fears hiding among the branches, these rarely entered his mind. Leif knew he was alone out here.

Today was the day this notion would change. This was the day the woods became haunted.

'It sounded like a scream, didn't it, girl? It wasn't a loon or a nasty old crow, was it?'

The dog's pinned-back ears told Leif all he needed to know.

On the way, something snagged his attention. Leif and Petra passed this way most days, when he was home from his studies, and this anomaly in the familiar interplay of bark and foliage seemed as blatant as a scratch across the paintwork of a new car. It was something carved into a tree, something which had caught his eye as surely as if it had been a face.

It *was* a face. Or a suggestion of one. It was gouged deep into the bark of an elderly sycamore, its edges oozing sap. There were slashes for eyes, a mouth, and a long, thin face. Something about the image seemed slightly familiar, but it repelled him. Someone had done this with a long, thin blade.

He glanced at the stick in his hands. Perhaps a blade like that would be able to chop right through this branch.

Another face popped up on another nearby tree, and another. The same expression, the same baleful features.

The girl had said there might be a sign – but surely not these grotesque things. The images had been carved into the face of the trees fringing the path, about half a dozen or so, and seemingly at random. They were all fresh – done in the past twenty-four hours.

So someone had been here. Without Leif knowing. Probably at night.

Then the scream came again – definitely a scream, there could be no doubt. Petra's back arched like a cat's, and she growled.

He stayed her with a firm hand at her neck. 'No. Not yet. Easy, Petra. Let's go and take a look. Be quiet, girl. Take it easy.'

There was no need for a leash out here; never had been. Petra obeyed, loping along close to Leif's legs.

The path gave way to a clearing, and here you could hear, but not see, the brook pattering through a defile in the land. Something in Leif shrank back from this exposure, even though the sun was high and bright, a beautiful May morning. Had he ever been frightened before, in these woods? He had been startled, but never scared. Not the kind of fear that clutched at your guts, and then your throat. The fear he was experiencing now.

A fresh scream echoed out through the trees. It was a crazed sound, like jammed machinery on the verge of an insanely dangerous disintegration, something born of panic, not pain.

'It's a girl, I think,' he said softly.

Terribly, terribly slowly, a connection was made, and a light blinked on. In his pocket, still sweetly tinctured with jasmine and rosewater, was the letter, the instructions. Leif was hours early, but there was still a chance, an awful chance—

Petra barked, four times, her body tense against him. He did not command her to be quiet, this time.

Someone was coming through the trees, opposite the clearing. It was particularly thick with ramrod fir trees at the verge, a band of dark green running to black on the inside. One of the shadows detached itself from this barrier, and fought its way through a wicked tangle of bark. The figure grew more distinct. Then it fully emerged, tearing across the bright green grass in a flaring oasis of sunlight.

Only a girl, indeed – but she was wearing... she was wearing nothing, he saw. The dark red splashes covering her body were surely blood. Her face was a mask of it, her hair clotted thick with dried brown clods. Through this hideous mask, a pair of eyes bulged in stark, raw panic. Her hands were outstretched, her legs sodden to the knees with mud and detritus, and she screamed, terrifyingly loud, bearing straight towards him.

'Wait! Wait!' he cried, hand outstretched, uselessly.

Petra shrank back, growling.

'Help!' she screamed, in English. 'Help! He's coming!'

# 16

Now

Edwin Galbraith pulled into his garage, engaged the handbrake, killed the engine, then watched the world close over his head as the garage door retracted. He sat for a while and listened to the car tick, until the muggy heat became unbearable.

Anyone watching video footage of Galbraith as he paced up and down the garage – for there were three security cameras on him at that moment – would have spotted an agitated man, like a deranged animal stalking its cage. He tore at his hair and mumbled to himself, and the stark strip lighting lent an oily sheen to his sweaty forehead. Finally, he checked every corner of the garage, made sure the door was secure, and let himself into the house through the garage door.

It was a huge property, far into the flat countryside outside the capital. Private wealth had ensured a massive home, while his much-derided MEP's salary had maintained it comfortably. If anyone was monitoring his phone usage, it would have showed Galbraith contacted his two children by text and then placed a phone call through to his wife at her work, while he stood in the hallway. Then he moved to an area which was not covered by security cameras, and emerged holding a faux-effect wooden trunk with a brass latch, the sort that a pirate might keep his booty in.

With more haste than ceremony, Galbraith burned its contents in a red brick barbecue built into a square courtyard in the centre of the property, a place of concrete and dry stone he called his garden. There was no greenery within that stolid arena bar the more stubborn weeds.

Galbraith sank into a garden chair, still in his work clothes, and watched the flames engulf everything in the trunk. As an afterthought, he added the trunk, dousing it with lighter fluid and watching until it splintered in a red torrent of ash and grew indistinct from the embers of the kindling.

The activity did not calm him, and he repeated many of the gestures he had displayed in the garage – pulling and tugging at his hair, gnashing his teeth, occasionally uttering portions of sentences only he understood. He continued to sweat. Several times, he scrolled through his phone, weighing it in his hands, but records would show that he did not text or call anyone else.

Galbraith considered a beer, then had one out of the fridge. It was a clean, but mean German Pilsner, and he became calmer after gulping half of it down. By the bottom of the bottle, he was almost confident. He went into the house for another one, and saw that despite the alarms, the cameras and the security lights, the sliding door separating the inner patio from the kitchen had been left ajar. Galbraith always, always closed this door.

Galbraith did not hesitate – he dropped the empty bottle and began to run for the door at the opposite side of the room.

A shadow detached itself from the corner and intercepted him, tripping him flat on his face.

Galbraith turned over and lay on his elbows, gasping, glasses knocked askew off one ear.

'Come on, Edwin,' said the newcomer.

'No.'

'Come on, now,' the shadow said, grinning. Then he showed Galbraith the knife. 'You knew I was coming. Let us be quick about it.'

# 17

The coffee was far too strong. It disagreed with Becky's tummy and thickened, rather than quickened, her blood. But the café was a delight – stone floor, scrupulously clean surfaces, waiters immaculate in crisp black and white. The chat among the clientele had a wonderful fluidity to it, a pleasing rhythm which, in her mind, she tried to break down into digestible language, so as to be prepared for the conversation to come.

Flowers garlanded the windows, and the sunlight streaming through blessed them with the effect of stained glass. A stainless-steel coffee machine would not have looked out of place in a black and white movie set during the war; the old lady with the Pekinese who caused a fuss over her *torte limon* looked as if she might have had a bit part in it. Although the subsequent argument streaked far ahead of Becky's comprehension, the cadences pleased her, too. She could not think of an English equivalent of this place, this scene.

She had lured him here on the promise of a date, somewhere very public, and very open.

Leif Fauré blew on the surface of a black coffee, his nostrils inflating to take in the scent. His eyes rarely left hers, deep, black and frank. The dog lay at his feet, beneath the table, unseen but present, like the shark in *Jaws*. Becky had heard sheepdogs were clever and obedient, if a little jealous.

'Why are you here?' Leif asked.

'You know why.'

'I know all about the date. It doesn't explain why you've contacted me this way. Was it a joke?'

'Sorry about that. I had to be cautious. Hey, for what it's worth – your dating profile *is* a winner.'

He studied her coolly, then took a sip. 'I spoke to the police – maybe about ten days ago. They made me go through it all again. It wasn't a nice experience. Are you helping them? By being here, I mean?'

She shook her head. 'I'm here for myself, no one else.'

'Perhaps you could speak to them, instead? They may have something for you.'

'You'll understand why I take an interest. I'm curious about some things. I have a few questions I need to ask.'

'I have nothing to say to you. I hope you do not mind me being blunt. Seeing you... it's not healthy.'

'I'm sorry you feel that way. I don't mean to upset you.'

'I know what you went through. I was there.' He scratched his head, suddenly, much as a dog might score its own ears in brute irritation. 'It's just that I don't want to revisit it.'

'I don't want to go through it all again, either. That's not my intention.'

He sipped his coffee, saying nothing.

'I just wonder... how long have you been doing online dating?'

'What?' He barked the word.

'Were you always on websites? Maybe you tried other kinds of dating, when you were younger. Pen-pals, maybe?'

He shifted, uncomfortably. Underneath the table, the dog sighed, as if disturbed by something it dreamed. 'I don't see what it has to do with you.'

'I found you, didn't I? This is a date, isn't it?' She smiled.

He didn't reciprocate. 'Please be brief. What do you want?'

'Like I said – just filling in some details. If I was to say the name Fabrice... would it mean anything to you?'

'Well, in a manner of speaking. I know some Fabrices. It's a very common name – like William or John in England.'

'That's not a name you've ever used on a dating profile?'

'No.'

'Intriguing that you use fake names, I have to say. Strange, as Leif is a lovely name. Kind of odd. Not recognisably French. Is it Scandinavian? Norwegian, maybe?'

'Finnish. On my mother's side. That was her grandfather's name.'

'Why not use your own name? I'm just wondering. Why do you need to...?'

'Wear a mask?'

She flinched. 'In a manner of speaking,'

He considered this a while. 'For you, I guess this part of the world must seem like a nightmare. But for me, this place is my home. Always has been. I've never wanted to leave – even after what happened. Even knowing he could still be out here, somewhere.'

'I doubt that he's still here.'

'You don't know that for sure. Maybe that's why you've come here? To try to find him?'

She nodded.

'Okay. So you've come back. But I stayed. Now, I wouldn't equate my experiences with what you went through. That was the worst of all things. It was hell. But it had an effect on me, too. It changed my life. It'd change anyone's life, to see what I saw that day. To have to recount it, again and again. But then, things actually got worse. To be treated as a suspect…' He shook his head. 'I remember reading one line in a newspaper. "A 20-year-old man is being questioned by police." Or, what is the term used in English? "A man is helping police…" What is it? You must know.'

'Helping police with their inquiries.'

He clicked his fingers. 'That's it! I like that. *Inquiries*. It's subtle. Yes. I helped police with their inquiries. And when they made sure that I had nothing to do with what happened… I had to go back home. Return to my life. But that wasn't the end of it. People who live here had questions to ask. They made *inquiries*. How would you feel if someone you knew was questioned over murder – the worst kind of murder, the worst thing in the world? You might accept they had nothing to do with it. But you would still wonder. And people here wondered. And so did their daughters.

'That's why I use the false names. Google can prove annoyingly persistent when it comes to this case. Particularly with the anniversary having passed. And now the new appeal. These new *inquiries*.'

She sipped her coffee. 'It must have been terribly inconvenient for you.'

'I know how that sounds. I know what you must think of that. It's just how it was, for me. This is how I was treated. As a suspect. And that was after the police had come and gone, and retraced my every movement, and bagged up my clothes, and spoken to everyone I'd ever known, and taken swabs and hair and blood samples, and torn our home apart.'

'Please don't worry. I understand everything you're saying.'

'Just… it's hard to meet a girl when you have a reputation. Whether you deserve it or not. Or even worse, if you do meet one, it's the wrong kind of girl. The ones who are attracted to a known name. Whatever the reason.'

'Pardon me for asking, but why didn't you leave?'

He frowned. 'Why should I? I come from old farming stock. We've been in this valley for centuries. My father built up the farm. When he sold some of the grounds and the stock, he was a rich man. The farming went bar the odd field to keep my father busy – it was never my thing – but the four walls stayed and were passed on to me. And I love those four walls. It's my home. I've never lived anywhere else, and I've never wanted to, either. And I love the woods, too, and the valley. All except one part of it.'

'I get what you're saying. But you had a habit of hooking up with people in the past, didn't you?'

'I'm not sure what you mean.'

'Letters. To English girls.'

'I don't think I ever did that.'

'No? You never went by the name of Fabrice?'

He scanned the far wall, over her shoulder. 'As I say, no. I never did that.'

Becky slid some photocopies from her pocket. They were typewritten, double-spaced; the only thing scripted by hand was a signature at the end. 'You don't recognise these?'

Leif scanned the sheets, holding them close to his face. Perhaps he was vain, Becky thought. Too cool for glasses. The tragedy was, he might have suited them.

After reading a few lines, his face relaxed. 'I have never seen these before in my life. That signature is not mine, and I've never posed as a "Fabrice" before in my life.'

'You're sure?' She took the sheets from him.

'Positive. It was a long time ago, I would guess, but I would have remembered something like that. What does it have to do with you?'

'They were written to my sister. The person who wrote these letters was trying to arrange a rendezvous. He was her pen-pal. As you can see, he was a French boy called Fabrice.'

'I was meant to meet someone that day. It was someone I wrote to, yes, and she wrote back to me. But she was American, not English. I was meant to meet her two days later, when her family was passing through the valley. Her name was Theresa. She wasn't your sister, Becky. I know what you might be thinking, but it wasn't her.'

'And you told the police about this?'

'Of course I did. They know all about it. They know everything about me from that time. They looked at the letters from Theresa. They know what clothes I was wearing on what days. They know it all. And I am telling you – I know nothing about Fabrice, and nothing about the letters.'

'It seems like an amazing coincidence. Because they were mailed from your house.'

This gave him pause. 'I can't explain that. It must be a mistake. I did not write to any English girls.'

'I find that difficult to believe.'

This statement caused no anger. Instead, weariness seemed to bear down on his shoulders. For a moment, he looked older than he was. 'It's a set-up, of some kind. That was the official line. They investigated it thoroughly. I had nothing to do with it. That isn't my handwriting. They cleared me, can't you get that into your head?'

'Put yourself in my position, just for a moment. You must admit it's too much of a coincidence.'

'Not if the killer knew who lived in the area. And needed an excuse to draw the family in, in some way. And anyway, it seems no more a coincidence than your sister meeting a boy she had been writing to called Fabrice, where your family happened to be going on holiday.'

'You're right – it is a little chicken-and-egg. I did wonder how much influence Clara had on my mother and father, whether she pushed the idea to come here onto them. She could be persuasive in her own way. She was used to getting what she wanted.'

Leif finished his coffee and set it back down on the saucer. 'That's for you to figure out. I'm sorry I can't be of more help. I have a number for the cold case police who I spoke to, the other day. I can pass it onto you, if you like. I discussed this and many other matters with them.'

'I'd appreciate that. How about your number?'

'What for?'

The question seemed absurd. 'Well... in case I need to contact you.'

'I'm sorry to say this... but I don't want to give you my number. I'm not sure I want to speak with you again. Now, I've given you my time. I have some business to attend to this afternoon.'

Becky nodded, and rested her elbows on the table. 'I understand all that. I know this is uncomfortable. If it wasn't important, then I wouldn't bother you. But the truth is, we're connected. It's not a nice connection. I'd rather it didn't exist. I wish our lives had never intertwined. But it's a fact. There is a line drawn between you, me, and the devil. I can't ignore that. Not until they find him. Do you understand?'

'Yes, but...'

'Just one more question I want to ask you – about the carvings.'

'Carvings?' He frowned.

'Yes. There was a sign, left on a tree. Fabrice had carved something in a tree for Clara. Like a patrin. A traveller sign. Gypsy stuff. I think she'd read about it in the *Famous Five*. It was cut into the bark.'

'You mean like the faces?'

'Excuse me?'

'The faces. There were faces, cut into the tree. I found them in the woods, right before I saw you.'

'No... these signs were stars. Pentagrams. Like devil worshippers have. Or pretend devil worshippers. Like you see in Hammer horror movies. Sorry, faces, did you say? Someone cut faces into the trees?'

'Yes. Like a mask. Like the one... you know the one I mean.'

Becky's nerves snapped taut. She sat bolt upright. 'I've never heard about these faces. Where was this, exactly?'

A tremor passed across his brow; his flesh crept. He stammered, 'Near the clearing. The path to my house. Listen... I have no more to say. I don't think I should say anything else. I really must be going.' He slid a banknote underneath the saucer and nodded to a waiter. 'I can give you the number for the cold case team if you'd like to feed it in your phone.'

She did so, typing in a number he read from his own handset, all the while thinking of the faces on the trees. 'Are you sure I can't have *your* number?'

Leif shook his head. Becky reached out and placed her hand on top of his. 'Please. It would be a help.'

His eyes locked on hers for a moment. At his feet, the dog whimpered and grew restless.

'At least let me give you mine. Here's my card – it's within your power, then. I want to talk about that day, Leif. I need to talk about your house, the woods, the path, about the American girl... Theresa? Everything. If you owe me anything...'

He tucked her business card into his top pocket. 'I owe you nothing, Becky. I wish you well in your life.'

'If you think of anything, please call.'

Leif paused a moment, then withdrew a pen. He scribbled a number down on part of Becky's card, then tore it off and threw it at her. He got up to leave, throwing on a light jacket. 'You know, my life was ruined that day, as surely as yours was. Nightmares. Social phobia. Pills, doctors. I was a sensitive boy. It ruined me. I don't expect you to feel sorry for me. I know how laughable it must seem, compared to what happened to you and your family. But it's true. So if we're connected, then that's the connection. That's our link. A lifetime of horror. I am so sorry for what happened. I am sorry about your life. But I don't think we should speak again. Goodbye, Becky.'

Before the door to the café had closed behind Leif and the dog, Becky was scribbling shorthand notes into a pocket journal. *Faces in trees? The woods? Local police?*

She switched her phone back on. The 'answerphone' symbol throbbed in the top corner, with a number 4 attached to it. There were also several missed calls. When she saw the same caller ID was attached to each one, she frowned, and hit 'call return'. A woman answered in heavily accented English – French, she thought. 'Hello? Becky?'

'Who's this?'

'Detective Inspector Labelle… I'm with the French *Police Nationale*. We have a number of things to speak to you about.'

'Like what?'

'First of all, we want to update you on your case. And we want to talk to you about Edwin Galbraith.'

Her pulse twitched at her throat and temples. The words tumbled out in an embarrassing rush. 'I'm sorry, I'm afraid I'm on holiday.'

'Yes, we know. You're on holiday not far from us, and we're coming to speak to you.'

'Why do you want to speak to me about Edwin Galbraith?'

'He's dead, Becky.'

# 18

The interview room was bare except for a table and chairs and the recording device. Although it had been shirt-sleeves weather when she arrived at the *gendarmerie*, she felt like she should have had a musty blanket draped over her head.

The woman sat opposite said, 'Becky, I want to have a formal introduction as I run the tape.'

She was about as tall as Becky, but a little heavier. Her straggly blonde hair was pulled back into a severe ponytail, as if she'd been called out of the gym. Her eyes were sheer chips of ice, Siberian husky-blue. She might have been a Ukrainian beauty queen in her cold glamour, if it wasn't for some unfortunate acne scarring across her face. 'I am Inspector Labelle, and this is my colleague, Detective Inspector Marcus.'

The man beside Labelle was tall, with black hair cropped high at the back and parted in the middle. This reminded Becky of George Orwell, though his heavy eyebrows and thick-lashed eyes were more Ian McShane than country vicar. A lopsided smirk was permanently installed on his face, which did not fade as he nodded in acknowledgement, arms folded across his chest. He was handsome, but he reminded Becky of a poorly-painted action figure.

'You are being interviewed regarding the death of Edwin Galbraith,' Labelle said. 'You are not being held on any formal charges, and are under no obligation to speak to us. You may terminate the interview any time you wish, though anything you do say to us may be used in evidence at a later stage. Is all of that clear?'

'Sure. I'm here of my own free will.'

'She didn't ask you how you came to be here,' Marcus said. 'She asked if everything had been made clear to you. Answer yes or no, please.'

'Yes,' Becky said, frowning. 'It's clear.'

'Good.' He made a note in his pad.

Becky smiled.

'Something amusing you, Becky?' he asked. 'This is a serious matter. We're dealing with someone's death.'

'I'm just wondering how long the pair of you are going to pull the "good cop/bad cop" routine on me. It's not that good a tactic, to be brutally honest. Even the thickest criminal has watched *Law & Order*.'

'Just answer the questions you're asked,' he said, irritably.

Labelle laid a hand on his arm. 'Becky,' she said, 'I'd like you to tell us how you came into contact with Edwin Galbraith.'

'I joined a mailing list, used my contacts, and emailed him directly. The party had advertised for a media and PR officer. I put myself forward for interview.'

'And why was this?'

'I'm working on some articles – it might even make a book – about the rise of the far-right in Europe, and the disintegration of the European dream. I wanted to infiltrate his team, see what I could find.'

Marcus scribbled notes; Becky strained to see if he knew shorthand. He asked, 'What were you hoping to find?'

'Dirt, frankly. I want to know what their secret is. Why this politics hasn't gone away, given everything Europe has been through in the past hundred years. The wealth of information there is on it, out there. Memories are short, but not that short.'

Labelle's eyes twinkled. 'Do you have a theory?'

'Human nature. Either that, or simple economics. I'll think about it in more detail once my research is complete.'

'Two broad categories, if you don't mind my saying so,' Marcus mused. 'So, this book?'

'It's not a book – at least, not yet.'

'You'll have extensive notes, I take it? Have you started writing your… project, or is it just an idea you have?'

'I've written a hundred-and-fifty pages or so.'

'Could we see those pages?'

'Sure, I've got them right here.' She fished in her jacket pocket and produced a pen drive. 'This is a copy of a copy of a copy, but it's a work in progress. I can email you a file if you like. But feel free to take a look.'

Marcus blinked in surprise, but took the pen drive, turning it over in his hands. 'Do you have a book deal?'

'Not yet. I got some positive feedback from an agent, but I have to produce some work before they can move forward. You've got the story so far in your hands.'

'When was your first face-to-face contact with Edwin Galbraith?' Marcus asked.

'I met him at the parliament last Tuesday. We had lunch, and he offered me a job. We met at the Atomium on Friday morning to discuss some terms, and had planned to agree on a starting date. But he was called away.'

'How long did you speak for?' Labelle asked.

'Couldn't have been too long.'

'How did he seem?'

'A little agitated, truth be told. I was annoyed that he had dragged me all the way out there and then left so quickly, but I understood his problem. Business is business.'

'He didn't discuss things with you in any detail?'

'No.'

'He didn't finalise the terms and conditions of your attachment?'

'Nothing that had been put in writing.'

Marcus's smirk angled downwards at one corner. 'Did you discuss the fact that you used a fake ID to speak to him?'

'No.'

'He appeared to be well aware that you were a fraud. It had been discussed in his office.'

'Then my cover story wasn't as good as I thought.'

Labelle's eyes narrowed. 'Why did you use the fake ID?'

'That much should be obvious. I was undercover. I surely don't have to explain this to detectives?'

Marcus sniffed the air; Becky fancied that his nose actually turned upwards. 'Does it strike you as being in any way strange that Edwin Galbraith should turn up dead within hours of meeting you?'

'I have no knowledge of that.'

'Again, answer the specific question.' He sat forward in his seat, still smirking. Becky wondered how many times he had been punched in his life.

'Of course, it strikes me as strange. I was shocked when I heard. But beyond the two meetings I had with him, I don't know anything about the guy.'

'And in the course of your meetings, you didn't say anything that should upset him?' Marcus asked. 'There's no secret information you may have had which might have caused him to become agitated?'

'Absolutely not. I was looking for a job. I admit that this was for research purposes, and not to take up the role as advertised. I've explained why I did this. You have a copy of the manuscript I was working on.'

'All right,' Labelle said. 'One question I want to ask you in particular – what are you doing in France?'

Becky sat back and rubbed her eyes, suddenly exhausted. 'You have to ask me that? Seriously?'

'We might ask you lots of questions,' Marcus asked. 'The reasons are our own.'

'Just to confirm… Labelle and Marcus, was that it? You're on the cold case review team, under Inspector Hanlon. I carried out some checks, before we met. Is that correct?'

The two detectives froze. Marcus broke the silence first, leaning forward and steepling his hands. 'That is correct, Becky. We are assigned to Inspector Hanlon's review team. We're here because of our knowledge of English, and to assist our colleagues in France – we were handily placed to speak to you about your contact with Edwin Galbraith, and to gather a more detailed statement.'

'Seems highly irregular to me. Wouldn't you say?'

After another pause, Labelle nodded. Those pale eyes studied Becky keenly, taking in every gesture and movement.

'Okay.' Becky sighed. 'I'm here to see the scene of the crime. For the first time since it happened. Is that why you're here? In this part of the world?'

'We're investigating,' Marcus said, almost incredulously.

'Why are you asking me about Edwin Galbraith?'

'Seems a bit of a coincidence, this, doesn't it?' Marcus said, acidly. 'A bit like you combining a trip to the crime scene with a writing project about... what was it? The far right in Europe?'

Becky cocked an eyebrow. 'Funny, I've spent a lot of time with Hanlon and his team recently. I don't remember either of you guys.'

'There are a lot of people working on your investigation,' Labelle said. 'It isn't just a case of one or two guys knocking on doors. The team is huge.'

'Still, it's a bit odd.'

Labelle smiled. 'Perhaps we should schedule a meeting on a less formal basis? I can take you through some of the progress we have made. We work closely with Hanlon. He's being briefed on what you say to us today.'

'I'm absolutely fine with that.'

'We are working hard on this case, Becky. There are one or two developments we'd like to share with you, but not right now – things are at an extremely delicate stage.'

'I'd appreciate that. Are we done here?'

Marcus scowled. 'Yes. For the time being. We'd like a detailed itinerary of your movements in the next few weeks, so far as possible. You may be called in for more thorough questioning, regarding Mr Galbraith's death and other matters.'

'My time is my own, as you'll have learned already,' Becky said. 'My work on the far right is done for now. That aside, I'm paying my respects to my family. From there, I'm going on a tour. They used to call it inter-railing. I have a number of weeks off work, and I want to make the most of them.'

'Fine,' Marcus said. 'But don't be disappearing. You will most likely have to appear at the formal inquiry into Mr Galbraith's death.'

'Suicide, right?' Becky said.

'That's for the coroner to decide.' Marcus said stiffly.

Becky saw herself out.

Once the door was closed behind her and the tape was switched off, Marcus tilted his head back and sighed, as if blowing a plume of imaginary smoke. His posture softened and the smirk vanished from his face. 'I think we'll be seeing a lot more of her.'

Labelle looked up from her notes. 'Why's that?'

'Are you kidding?' Marcus jerked a thumb towards the closed door. 'She's a liar. Clear as day.'

'Are you sure about that?'

'As sure as I am about anything. What did they teach you where you used to work? Cheese farming? Wine press techniques?' His smirk returned, but on the other side of his face.

# 19

The countryside galloped past her, a riot of rude colour interrupting the lush green. The train seemed bigger and faster than what she was used to in Britain, and scrupulously clean. Something had gone badly wrong with the railways in the UK, she thought.

It might have been a pleasant journey, were it not for Devin McCance hissing steam in her ear through the phone.

'Five hundred words you sent me on Edwin Galbraith. Five hundred words, I suffered through. So boring, they would have been rejected from the fucking agencies!'

'What do you want me to say, Devin? Make stuff up? Say he was upset about something? We had a couple of boring meetings. Nothing interesting came up. He didn't even flirt with me.'

'So you meet one of the UK's best-known politicians, he dies within hours of meeting you, and... nothing? Nothing of note? No interest?'

'Honestly, nothing. I don't know what you want out of me. I'm on sabbatical, as I keep telling you.' *I want him to sack me*, she realised. *I want him to do it.*

'That's fine, Becky,' Devin said brightly. Something in this tone gave her pause. 'Let's lay that aside, for the time being. Now, let's talk about your real name.'

Becky swallowed.

'It's not Becky Brown, like you've been telling us. Or 'Marion Clifford', as you used to have it, years ago. Becky Morgan is your real name. That's something that's been in the news for a while, now. I can't think why... oh. What's this? What do I have here?' Paper was shaken close to the handset, dissolving into an unpleasant crackle. '*The Salvo*, no less. Page one. And who's this I see in the photo?'

'*The Salvo*? What in god's name are you talking about?' Beyond the window of the train, the scenery seemed to throb.

'Why, it's you! There you are. And guess what I discover you're up to? You're in France. On the anniversary of one of the most notorious murder cases in recent times. A murder involving your family. And that's you, on the front page of *The Salvo*, giving them a fucking interview!'

The blood leached from her face. 'I don't know what you're talking about. *The Salvo*? And it's me?'

'It's you, all right.' He cleared his throat and read. '"Becky Morgan has stayed out of the spotlight in recent times – but with the twentieth anniversary of the murder of her mother, father, brother and sister approaching, she's heading for the continent – and out for justice." Out for justice, it says. All caps.'

'Devin, I swear to god, I have not spoken to anyone... This is news to me.'

'It says you have, here. Exclusive interview. "I need closure on this," you said. "I want to find out who did it, if it's the last thing I ever do." Your face is on *page fucking one*. You look a bit pissed, to be fair, but it's you, all right.'

'I've spoken to no one.' Then she found her fury. 'And what does it have to do with you, anyway?'

'Oh, nothing, Becky. And before we go on, I'd like to offer my sincerest condolences. The very sincerest. But you might want to give us a call when you've collected your thoughts. And explain why you thought to tell *The Salvo* this, but not us.'

She had a moment of sudden, beautiful clarity. 'Aw look – I quit, Devin. Quit. We're through. Cancel the fucking sabbatical. We're through. I'm not coming back.'

'Oh, you're coming back. Don't fool yourself.' She could picture the grin. 'What else do you know but our paper? You'll be back. I'll give you four hours before you file the next instalment of your exciting adventures.'

'And I can tell you—'

He hung up.

After a full minute of cradling her head in her hands, Becky opened up a web browser on her phone. It would cost her a fortune to access the net this far from anywhere, but *The Salvo*'s front page – one of the most-browsed news sites on the planet, mainly thanks to a focus on celebrity side-boob shots and beach holiday fat-shaming – soon opened up.

And there she was. Looking drunk, as advertised, with a blood-red cocktail on a table in front of her. The drink rang a bell – this had been a month or so ago. A nasty evening which had taken her two full days to recover from. There had been a man, a photography student, perhaps, someone who hadn't stayed at her flat for a proper sleep, far less breakfast. She swallowed… was it him? Had she talked? Had he gone to *The Salvo* with it?

But someone else was in the mix, too. Someone she'd talked to all night. She'd assumed they were part of the group the photographer had been with. It was indistinct – one of those nights that seemed to be going wonderfully well at the time; less well, in retrospect. Bright lights, dancing, even singing at the top of her voice. Who had the other person been?

The countryside unfurled past the train window, relentless.

'The big secret's out,' she whispered to herself. 'One of them, anyway.'

She checked the byline on the article: Rosie Banning. A clickable thumbnail enlarged on Becky's screen. The young woman had dark hair and glasses, but the face meant nothing to her.


A hire car was needed for the rest of the journey. Becky parked up in a deserted truck-stop a mile and a half away from the woodlands, still discomfited by a close encounter with an angry man in a baseball cap driving a puce VW Golf with his own skull decals. He had tailgated her with inch-perfect precision for at least a mile, even with a wide, clear space in which he could have overtaken. Becky had noted the licence plate, heart thumping, but he was soon gone.

He was no one special. Just another arsehole on the road. She wanted to blame France, continental drivers, and as many as half a dozen other equally bigoted reasons, but these people were everywhere, after all. '*Gardez-vous,*' she'd muttered, as the car disappeared over the hill.

The parking area was new, as was the sign advertising a camp-site, 300 yards away at the top of the hill. Through the trees, there were no tents set up in the clearing, and no other cars parked either. Becky wondered if this place's reputation preceded it. It must be difficult to set up for the night, knowing that the person responsible for what had happened to her family might be close by, even today.

She had expected to be shocked by a sensation of sudden recognition, or even worse, assailed by flashbacks, visions of what had gone before. The opposite was true. Heading into the pathway, she felt no sense of returning to a place she knew. Had the path been so well-kept back then? She remembered an overgrown place, limpid with ferns and waist-high weeds; now there was a stony path, bordered with white stones. Birds fluttered from branch to branch. A bright blue dragonfly hummed past her, a tiny flash of lightning, feather-light on the sparse wildflowers that grew in the sun. Somewhere in the midst of the pine trees, a woodpecker hammered out his lunch. It was almost enough to make her forget that, about a quarter of a mile up ahead, was the boating pond. Beyond that was the *gîte* – still in use, still occasionally hired out for a few months a year, though with a different owner. And somewhere in the middle, very close now, was the clearing, hemmed in on all sides by thick woodland, a frown in 360 degrees, and the stone circle.

Where it had happened.

Though this scene might have portended nothing more than a brisk hike up a gentle slope in the middle of a bright spring day, Becky's heart thundered in her chest, and sweat trickled down the back of her neck. She controlled her breathing, but the anxiety was strong today, overpowering. Had she been required to speak to someone, her voice might have wavered. Or it could have clicked in her throat, stoppered fast.

The sun-dappled forest floor seemed to writhe with a life of its own; every shadow, every flickering branch, required watching. As she climbed towards the clearing, Becky was reminded of a time when, as a young girl – before *it* happened – she had walked across a railway bridge. This was in broad daylight, but the acoustics in the enclosed pathway had played tricks on her ears. She'd been sure someone was following her. Here, every crack and rustle were the result of her own footsteps, but the illusion of pursuit was visual rather than aural. It was like a stray hair blown across her forehead and into her field of vision, or something in her eye. There! A bird took wing, and a branch rebounded. Or there! Something scuttled down a tree bark, spiralling completely around the timber and parting the ferns as it escaped.

Just as she began to acclimatise to the forest and its perpetual furtive movement, she saw something duck down, just over her shoulder.

Nothing. There was a natural aperture in some brambles, set behind the treeline. A branch had moved in the background of this space, perhaps; her imagination and her nerves did the rest.

When she discerned another movement, from roughly the same position, a little further up the slope, just where the path began to flatten out towards the clearing, Becky stopped doubting herself. She turned round, bent down to tie her shoelaces, and stared into the undergrowth.

Again, nothing. No sprung branches. No disturbed birds. No quick-darting deer, no dextrous squirrels. She stood up, popped a stick of chewing gum in her mouth, unzipped her waterproof jacket, turned, and darted up the path. At the last moment, before the brow of the hill was reached, she angled into the treeline, and squeezed between two elms.

Becky crouched low, behind a huge tree whose girth was easily greater than her own, taking care not to crush a crop of nut-brown mushrooms whose fingers poked through the moss at her heel.

Something tore through the trees down the slope, following her passage. The trees obscured the details, but there was no doubt it was a person.

The footsteps slowed. Someone was breathing heavily. They took a step or two forward, then stopped. The unmistakeable sound of a smartphone screen being tapped followed; then came a low curse, somewhere between the level of a gasp and a sigh.

The intruder was close, just to the right, out of view. Becky allowed her mind to clear, listening to the footsteps approach.

There was that same feeling of something lingering just out of vision, a maddening foreign body, just as a shadow fell across the moss, to the right of the tree.

Carefully, a figure stepped into the light. Then Becky pounced.

## 20

The figure was that of a short, slight woman in her early twenties. She was dressed in a black hoodie, but she was no one's idea of a mugger, far less a killer.

Nonetheless, Becky was fully committed.

The girl's large green eyes flared as Becky gripped her shoulder, pivoted hard with one foot planted on the forest floor and hurled her to the deck.

It was a rough landing for the girl. Laid flat out on her back, her hood slipped off her head as she got onto her elbows, blinking, utterly astonished. She wasn't out of shape but was certainly out of breath, the armpits of her top dense with sweat. She rolled over and lurched to her feet.

'What in god's name are you doing?' the girl asked, in English, with a Liverpudlian accent.

Becky remained poised, ready to strike, bouncing on her feet. 'I'll ask the fucking questions. Why were you scurrying around after me? You following me?'

'I was just minding my own business, you crazy bitch! What are you talking about?' The girl stooped to pick up something she'd dropped; a Nikon with a long lens. 'This better not be broken!'

'Take one picture of me and I'll break it, and then your neck.'

'You're tapped, love. Mental.' The girl backed off but did not raise the camera.

Becky relaxed and narrowed her eyes, taking in the pale features, the heavy eyebrows. The girl's eyes were wider than they had seemed in the photo byline, but there was no mistaking those eyebrows.

'Your name wouldn't be Rosie Banning, would it?'

'None of your business.' The girl slung her camera strap round her neck and made for the gap in the trees.

'I think it *is* my business, if you're going to splatter my name all over the front of a paper. Hey – I'm talking to you!'

*I'm talking to you.* How easily the language sprung forth. How the bullies spoke; how they made you stop what you were doing, pull you up short, snagging the breath in your throat, triggering that awful fear. Becky felt a tug of shame as the girl paused. She brushed dirt off the side of her leg where she'd landed. 'Don't come any closer,' she said, querulously. 'That's as far as you go. You'll be lucky I don't report you for assault.'

'Where did the interview come from? The one you put on the front page. We've never spoken before.'

'We have. You were just too drunk to remember.'

'When?' The red drink. The cocktail. Blood red. Becky remembered that about the evening in question, if not much else; some triangulation was possible, calculated from the work clothes she'd ruined by spilling the stuff. She'd drooled some of the stuff, deliberately, allowing it to spill down her chin. *Look at me. I'm a vampire.*

'Bar Skeelo?' Rosie Banning smiled. 'I'm not surprised you don't remember. You were blazing drunk. You could still talk, though. You talked a lot.'

She grinned – a silly, schoolgirl sort of grin, which triggered something unpleasant in Becky. She strode forward, but before she got there, Rosie Banning reached into her hooded top. Something sleek and silvery glinted in her hand: pepper spray. Irony of ironies, if she blasted her with that.

It was a canister of some kind, with a nozzle attached to the top.

But instead of triggering noxious vapours, the silvery object emitted a terrific noise. Rosie Banning stood fast, defiant.

'What the Christ is that?' Becky yelled, not quite above the clamour.

Her chin upthrust, the girl continued to press down on the canister, and it blared on, startling every living creature in the vicinity. A fox tore out of the undergrowth and sped away.

'What?' Rosie mouthed, suddenly realising Becky had spoken.

'I said... what in the Christ is that?'

Rosie Banning let go of the trigger. The whole world seemed to whine with the sudden absence of the sound.

'Attack alarm,' Rosie said, diffidently.

'And it's meant to *stop* people attacking you?'

Rosie shrugged. 'It works on dogs.'

Becky snorted. Then laughed.

'What's so funny?'

'I've got me an idea. How would you fancy another scoop? This one's on the record, and we don't have to go drinking.'

Rosie took lots of photos, from every angle. The light was good at this time of day; the trees formed a natural crucible round the grassy clearing.

'I don't know how you can stand to be here,' the girl said. 'Honestly. *I* don't even want to be here, and it's the middle of the day. This is it? This is the place?'

'Yeah. This is where most of it happened.' Becky pointed towards the rocks embedded near the back of the clearing.

'What are those? Standing stones? Like Stonehenge?'

'They're not sure. The rocks had to get here somehow, they're not native to the geology of this place. And they don't form any kind of pattern you see on these type of stones – they don't align with the sun or the moon. No one can be sure. It is a natural arena, though. There was a lot of druidic activity here.'

'Druids?'

'Yeah. You ever read Asterix?'

'Who's he, a philosopher?'

'Yeah. Modern-day. I believe he played football for Nantes, too.'

Rosie continued snapping. 'I guess you did your research.'

'Always.' Becky bit the side of her mouth.

They approached a lump of rock, slanted down one side, bleached in the sun. Things had been scored into the surface of the rock – love-hearts mainly, true labours of love. Time and the elements had smoothed them over, an effect Becky recognised from tombstones in the churchyard at Whitby, edifices sanded off by the elements.

'Was it here, that…?'

'This is where they died, yes.'

'Are you sure you want to do this?'

'Let's do it quickly.' Becky had taken to the girl, despite herself – she had pluck, but also a basic sweetness in her broad, honest face. In another life, they might have gone drinking. In fact, in another life they *had* gone drinking.

But Becky had to be firm. 'I'm happy to speak to you, and I'm well aware you're going to publish regardless. Here's your first and only warning: get it right. Don't misquote me. Don't fill in the gaps, like you clearly did in your big splash. Assume I'm recording all this.'

Rosie blanched. '*Are* you recording this?'

'Assume I am, I said.'

'Okay then. I'll start with the big question. Why are you here, exactly?'

Becky shrugged. 'I'm marking the anniversary. Wouldn't you? It's my family.'

'Don't you ever wonder if… *he* might be here? Right now?'

'It's crossed my mind. He's somewhere, isn't he?'

'Does that worry you?'

'Think back a few minutes. Do I seem especially worried?'

Rosie shifted her stance, taking a wider shot of the trees. 'I'd say you're quite handy. Do you know self-defence? Karate? Kung Fu?'

'One or two different disciplines, but I'm no master. I've studied Krav Maga, but I'm a bit rusty.'

'Not so you'd notice,' Rosie said, sullenly.

'I competed as a kid, but my training was long ago.'

'What belt?'

'Blue.' Becky smiled. 'Or maybe black. One or the other.'

'You aiming to kick his ass?'

Becky shook her head. 'I never, ever want to encounter him again, until I read about him being put behind bars.'

Rosie's smile slipped out from behind the camera. 'You know something? I'm not sure I believe you.'

'I don't care what you believe. That's what you put down in the paper. Understand?'

'Whatever you say.'

'I mean it.' Becky's face hardened.

'I'll need a photo. The main image.'

Becky trailed her fingers along the pitted surface of the slanting stone. The place of sacrifice. 'This is the best spot, I suppose. I think, for a front page image, I—'

She was interrupted by a click, and looked up, startled.

'I've just taken it,' Rosie said.

'Okay. Just make sure I don't look too chinny, though, will you?'

She smiled. 'I'll do my best. I think it's your best side.'

Becky surveyed the stones, the unruly lawn in the centre of the circle. It felt a little like seeing your old primary school for the first time in years, she thought. Everything seemed a little bit smaller but was utterly saturated in memories.

'I have to ask,' said Rosie, 'what's going on in your head?'

'Ah... all sorts of things. I'm seeing it happen, really. I'll never forget it happening, much as I want to.'

'You seem calm. I think I'd be on the ground by now, if I was you. I don't think I'd want to get back up.'

Becky's lower lip quivered. It was a flash flood, sometimes; out of nowhere the dam could burst. She might be on the floor, indeed. She bit her lip and turned her head away for a moment. 'You never quite get over it. It's like any kind of grief. You learn to live with it. You scar over.'

'There's grief, and there's what happened to you,' Rosie said quietly.

'I've learned to cope. It takes time. As long as it needs to. I've suffered, I won't kid anyone on. PTSD, anxiety disorder, panic attacks….' She swallowed. 'And problem drinking. You name it, I've had it. I needed counselling, therapy. I wasn't right for years. More than a decade. Sometimes I still don't think I've got to grips with it. I was lucky – someone spotted I was struggling at university. They set me on the right path.'

'Are you sure it's a good thing that you've come here?' Rosie said, abruptly. 'We can go if you want. Just get out of here.'

Becky shook her head. 'No. This is necessary. You have to face what frightens you, sometimes. I'll take you through it.'

Rosie held up a digital recorder. 'Take your time. Anything you don't want to discuss, or strike from the record…'

'It's fine.' Becky looked Rosie in the eye. 'He used Howie to coerce us. Held a knife to his throat… said he was going to kill him unless we did what he wanted.'

Rosie said nothing.

'So of course, we did what he wanted. Except my dad. My dad fought. He was clever. He waited until he had a chance. One hand free. For a second or two, I thought he was going to win. But he didn't. He had his legs broken. He still fought. My dad was a brave man. The bravest man.'

Becky and Rosie stood stock still. A breeze stirred the grass.

'From there, he made Clara cut herself. He told her to slice her own face, and she did it. Then he told her that she wasn't doing it right. At one stage, all I could see was her eyes. But she did it. You would. Anyone would. But he made her do it.'

'Jesus,' Rosie whispered.

'Then he took her away into the bushes. We heard her scream. By then he'd already tied the rest of us up.'

Becky saw tears pooling in Rosie's eyes.

'Then he killed Howie. In front of us. That was the worst, that…' Tears spilled down Becky's face, and she sobbed. 'He didn't suffer long. I can say that for him, if nothing else.'

'No more, Becky. You don't need to tell people this.'

'I do. Maybe I kept quiet too long. Maybe that's a big part of my problem.' She took a breath. 'So he killed Howie and we lost hope. Then he untied me and gave me this.' Becky turned and pulled her collar away from her neck. 'See that scar, there? You can see the start of it. It extends from the meat of my shoulder down to my hip on the other side. They call it a flesh wound. No nerve damage. He did it deliberately. Slowly. He wanted to see my reaction, and my parents'. They were watching their last child being tortured, and worse. But my mother thought on her feet. She tried to coerce him, to distract him. Again, he made it look like it could work, that she might get a chance to… I don't know. Get away. Take the knife off him. But it didn't work, and he killed her too. I think they mentioned in the news reports that my mother was suffocated, and she was. It's just that he... he sat on her head. He pushed her face down in the mud. That's how she died.'

'You got away, Becky,' Rosie said, thickly. 'You made it. It was a miracle.'

'No miracle. I got lucky. He stumbled. Before she died my mother told me to run. He left me untied, when he... when my father died. So I did run. He thought I was frozen to the spot. And I was... until I wasn't. Something snapped, and I ran. It took him by surprise. He fell, and that bought me some time, to run into the trees. I hid. I had to lie in the bushes, hardly daring to breathe. Covered in bugs and spiders. I couldn't make a sound. I got away. I ran into someone in the forest, found someone, and they saved me. The killer had got away.'

'Your dad... your dad didn't die like the others?'

'No,' Becky said, sharply. 'No, he died quickly. If you take away the fact his legs got broken.'

'Jesus, Becky. What can I say? What can anyone say?'

'Nothing. Just write it all down. Put it out there.' She wiped away a tear and rummaged in her bag for a tissue.


The nearest place to grab a coffee and a slice of cake was several miles back down the road. In Britain this might have been a truck stop, a concrete box dumped in the earth distributing bacon rolls and tea thick as trench mud to truckers. In ancient days, it could have been a Little Chef. The truckers were still here, of course, a preponderance of beefy men in plaid shirts, and some of them were British. But the coffee was first-rate, the floors and tables spotless, and barring the odd glance or two, the clientele mostly respectful of the two women.

Becky studied each and every one of them, her back against the far wall. Their height, their limbs; she didn't pay too much attention to the extra weight clinging to their chins and inflating their waistlines – behind every wheezing fifty-year-old grizzly lurked the frame of a whiplash-thin young buck, after all.

Meanwhile, Rosie Banning polished off the last of her pastry with a beautiful, unashamed gusto. Becky wondered how young she was; no older than 25, surely.

'There are theories, about what happened,' Rosie said, wiping her mouth with a napkin, 'if you'd like to hear them.'

'Go on.'

'First – the Crandley theory.'

Becky shook her head. 'Debunked, a long time ago.'

'Hold on, hear me out. Miles Crandley wasn't a DNA match, but his psychological profile was a close fit. And he did own property in Provence.'

'It's not just the DNA evidence which ruled him out – but the fact that he wasn't in the country when my family were killed. He was in the UK. Miles Crandley was a rapist, a murderer and a psychopath. But he didn't kill my family.'

'But we know that he had a business associate who sometimes used Crandley's account to stay in hotels, and signed in some places under Crandley's name. This other guy's now dead, so we can't know for sure. But it's possible Crandley was still in France at the time.'

'The MO doesn't fit. He didn't use a mask. He didn't tackle whole families, just single career women. He didn't draw out their suffering, either. It's too much of a leap. The patterns don't match.'

'Hold on a minute. You say he didn't use a mask – but he did. A girl who survived one of Crandley's early attacks said he used a ski mask or a balaclava. Not as theatrical or as horrid as the one the killer used in your case, but he might have graduated to using that. Crandley's other victims aren't around to tell you one way or the other. Then there's the... well. The manner of death, for one. At least, in Clara's case.' Her voice tailed off, and her cheeks coloured. 'Sorry.'

Becky waved her concerns away. 'There are a couple of coincidences. But if that's true, how do you explain the DNA evidence? It wasn't him. Wasn't his saliva. Wasn't his hair. Wasn't his semen.'

'That brings me to a new theory.'

'One that I haven't heard before?' Becky smiled wryly. 'Go on, then.'

'There were two killers, not one. Maybe even more than two.'

Becky shook her head and sipped at her coffee. 'There was only one killer.'

'With respect, there is some evidence that suggests maybe more than one man was involved. You *saw* one killer, but...'

Frustration bunched Becky's shoulders, but she kept her voice level. 'With respect, I was there. In the teeth of it. I know. And there was only one killer. It was the same man, all the way through.'

'But you didn't actually see his face – you admit that. You can't even be sure what colour the hair on his head was, what colour his eyes were.'

'His eyes were black. I looked into them.'

'It would have been easy to make a mistake. You looked into a mask...' Rosie hesitated for a moment, then laid a hand on Becky's. 'I'm not saying this to annoy you, okay? But you have to consider every possibility. You said it yourself – your guy is still out there, so something, somewhere, has been missed.'

Becky took a deep breath. 'Okay. That seems fair enough. I'm listening.'

'You say there was only one guy there, and that you recognised his voice and his accent, and would do again. I believe that. I believe there may have been only one person who dealt with you. But there are gaps, leaps of logic that don't make sense.'

'I've heard all this before,' Becky said. 'On some dark nights I start to wonder if it's true. You could see how someone would entertain those ideas. I mean there were five of us, right? How could one guy stop five of us? But I can tell you how; he threatened to kill my little brother. Anyone does that in front of you, then you do what they tell you, and you don't run. And on top of that, he tied a very good knot. I know that from experience. We couldn't escape. What he did was crazy, but he was methodical in setting it up, systematic in the way he carried it out. He'd planned it, well in advance. Possibly he'd had lots of practice.'

'There are theories about all that, too.' Rosie paused. 'And about why your evidence might be unreliable.'

'I know all about those, too. I've read the same websites as you. There's the theory that I grew confused; that I was stressed; that I lost my mind; that a lot of my evidence can't be taken seriously. "All perfectly understandable" – that's how they qualify it. Someone hypothesised that I passed out for a whole day through thirst and hunger, before he returned… but I didn't. I know what happened. The theories are just that, only theories. Only one man was involved. It seems hard to believe, but it's true.'

'You have to look at the places where the patterns don't fit, surely. That might bring us closer to the truth.'

Becky bit the inside of her mouth. 'Listen. If I was to hold a knife to your neck… a long, sharp knife, the kind you might use to gut a deer… and then hold it to your sister's neck, or your mother's… then you'd get an idea of how I felt. And then, when you see him do what he did to my father, when you understand what he is capable of, then you might know why we didn't try to fight, like he did.'

'I understand.' Rosie's enthusiasm for the topic had given way to anxiety. 'I'm sorry. I don't mean to hurt you.'

'It's… fine. I get what you're saying.'

'One thing you maybe don't appreciate… we're only trying to help.'

'Who's "we"?'

'The community. There are groups dedicated to crowdsourcing solutions to unsolved crimes. I'm involved in one of them. Have you heard of the Dupin Collective? Maybe you've heard our podcast?'

'I've heard about that. Read a few articles. Mostly to do with my family. But I'm afraid I don't see many master detectives at work, there.'

Rosie folded her arms. God, Becky thought, she's actually in a huff.

Becky continued, 'Meaning… you seem like enthusiastic amateurs. It was a little bit grim, though. Well meaning, but sensationalist.'

'We want to help,' Rosie said, solemnly. 'I don't deny there are a few ghouls who are into true crime, the horror of it all. And there are plenty of people turned on by serial killers and freaks, crime scene photos and the like, but... by and large, we want to solve your case. We hate what happened, hate the fact that he's still out there, hate the fact that you went through that godawful nightmare. It's a case of morality. We're not playing. We want him caught.'

For a moment Becky felt a wave of self-pity lifting her up, a sudden swell that usually occurred to her while she was drunk or getting there.

'Me too,' she said, at length. 'That's why I want you to be very careful with the article. Understand? I'll give you some quotes. I want them printed verbatim. It's important.'

'You'll get your quotes. I promise.'

'Any distortions or misinterpretations, wilful or otherwise, and I'll sue. That's not a threat. It's a guarantee.'

It was Rosie's turn to be irritated, her thick eyebrows bunching together. 'Hey – we're talking world exclusive here. I'm not going to pass it up, am I?'

'Good. All right then. Give me a moment to think about it, then once it's down, we'll go over it.'

'Not a problem. By the way – what name are we using? I know you changed it somewhere along the line. It's been a hard job tracing you on the electoral roll or phone records.'

Becky hesitated for a moment. Then she smiled, on open, warm smile. 'I've only got one name. Use it in full. Rebecca Morgan.'

# 21

Rupert wore a virtual bear mask, a fuzzy brownish haze with a dewy nose that was possibly meant to look cute.

'I've seen your face, Rupert,' Becky said, folding her arms. 'What's with the stupid get-ups?'

On the computer screen, Rupert's hand disappeared into the cartoon fuzz, possibly to scratch his real chin. 'I don't know... I guess because it makes me feel better when I'm doing all this illegal stuff, maybe?'

'It's childish and it puts me off.'

'Would you like me to wear a proper mask?'

'Is that supposed to be funny?'

'Sorry. Maybe we should just talk business, and take it from there?'

'That's probably for the best.'

Rupert tapped at the keys, then the bear mask disappeared, and the face she'd seen during their last contact reappeared. She could see him sifting through some sheaves of paper – a series of handwritten notes, rather than printouts. She settled back, the wood-panelled walls of her cottage in the woods creaking at her back. The encounter with the girl from *The Salvo* had discomfited her, almost as much as the news about their front-page splash. Becky had planned to put her head above the parapet at some stage, but not quite so soon.

'First things first,' Rupert said, 'the tip your late friend Mr Galbraith provided… the January Orchestra. Whew.'

'You got something?'

'I got *something*. It's an odd name. At first, the only thing that came up was spelling mistakes. I'm not just talking Google, either – I mean the dark web. The kind of clubs where the gangsters, child molesters, jihadis and thrill killers hang out and do their business. Then I began to realise there's a reason it's so hit-and-miss. I carried out some fuzzy searches, looking at variations in how you spell "January" … numbers in place of letters, alternate spellings… and… well. See note one.'

Becky clicked on a thumbnail which flashed up on screen. It contained three screengrabs, all from fairly nondescript front pages of websites. They all showed the same graphic – a set of closed doors, with shiny brass handles – but in different colours. One door was white, one jet black, another a gaudy shade of purple. In the top left were what appeared to be the same words, in the same subtle script, in white or black depending on the background. The spellings in each case differed in subtle ways. Sometimes there were capitals in odd places, or numbers in place of letters, like 'J4NU4RY'. Colours aside, the basic template image of the site was the same on each occasion.

'So they change the name,' Becky said. 'It's different every time.'

'Exactly right. Standard practice really – the address changes, and even that's a jumble of text that you couldn't type in by mistake if you tried a billion times. It's like if you reconfigure your password regularly – it makes it more difficult for hackers to steal it. Still one of the best defences you've got, such as they are.'

'*You* got in, though?' On the screengrabs, at the bottom, she noticed there was a log-in box, the same colour of the background. Only a solid cursor gave away its position.

'Well, not quite. First of all, these are cached versions. I found them backed up on a message board. The content itself is long gone – I would say whatever tunes the January Orchestra played, they changed the name of the band long ago. Wonder what they mean by January?'

Becky shrugged. 'I guess most people have a hard time in January. So does anyone who sees their performance.'

'I was thinking... January... comes from Janus... a god with two faces.'

'Interesting,' Becky said. There was something there; some insight she'd missed. She made a note. 'What about the message board? What did it discuss?'

Rupert hesitated. 'Snuff movies,' he said quietly.

'Murders? In real life?'

'Yes.'

'Where did you find the data?'

'They were stuck in a file originally saved at a local Spanish police office. Just the one file, buried away. Part of a dead-end investigation into a child abuse ring. A tangent, you might call it, nested among a bigger discussion. The message board was in Spanish, and it's from a few years ago.'

'What was the discussion?'

'You can see for yourself. I don't know what your Spanish is like...'

'Passable. Where is it?'

'Hold on a second. Look... there was an image attached with it.'

'So?'

'I'm just warning you, all right?' Rupert's fingers rattled on the keys. Another clickable thumbnail appeared on Becky's screen. She opened it.

It was similar to a Reddit discussion, but with red lettering on a black background. The screen IDs of the people on the boards had no images attached to identify them, not even a concession to irony in the form of crazy avatars. Becky began to translate some of the screeds of text. It was unusually detailed, with not much in the way of internet contractions, text speak or coding slang, which probably denoted older users.

And then the image stopped her dead.

'Oh, good Christ.'

'I did warn you. It's...'

It was Clara. Becky's throat was dry. Her hands began to shake, uncontrollably.

The black and white JPEG was in very fine grain. The hair was unmistakeable. The fringe was whipped over the eyes and nose, and what was visible of the face was completely ruined, of course, the way it was when Becky had last seen it in the flesh. But there was something about the way the upper teeth protruded slightly over the lower lip that gave the game away. It was this expression in particular, rather than the pooled blood and the gory muddle below the point of the chin, which had excited the people on the message board.

Becky composed herself; forced herself to look at the image; accepted it; exhaled. 'What did you find out about the January Orchestra?'

'Very little. But I would say, it looks like a point of contact of some sort. Heavily encrypted. There's no battering ram I can think of that would get through those doors. You have to know people, basically. A passkeeper. Probably not too many of them. Except it looks like someone on the message board knew all about the case and shared the picture with some like-minded souls. He also shared an image of January's log-in page.'

'What for? To make money?'

'More likely just a sicko. The real stuff can be hard to get hold of. Especially from famous murder cases.'

'When is this dated?'

'Eight years ago. The system it uses is long out of date.'

Becky scanned the handles. 'What about the ID? The guy who shared the picture? "Pedro L"?'

'I did some digging. Pedro L was a little bit slapdash, it seems. Prone to boasting, here and there. He didn't share this image again, but I got some details.'

'Who was he?'

Another thumbnail appeared. The image of a jowly but handsome man opened up, his hairline still dark but badly receded, Hispanic in complexion. There was an official title: 'Henrique Lopez'.

'Worked in government, would you believe,' Rupert said.

'He was a politician?'

'No – more in the line of the Spanish civil service. Justice department.'

Becky scanned the job title appended to the picture; she scribbled notes. 'Where is he now?'

'Six feet under, I'm afraid. Not long after he posted this photo, he ended up dead.'

'Killed, you mean?'

'Well, not by anyone else. But I must admit, my ears pricked up when I read about how he did it.' Another thumbnail – this time a Spanish language newspaper.

She scanned the tight print, read the headline and the first three paragraphs over and over. 'Jesus. He killed himself. Carbon monoxide. In his garage.'

'Stunning coincidence, I'm sure.'

Becky gripped the arms of her chair. 'It's a link. God almighty, you've got something. Was there an investigation? Anything untoward?'

'This is the really suspicious thing. In official and unofficial communications, from the coroner's office through to the police, through to what his wife said on the emails I dug out... There's nothing. No suspicious activity. Nothing on his computer equipment that would indicate anything untoward – not even any garden variety porn. He was clean as a whistle.'

'Why does that make you suspicious?'

Rupert laughed. 'Who in the name of god doesn't have something nasty on their search history? It's so easy to call up something questionable purely by accident. My guess is, he was ultra-careful. Separate computer, nothing that could be tied to him, somewhere well off-grid. Something untraceable, should he get caught. You know that old joke about assigning a friend to clear your search history if you should die suddenly? It's kind of like that.'

'Was he anything to do with the January Orchestra?'

'He definitely knew something about it. If he was in the Orchestra, then Mr Lopez would have pissed his fellow performers off. They are a very clever, very cautious bunch. Curtains behind doors behind walls, and all of that hidden behind passwords and codes, keys and locks. It seems to change and shift and move houses at random times and places. It's probably a cryptographer's nightmare – or wet dream, depending on how you look at it. My guess is, even if I cracked January wide open, I wouldn't find much bar gobbledegook and nonsense – something abstract that means something to them, rather than anyone or anything specific. Euphemisms and innuendo. I'll say this, though; the fact they're so sneaky and secretive about it means they are up to absolutely no good. QED – it's on the dark web.'

'So what's the point of the site?'

'It wouldn't be to share videos or still images. My guess is, it's a point of reference. Something that points towards coordinates, times and events. Places where they meet up. Something that might be explained away should anyone ask questions.'

'Where did the picture come from, do you know?'

'The girl's head? I'm not sure who took it, but I know where they got it from. The picture is from the crime scene photos. The English family who were killed in France.'

'You know this for a fact?'

'Yes. Because I've got the crime scene photos you asked for. All the data. All the suspects, all the interviews. Everything on that case. Everything. And a few more cases besides. I hope you haven't eaten anything lately.'

## 22

'There's a lot of stuff here,' Rupert said. 'I can't pretend I've gone through it in any kind of detail, much less catalogued it.'

'Not a problem.' Becky scrolled past folder after folder as they appeared on-screen. A virtual filing cabinet-full. 'How long will it take to download?'

'Could be a while, if you're pushed for time. I've sent a link to the email address you gave me. Did you keep it clear of other emails, like I asked you?'

'I don't think I've even been spammed yet.'

'Excellent. It should all fit on a decent data stick.'

'I've got a few of those.'

Becky wanted to delve into it; one folder was marked 'suspects', and she couldn't resist. Inside, a sub-folder of files and thumbnail pics fanned out. There were dozens of them.

'It could be a long day for you, so I'm going to get back to reality now,' Rupert said.

'This is great. Ideal, in fact. Thank you.'

'Hey, you're paying, I'm providing.'

'If I need you for anything else, can I contact you in the same way?'

'Of course. I'm kinda curious about the January Orchestra now, myself. I can think of some dudes who would be very interested in that little band's back catalogue. They're up to no good.'

'Please stay in touch – and let me know if you find out anything else.'

'Of course.' He grinned. 'What would you do without me, Rebecca?'

She started to protest, then smiled. 'You got me. Rebecca it is.'

'Aren't you just?' Rupert winked, then signed off.

As she scrolled through a grisly cavalcade of bodies and blood contained within Rupert's files covering many cases, Becky did not altogether dislike the feelings of disgust, or the sense of shame at having witnessed things no normal person should have to see. It was a reminder, she supposed, that despite everything, she was still human. She could experience these sensations, feel the wounds inflicted on her soul. Not everything had been taken away from her.

She thought about the people who had had to take these photos. Nothing new under the sun, they said, which was fair enough, until you had to look at a woman who had been trussed up like deli counter poultry, with her head removed just as obscenely. Then she considered those who had found the bodies in the first place – the long-distance partner, who had driven thousands of miles in the hope of surprising one woman with an engagement ring, only to find the front door ajar and blood seeping out beneath the crack of the kitchen door. Or the elderly widowed housekeeper who was struck absolutely dumb with shock, after letting herself into her glamorous wealthy client's house, only to see... to see...

She'd needed her parish priest with her, twenty-four hours a day, in the immediate aftermath.

People came back from these things, Becky knew. She was proof of that, of a sort. 'Recovery' was the wrong word to use, but you could come back, put one foot before the other, and start to move again. You could laugh, you could drink a glass of wine, you might even eat. You could have lovers. But nothing would be the same inside.

One typewritten note had been underlined, in the case of the woman found butchered in a holiday home in Auvergne.

Check out links to Krnczr family.

Becky searched the files for the term, and found nothing apart from the initial reference. A prompt at the bottom of the screen asked if she meant 'Kranczr'. This pathway led to one folder under 'Possible Correlations'. When Becky clicked on it, the file was empty.

Frowning, she made a note of the name, and underlined it: <u>Kranczr?</u> Then she added: *Everything removed? Deliberate?*

The 'Known Associates' file interested her, but they were mostly oblivious friends, relatives and business colleagues of the victims. One of them, a married man with children, had accompanied the thrill killer Miles Crandley to brothels, but he had admitted as much when he spoke to police, and had also been completely forthcoming in his evidence at the trial.

Faces of sex offenders drifted by. A couple she ruled out by sight alone, but she pledged to go back and systematically look through the files.

*Are you here? Have I already seen your face?*

Leif's face was visible in a thumbnail attached to the 'suspects' folder. A record of his seized correspondence was also inside.

It seemed the American girl 'Theresa' was not the only girl Leif had written to.

'Pants on fire,' she said, tapping his mugshot with a fingernail.

Theresa's signature lurked at the bottom of several of Leif's love letters. She zoomed in and took in the final letter 'A' in the name, fashioned into a love-heart, the kisses at the bottom.

Becky covered her face for a moment, eyes blurred with tears.

Then there was the letter he had in his pocket on the day he saw Becky running through the trees. It was from a 'Theresa' – the handwriting different, the letters squeezed close together.

The language and tone of the letters was silly. There were references to his body, a hint that they might make love, although shaded in crude innuendo. There was no longing in the note, nothing she might have associated with teenage crushes and flirtations. The closest it came was a reference to farming by Theresa, followed by: 'I would like to know what your prize *coque* tastes like.'

This was not Clara's style.

Becky read it over again, dispassionately. The letter had the instructions, details about where and when they would meet. This was the letter police had found on him.

'Something wrong here,' she muttered. 'The coincidence... it doesn't fit. At all.'

Leif's file had been recently updated, she saw. Then she saw a file marked 'convictions'.

Becky clicked on it and read over a few lines.

'Leif... Oh dear god, Leif,' she whispered.

## 23

Bills awaited Becky upon her return to the flat, sober white slips in between the gaudy fast food advertisements and other folderol. How could pizza shops afford better junk mail than payday loan firms?

Once she'd sorted through the mess beneath her letterbox, she turned on her work phone, bracing herself for the tickertape parade of missed calls and messages on the touchscreen.

One or two of the voicemail messages from Devin McCance were particularly amusing; Becky wondered if there was a way she could transfer it to an audio file. Hers to keep forever. She might ask Rupert about that.

She knelt down by her bedroom door and checked the hair she had glued across the crack. She's seen this done on James Bond and had read it in comics as a girl, but had never done it until now.

The thin strand was in place, of course, but she still checked the tiny security cameras she had fitted in both her bedroom and front room to be sure.

After moving some files from memory sticks onto a laptop computer, she had some black coffee in the kitchen. This followed a brief consideration of a four-fifths finished vodka bottle which was the only major inhabitant of her fridge – discounting some desiccated onion skin, tear-shaped garlic cloves and a tetrahedral butter escarpment brocaded with toast crumbs.

The kitchen window faced onto another block of flats similar to hers – high-maintenance for now, probably gone to seed within twenty years. High windows granted an excellent view of the main road below, and the cars which were parked in it. One of these she hadn't seen before; as well as this, a figure could be seen inside.

Becky noted the make and colour, but before she could get any further details the car started and turned up the street.

'Could be nothin',' she muttered.

Sitting in a shaft of sunlight, she took a deep breath, then cracked open yesterday's edition of *The Salvo*, which the concierge had fetched with a dipped gaze which led Becky to believe that he had read it and knew all.

As promised, Rosie Banning had published the picture and the quotes which Becky had sanctioned, though she noticed that one or two unauthorised ones had been sneaked in. In one of the shots, Becky saw a face she did not recognise; her own, lost in thought, and looking so sad that her instinctive response was to think it had been posed. She had no recollection of this being taken. Rosie Banning's photo byline was bigger than before, she noted.

Before the coffee was finished, the buzzer sounded.

'Hello?' she said into the intercom.

She'd been prepared for press, or even a frontal assault by some of her editors, but not for Aaron Stilwell.

'We need to talk,' he said.


They had more coffee, and even pastries, sitting outdoors on a sunny but breezy day. The café was in a part of town that was unrecognisable compared to even five years previously. Apart from a break to allow for the height of the financial crisis, steel and glass monsters had blossomed in this district – hotels mainly, with the odd bar and restaurant lodged on the ground floors. The planners had cultivated a continental atmosphere, and on a day like today, they largely got away with it.

'Don't you have work to go to?' Becky asked. 'And how did you know I was back?'

Aaron was dressed in a white-and-blue-banded polo shirt over jeans. He might have looked like a football hooligan, except he still had most of his hair. 'Number one, it's my day off. Number two, you answered the buzzer.'

'Odd coincidence, you just happening to pop by like that.'

He leaned forward. 'Look, I was worried about you. All right? I've been calling, dropping by. I saw the papers. Becky… I don't know what to say. I had no idea.'

She smiled warmly. 'You don't have to say anything.'

'It's horrifying. I remember the case. If I'd known… You never said a word. Not a damned word.'

'I never wanted you to know.' A gust of wind ruffled her hair, and she fought to keep it from scrabbling at her face. 'I always needed you as a mate.'

'But Becky... it all fits in. It's classic. The destructive behaviour, the drinking... You need more help than I thought. AA isn't quite enough. The stress you've been through...'

'It's all in hand. I told you – I'm in control.'

'Going through all that stuff again is bound to have had an effect on you. You should be in therapy, some kind of counselling.'

'Aaron, stick any kind of therapeutic label on it, I've done it. I'm fine, I promise you.'

He sipped at his coffee. 'Do you ever think he might come after you?'

'Why would he? He's mad. But he's not stupid. If he wanted to, he would have done it long before now.'

'Bastard. Hopefully he's rotting in jail for something else. They might get him yet, you know. You hear about cold cases being solved all the time now. They've got the science to get these creeps, years later.'

'They will. Don't doubt it. Some DNA breakthrough, maybe after his son gets caught shoplifting. Or loyalties change, and someone who knows about him comes forward. Or he tries to do it again but gets caught this time. I don't know. I want to see his face in open court. I want to look into his eyes when they jail him.'

Aaron shook his head. 'And some people think they've got it rough. I dunno how you manage, I really don't. Carrying *that*.'

She caught the tone in his voice. 'Carrying what?'

He grinned. 'That false name you gave me, when we first met. The one I've got saved in my phone. The name

I thought you actually *had*. Becky Roman? Of all the false names you could have picked, you went for Becky *Roman*?'

She laughed. 'It was a book on your shelf. *Rise and Fall of an Empire*. There was a spear on the spine. It might not even have been about Romans. If I'd thought harder about it, I might have chosen a really silly name. Becky Bungle. Becky Stigmata. Something like that.'

'Becky Thump?'

She ruffled his hair. 'Silly boy.'

'I'll be back with more after this short commercial break. You know where the dunnies are in here?'

## 24

Becky sighed and rubbed her eyes as she was rudely awakened by her phone. She'd needed a nap – a new development of her thirties.

Seeing the name, she clicked answer, switched the mobile phone to her other ear and kicked her shoes off.

'Let's hear it Rosie,' Becky said.

'In a word... assassins.'

'Assassins? Sorry?'

'Organised crime. Your parents were murdered to order.' After a pause, she said, uncertainly, 'That's the theory.'

'*That's* what your big development was?' Becky asked. 'That's what you phoned to tell me?'

On the other end of the line, Rosie Banning paused for a second or two. 'It sounds silly. But every theory has to be entertained. And I know that's what you're doing, trying to find out what happened. Don't even try to deny it. One of them could hold the key – you know this.'

'I'm thinking you're going to tell me it was aliens soon.' After another pause, Becky added, 'And this is the part where you tell me there is an alien theory.'

Rosie giggled. 'Of course there's an alien theory. It was one of the first ones posted on the site.'

'Which planet are they from, out of curiosity? I want to rule out every alien species systematically.'

'This new theory isn't on the same scale of nuttiness.'

'I'll need convincing.' Becky drew her legs up and lay back on her bed. A breeze from an open window ruffled the net curtains. 'But it's a little far-fetched to me. Why would my parents be the target of international assassins? Never mind my brother and sister?'

'Well, wasn't your father involved in property?'

'That's true, but it was all legit – he wasn't mixed up in anything criminal. Unless you're referring to the property market as a whole.'

Rosie's voice grew higher the more she warmed to her topic, reminding Becky of a primary-school-age girl imparting gossip in class.

'Well, nothing criminal… *so far as you know*. A lot of people lost out in property a few years before. Your father was known to have liquidised a lot of assets not long before the market dropped. It's not out of the question he could have fallen foul of people who lost out not long after buying property from him.'

'And you have examples, I'm guessing?'

'Of course. Your father sold several flats in a new development to Patrick McGlinchey in 1990 – he's a well-known Irish Republican with links to the underworld in

Dublin. That's just a start. Some of the London property went to some very nasty types from the East End. The sort of builders who use skeletons for the foundations.'

Becky yawned. 'It's interesting, I guess. But trust me – my father was straight as a die. He was lucky in property speculation in the eighties. If he'd been greedier at the time it might have gone badly for him, but he kept a lid on it and did all right. There's no question of any bad deals or bad associates. What happened to my family was a lust murder, Rosie. I can tell you that for a fact. Any theory you've got, I'm happy to hear it, but – and this is my official line, if you're quoting me – my family were murdered by a pervert. A thrill killer, someone who'd done it before, and most likely did it again, and might still be doing it, for all we know.'

'Well. It's a theory. It might be worth looking into. Look, here it is, all right? I want to catch him, same as you do.'

'I understand.'

'What's your next step?'

'I need to go back to France. There's something that doesn't add up. I want to speak to someone.'

'Okay... you keeping that one close to your chest?'

'Yeah.'

You'll let me know if you get a tip?'

'Of course. Take care, Rosie.'

Once she'd hung up, Becky turned to the whiteboard in her kitchen. It had started life as a kitsch equivalent to a noticeboard, and for the most part she had used it to write obscene messages to herself after drunken binges. Now, it had a practical purpose; it bore various notes about her case, with paperwork and printouts pinned to the surface by magnet. Uncapping a marker pen, she made a note on the board. *Property deals? Hitman?* She drew a sad face beside this, then laid the pen down as an alarm buzzed on her laptop.

It had powered down since she'd taken the call from Rosie Banning, but was primed to wake up when someone contacted her through the video messaging system.

And on this computer, there was only one person it could possibly be.

'Rupert? I thought we agreed – telephone contact first, then a meeting?'

On-screen, Rupert sat in his cluttered room, the same as before. His face was uncovered, and he wore all black, the tips of his straggly ginger hair tickling his shoulders. He was sat a little further away from the camera than usual, and situated to the right of Becky's screen. Quite apart from the unmasking, the break in the normally scrupulous composition of Rupert's on-screen appearance was discordant.

He said nothing, his face pale but composed.

'Hello? Rupert, can you hear me? How did the Leif stuff go?'

'Hello, Becky.' Rupert grinned. His eyes darted in the flickering light of a candle; the huge dark pupils caught the flame in stark white pinpricks. Her initial thought was that he was high.

'You've got your real face out again, I see. Everything okay there?'

Rupert grinned and swallowed. His back was rigid, a markedly different posture to his usual slouch. Finally, he said: 'I want to welcome you to what will hopefully be the first of many points of contact. I cannot tell you how wonderful it is to reacquaint myself with you. It has been a long journey for us both, but a worthwhile one. That, I can promise you.'

Becky sat upright. Fear clutched her stomach, chest and throat. 'What is this? Are you reading this off a card?'

Rupert's eyes watered. 'I know that you are keen for us to have a meeting, and I can totally understand that.'

'Rupert? Is someone in the room with you?' She leapt forward, covering the in-built camera with her thumb while she tore off a spare piece of notepad paper with her other hand. While she folded this into a crude covering for the lens, Rupert continued.

'We *will* meet, Rebecca. But there must be some rules in place before we do. And also, I hope we might have a little fun.'

'Rupert – I'm going to call the police, and I'm going to shut down this connection. Tell me where you are.'

'Here is a quick reminder of how acquainted I was with your mother. It will hopefully help your memory, as I know it kindles happy ones for me.'

Rupert remained seated. Then a figure blocked out much of the light, obscuring him from view.

A gloved hand stabbed down towards the keyboard, before the figure withdrew.

Inset into the video window was an image of Becky's mother. She was naked on all fours, looking back towards whoever was taking the photo, her face screwed up in pain and misery.

'No.'

'A blissful day for you and me both,' Rupert said, in a choked voice.

'Is he there? Rupert, is it *him?*'

Rupert spoke more quickly. 'Just so that you understand exactly who you are dealing with, we will now have a short demonstration...' He looked away from whatever he was reading, glancing upwards. 'No,' he said. 'That's it. I've done it. Come on, man.'

He crumbled, then, his face contorting into a babyish expression of misery that might have been funny in almost any other context. He wailed, 'No, you promised, no!'

Becky clamped a hand over her mouth as the second figure came into view. Rupert must have been tied up tight to a chair, arms immobile; the dark figure disappeared behind him as he tried to twist his head round to get a better view, tears rolling down his cheeks.

A long, wicked-sharp hunting knife appeared in one of the intruder's hands; the other caught Rupert by the chin, tugging it brutally upward.

'Wait!' was all Rupert said. Then the knife quickly and expertly plunged home just under the jawline.

Rupert's body tried to arch backwards, but it was held immobile. His eyes screwed tight and his teeth clamped shut. He emitted one quick snort of pain or astonishment as the blood gushed out.

Another savage thrust from the knife, and the blood gouted in a surreal, near-horizontal splatter, dousing the stacks of data CDs in the background.

Becky watched as the figure standing behind Rupert began to saw at the gory ruin of his neck, rills of blood coursing over the fingers of two large gloved hands.

She sat there in complete stupefaction as the blade reached bone, finding a seam somewhere and sawing through with a sound like skis slicing the snow. She heard heavy breathing, then a wet wrench, and then she finally remembered to clamp her eyes shut.

After silence returned, she made herself open them.

She saw Rupert's body, shoulders relaxed but nothing above them, his black clothes having taken on a soggy sheen in the flickering gloom.

She saw Rupert's head placed on the desk, in extreme close-up, his expression blank, jaw sagging, eyes closed.

She saw a pair of bloody hands, smoothing away stray hairs from Rupert's brow.

She saw one finger dipped in the spreading pool of blood beneath the head, then tracing two tear-tracks down each cheek.

The fingers forced Rupert's eyes open. His head was glaring right at the screen, at Becky. There was no light in those eyes now.

The killer spoke. Deep, harsh, rasping.

'Can he still see? I like to imagine that he still can. There may be a crackle of activity in that brain of his, even now. Some little spark.'

It was a voice she knew.

Becky could not muster her own voice; it had been stolen from her throat.

Then the killer bent down and levelled his head close to Rupert's.

He wore the mask. It had to be the same one; the skull of an animal, maybe a stag, possibly a bull, but sewn up and reconstituted in sections, a yellowish patchwork death's head. Behind that black-and-white pattern were the eyes she could not forget – huge, black, with just a hint of white, like the corona around an eclipse. They radiated hate, malice, perhaps a trace of amusement.

A finger pointed towards one of Rupert's eyes.

*'I'll see you soon.'*

He raised a hand, the material of the glove infused with blood, and wiggled the fingers – a child's goodbye.

Then the connection was cut.

# 25

Becky had never liked the white, ergonomically designed edging on her kitchen table, so she had no problem with obliterating the laptop against it. One swing was all it required; she gave it everything she had, raised overhead, crying out as she brought it down.

The machine exploded in shards, splinters and wiring with an alarming crackle. She stamped on the hard drive until its front end appeared melted, and then flat. She brought her heel down on anything that looked in good working order, then snapped the pieces. Keys broke off like squares of chocolate, a jumbled snowstorm of characters; an exclamation mark cartwheeled across the floor.

After sweeping up the bits she turned to the mobile phone Rupert had called her on. Her breathing and heart rate were not under control, nor would they be for a while. Tears dripped off her chin and the end of her nose. She had just placed her finger on the off-switch when the phone went off.

She allowed it to ring for a few moments, numb in the flashing blue glare. Whoever was calling wasn't using Rupert's phone.

And Rupert was the only person who had ever had the number.

She answered. 'Hello.'

The breathing told her everything she needed to know. It was someone slightly winded by exertion. She could tell by the muffled quality of his voice: *he was still wearing the mask*.

'Hello again, Becky.'

She knew the voice immediately, of course. It was one you wouldn't forget no matter how long you'd waited to hear it again – like a hated teacher, an old friend, or perhaps your aeons-dead father.

European – eastern, surely. Very rough; perhaps a smoker's voice, but not uncultured. Maybe the passage of time had smoothed some edges, or roughened others, but it was clear as day.

As he spoke, Becky's head felt like the inside of a bellows. It might reverberate forever, from this moment on.

'Who is this?'

'You know who I am.'

Becky said nothing. There was no point; there was no doubt.

'I killed your mother. I killed your father. I killed your sister. I killed your baby brother. And it was the best day of my life.'

No phrase came to her lips; no riposte, no comeback, no glib retort. Yet she couldn't bring herself to cut the call.

'And now, I've killed your red-headed friend here. Do *you* have anything to say? After all this time?'

There was nothing. He might as well have had her by the throat. Everything in her flat was unfamiliar, warped, a hall of mirrors, a funhouse after dark. All that was familiar now looked alien; every shadow radiated threat.

'It seems you are trying to find me.' He sounded amused.

She croaked, 'It seems I was getting close. You wouldn't have done this otherwise.'

'Did you miss me? Do you want me again?' He chuckled dryly.

'Perhaps we should meet up? I'd like that.'

'That's good! You're thinking. That's a start. I knew I had a bright spark. I spotted your talent, all right. That's why I let you go, of course.'

'I escaped.'

'Did you really? I plan very well. I know every path, entrance and exit, where I carry out my work. You wouldn't have got away. You know that by now, don't you? I was meticulous.'

'I don't buy that. I think you got sloppy. You made mistakes, and I got free. Maybe you got over-excited?'

He paused. 'You know, there are times when I look back, and I wonder... You were so very young, of course, but... perhaps I awoke something in you? Only you can know for sure, of course. Tell me: at night, do you still dream of it?'

Becky made a fist with her free hand. She forced herself not to disappear into the flashbacks, into the memories that still haunted her. She clenched her teeth for a second or two before speaking. But her voice was calm.

'You left a loose end, didn't you? That loose end was me. I think you're going to have to close it. I'm the danger you can't afford to have. So long as I'm alive, there's a chance you'll be caught.'

He exploded, in what sounded like genuine mirth. 'Oh, you are a loose end – but a deliberate one. When I started to build my career, I began to crave more and more intense pleasures. Higher stakes. There were a few near-things, but I was just too well prepared. Too well controlled.'

'You weren't controlled. Not that I remember. You were the opposite. You were an animal.'

He ignored this. 'One day – not long before I met you, in fact – I decided that there was one thing I hadn't tried yet. One high that I hadn't sampled. It seemed such a simple thing – I wondered why I hadn't thought of it before.'

Becky remained silent. *Keep him talking. Take something, anything from this.*

'I realised: what could be better than to leave one alive? It's a great pleasure to take a life. It's an even better one to make them suffer first. You know, your sister died with the most beatific look in her eyes? It was like a figure from Caravaggio. Well, ignoring what happened to her face. I admit, even for me, that was harsh. But I do appreciate beauty. And she was a beauty. That's why I chose to keep you alive, and indulged myself with her. She had something you don't. I took more pleasure in her.'

'You *didn't* choose to keep me alive. It's a lie. Why keep saying it? I know the truth.'

'Think about it, Becky. Tripping on a tree root? You think that would have slowed me long enough to let you go? The little double-bluff you pulled with the knife dropped beside the hawthorn bush, while you ran the other way? Smart thinking; when we are pushed to our limits, we find solutions, don't we? But I let you escape. I used the time to prepare the scene for my departure. Though I admit, seeing your terror... hearing the sound you made... that cry of fear. You know, there are some sounds that touch human souls to their very core. Babies crying. A cat purring. Or a young girl screaming in terror. It's a pitiful sound. You can't help responding to it.'

She took to her feet, pacing the flat. 'Interesting hobbies you must have had as a child. So tell me this, genius. If you wanted me to escape, why did you scrabble round, shouting and bawling? I heard you do that. You didn't sound like a man with a plan. You sounded like the kind of lunatic you see under a bridge. Roaring at the traffic.'

'Wasn't it convincing? I'm a fine actor. I have to be, in my chosen career. The mask has to fit. It's all part of a very careful plan.'

'And I guess you just happened to plan for someone to come along at the right time to save me? Did you set that up, too?'

'You haven't asked me why I kept you alive.'

*And you haven't answered my question about Leif.* 'Whatever you say, it'll be bullshit. So spit it out. Get it over with.'

'I kept you alive because you're my ultimate goal. You're my masterpiece. A life I created. You're my dark daughter. Every single day, you fight against the darkness. I am that darkness. I made it; I gave it to you. Because of it, your life is mine to control. All of this stems from that one fine morning, in the deep dark forest.'

'Your masterpiece,' Becky said, numbly.

'That's right. The nightmares you suffer... the post-traumatic stress ... the dark shadow cast over every single human interaction you can ever have... the memories that haunt you when you make love... the panic, the hand about your throat. The blood that roars in your veins, the stutter in your brain chemistry, the barrier you can't climb over. The heart racing in your chest right now, *right fucking now*. I am its maker. I can almost hear it. Is your heart beating fast?'

Becky resisted the urge to snatch the phone away from her head and finish it like the laptop.

'I made that happen. That was me. I was the creator. The architect. You belong to me. I *own* you.'

'So what is the end goal? What's the purpose? There must be a reason. Shall we meet and talk about it?'

'We'll meet when I wish it, and not before,' he said simply. 'What I want you to do for now is *exist*. I want you to keep going, and to know that the hand which grips your shoulder belongs to me. I can keep you fixed in place or push you in other directions – or off a cliff, if I choose. I am still here, I am still watching, and I am always waiting.'

'I'm not buying your explanation. You tried to kill me. You told me everything you were going to do to me, just like you did with Clara. Keeping me alive... your masterpiece? It sounds like something you told yourself to feel better about fucking up. The word is rationalisation.'

'That sounds like something your therapist told you.'

'I am looking for you. There's only so long you can stay hidden.'

'Indeed. So are the police, I see. Lord, but they are persistent. I drove at least one of them to his grave, you know. A drinker. Well, if he wasn't before, he was after he came across my work. But the question for you is… do they know about *your* handiwork?'

'What?'

'Did you ever tell the police what *you* did, Becky? I wonder if they ever knew. I always assumed they had buried it. Perhaps they realised it was a horror too far; they turned a blind eye. They understood. It was never made official, was it? But it strikes me that they simply *didn't know*. That you didn't ever tell them. And that interests me. That interests me very much. Perhaps, if they knew, you would be a suspect?'

Becky's fear had almost fully worn itself out, now. It had been substituted for a cool, clear river of anger. She stood tall and straight, shoulders taut with tension.

'I can tell you one thing that is the absolute truth,' she said. 'You're scared. Aren't you? You've just done something desperate. That's not the work of a rational man. You have things to lose. That's why you've acted. You've tried to shut me down because I've got close to you. And I want you to know: I'll get closer. I'll get so close, you won't even see me.'

'You can't stop me. It's impossible.'

'Oh, shut up,' she spluttered. 'What are you, I wonder? A banker? Civil servant? Someone with a home, a mortgage? You've probably got a family. A wife, drugged to the eyeballs, maybe self-medicated. Too scared to leave. Or too stupid.'

She heard only breathing, in response. She allowed this to continue for a couple of beats.

'She'll be a doormat. I doubt you're the tolerant type. Do you have a son or a daughter? They'll turn against you, for sure. How does a mass murderer deal with a stroppy teenager? Sweetness and light? A soft touch? It's all going to come crashing down. You must know this. The end is coming.'

He sighed. 'So sad. You don't know what's coming your way. You don't realise how tightly I have you on a leash.'

'Really? What am I going to do next?'

'Well, if I was you, I'd contact your French friend. But now I must take my leave; I have one or two duties to attend to here. I do hope you'll excuse me. But we'll speak again, child of mine. Dear, sweet, fresh Becky. What are you like, with a few years behind you, some miles on the clock? A wild one, I bet. *My* wild one.'

He hung up. She didn't hesitate. Becky picked up one of the burner phones, set up in a row on the kitchen tabletop.

'Hello?' He was outdoors, somewhere public, going by the voices. Perhaps a market; a distant machine-gun burst of French in the background sounded like a sales pitch.

'Leif? It's me. Becky. The English girl. Don't hang up. Your life is in danger.'

# 26

Inspector Hanlon should have been a butcher, Becky decided. That was who he would have been in a children's picture book, rather than a policeman. His ruddy complexion, the girth, the hair bristling at his earlobes, and the tweed jacket, all spoke of flesh, sizzling fat and bloody greaseproof paper.

At that particular moment, anger had made him even more rubicund, and he tucked his shirt in and squared his shoulders before speaking.

'I'll be honest, Becky. I suspect you might have gone ever so slightly off-message. Trips to Europe... this stuff in the papers... the detail... There are some things we hold back. And with good reason. People get in touch, you know. People pretending to be involved. There's been a few already. Nutters, for want of a better word. Attention seekers. They don't help. We have to check them out. These details are how we weed 'em out.'

'I didn't let slip every detail. I hope you're not telling me what I can and can't say to people, Inspector. The goal is to catch this guy. Nothing else matters. I recall you saying that in the run-up to the *Crimewatch Special* appeal.'

There was silence in Hanlon's office for a moment, aside from the gentle roar of London traffic outside. The room was a complete mess apart from the desk, which Becky supposed had been swept entirely clean, papers, coffee cups, dirty cutlery and canteen trays all shovelled into the drawer at his knees seconds before she entered. Inspector Hanlon rested his elbows on the desk and leaned forward. His shoulders seemed to block out the light; Becky decided she wouldn't like to see him lose his temper.

'Becky, I can't stress how important it is that we cooperate fully. There are a number of reasons for this. First of all, we need to liaise constantly. There is a danger in putting yourself front-and-centre like this. If this guy is still out there, there's every chance he could come after you. It's unlikely, but given the nature of the crime, and the type of person we're dealing with here, it's not impossible. I like to have every possible angle covered.' He sighed, and the shoulders relaxed a little. 'I'm not trying to curtail your human rights. I'm not trying to disrupt your freedom of speech. I want you to be safe.'

'I want you to catch this guy – I'll share everything I know with you. We want the same thing, I can guarantee you that.'

A cough came from the side of the room, where Hanlon's other two guests sat tight against the blinds. Seated against the back wall were Labelle and Marcus.

Inspector Marcus, he of the lop-sided smirk, said: 'I don't think you're telling the truth, Becky.'

'I don't follow.'

'Well...' Marcus consulted some notes. 'It looks like you didn't mention a word to Inspector Hanlon about your trip to Europe. That's hardly close cooperation.'

Becky sighed. 'I've already explained that to you. It was research for an article. I've even given you a copy of what I've written so far – my editor would blow a gasket if he knew that.'

Marcus held up a hand that was probably meant to be placatory but came across as patronising. 'Okay. We appreciate that. But you also met up with the reporter, Rosie Banning, did you not?'

'It wasn't a rendezvous. I'd never met her before in my life. She followed me – she's probably been following me for some time, in fact.'

There was a death-ray chill to Labelle's eyes. She said, 'You also contacted Leif Fauré, did you not? More than once, in fact.'

Becky's guts contracted. Leif must have got in touch with the police, after she'd called him. But why, then, had he arranged a meeting with her? 'That's true, yes.'

'Why was that?' Labelle asked.

Becky closed her eyes for a moment. 'He's the missing link.'

Marcus raised an eyebrow.

'He's a straight line between me, the killer, and that place. He is the missing piece.'

Hanlon had studied this exchange warily. 'It seems to me that you're taking an awful lot on, Becky. If I was to suggest you were carrying out an investigation off your own back, how would you respond to that?'

'I'd ask you to tell me what I'm doing wrong.'

Hanlon ran his fingertips through what was left of his hair. Below, worry-lines stretched across his forehead like bars of music. 'You are putting yourself in danger, that's for a start. And, whether you like it or not, you're interfering with an ongoing investigation. I'd like you to stop. Is that clear?'

'I can't promise you anything,' Becky said. 'All I know is – I'll share any information I find. As it is, I've found nothing.'

Marcus leaned forward. He did not have a good poker face; a feral light seemed to blink on in his small, dark eyes. 'What do you know about computer hackers, Becky?'

'Not much beyond what some of our national newspapers got up to. I'm sure Inspector Hanlon here knows more about it than I do.'

'That's odd,' Marcus said, consulting his notes again. 'It seems that one or two European databases were compromised in recent weeks. Files relating to several cases were accessed – including those relating to your family.'

'What would that have to do with me? Surely you should be on the lookout for whoever accessed them? That might be your killer.' She was surprised by how level her voice was, a counterpoint to the clamour of blood in her ears. She had said nothing to anyone about Rupert, or the subsequent telephone call; aside from what had happened to Rupert, it would tie her in with a major hacking event.

'Nothing,' Marcus said breezily. 'Nothing at all.' He scribbled one last note, then closed over his notebook.

Becky turned to Labelle. 'When we spoke before, you told me there were new developments in the case. What were they?'

Labelle looked to Hanlon for guidance; after the big man nodded, she said, 'A possible link to a known serial killer has emerged.'

'Miles Crandley,' Becky said.

'We'd rather not say,' Labelle countered. 'But the evidence has changed the course of how this investigation is going.'

'Okay. So – are we talking an active serial killer, or one who's already in jail?'

'The man is currently in custody over other matters, yes,' Labelle admitted.

'So, Miles Crandley, it is. And what is this evidence? Short of a full confession and a bloody knife, I'll take some convincing.'

Marcus said, 'Bloody knife is not far off the truth. But there were also new pieces of information from the public following the television appeal.'

Becky said nothing. *I know. I know it's not Miles Crandley. There's no doubt about that, now.*

'We'll keep you updated,' Labelle said. 'Forensic investigations are under way at several locations. We may be close to a solution.'

Hanlon cleared his throat. 'Becky, I'll say this to you one more time – be careful, and please leave the police work to the experts. We'll get your man – I'm confident of that. I'll say no more about it. What I will say is… you look tired.'

Becky burst out laughing. 'And they say policemen can't be charming!'

'I mean it. I see a change in you. Try to rest, as far as possible. Take it from me. A case like this, even if you've no personal involvement… it can eat you up.' For an absurd moment, Becky though the big man was going to cry. After a pause, he said, 'I retire in two years' time. I've seen a lot of unpleasant things in my line of work, dealt with some unpleasant people. I've never been in the position of being a victim, but I've seen what cases like this can do to the people investigating them. I've seen good men go to drink and drugs. One of them even killed himself. So what I can tell you is, don't put that pressure on yourself. Not on top of everything else you've suffered. Clear?'

Becky nodded. She didn't want to lie to Hanlon. Not openly, anyway.

The interview being concluded, Becky saw herself out. While she waited for the lift doors to close, someone ran along the corridor outside, stabbing at the buttons. The doors halted, then slid back open.

A pair of unearthly blue eyes appeared.

'Now – about that informal chat I promised you,' Labelle said.

'Seriously? I'm tired. I need to sleep. I've had a long few days.'

'Yes, I can see you're tired.' Labelle stood beside her in the lift. 'And I suspect you're hungry, too. Are you hungry?'

'I am,' Becky said, a little hoarsely.

'Come on then. Lunch. My treat. It's on expenses. Let's go big. All right?' She squeezed Becky's shoulder.

'You're on.'

# 27

Becky dabbed her lips with a napkin. She'd demolished lunch; only debris remained. She scrunched up her napkin, added it to the paper carton of fries, and squashed the lot inside her burger box. 'You finished?' she asked Labelle, her mouth still full.

Labelle, in the driver's seat, nodded. Becky took her rubbish, dumped it in the bin of the drive-through car park, then got back in.

'Not to be culturally insensitive,' Becky said, buckling her seatbelt, 'but that seems a blasphemous kind of lunch for a French person.'

'Sometimes you crave it,' Labelle said. 'It's so hard to avoid temptation, once the idea is in your head. I hear they even do home deliveries, these days.'

'Let's never speak about this again.'

Labelle smiled, and started the car. 'To your hotel, then?'

'Only if you're happy with the drive.'

It was a hire vehicle, and the policewoman struggled with it, with the traffic, and finally with the very existence of those who darted out in front of her. Becky tried not to smile as Labelle swore mellifluously.

'Goddamn it, congestion charges, speed cameras... and these zombies, now, appearing in front of the car. How do people live in this nightmare city?'

'They don't live. They exist. It's not so bad if you take the Tube.'

'I'll remember for next time.'

The car lurched to a halt at a set of traffic lights. Labelle tapped her finger on the wheel, in time with the ticking indicator. LOOK RIGHT, said the road.

'There's no need to take me back to the hotel,' Becky said. 'I would have taken a cab – we could have stopped off for a coffee on the way.'

'A beer would have been preferable.'

The rain grew heavier, an insistent drumming on the windscreen. They turned into a steadier stream of traffic heading south, after some gentle advice from the sat-nav. Its voice was familiar, probably from films or TV; Becky wanted to identify it for herself before asking Labelle for confirmation.

The driver eased back into her seat, more relaxed with a less frantic pace on the road. 'I want to say – that was some performance.'

'When?

'With Inspector Hanlon. Just about everything you said to him. Masterclass.'

'It wasn't a performance, it was the truth.'

'Sure.'

'Now you're starting to sound like Marcus. Why isn't he here with you, incidentally?'

'I'm not sure what the deal is with him. I mean, in general. We haven't worked together long. He wanted to do some digging regarding you and Edwin Galbraith; I had some bones to pick with you.'

'Such as?'

'I want to know why you're lying to everyone.'

Becky sighed. 'Look, just pull up at the next bus stop, would you?'

'Okay. I'll share some ideas. You don't have to say anything at all. I'm just going to say what I think.' Labelle steadied herself, spreading her hands evenly at the top of the wheel. 'I think you're looking for him. The killer. I'm not sure what you're doing exactly, but your activities have been strange, to say the least.'

'And totally, logically explainable.'

Labelle held up her hand. 'Please. Just listen. If I was you... if it was *my* family that happened to... I'd think I could launch a little investigation of my own. I'd think I could pick up that detail everyone else missed. I'd think I could crack the case, all on my own. And if I did... I wouldn't think to pass the details on to anyone else. And I think if I actually caught this man, if I found out where he lived, if I cornered him... I would kill him.'

Becky kept her eyes fixed on the road and said nothing.

'I wouldn't blame you. I've seen the pictures, read the details. What happened was... beyond perverse. I do not know how you could survive something like that happening to a loved one. I cannot imagine the courage it would take, to put one foot in front of the other. To function as a human being. He was a sick man, sick in all the worst ways. There could only be a handful of people on the planet capable of doing something like that. You had the most dreadful misfortune to run into him. So if it was me, and I caught him, it would not be quick. He would know fear and terror before he died. This is something you've thought about. Isn't it?'

'Is this leading somewhere?'

Labelle nodded agreeably. 'It's quite all right, you know. It's only human nature. Who wouldn't want to take revenge? You'd need to be a saint or an angel not to consider it. But here's my advice to you. If you were to meet this man or find out where he lived – tell the police. Anything at all that rings a bell, any suspicion. Above all, if there is any contact from a strange person... then let us know. Anyone. Even Marcus. You're a tough cookie. You're strong. But this idea you might have about taking him out... that's not something you want to experience. You'll be face-to-face with a man who is capable of anything. You haven't tested yourself against someone like that.'

'Apart from the last time I met him.'

Labelle took a breath. 'I don't say this to insult you or belittle you. It's the cold, hard truth. When I started out with the force, I saw so many bodies of men who thought they could do better. That they were tougher than the other guy. Loudmouths in bars and nightclubs. Guys who answered back when they would have been better walking on. One swipe, one cut, one punch later, they are on their back. Forever. Don't let this be you, Becky. Hanlon is a good, honest man, but perhaps he's not honest enough with you.

Let us do our jobs. We're happy to have new information – we wouldn't solve any crimes if people didn't call us. Tip-offs are our saving grace. Wouldn't you prefer to be the person whose input allowed the professionals to capture the man who murdered your family?'

The swishing of the windscreen wipers answered her.

*'Travel 400 metres… you have arrived at your destination,'* said the sat-nav.

'Good god,' Labelle muttered, eyeing up an unappealing beige block. 'This is where you're staying? That thing is a *hotel*?'

'After a fashion. Thanks for the lift. Are you staying in London for a bit?'

Labelle smiled sweetly. 'I'm not sure, Becky. You're not going away anywhere soon, are you?'

'If I do, you'll be the first to know. I promise.'

# 28

He was waiting for her when she came through the arrivals gate at the airport and spotted her before she spotted him. He folded a newspaper and tucked it under his arm.

He shook hands like an Englishman, she thought, as he took her hand, head back, shoulders straight.

'Nice to see you Becky,' said Leif. 'I've got the car. Let me take your bag.'

Leif poured a measure of brandy into a shot glass, then tipped the bottle towards Becky.

She shook her head.

'You're sure?'

'Absolutely. Water's fine. Tea would be better.'

'Tea. Ah. I forget you're English.'

'I'm cutting down.'

'On drink, or being English?'

Leif crossed over to the spigot-style taps and poured a glass of water for her. The kitchen, like the rest of his house, was simply but elegantly laid-out. It was either an ancient farmhouse that had been totally refitted recently, or a brand new property which the builder had tried their damnedest to turn into a rustic idyll. Oak beams spanned the roof, and a heavy, studded table out of a medieval legend stretched across the far wall. Everything about the place, from the windowpanes to the subtle oatmeal texture of the wall cupboards, spoke of solidity and wholesomeness.

It was a bit too glossy-catalogue for comfort, Becky thought. She wondered if it was someone else's idea, imposed on him.

Early evening sunshine filtered through the trees outside the kitchen window and scattered golden embers across the wall. Light flared across Leif's cheek as he held out the glass.

Becky took a drink. 'I won't take up too much of your time,' she said. 'I already told you that your life is in danger.'

Leif sat down and took a sip of the brandy. 'Sure. But you didn't really convince me.'

'There are some details that aren't safe to go into. But I'll say this: I've been searching for the killer. And I think I've got close to him.'

Leif frowned. 'How close? Do you have a name? An address?'

'Not yet. But... all I'll say is, I've had some contact.'

'Has he spoken to you? How?'

'There's been contact, and I believe he may have been involved in other crimes. More importantly, he seems to be aware of you.'

'In what way?'

'He probably knows your name, he knows you're involved, and so long as that's true, he'll come for you. I can't say any more than that.'

'You've told the police?'

'You mean like you told them I'd already spoken to you?'

Leif shrugged and took a drink. 'I have my own interests to look out for. If I decide to tell the police you contacted me, that's my choice. You could forgive me for being a little bit nervous when you showed up, out of the blue.'

Becky sipped at some water.

'As for the killer, what possible reason would he have for coming after me? I'd imagine it's better for him if I was still alive and well. Slinking around in the woods. Wouldn't you agree? I make a nice suspect. What's the term? In English? A red herring. Or am I?' He grinned and finished his brandy.

'Don't play games with me. I'm telling you the honest truth. I'm here for your own good.'

Leif poured another. 'Maybe you are. But you're also here to find out something. Some loose end you didn't tie up before. So what is it?'

'How many brandies do you normally drain before dinner, Leif?'

He frowned. 'Answer the question, please.'

'Okay.' Becky gestured towards her glass. Leif poured a measure and handed it to her. She sniffed at the contents and shivered as it scorched her nostrils.

That most agreeable burn. She had promised to have no more drink while she was investigating. She let the glass rest on the table, without taking a sip. 'I want to know about the legal trouble you ran into. Early noughties.'

Leif's face registered no shock, only a grim acceptance. 'You mean the girl from Beauvais?'

'That's right. She was 15. You were, what... 22?'

'I was not charged with an offence. No sexual contact took place. I was warned by the police for my conduct, but it was a simple misunderstanding. She claimed to be older than she was; we began a correspondence. After we met, I realised my mistake. I was astonished when the police knocked on my door. You already know that I was fond of writing letters. No harm was done.'

'Not according to the police files, Leif. The girl said there was some sexual contact, but there were no witnesses and no evidence, and so no case to answer. And then there seemed to be other letters, written to other girls. Aged 14, in one case, though the others were admittedly older. Old enough, anyway.'

Leif shrugged. 'They contacted me. They lied about their age.'

'Did you target those girls, Leif? Look at me.'

He looked her straight in the eye. 'No.' Then he smiled. 'But really, in your deepest darkest heart, ask yourself: if something had happened, then so what?'

'So *what*? Under-age girls?' Her arms, hands and finally her fingers betrayed her, curling round the shot glass. And so did her lips; one swift, deadly kiss. Quick as a cobra strike, the agreeable burn scorched her tongue and cauterised the back of her throat.

Leif tapped a brass stud on the tabletop. '"Under-age girls" is technically correct. But tell me, when you were 15 years old, did you have a boyfriend who was 18? Maybe even older? If not, did you know someone who did?'

'That doesn't make it right, Leif. It's still against the law. And I don't care what you think – 22 is old enough to know better.'

'But I didn't know better. It was an honest mistake, that's all. I'm not lying. I would have been charged if I had behaved in any way inappropriately. And I'd have deserved it, too. Now let me guess; you think that somehow, that incident puts me in the frame for what happened to your family? You think I was somehow involved? You know that can't be true.'

'I don't think you had a hand in the murder. Not wittingly anyway. But I want to know about who you were writing to, at the time. Theresa.'

'I already told you. She was American. We had arranged to meet on the day, in the forest.'

Becky took another sip. The fire had spread, a pleasant throb in her bloodstream. 'And whose plan was it – yours or hers?'

'Hers, I believe.'

'Where was she? What became of her?'

'No one knows – she was never traced. The police ruled that she probably didn't turn up. It was a dead end, all done through the postal service. The name led nowhere.'

Becky shook her head. 'It's too much of a coincidence. All of it. My sister... the mysterious other girl... you showing up... He claims he planned it all, you know. Right down to the moment you appeared. He might be telling the truth. It's possible you were writing to a murderer, all along. Maybe he was manipulating you, making you part of his plan.'

Leif drained his drink. 'But why involve me at all?'

'My theory is: plausibility. That having you there caused some kind of distraction. It let him get away, or gave him a head-start, at least.'

'I don't follow. You mean he wanted you to escape? For someone to find you?'

'So he says.'

'That doesn't make any sense. Why would he need me? He could just let you go, if that's all he wanted. It could have taken hours for you to get help, if I hadn't arrived. Or he could simply kill you. Why take the risk?'

'Because he wanted me to survive. Ensuring you were there meant I would make it. Leaving someone alive was the ultimate turn-on. Knowing that I was frightened of him. Knowing that I'd spend my entire life looking over my shoulder.' It was too soon to say all this. Becky frowned. 'Are you keeping all that brandy for yourself?'

Leif poured another measure for her and said, 'Something else occurs to me. You say, he told you about me. So he knows who I am, and probably where I live. You got in touch with me again. And you came here to tell me. Is it possible he's waiting for you to come out here?'

Becky drained the glass in one gulp. It was more than a fire in her blood, now; it was a molten river, every heartbeat an eruption. 'I'm counting on it,' she said.

'Interesting.' Leif drummed his fingers on the tabletop. 'I'm getting a clearer picture of what you're trying to do. I'm not sure I like it.'

'I can't pretend I'm interested in what you like or don't like.'

Leif considered this a moment. 'I think perhaps we should head out. I love this house; three generations of my family have lived and died here. All that we are is within these four walls. And I'm the last. But let me tell you – it's no place for a party.' He twirled his car keys on his index finger. 'Come on. I've got an idea.'

'What – you're driving? You've had too much, Leif.'

'I know these roads. Whether I've got a couple in me or not. Come on. I can take you to someplace a lot less quiet. Let's get out of here. You can ask me anything you want. We'll have background noise. Better than a ticking clock, eh?'

Perhaps if Becky had had just the one inside her, or less, she'd have said no. But she'd had a couple. And a couple was all it took to spark something utterly unquenchable in her.

'You're on.'

Outside the kitchen door, Leif's dog pawed the door and whimpered.

# 29

He drove far too fast with the top down on his sleek little Mazda. Becky did not complain at all; her hair scattered in the wind. His own silvery-black locks furled to and fro as if underwater.

This was a sly taste of the old life, the reckless life. She wanted more.

He grinned at her with even white teeth. 'How do you like the air conditioning?'

The trees crouched ahead of them, readying for summer, shocking green in the headlights. Creatures scurried out of the way only just in time, a flicker of eyes reflected, then a twitch of foliage, then safe. Leif did not slow down for any them.

'Let's hope we don't run into any deer,' Becky said.

'Or a wolf.'

The lights of a town appeared. It was not the place they'd had coffee before but had no less of a picture-postcard effect. Its thoroughfare was thronged with young people along roadside cafes and bars.

She needed another drink, fast, and said so.

'Yeah, it's good brandy, isn't it?' Leif yelled above the roaring wind. 'A little spark. Lights something in you, no? I know a place where they serve it.'

Leif knew just where to park, a leafy spot round the corner from some immaculately-kept white bungalows with bright red Spanish-style slated roofs. From there they headed through a doorway in an elderly block of flats, and then downstairs, towards the music.

Becky kept her distance from Leif, allowing him to descend into the gloom ahead of her. Her mind raced through different possibilities, combat scenarios. The treacherous urge to plant a kick on the back of his head and watch him sprawl was strong, telling her that she should not take this chance. Not after everything she'd seen and heard in the past few days.

But instead, she followed him into the light of a basement bar. She always seemed to find her way into these, when she didn't want to.

It was not as dingy as the entryway had advertised, smart, bright, well-kept, and loud. The building backed onto a canal embankment, and late evening light flooded in from large windows. Children were still out and about there, enjoying the warm air, bicycles surging past on the waterside track. The bar itself was filled with young people, mainly stylish looking couples, talking loudly to make themselves heard over the music. The tune was something new she didn't recognise, possibly the Chemical Brothers – if they were still around. Perhaps their sons.

Leif knew someone at the bar, a tall West African man with green and white braids in his dreads and a red and orange shirt that would have looked silly on any other person in the room. The two men clapped each other's shoulders and jabbered for a while. Becky ordered vodka while they were talking, drank it, then considered another.

*Control*, said a small voice at her shoulder. *Remember control.* But the urge was on her now, sudden and bright like a petrol bomb. The small voice grew distant, and her heart took over.

They chose a booth near the windows, as far from the pounding speakers as possible. Leif offered her a beer. 'You haven't told me why you came back here,' he said, bent close to her.

'I need to see the letters, Leif. The ones from Theresa. Some are missing from the police files. Do you still have them?'

'I told you, no. The police seized all that stuff.' He frowned. 'How do you know about the police files?'

'I'm a journalist. I have my sources.' She sipped at the beer. 'Here's the thing, though. Your house is lovely, but you've lived in it all your life. The fittings are old. You've still got your dad's books on the shelves, and he died years ago.'

'So?'

'So, you're a pretty conservative guy. The type who hangs onto things, people and places.'

'But I don't have the letters.'

'What was Theresa like?'

'I don't really remember. It was all very innocent – this is something you don't get. I know the world is different these days. Mobile phones, dating apps. Everything is so explicit. This was different. It was... tender.'

She grinned. 'I get you now. A sensitive artist! A budding Sartre.'

'It was what it was. I enjoyed communicating. It appealed to me. I enjoyed writing to women, but couldn't talk to them. I was more shy than I am now.'

'So you didn't talk about sex?'

'Only if kisses count.'

'A young guy, talking about kisses? Now I know you're full of shit.'

He sat back abruptly. 'You believe what you like. It was innocent, so far as it went. I enjoyed writing letters. Remember, no one had email at this point. No one had text messages or emojis or webcams.'

'I want to know about her. What did you talk about, apart from kisses?'

'Cycling. She liked the Tour de France. She also claimed to like poetry but knew nothing about it. I don't remember much else.'

Later, Leif introduced them to a couple with matching side-parted hairstyles. The man had an even more amusing beard, like an ice cream cone turret stuck to the end of his chin, or some exotic shellfish. He wore John-Lennon-style sunglasses indoors, though the sun had long disappeared. Becky found this amusing, and told him so, wondering what the French was for 'hipster'. He took this in good sport, although his girlfriend did not. Both asked her to say French phrases in an English accent, which broke the tension and caused so much mirth between the three of them Becky didn't see Leif drift away.

For the space of three rounds of drinks, she saw him talk to several different women. She took in their non-verbal cues, things which could mean nothing, or a lot – hair played with, hems tugged, shrill laughter. Leif never grew more animated than wry amusement, his smile broad but his eyes narrowed. At some point UV was switched on behind the bar, something of a nineties' accoutrement, Becky supposed. It threw Leif's spikes in sharp relief, his silvery crown as distinctive as a shark fin cutting through the bobbing heads.

The music grew louder, and blank spots became more frequent. Becky's brain began to repeat on itself, like an alarm in a 'snooze' mode loop. *Beware an older man, anyone over 40. Anyone at all.* She found herself glaring at a round-bellied barman, who did his best to avoid her eyes. He didn't look tall enough, but everyone was a suspect.

She was then distracted by the West African man with green and white braids. His name was Patrice and he was originally from Paris. He hinted he was the owner, although Becky wondered if this was a lie. He was confident enough. A light sweat made his skin slick in the light, and in the close atmosphere she could smell sweet alcohol on his breath as he told her about DJing in Manchester and London. She asked what he was drinking, and she ordered two of those. Patrice placed his foot on the brass rail at the bottom of the bar and leaned close to her. At the same time, his hand stole across the top of hers. She noticed Leif watching her from one of the corners of the bar, while an excitable girl of no more than 18 yelled something in his ear.

Becky decided to kiss Patrice; he was not surprised, and their tongues touched in controlled, unabashed flickering. She tried to put her arms round him, but Patrice was in no hurry; he only ran his hands through her hair and drew his fingers down the length of her jaw.

She glanced over to Leif but he only grinned and raised a glass.

Something happened then – an argument between Patrice and a man in a long corduroy coat. The thread was difficult to follow in the noise, but Becky gathered it was something to do with a girl who was not in the building. Patrice tried to placate the man, but he grew utterly furious, jabbing a finger at Becky.

She withdrew to the far side of the room. She flinched when Leif patted her on the shoulder and leaned close.

His lips were very close to her ear. 'If you're trying to impress me, you'll have to do a lot better than that.'

On the drive back to the farmhouse, he drew a hand up and down her thighs without once glancing away from the road as it bucked and twisted under the headlights. It was a firm appraisal which put Becky in mind of farmers examining livestock. Only very slightly nettled by this, she replied in kind, clutching at him until his lips parted in one trembling breath.

Out of the car, they kissed long and hard, his hands everywhere. He lifted her clean off the ground and settled her on the bonnet of the car, its headlights marking out the narrow path through the yard, their shadows intertwined serpents writhing on the walls.

'Be careful,' she tried to say. 'Watch out.' But his mouth smothered hers.

Inside, he slowed down to undress her, pausing to examine the scarring that crossed her shoulder with light fingertips. It seemed more of a wrinkle than scar tissue now, like laugh lines or stretch marks.

He had seen it once before, of course. When it was fresh.

'Here?' was all he said. She nodded. He kissed it, starting from the tip, all the way down to her ribs and underneath her arm. The time it took for his tongue to travel that kinked path was roughly similar to the time it had taken for the wound to be inflicted. She shuddered, but was not disgusted, an act of sublime treachery on her body's part.

Much later, she watched him sleep. He didn't snore; his nostrils twitched like a rabbit's with every breath he took. She stared at his face for a long time, then whispered, in English, 'This means nothing. If I ever find out it was you, I'll torture you. I'll record it, every moment, up to your death and beyond, until you are bones. And I'll drink a toast every time I play it back.'

Only his slow, deep breathing answered her. Finally, she lay back down in bed, and closed her eyes.

# 30

Long after breakfast, with the coffee finished and the plates put away, Leif said, 'I've something to show you.'

He turned towards a darkened alcove in the room. After a brief rattle of his keys, a door grated open. He clicked on a light; Becky saw a long, narrow staircase.

'A cellar? I'm not going down there, Leif.'

Leif shrugged. 'Suit yourself. Here... in case you don't trust me...' He opened a cabinet, then pulled out a shotgun. He handed it to her, then disappeared down the stairs.

Becky tried the weapon for weight, then frowned and set it down on an ancient telephone table.

After a while, Leif returned, holding a buff-coloured folder of the type she hadn't seen since her schooldays. 'I had a few examples of what you wanted. I looked them out the other night. I was going to send them on to you, I promise.'

Becky glanced inside the folder; they were letters, written in a careful hand, neatly folded into squares.

'That's all I have left. I thought they may be of sentimental value. If they can help you find the man you're looking for, all the better.'

'These are letters? From Clara?'

He nodded.

'So you lied. All along, you lied. Why?'

'Once I lied to the police, I had to maintain the lie. I made a stupid decision when I was younger to hide the letters, to keep silent about them. I thought the police might blame me for the killings. You were right. It *is* too much of a coincidence that she arrived here, and then your family were killed. It would look as if they were lured. But I had nothing to do with it. I was scared.'

She delved into the letters. 'These are from my sister? All of them?'

'No. Some are from the American girl. Theresa. I was writing to both of them, at the same time. Now I've given you what you were looking for. And I want you to leave. Understand? I want you to leave, and I don't want to see you back here for a very long time.'

Becky had already tuned him out. There, in lined school notebook longhand, was her sister's looping script, the love-hearts and kisses, the comic faces scrawled in the top left corners.

Then she turned to the American girl's letters. She had seen the writing before, in Rupert's stolen files, but she hadn't recognised it then. The script was more compact, and slanted in the opposite direction to Clara's letters. Becky had gazed upon this script many times, in birthday cards, in the margins of an old tomato-splattered recipe book, and in the address book she'd salvaged from her old family home and kept close. Even at that, she might not have recognised it, despite the script on the paper in her hands. How often did you memorise another person's handwriting, after all?

But then came the giveaway – a final flourish in one of the letters: a series of kisses, forming the shape of a diamond. That's when the pieces fit together. That's when she knew.

The handwriting was her mother's.

# 31

Back at the flat, Becky had circled two names she'd written on the notice board: KRNCZR? KRANCZR? The names had come from the file of related cases. She'd grown used to some of the names in the inquiry; the Bells, the Jameses. They'd come up again and again. But KRNCZR/KRANCZR had stuck out, precisely because it was a loose end. The names went nowhere; they appeared nowhere else.

One of her phones rang. It was Rosie.

'You seen the newsletter?'

'Newsletter? You spamming the internet on my behalf now?'

Rosie sounded put out. 'It's for your benefit, you know.'

'Is this your podcast? What is it, the Dupin Collective? I haven't had the time, Rosie. Been busy.'

'Oh. With your mysterious friend in France.'

'C'mon, out with it.'

'One of them turned something up. The Kranczr family. They were murdered in Romania. You'll never guess how.'

'Same as my family?'

'Yep. And they never caught the killer.'

'You're kidding. How did you find this out?'

'One of the group has family in Romania. They knew all about it. Even better... they've managed to turn up a connection. But it's not in Romania.'

'Where is it, then?'

Rosie cleared her throat. 'Just remember... when I tell you this... you owe me one.'

'I don't think I do!' Becky spluttered.

'You do, though. You owe me one.'

'I could just wait for the podcast.'

'Won't be out for ages.' Was she laughing? Becky couldn't be sure.

'What do you want?'

'I want in, Becky. Let me come on board. We can team up. As if we're superheroes.'

Becky sighed.

Two hours later, Becky checked her online boarding pass was stuck tight inside her passport, turned off all the lights, punched in her security codes, and whistled *Viva Espana* as she locked up the flat.

The road curved its way around a rust-red mountain which might have been transplanted from Mars, were it not for the phone mast right at the top. The view over the brow as the car eased across it was spectacular; a broad expanse of ocean, tropical blue, glittering in the late afternoon sun.

This was a place which had tourists, but only a select few. A distant tanker clung to the outermost edge of the horizon, a lonely plume of smoke reaching up into the merest haze of cloud above, but there were few other boats to be found on that flat calm.

The car's air conditioning roared, blowing Becky's hair out of her face and freezing a trickle of sweat that ran down her back.

The house was set in a narrow valley with a view of the sea. It was a grand place, the seaside residence of a childless rich man who had bequeathed it to the state. It was welcoming, if one ignored the wrought iron gates, topped off with ornate, but mean-looking spikes. On a neat lawn outside, old men wearing blinding white clothes played *petanque* in the shimmering heat.

They were expecting her at the front desk. A pretty young girl with light almond eyes and a wicked smile checked Becky's paperwork, before passing her on to an orderly with heavy Greek eyebrows and thick neck hair clambering over his collar.

He led her through the cool corridors to where the old lady lived.

The orderly gave a cheery greeting as he rapped the door. The woman inside the room answered him in an alarmingly frail voice. She was sat upright in a chair, perched on teetering cushions like a fairy tale Sultan. A fan whirred, stirring her hair, surely too close to her for comfort.

She was heavy-set, but had extraordinary braids of long silvery hair over her shoulders. These reminded Becky of a daguerreotype photo of a Native American woman.

There were few ornaments or personal decorations in the room, although a stack of books in a language Becky didn't recognise clung to the edge of a dresser.

'Someone to see you, beautiful,' said the orderly in a bright voice. The old lady's eyes opened a little wider, as if she'd been asleep. She smiled at the orderly, then turned her gaze upon the newcomer. Her skin was sun-damaged, Becky thought, her colouring slightly mottled in the air-conditioned atmosphere.

'I don't think I know this one,' the old lady said. She reached for some glasses on a table by the side of her armchair, but the orderly was already there, fixing them over her ears with the easy dexterity of long practice.

The lady's eyes were comically magnified under the lenses, but their shade was still beautiful, a delicate green flecked with hazel. Gypsy eyes; added to the well-tended hair, Becky wondered if she had been beautiful.

'No... I don't know this one.'

'I'm from England,' Becky said. 'I want to talk to you about your time in Spain. I'm a writer, researching a book on the ex-pat life. I understand you've been in Spain for a number of years?'

'That's right,' the old lady said. 'Nearly thirty years. Sit yourself down, girl. Gregory will get you some water, if you wish?'

'Water would be lovely, actually.'

She glanced at Gregory, who poured her some water from a carafe near the sink. To Becky's annoyance, he remained in a far corner, paying close attention to the exchange.

'My name is Jane,' Becky said, flashing a doctored NUJ press card at the woman. 'My book is about how life in Spain has changed since Franco. Can I ask your name – it's Elizabetha, is that right?'

She nodded.

'And your second name is?'

'Grillo.'

'That's an Italian name?'

'I'm not quite sure.' Her eyes were questioning, as though searching her brain for the knowledge behind the name. 'My husband was Spanish, though.'

'And where did you meet him?'

'In Seville. Before we go into that... can I ask how you got my name?'

'I was researching families who had moved to Spain from lots of different places. But I'm particularly interested in people who might have come from Eastern Europe.'

'Eastern Europe,' the old lady repeated.

'Yes. Specifically, the former Communist states.'

'Former Communist states.' The woman did not change the pleasant intonation of her voice; she might have been making an empty inquiry about how a great-grandchild's day had gone at school. But the eyes had taken on a curious animation now, a gleam of activity like slow traffic crossing a bridge at night.

'Indeed. I'm interested in your original name. Where is it you said you were from?'

'I didn't say I was from anywhere.'

'Ah right. Was it Bulgaria?'

The old lady laughed. 'No, Romania. Though the name was from Croatia, originally. Or what you now call Croatia.'

'Oh. Sorry. I had some bad information.' Becky scored something out on her notepad.

The old lady chuckled. 'I hope you are a better writer than you are a liar, miss.'

'I'm sorry?'

'This book you say you are writing... the life of ex-pats, you say? Living in Spain, from Eastern Europe?' She turned to the orderly and laughed, uproariously. 'I cannot say I am looking forward to the movie, Gregory. Are you?'

Gregory was deathly serious. 'Do you want me to ask her to leave, beautiful?'

Elizabetha raised an arthritic hand like a knotted fencepost. 'No, my love, peace. I'm curious now.' With an effort, she sat forward in her chair. 'Why do you really want to speak to me?'

Becky smiled. 'You're sharp as a tack. I am lying to you. I'm not really writing about ex-pats. I'm writing about unsolved murders.'

Elizabetha's kindly expression faltered. 'Murders?'

'Yes. I'm looking for information about an incident which took place outside of Galati in 1980.'

The old lady glanced at her hands, then turned them over.

'It involved a family known as Kranczr.'

She drew breath to speak, then settled herself.

'Elizabetha, I am trying to find the man who killed the Kranczr family.'

'Kranczr... I do not know that name.'

'The Kranczrs had a son, Constantin. He was active in underground politics, which was how I was able to track back to the case. The curious thing about the Kranczrs was that I only found out about what happened to them because Constantin was known as a traitor during the Ceaușescu era – or at least, those were the references I discovered. Many of the press cuttings and online references have been obliterated. This was something I came across several times in reference to murdered families across Europe from the eighties to the present day. I managed to find out that Constantin had three younger sisters, the youngest being just 10. They all died along with Constantin, as did his father, Adrian. Only the mother survived. You. That was your family, Elizabetha. Yes?'

The old lady's hands shook. She covered her eyes with them, then drew them down her face.

Gregory's thick eyebrows concertinaed, a fuzzed line of static across his brow. 'Enough. This interview is over.'

'I know you found them, Elizabetha. I know it's hard. Believe me, I know. I think the same man killed my family. He killed families all across Europe. I need to make the connection without making official contact with the police. How did you survive?'

'I was late,' the old lady said, eyelids quivering. 'My friend at the factory, Masha, had an accident as we got off the bus. She twisted her ankle. I had to help her. We had no telephone. It took hours to get her to a doctor and have her leg put in plaster. If that had not happened, it should have been me, too…'

'You found them, Elizabetha. What was marked on the walls? Was there a mark?'

'Words… "This is how sluts end their lives". Then a marking… a face, or an animal. Maybe an insect.'

'Was it like a face? Or a skull?'

'Yes. It could have been.'

'And what else did you see? Elizabetha, how did they die?'

'Their heads. He took their heads, after he had his way with them.' Her voice was barely above a whisper. Then, with feral suddenness, the old lady's face twisted with hate.

Yellowed teeth split her lips as she growled: 'God's curse be upon you!'

Gregory's hands gripped Becky's wrist. He tried to pull her to her feet, but with a flick of her arm she was free. She gave herself some space, and took an aggressive stance, her pen locked rigid at the knuckles between her second and third fingers.

'Don't touch me again, Gregory. Or I'll split your eyebrow in half.'

'Get out,' he said. 'And never come back. Don't make me call the police.'

Becky charged along the corridor, trying to ignore the wailing that grew shrill at her back.

# 32

Becky drove too fast on the way back over the hill. She tried to forget the woman's final imprecation and focused on what she'd gleaned.

The decapitations fit the MO nicely, though she tried to swallow the rising tide of enthusiasm.

She imagined what Elizabetha might have said to Rosie Banning, had she spoken to the woman in the nursing home and not Becky. *'There's no absolute proof just yet, just coincidence,'* Becky might have said, once Rosie had reported back. But there was no denying that Elizabetha's corroboration was a good start. So there was that killing, in Romania, early eighties; then the Polish family in 1982; after that, the Baumlisch family went missing in 1988, never to be seen again. The murders moved further west, including a case in France, then one in Spain in 1992 – a family of four, mother and father, two daughters under 16.

Families were the link; that was what he wanted to destroy.

But there was little physical evidence connecting any of these cases, and few breakthroughs in the inquiries. More intriguingly, someone had been convicted for the Vladek family killings in Poland, and the murderer had subsequently been garrotted in jail. That case seemed very firmly closed. And if the families had been killed in the midst of some problems in their business dealings – even Elizabetha's family were implicated in fraud, as well as their political difficulties – then that broke the link between that string of cases and the one involving Becky's family. There had been no business problems linked to Becky's mother and father, real or imagined.

The all-media search accessed through her still live connection to the newspaper had been uncharacteristically slow in dredging up prior material on these cases. In instances where bodies had been found, the details were scant, particularly in the former Soviet states – especially the Gursky case from just recently.

In the western murders, there was always room for doubt; a family in debt, links to the criminal world, people trafficking, a suggestion that missing girls had been sold to slavery while the parents were butchered.

In most cases, the families had simply vanished. You never could tell without bodies, without solid witnesses. But Becky had to admit, some patterns made a compelling fit.

Being in Spain to check out the Kranczr link gave her the chance to kill two birds with one stone, having spoken to Elizabetha. Now she could head to the fishing town where the Ramirez family had disappeared without trace in 1992. That was the final case Becky had been able to uncover before the killing of her family, which took place a few years later.

'God bless you, Rupert,' she murmured.

She was adjusting the sat-nav to direct her to the nearest petrol station when she noticed the car keeping a steady distance behind her. The vehicle was nondescript, a dark smudge trailing a sirocco of dust in its wake. It was only a couple of hundred yards above and behind her as the crow flew, growing to half a mile taking into account the weave and twist of the mountain road. There was nothing especially dodgy about this, but the past few weeks meant Beck knew she should cleave to any suspicion whatsoever.

She increased her speed on the straights, braking hard when the corners approached.

A quick glance upward told her there was no appreciable difference in the speed of the black car.

The mountain route flattened out after a spell as the road twisted through the valleys, still well above sea level. Becky would have enjoyed the splendour of the ocean view but for that blocky pursuer in her rear-view mirror.

The blur remained a steady presence behind her.

'I've seen too many movies,' she muttered. A quick glance at the red thread running through the sat nav screen revealed a petrol station a mile or so ahead.

Easing up a little on the speed, she waited for the car to come closer in order to get a better look at the details – or better still, the driver. But the car kept its distance. It might have been a dirty mark on her wing mirror, bad enough to risk wiping while in transit.

When the sign for the petrol station appeared, Becky pulled in much too fast, without indicating, and stopped in one of the empty parking bays.

She kept an eye on any traffic coming in. After maybe twenty seconds or so, with the inside of Becky's hire car still ticking in the heat, the dark smudge rocketed past.

It could have been one of the blockier VWs, or maybe even a Mercedes, either black or inky blue, but there was no way of making an accurate assessment. She waited, drumming her hands on the steering wheel, before moving the car into the filling area and topping up the tank. Soon she was back on the road.

Becky hadn't consciously decided to keep an eye out for a dark smudge anywhere as she pulled back out onto the motorway, but she kept her speed low in any case.

When the same car pulled out behind her, emerging from the shadow of a truck parked in a lay-by maybe three hundred yards away from the petrol station, Becky felt a curious thrill of satisfaction.

'Now it's a game, my friend.'

She did nothing out of the ordinary until she reached the nearest town, a quiet place with villas poking out of the hillsides, flecked with sparkling blue shards of swimming pools.

The dark blur swung onto the exit not long after she did. There was a suggestion of a single occupant, probably a man, and a tall one at that.

Then she reached a roundabout, slowed right down, and made a full right turn, back onto the opposite side of the road she had just emerged from.

The blur had followed her, but slipped back a little in her mirror, perhaps to buy some thinking time. This was a mistake, as it allowed Becky to get a good look as she passed him going in the opposite direction.

A man, for sure; dark-haired, white, possibly wearing a collar and tie.

Becky smiled grimly. Now for the clincher.

Once on the motorway, with the bluish smudge at its regulation distance behind her, Becky took the next available exit and doubled back on herself, heading back into the town.

The car followed her.

'Schoolboy stuff, this,' she said, chuckling.

Heading through the town, her plan seemed to arrive fully-formed, based on a strange icon which popped up on her sat-nav screen. A sign and a set of lights confirmed her initial impressions, and she sped up as the road narrowed on the edge of town, heading towards the mountains.

In a valley just ahead, a set of lights flashed a warning ahead of some barriers.

Perfect.

Becky scanned the trees at the side of the road; coming up to her right was a brown track, edging into the cover of some desiccated pine trees.

She jammed on the brakes, overshooting the dirt road, her head lurching towards the wheel and her guts following in tandem. Now things had got more real, less detached; she spun the wheel frantically and reversed, expertly pulling the car into the dirt road. It was stony, the car lurching to and fro over it and her backside bouncing in the seat. Becky cursed the light plume of dust stirred by her wheels, hoping it would settle before her pursuer arrived.

She stopped the car on a bend in the dirt road, keeping her eyes on the level crossing visible through the trees. The barriers were down, but there was no sign of the train just yet. Becky palmed some sweat off her brow, unzipped her handbag, and waited.

The dark blue car crept along the road, slowing down as it approached the crossing. The man in the car was wearing shades; a slim tie lolled like a dog's tongue beneath an open collar and bulky shoulders. He didn't look good in a suit – he was built like a prizefighter, and sweating like one, too.

The car reached the crossing and the man stopped and got out, running a hand through longish dark hair, glancing up and down in irritation. He checked his watch and cursed in English. Then he spotted the dirt track, his expression changing from anger to confusion. He started up the path, and quickly spotted Becky's car.

Becky was not in it.

He did not approach the car, flipping open a phone while keeping a close eye on it. 'Yeah,' he said, in a south London accent, 'Level crossing. Not sure where she's got to. I reckon it may be time to pull out. I'll get someone else to pick it up later, I think she's spotted me. She ain't daft, mate, I'll tell you that for nothing.'

Becky waited until he'd flipped the phone closed and placed it in his pocket before shooting him.

The twin prongs of the stun gun dart punched into the back of his neck, in the middle of the hairline just above the collar. Becky had only seen the death-ray effect once before in the flesh, but it was no less fascinating.

The man's body jerked like a fish on the line, just as the report of the weapon sounded, a near-subliminal crackle. He fell awkwardly, dark glasses tumbling across the dirt, landing face first, and hard.

Becky pulled out the stun dart and reeled it in while the man lay flat, panting. Puffs of dust rose above his gasping mouth like tracer fire. When he managed to lift his head, Becky had swapped the stun gun for the mace; one quick blast into the mouth, and the game was over.

With some difficulty, she dragged him into the treeline, her back and shoulder muscles taut with the strain. He did not scream too much; neither did he protest to any great degree when she rummaged inside his jacket and pulled out some ID. She took a photo of everything with her phone – bank cards, driving licence, even a library card – while the man lurched upright, drooling. His cheeks were sodden with tears while an altogether more unsightly shadow crawled across the front of his trousers.

Becky took aim with the stun gun. 'I don't want to hurt you any more than I have. So let's make this quick.'

The man gasped; when he managed to open his eyes, they were Hammer-Horror red.

'First, tell me who you are, and who you're working for. Then you can have a nice glass of water.'

The man shook his head.

'Aw, don't be shy. What I can do now is make a citizen's arrest, and contact the Guardia Civil. They really enjoy processing people like you. How's your Spanish, incidentally? All right?'

The man said nothing.

'Bit shy. That's okay. Know what else I could do?' Becky gripped one of his ankles, and dragged him through the dust, teeth gritted, muscles straining at her neck.

'Hey,' he wheezed, arms flailing. 'Wait!'

'Let's take a look at this train. It can't be far away.' She dragged him up the bank of the rail track. He still didn't have full control back of his limbs, though he clutched uselessly at the loose stones. Above them, shimmering in the heat, the rail lines quivered.

The man's eyes were trying to crawl from their sockets, and he gaped and flapped at the ground like a landed fish.

'Sounds like an express,' Becky said. 'It'll come through here at a fair old lick. The trains over here are awesome, aren't they? Put the ones back home in the shade.' She braced her foot on the stones bordering the tracks, gazing into the heat haze in the distance. 'I'm not kidding. You'll just be another suicide. I'll leave you on the track. You'll be another mess to clear up. All you have to do is say a name. If you can. Just one name. Who are you working for?'

'Tullington,' the man wheezed, at last.

This hit her so hard, she cut it very fine, only remembering to pull the man completely away from the tracks when the train appeared on the horizon. It hurtled past them, at a scarcely conceivable velocity, and if any faces gaped at the two figures on the verge, they were lost to a blur of momentum.

# 33

Rosie Banning sucked down the last of the pina colada until it gurgled. The sun had brought out a light dusting of freckles on her cheeks which reminded Becky of a favourite dolly in her childhood. Becky recalled that if you'd rubbed the dolly's belly, it gave off a whiff of ice cream and strawberries.

'I quite like these,' Rosie said, pushing the foam-rimmed glass aside. 'I'm surprised. I thought they were like something your grandma might drink.'

Becky sipped her fresh orange juice. 'You remember the song? Radio 2? A Ken Bruce classic.'

'Who's Ken Bruce?'

'I hope you're joking. Never mind. What have you got for me?'

They were still in Spain, in the fishing town where the Ramirez family had vanished in 1992. A Tiki bar on the seafront had seemed a little gaudy when they'd driven past it first time, but it had drawn them in nonetheless. Inside, everything gleamed; it had only been opened a matter of weeks, and the leather on the benches was smooth and the pinewood tables and fittings largely unmarked with graffiti. It had been marketed for surfers and many of the people who passed in and out were in neoprene bodysuits, their hair sometimes clinging wet with the sea.

There was even a place to park one's surfboard, right next to a freshwater shower on the edge of the beach. Becky had felt a dull ache upon first sight of this place, which had only just begun to show up on tourist websites and yearly 'best-of' lists in Sunday supplements.

The weather was perfect. It couldn't have been less of a holiday, but Becky's brain was duped by the blue water, the rising heat, the sugar-candy sand, and above all, the white-crested waves.

Rosie turned round a laptop computer. 'Your theory has made a bit of a splash in the community.'

'I'm amazed no one put it together before now.'

'This is the point – no one had *heard* of these other cases before now. There's so little information out there. And the police wouldn't admit to anything.'

'I got a very polite "we'll check it out", when I told them about it. The cases that are unsolved are said to be unrelated. There's just a little difference in each case, something off about the MO – enough to raise doubt that it's not the same killer. Then there's the knife traced to Miles Crandley. That's the new evidence they thought they had turned up. It seems the DNA evidence is inconclusive and probably couldn't be used to bring a prosecution. And there's DNA evidence here and there that doesn't match, which I must admit counts a lot of cases out.'

Rosie almost bounced on the bench in excitement. 'But that's where you might be wrong. A couple of our guys reckon a lot of these murder scenes were staged to raise doubt in anyone who might be looking for a link. The knife left at the scene in the first French case, with the fingerprints no one can match. He might as well have painted "Red Herring Here" on the walls. It's far too convenient. But that's by the by. You haven't asked me for my news.'

'Don't keep me in suspense.'

'We reckon we found another case. In the UK.'

Becky raised her eyebrows. 'Oh yeah?'

'Orkney. 1984. It's not as well-known as you would think.'

'The Sloans. I know it. I had heard something about that before... but details were hard to find. I spoke to one of the local police, and he basically shut the door on me. Couldn't work out if he was scared, or just tired.'

'Well – it's a big connection. The case involved a family of self-sufficiency nuts, with their own farm. Watched a bit too much of *The Good Life*, maybe. Went off-grid. Mother and father, six kids. All of them dead; heads removed, bodies burned. All except the father, who seemed to have done it; he hanged himself from a tree just outside the farm. Ritualistic elements, they say. A fatal accident inquiry determined it was murder/suicide; he'd gone mad up there during a hard winter after a lot of their livestock died. Self-sustaining wasn't sustainable. Not enough for them all to eat, the dream dying, kind of thing. But there was one other thing that rang alarm bells. This was found written in blood on one of the walls which survived the fire.' Rosie clicked on the mousepad and turned the laptop round.

'Jesus Christ. It's him. Or damned close to it.'

'That's what we reckoned. Given the year, we could be looking at a prototype version of your friend's motif.'

On the screen, sketched in thin, brutal strokes, was something very close to the bone mask.

'Looks a bit like the devil, too, of course, and that's what the police and the media focused on. Devil worship. Paganism. Self-sufficiency nutter loses his mind, chops up his family. A sacrifice. Some even saw significance in the bloke's manner of death. He's the right way up, but his leg was in a funny position. Like the Hanged Man, from the Tarot card. Um, I guess I should warn you, this next shot...'

Becky waved her away. The next image on the laptop was a dead man. Even in black and white you could make out the unearthly tinge and the swollen tongue which gave away anoxia as the cause of death; there was an almost comic leer in the blood-suffused eyes and the jaunty tilt of his stretched neck. He was young, Becky saw, younger than she was, with long naturally curly hair which Marc Bolan would have envied. Helpfully inset, was an image of the Hanged Man Tarot card. Becky scribbled down some quick notes, intrigued.

'The Tarot thing is new.'

'Could just be a coincidence,' Rosie said, frowning. 'He might have set that way depending on how the wind was blowing.'

'What does the card mean, again? Is it like a choice, or a contradiction?'

Rosie smiled. 'Hard to say. The Tarot is like that. Open to interpretation. Could mean a dilemma, a fork in the road. Could refer to an old way of punishing a traitor, and nothing to do with the Tarot. Thought to refer to Judas.'

'So if our guy was behind this, Mr Orkney could be an associate? Punished for something?'

'Bit of a leap, there, Becky, but it's possible. As far as the police are concerned, there's nothing sinister about it, though. Nothing beyond your regular family murder/suicide, anyway. What was more interesting was the location.' Rosie called up an online map.

'A stone circle?' Becky asked.

'How did you know?'

'Oh... just a hunch.'

'Yep. Standing stones. Thousands of years old. Early Celts, druids. Picts. Whatever you call them. Hardly any of them left, now. It's kind of overgrown.'

'Have they accurately dated the stones?'

'No one's quite sure. They reckon about the same time as the Callanish stones on the Hebrides. Neolithic. Ritual space. So that's a direct line between where two families died, taking into account what happened to yours. It's not an exact fit, but it ticks plenty of boxes – certainly there are more direct links than folk ever cottoned on to. The drawing on the wall is the giveaway, for me.'

'This is good stuff. Any sexual element to the Orkney family deaths?'

'No one knows. There wasn't much evidence left after the fire. The house and all the bodies were burned. But their heads came off at some point, we know that much.' Rosie raised the straw from her glass, and let the final drops spill out. 'I think I'll get another. You fancy one?'

'I'm good with OJ, for now.'

Rosie gathered her ankles and slid off the table. With a two-piece bikini, a sarong and a frankly ludicrous sunhat, Becky couldn't decide if the girl was over- or under-dressed for the occasion. She had fine, shapely legs which certainly drew the attention from many at the bar and elsewhere. Something in Becky – either predator or prey – was grateful to have Rosie running some interference.

Since the episode with Leif, Becky had wanted less complicated company around. Rosie had been delighted with the request to come to Spain. She confessed early on that she wanted to write a book about the case.

Without telling her what had happened to Rupert or the phone call, Becky had warned Rosie that being round her could be dangerous.

And at that point, Rosie had simply smiled at Becky, gestured round the bay, and asked what she was drinking.

Orange juice, was Becky's answer. From now on.

A group of surfers were stationed to Rosie's right as she ordered her drink – loud, brash and florid-faced after their brush with the elements. One of them, a tall, brawny blond man with thick red cheeks that gave him an incongruously babyish aspect, approached Rosie. He had a deck of cards in his hand, and he used them to facilitate a clumsy grab for her attention. Some trick or other, one hand gesticulating, the other going about its furtive work, expertly separating the card Rosie had chosen from its fellows. Rosie watched the trick, and even gave polite applause before collecting her drink and returning to the table. The blond man pouted for a second or two, then shrugged. In the drama of this gesture, he'd managed to conceal his deck of cards without Becky noticing how or where, which annoyed her.

'You always look at the hand which isn't doing anything,' Becky said, as Rosie returned. 'That's the one that's working the hardest.'

'I guessed that. I was thinking about saying a completely different card to the one I picked out, just to fuck with him. But some guys see humiliation as encouragement, or a challenge, and he looks like a nuisance. Anyway. Fair exchange: I've given you my news. How about yours?'

Becky flipped back a few pages on her notebook. 'Okay. Letters. There's been a new development. It seems that Leif was Clara's mystery pen-pal, after all.'

'Leif lied?'

'Oh yeah. Leif lied. But that's not the most interesting thing. I'm 99 per cent sure that the handwriting on the letters from the American girl belongs to my mother.'

'Christ. That's big. What's the connection?'

'There are loads of possibilities. I'm not ruling anything out. It could be complete coincidence, and Clara and my mother were looking for the same thing and ended up writing to the same kid.'

'You mean... your mum was looking for men through lonely hearts' columns? And got the same man as your sister?'

Becky nodded. There was no hint of annoyance in her voice. 'Unlikely, but that's the obvious conclusion to be drawn. We'd be silly to ignore it.'

'And what do you reckon Leif has to do with the killings?'

Here, Becky's expression clouded. 'Again, possibly nothing. But it's something we can explore. He admitted it himself – even before you factor in the murders, it's all too much of a coincidence. I'll rule nothing out.'

'Okay... that's interesting. I'll get looking.'

'I want nothing in the papers on that one, just yet.'

Rosie smiled. 'It's for the book. After we catch him. I promise. Scout's honour.'

'You were never in the Scouts, love.'

'What else have you got?' Rosie continued, ignoring Becky's jibe.

'I was followed the other day, on my way back from the rest home where the Romanian lady was living.'

'You any idea who it was?'

'I can give you his National Insurance number and blood type, if you like. His name is Michael Laurel. Private investigator. He was hired by a family friend. A journalist who was friends with my father; his name is Jack Tullington. Semi-retired.'

'You know him well?'

'Better than well. He's like an uncle to me. You could even say he was a father figure, and I wouldn't get annoyed. He helped me out a lot in the years after it happened. He brought a lot of good things to my life, some good lessons. Plus I was never stuck for somewhere lively to go at Christmas, or somewhere to chill if things got a bit tense in my aunt's house. I owe him a lot.'

'So, this father figure... He was spying on you?'

'I would guess, like everyone else on the planet, he was concerned about my welfare and had decided to check up on what I was doing.'

'Plausible enough, I suppose.'

'Yeah. He's worried I'm going to draw the killer, with no one to protect me.'

'So you haven't talked to him about the fact he hired someone to tail you?'

'Not yet. It's a tricky one.'

'How'd you find out the detective's name? Or that he was a detective?'

'It was easy enough. I just asked a polite question or two after I'd caught up with him.'

Rosie laughed. 'Yeah – just like you asked some polite questions when you caught up with me. I remember you, Kung Fu girl. You threw me onto some nasty old rocks sticking out of the ground. You know how long those bruises took to fade on my arse?'

Two hands slammed down on their table, jolting them. A tall figure in a neoprene suit stood at the edge, then lowered himself down so that only a thick, blond head of hair remained at the level of the table. It was the card tricks guy from the bar.

'Good afternoon ladies,' he said, in a South African accent. 'I was just wondering if either of you fancied coming to a party later on?'

'You know, that's a little bit rude,' Becky said, irritably. 'You interrupted a private conversation.'

'I'm terribly sorry.' He grinned, revealing chipped front teeth. His gaze briefly crept over Becky's neoprene suit. 'You here to catch some waves?'

'No, I just enjoy squelching whenever I sit down.'

He grinned again. 'Okay. I guess you're a no for the party, then. How about you, Miss… I didn't catch your name?'

'Bob,' Rosie said.

'Bob. Hmm. You don't look like a Bob. Is it because you're a competent swimmer?'

'I was named after my mother.'

'I bet Bob had the pick of the boys in class.'

'To answer your question, no, we're not interested in going to your party,' Becky said.

'Oh, don't listen to her,' Rosie said. 'Tell me when and where.'

The head resting on the table beamed. 'Great! It's down by the Banana Boat hut. Maybe half a mile from here, heading east along the beach. You can't miss it. Big yellow shed, blue letters. Bring yourself. And lots of beer.'

Rosie noted it all down.

A deck of cards appeared in one hand. 'Hey, can I show you a magic trick?'

Becky raised a hand. 'Actually, no, you can't. We're busy here.'

'Just one?' The head turned to Rosie and winked.

Another figure approached them; a tall black man in thick-rimmed glasses and a well-tended Afro, wearing a faded Grateful Dead tour T-shirt and knee-length khaki shorts. This man was so skinny that the clothes might have been draped over his frame to drip-dry.

He cleared his throat and said to Becky and Rosie in an Australian accent: 'Excuse me. I was wondering – is this man bothering you?'

The blond head on the table turned towards the newcomer; although the flushed pink cheeks remained, the eyes lost any trace of warmth. 'Say again, mun?'

'Um, I said, to these two ladies, "is this man bothering you?"' A tremor had crept into the newcomer's voice, and the large brown eyes took on a molten quality.

The blond man stood up sharply. He wasn't as tall as the black man, but the difference in girth between them was painfully clear. 'Maybe I am. What's it to you, four eyes?'

Becky stood up between them, a finger raised. 'You know, that's prejudicial against people who wear glasses. Some of my best friends wear glasses, and I'm offended on their behalf.'

The blond man glared at the newcomer just a moment longer. The black man was actually quivering out of the corner of Becky's eye, his lips twitching. Shivering bones, she thought.

Then the blond man grinned and backed off. 'Hey, no offence meant. I apologise, on behalf of all non-spectacles-wearers. I'll see you at the party later, yeah? Even you, if you like, four eyes.'

'God, I hope not,' Becky said, smiling. Once the blond man had rejoined his friends, she turned to the black man.

He flinched at the sudden movement. Becky wondered if he might cry.

'Listen, that was awfully nice of you,' she said, 'but at times like this, you need to remember *Mad Max*.'

'*Mad Max*?' the man said, biting at his thumbnail. 'How's that?'

'Think Thunderdome. Think mullets. Think Tina Turner. 'We don't need another hero'. Okay?'

The black man mumbled, 'Just looking after you, that's all,' and returned to the corner table.

'Worst tough guy act ever,' Rosie remarked, under her breath. 'And I've seen a few belters.'

'I'm sure it went really well, in his mind. Even better when he emails his friends about it later.'

'If he has any. He's been sitting there on his own since we got here. Nice thing to do, all the same. Does it actually make you braver if you confront people, and you're a bit of a coward? I think it does.'

'He could simply be stupid.' Becky scooped up her notepad and stuffed it in her backpack. 'Besides, we don't need help. We're not damsels in distress. Jesus, to think I came here to escape the drama for five minutes.'

'I did wonder if drama followed you around,' Rosie said. 'Bit uptight of you, all the same. We got invited to a party. Big deal.'

'*You* got invited, Mrs Sunhat and Two-Piece.'

'Well… you're an excellent wingman, I'll say that for you.' Rosie sucked down her second pina colada.

Becky got to her feet. 'I think I'll go and catch some waves. Who knows, I might drown, and that'll be the end of the whole business.'

'It'd make a hell of a twist at this point of my book,' Rosie said, poker-faced. 'How about a shark attack? Who would see that coming?'

# 34

Later, with the neoprene ditched in favour of something lighter, Becky and Rosie sat on the beach. Night had fallen, with a blanket of stars hung out to dry high above them.

They were a fair distance away from the flames, laughter and occasional howls of the beach party, sat close to the Blue Banana café. The shoreline had come alive after dark. Someone had a guitar. An even more daring individual had brought bongos. Beer bottles clinked, and a fug of sweet smoke did its best to linger overhead in the face of the sea breeze.

Teenagers dotted the shoreline all the way down to the pier and the flashing lights of the seafront a mile or so down the coast – hyenas too young to take part in the feast, but too bold to stay away.

At the main party round the fire, the South African guy's blond head flickered around the fringes of the group like a torch. He hadn't removed his wetsuit; some of his friends had even taken their boards out into the soughing darkness just beyond the shoreline.

'Loons,' Becky said, sipping at a bottle of water. 'Some of them will be lucky to come back.'

Rosie – who was dressed for an evening out somewhere there were lights, music and a roof – sipped at a beer, and shivered. 'Sharks? I've heard you shouldn't surf after nightfall or early in the morning.'

'I was thinking more of them being pissed, falling in and drowning.'

Rosie shook her head. 'I can't believe that dope earlier on today. The skinny guy who tried to save us in the café. He'd clearly never surfed in his life. Lucky the lifeguards were on hand to get him back to shore.'

'Surfer wannabe. You get them – just like you get military wannabes, police wannabes, cage-fighting wannabes, whatever. They hang around and hope to catch the ambience. Hook up with someone gullible. Maybe tell their friends a tale or two about it later, whether they got lucky or not.'

'I don't think he's got any friends. Look at him – I don't think I've ever seen anyone so stringy in my life.'

'Where is he?' Becky strained her eyes. There, away from the fire, circling the periphery, on the edge of the group, was the tall, skinny black man. He wore the same stuff he'd worn at the café earlier – which he'd worn in the sea, in fact. He gave the impression of not knowing what to do with his hands, or indeed any of his limbs. The word gangly might have been invented with him in mind.

He got close enough to the group for the others to notice him. The South African guy piped up: 'Hey, man!'

The gangly figure skirted away from the circle of light and its nucleus of bodies like a spooked cat.

The rest of the crowd called out in dismay. 'No, wrong way!' the South African man yelled. 'Over here – come get a beer, mun!'

The gangly man changed direction, trying to suppress a smile. Warm applause greeted him as he moved towards the group. And it was here that Becky imagined they would spring on him, hurling him to the sand, then piling in with fists and feet. How many times had she seen it before in life?

But the eruption never came. Someone handed the gangly man a bottle of beer; as it changed hands the golden liquid caught the light just so, just perfectly, and Becky could almost taste it herself.

Just one would be all right; just one would get her arse off this sand and into a more sociable frame of mind. Just one.

'I'm confounded, officially,' she said. 'They're being *nice*.'

'Hey!' the South African guy called out. 'The English roses! Yeah – you two, over there!' He held another bottle of beer out, waving it in the firelight. 'Come on over! Don't be shy.'

Rosie had a look of devilment. 'What do you reckon? Maybe we could head over. Safety in numbers, and all that.'

Becky frowned. 'What do you mean?'

'Well, if the guy… your guy… was trying to snuff us out over here, he'd need to be really good at it. Or they'd need to all be in on it. Which is unlikely.'

'I doubt our guy will be here,' Becky said. 'I'd imagine he's busy elsewhere. But I hope he *is* here. Right now.'

'You what?'

Becky checked her hip pocket. The knife handle was still there. 'It'd bring things to a nice finish. Then we can all enjoy a holiday after it.'

'You mean this *isn't* a holiday?'

'You have a beer if you want. But we're up and out tomorrow morning, early. If you're not early, I'm leaving without you. Your call.'

The South African guy approached, his barrel shape not quite flattered in silhouette by firelight. 'I come in peace,' he said, teeth glinting. He anchored two beer bottles firmly in the sand. 'Here is an offering in good faith. I'll even leave the bottle opener for you. If the offering is to your liking, come over and join us. If not, please be so kind to return the bottle opener.'

'Your grandma gave it to you, I presume?' Rosie said.

'She fashioned it from the bones of my grandfather.' He held out a hand. Rosie took it. She had been keeping herself topped up all day, growing used to the cosy benevolence of pina coladas and then, after dinner, white Russians. But she wasn't drunk, or at least not reckless-drunk. All through the late afternoon and evening, Rosie had kept her notebook with her and even looked interested as Becky explained her theory, and what she'd put in place to test it, right here, in this town.

The seaside was probably too much of a distraction. But then, Rosie didn't know about the phone call, about Rupert's dripping head.

No one could know about Becky's connection to that, just yet. A connection which felt uncomfortably like complicity.

Rosie got to her feet and cuffed the sand off the back of her dress. 'You coming too?'

'In a bit,' Becky said. 'You two take the beers.'

'You sure?' the South African seemed a bit disappointed.

'Absolutely. Have fun. Keep one cold for me.'

She watched them trail off towards the fire, burning high and hot; watched Rosie exchange greetings with the other men and women sat round it. Then she got up and walked along the beachfront, away from the light, allowing the darkness and the stars to take her. Only the odd beach house lit the way, or the occasional car passing along the main road. The darkness hid the signs of construction all the way along the coast; this resort was beautiful, still a little rough n' ready, and perhaps another two years away from being totally ruined. Becky enjoyed the feel of the damp sand sucking at her sandals, the white kindling of the surf as it slid along the beach.

She might come back here, Becky thought, when it was all over.

She only took a quick scan of the bodies that were pressed into the sand here and there. *If I was him, that's what I'd do to hide*, she thought. Might even curl down with a body, as camouflage. A willing one, that is. That would be just his style.

But the figures pressed together in the sand were mostly teens. Few of them looked up as Becky passed.

That she was being followed wasn't a huge surprise. She had got used to it. In its way, it was tiresome.

A quick movement tipped her off, something as sudden as a shoal of fish changing direction in the water. Someone was up near the sea wall, crouching low as she looked round.

Becky withdrew the knife blade and then angled away from the beach towards the wall.

The sand grew hard-packed beneath her feet. Once, she fancied something scuttled away just before she planted a foot down. Her eyes grew more accustomed to the darkness, to the sublime starlight and the crescent moon.

The figure picked his way along the wall, occasionally crouching as she glanced over her shoulder.

Becky reached the wall. It was around six feet high, and the concrete was brittle underneath her fingertips. Once she found purchase she vaulted it, shoulder and back muscles taut, easily absorbing the strain. Her knees scuffed the concrete, painfully, but then she was up and over, landing quietly on the balls of her feet along the narrow pavement on the other side, only a couple of feet beneath.

Here, she waited for her pursuer to try the same manoeuvre.

She was close to giggling when his head appeared above the sea wall, followed by one clutching, desperate hand. Then she winced as she heard a crunch which might have been splitting fingernails. After two more aborted attempts, he was finally up and over the wall, breathing hard. The he spotted her and gaped at what she held in her hand.

'Yep – it's a knife,' Becky said brightly. 'And I'll cut you from nipples to knees with it unless you tell me what you're up to.'

He straightened up to his full height, fiddling with his hands. The sweat glistened on his dark skin in the silvery light, his 'fro a dark halo above the thin face. His strangulated Australian accent seemed even more out of place.

'Just, you know... out for a walk.'

'You fancied some rock climbing, too?'

'I'm just making sure you're all right on your own.'

'Uh huh. Same way you were making sure I was all right out in the water? When you went surfing?'

'You can't be too careful, can you?' he mumbled. 'You especially. Dangerous people out there. I'm sure you know.'

Becky was utterly still for a moment. 'Enough of the bullshit. Who are you, and what do you want?'

He straightened up, shoulders back, and seemed to inhabit his frame to its fullest for the first time. 'I'm a friend of Rupert's. I know what happened to him. They said it was a drugs feud, but I know the truth. I did some of his research for him. I think the guy who did it was the same guy who killed your family. And I want the same thing you do.'

# 35

They took their time walking back to the party, with the sea sighing in the background, lost in the dark.

'Rupert was the best in the business,' her companion said. 'White knight, you know? Took on good causes, rather than disrupting things.'

'That's what I wanted,' Becky said. 'That's why I hired him. I'd asked around.'

'He was like a brother to me.'

'And who are you, exactly?'

'Name's Bernard,' he mumbled, kicking at a shell in the sand.

'Well, Bernard. You say you're here to protect me? I think you should protect yourself, first of all. I'm mixed up in something dangerous, here. Rupert knew that.'

'There's dangerous, and *dangerous*,' Bernard said. 'Rupert knew all about risks. He expected that one day he'd have his door kicked in by the FBI, someone like that. But he didn't expect to be slaughtered.'

'He knew there were risks. I was upfront about it.' But had she been? Guilt, that old enemy, loomed and flared like a cobra. Had she been completely upfront? Or was it just one more head to add to the pile – someone else dead on her behalf?

'He was careful, too,' Bernard said. 'Rupert's security was tight. How the guy traced him, I don't know. He's got skills, whoever he is. He knows systems, and how to get into them.'

'Our guy could be in the police. Or he knows someone who is in the police. He's been removing files, messing with evidence.'

'I want to help you. I want to catch him. I can help you with whatever Rupert was doing for you.'

'Didn't the police investigate?'

'It was reported as a drug dispute. Fair go – Rupert dabbled in that world. Brought in more money than hacking, that was for sure. It was played as if he'd messed with the wrong gang. They do that, you know. Places like Mexico, Eastern Europe. They take the heads.'

In that moment, she envisioned it again – Rupert's head. She'd do this as long as she lived. The eyes, with the lights switched off.

'It was recorded, surely,' Becky said.

'It was... and I believed the official version. At first. But here's the messed-up bit. The footage recorded showed that he confessed to messing with another dealer's turf. Then he got offed...'

'If that's what you saw, then why are you here? How did you find me?'

'Rupert had a kill-switch. If he died, or someone screwed with his files, an alarm would trigger, and I'd be sent a copy of his data, what he was working on. It sent me all your files. Your details.'

'How did you know I'm connected to what happened to Rupert?'

'Everyone who was anyone on Rupert's turf... they all denied it. Some of them even put out their own reward, to find out what happened. He was well-liked. Some of them even got rich because of Rupert. It didn't fit. Plus, he didn't make enemies, not among people from that world. He was a good guy, you know?'

The sights and sounds of the beach party drew nearer. Fires continued to burn on the shore; silhouettes seemed to flicker in sympathy with the flames.

'When he got broken into, Rupert triggered a kill-switch, with a note, explaining what he was working on. He'd prepared for something like that happening. Whoever killed him deleted Rupert's files manually, from what I can gather, but didn't know about the kill-switch. They knew enough to remove all traces of your case... but they still allowed the footage of the drugs confession and the killing to be released. That's when I knew the official line was bullshit. Rupert was reading from a script. He wasn't killed by gangsters, though the police seem to think he was. You were the link. I looked into your files... and I think we're looking for the same man.'

'We are.'

'You're all right with me tagging along then?' He looked uncertain, and his body language was all wrong; angled away from her, as if he wanted to take flight.

'You can help,' she said, 'if you want to. But I'll warn you right now – what happened to Rupert could happen to you. You saw what occurred. I can't take responsibility for another life. That's on you. So long as you understand that.'

'I understand.'

'All right then.'

'So,' Bernard said brightly, 'when do we start?'

'Tomorrow. Early.'


Rosie kept her huge sunhat clamped to her head, but this was at the expense of balance. More than once she stumbled up the steep slopes, stirring up a djinn in red dust.

'Hell of a place to put standing stones,' she wheezed. 'You'd think they'd fall over.'

Hat aside, she had at least dressed for a walk in hilly terrain. Beside her, Bernard looked like he was ready for another hapless day at the beach, even down to the mandals clamped to his outsize feet. In emerald green shorts and an ancient Brazil football top with the badge half-peeled off, he looked like the boy who'd deliberately mislaid his PE kit, only to be given the heartbreaking news that there was some old gear in a back cupboard he could use. Despite his ultra-lean frame, he was slick with sweat, and clearly out of condition.

'I'm guessing they'll be right at the top,' he said. 'The hill plateaus up there, right? Nice flat place for standing stones. They probably got them right out of the ground nearby.'

'That's right,' Becky said. 'The stones were so nice they decided to put the monument alongside them.'

Becky indicated a granite slab perched on a plateau in the hillside. Although they couldn't quite make it out from that distance, they knew that the word 'Saludo' was etched on its pitted face, the letters overlaid with stark white paint. An exclamation mark added to the end was in a slightly different script, somewhat fragmented and leaning to one side, as if reluctant to stand with its embarrassing peers.

'You're kidding. They put a monument all the way up there?' Rosie raised her sunglasses, peering towards the plateau. 'They must have been crazy.'

'It looks like a bit of an effort,' Bernard said. 'It also doesn't look like the kind of place that would suit our guy.'

That was how he was referred to, now. Not something they'd decided consciously, just something they fixed upon. No cute names, no diminutive. *Our guy.*

'That's what makes me suspicious,' Becky replied. 'It looks like something hidden in plain sight, to me. Come on. We've got to get there by 9 a.m. Miguel is coming to us from the other side of the hill.'

'Miguel?' Rosie bent her back to it and continued up the desert path. 'You didn't say anything about a Miguel.'

They'd started at 6 a.m., none of the three mustering much enthusiasm despite the cool of the morning and the breeze whipped in from the coast. They heard a lot of buzzing, chirruping life, but saw no signs of it in the air bar the occasional flies which harried them at a lower level.

Rosie had been suspicious of Bernard, at first. Becky hadn't fully explained their connection, of course, but had mentioned that he might help them with one or two unresolved technical issues. They had quickly fallen into an easy patter; once the shock of human contact was out of the way, the tall man soon became a warm, if not quite sensible conversationalist.

They reached the summit at a little after 9 a.m., the welcome sign looking a little less preposterous at close-quarters, if a little more guano-splattered. Beneath the sign, situated a dignified space away from it, were the standing stones. In a variety of shapes and sizes, the rocks were planted in the harsh earth, some leaning to one side, others scarred with scratched names and phrases, and a few reclaimed by mother nature, encrusted with lichen and strangled by weeds.

The menhirs had been planted centuries ago in a rough circle, reckoned to be in harmony with the lunar cycle. By day, and especially at this time of the morning, it was a shady oasis of loose desert scrub and bare rock, shielded from the morning sun by the rockier peaks in the distance. By night, Becky supposed, the place had a very different character. By night – when he had been here. Their guy.

'So who's Miguel?' Rosie said.

'Someone who can tell us a bit about the history of this place.'

'Christ,' Rosie spluttered. 'Guidebooks were available down at the bistro. They weren't cheap, I grant you, but better than dragging some poor bloke up here.'

'You're looking for the mask,' Bernard intoned, stepping forward. 'Somewhere among the stones.'

'Correct. The mask, or something like it.'

'I'll take a few shots, just in case we miss something.' He produced a compact digital camera and proceeded to photograph the stones, flitting round them like a great gannet.

'Bit hard to carve a face into rock, I'd imagine,' Rosie said. 'Our guy must have been patient to do it in the woods, that's for sure. But at least he could hide in there. There's not much cover, up here. Maybe not so much time, either.'

'Remember, this whole town is fairly new,' Becky said. 'The monument is too, though it looks like it's been here for decades. If our guy killed the Ramirez family and dumped the bodies up here, there would only have been standing stones here at that time. And no tourism.'

'Bit of a leap of deduction, that,' Rosie mumbled. 'You want to see if he's carved a face into the rocks?'

'It's worth a look at them, sure. But that's not the real reason we're here. We're here to see Miguel.'

'Miguel?' Rosie's eyebrows rose above her sunglasses.

'Yep. Miguel. In fact, I can see him coming now.'

Rosie shaded her eyes and squinted down another path, on the opposite side of the hill they'd just climbed. Two figures became visible in the rising heat of the day, churning up the red dust as they approached.

Becky raised her hand. Miguel raised his head, and barked in response, before his handler waved back.

# 36

Miguel's handler, Maria, had been harder to approach than she had been to bribe. Becky had to be patient, contacting her several times via email before a meeting was proposed. Several other handlers in the area had told Becky to sling her hook; one or two had threatened to have her arrested. To be fair to Maria, the promise of cracking a case seemed to entice her more than the pledge of a generous donation to a local community fund.

She was a heavily built girl, but not fat, and surprisingly English in appearance despite her thick local accent on the telephone. With frizzy blonde hair tied back and dusty dark green hiking trousers, with the hems tucked into thick socks peering out over her boots, she might have been a Pollyanna-ish scout leader, easier to love than to mock.

Miguel pulled heavily at the leash, but always came to heel with one sharp cluck from Maria.

'Police dog?' Rosie asked.

'Cadaver dog,' Bernard mumbled. 'Got to be, right?'

Becky nodded. 'It's a hunch more than anything else. But if our guy's got a thing for standing stones, ancient monuments and ceremonial sites, there's a good chance he'll have left a body or two here. The Ramirez family lived about thirty miles down the valley. Vanished in 1992, during the European football championships. I think the site was too close for him to resist. Probably he picks the killing grounds first, then the families.'

Becky intercepted Maria, shook hands and then petted the dog. Miguel was a black and white springer spaniel, bouncy and utterly indefatigable, as all springer spaniels are. Maria understood what was required; Becky stood back and watched as both dog and handler made their way round the stones.

'Surely any blood or other evidence has long gone,' Rosie said.

Becky shook her head. 'It's bodies I'm looking for, not blood. They'll be here. Maria is with the police – she's Miguel's trainer. Cadaver dogs can find remains decades after they were buried. There's still soft earth somewhere around the summit. If there's some bodies out here, Miguel will sniff them out. And we know our guy likes standing stones.'

'The stones...' Bernard said. 'Is that where he did the deed? With your family?'

Becky shot him a look; it was the first time Rosie had seen her so much as flinch when it came to the details of the case. 'In a manner of speaking,' she said.

'So it was a ritual, then? Some kind of cult thing?'

'I'm fairly sure of it. He behaved in a ritualised fashion, laid out the knives in a formalised way. I thought he'd uttered some sort of incantation or a spell, like an offering to Satan in an ugly language. I know now it was an Eastern European language. If he was praying, it was in his own language. He might even have been speaking to god, for all I know.'

Bernard backed away from them, shielding the glare on a palm-sized tablet computer. He looked from the screen to the sky, then turned forty-five degrees before repositioning the tablet.

'What have you got?' Becky asked.

Bernard waved her away in irritation; after a few moments he muttered, 'You've got me thinking. These stones and some of the others near the death sites are astronomical in origin – a way of marking the passing seasons, the solstices. Some of them have a lunar significance, or something relating to the night sky.' He gestured towards a large stone at the edge of the circle. 'If that's marking the position of the North Star, which should appear right here, tonight—' he gestured with his hand '—then there could be something in that.'

Becky nodded, and scribbled a note in her pad. 'It's as good a link as we can find, I guess. It's worth looking to see if there's any detailed pattern followed.'

Rosie asked, 'You reckon he's on a lunar cycle then? Some sort of worship linked to the stars? So he's like a druid?'

'Maybe. But ultimately, I don't think it's relevant. He's not really motivated by the stars, the moon, or little green men.'

'What is he motivated by?' Bernard asked, turning another ninety degrees.

'Humiliating, raping and decapitating people. Specifically, women. But it seems anyone will do, at a pinch. He's a sexual psychopath, so far beyond normal they'd have to invent a term to cover him. Star charts, ley lines, or anything else is just window dressing. It doesn't even stretch to an excuse.' Becky capped her pen and smiled sadly. 'And that isn't a theory. That, I guarantee you, is the truth.'

Miguel barked, skirting round one of the smaller stones at the back of the circle. Becky ran towards them, her heart pounding.

'Has he got something?' she asked Maria, as the dog sniffed hard at the stone.

Maria frowned. 'No... sometimes this happens. He can sniff out something, like a rabbit or another dead dog. But there's nothing here. He would have made it obvious.'

Becky checked herself, clenching and unclenching her fists in frustration. A hand touched her shoulder. Becky flinched for the second time that afternoon.

'Sorry,' Rosie said, withdrawing her hand. 'You have to admit it was a long shot. I suppose it was worth a go.'

Becky ignored her. 'Keep searching,' she called over to Maria, as she let the dog off its leash. 'All the way round. Every single stone.'

'Of course,' Maria said. 'But just so you know... don't expect anything.' She jogged after the dog.

A sudden gust of wind threatened to tear Rosie's huge hat off her head, and she clamped it down tight. 'Surely the local police department would have searched all over for missing persons? Even up here in the hills? First place they'd check after the sea, I'd imagine. Remote place, this, at the time.'

'You'd imagine. As I said, it's just a hunch,' Becky replied. She folded her arms, chilled for a moment by the breeze.

Bernard stared at his screen; he had barely moved save for flickering movement at his fingertips. 'What date did the Ramirez family buy the farm?'

'They vanished on July 2nd, 1992.'

Bernard clicked the touchpad again, then became still, almost as if he'd never spoken.

'Funny. It's showing that Mars came close to the earth round about that time. Could be something. Could be nothing.'

Miguel began to bark. The dog leapt in the air with each yelp, ears splayed in the sudden breeze. The animal had followed its nose far beyond the standing stones. As Becky, Rosie and Bernard broke into a run, stirring pale dust as high as their heads, they saw that the dog had stopped in front of the immense stone sign welcoming visitors to the new town in the valley below.

# 37

The sun had long disappeared, but the hillside was alive with lights and colour. At first some cars had arrived with their emergency lights, streaking the arid slopes an effervescent blue. Then the wavering white spotlight of a helicopter lit the scene – surely a news network – before the police managed to erect tents and overhead lights, whitewashing the monument in a steady glare.

Becky was on her own, her two companions having left not long before the first of the Guardia Civil had shown up. As discussed, she'd let Maria do most of the talking, making it sound like the entire investigation had been her idea, on a hunch from a contact. The officers had asked Becky questions, and she'd answered them as honestly as possible, if 'honesty' covered the great chunks of information she'd left out. Now it was a full day later, and things seemed to be moving at pace.

Aside from the ebullience of a possible breakthrough and her intuition perhaps paying off, she felt a measure of control at how she'd dealt with the situation.

The appearance of Inspectors Marcus and Labelle crushed this smugness. Jittery torchlight heralded their path up the same route Maria and Miguel had taken earlier. As they grew more distinct, forcing their way through the initial cordon, Becky could see them arguing, heads set close together.

Marcus' mouth was still sloped downwards from left to right, but he was showing some teeth too as he approached Becky. 'The mystery girl returns,' he sneered, sweeping stray locks of his floppy fringe back across his forehead.

'Good evening to you, too,' Becky replied, brightly.

'Mind telling us the story behind your hunch?' he asked.

'Just a bit of old-fashioned research, really. I looked at some cold cases, and followed my nose. I'd rather not expose my sources. I'm a reporter. You know how it is.' Even in the gloom, she could see a nerve jump at Marcus' temples. 'That's fantastic. And when did you qualify to serve with the police?'

Becky met his stare but said nothing.

'Did you even *consider* telling the police at any point leading up to this?' he yelled.

'What would you have done?' Becky spread her hands. 'Got right on the case? Diverted all available units? You'd have done nothing. Neither would the Guardia Civil. They'd have told me to take a number. It seems if I want something done in this case, I have to do it myself. So, I have done. And by the way – I don't hear anybody saying "thank you".'

'We've got no idea what's under here – it could be dead rabbits for all we know. Maybe an old gravesite from centuries ago. The dog might have got it wrong. And let me tell you – if it turns out to be nothing, I'll get you charged with wasting police time and obstructing our ongoing investigations.'

Becky clenched her fists. 'I'm getting tired of your attitude,' she said. 'And I'm really, really tired of your fringe.'

'I don't blame you,' Labelle said. 'I think he'd suit something a little closer to the scalp. But Becky, this was naughty of you, you have to admit.'

'There's nothing wrong with carrying out a private investigation under private means. I had an idea that a crime had been committed here, and I informed an officer of the law to look into it. And that, Inspector Clouseau,' she said, glaring at Marcus, 'isn't hindering an investigation – it's assisting one. I guess you'll be putting me forward for next month's community award?'

Marcus snorted, and a lemon rind smile broke through his lips. 'You know, I always loved those movies,' he said. 'I see myself more as the Herbert Lom character, though.'

Labelle remained focused and businesslike, and her intense blue eyes seemed to glow in the dark. 'You didn't come up with a hunch out of nothing. Have you been tipped off?'

'No. This is all my own work.'

'Then what brought you here, Becky? Marcus is right. If you're withholding evidence from us and cost us time and resources, well that's…' She shrugged. 'Very bad.'

'And naughty,' Marcus added.

Becky took a deep breath and allowed her jaw to sag. Underneath her clothes her stomach muscles rippled, helping the tension leak out from her frame. 'Take a look around you. What's strikingly obvious?'

Marcus made a point of scanning the horizon. 'Dust? Hills? Spanish castle magic?'

'Stones,' Labelle answered.

'Correct. Menhirs, obelisks. Standing stones. Ceremonial sites. Prehistoric, druidic, Celtic, Pictish. It doesn't matter. So long as it's old and some cavemen set them up, our guy wants to kill people there. What the significance of it all is, only he knows. Maybe it's just something he's into, like some people like to collect ceramic frogs. There's no obvious link, whether geographical, meteorological or astronomical, so far as I can tell. A different spot every time, but they have that vague feature in common. It's the same everywhere else he's struck.'

'Who?' Marcus frowned. 'Your guy?'

'Yes. Families. Slaughtered, like mine was. The heads removed. He's covered a few cases up very well, like one in Orkney in 1984. Made it look like a murder-suicide. This monument was built six months after the Ramirez family vanished. My guess is, they're buried under there. Deep.'

'We've heard a lot of these theories before, Becky,' Marcus replied. 'We know all about them. Particularly the one in Orkney. We've looked into cases with possible links. All of them. There's a more plausible theory that the Orkney case was a crime of passion, the work of a jealous lover, disguised as a murder-suicide by the real killer. But the evidence is clear. That family had money problems. It led to stress in the home. The wife complained of it to her doctor. She was worried her husband was cracking up – and with good reason. Two weeks later he killed her and their children, then himself.'

'That's what the initial inquiry says. I admit he did a good job, but there's been no proper DNA testing. Our guy was trying to cover his tracks, and he did it well.'

Marcus shook his head. There was a note of conciliation, even of pity, in his voice. 'We've gone through all that, Becky. Whatever you've heard from whatever sources, we've picked through the case in a lot more detail than you. I can promise you, the investigations were thorough.'

'They've never found any sign of the Ramirez family. Until now.'

'We don't know what's under there, as we've said.'

That's when raised voices echoed out across the mountainside, coming from the bleached white light tents where shadows occasionally bulged and twisted before moving lights.

'I've a feeling we will soon,' Becky said, under her breath.

# 38

You got used to a mouthful of dirt – after all, what harm could dirt do? It couldn't bury her, unless there was a serious flood, a biblical flood – the kind that gouged a chunk of land off bare mountainside. Minor floods seemed to be catered for, though – there was drainage, helped in a large part by the trees, so the mud wouldn't pool any higher than about ankle deep. Still some dirt got in her mouth, which had been horrific the first few times she'd tried to climb out. But you got used to it. You even got used to slipping off the walls and landing hard.

The same applied to bugs. She hadn't felt any particular hunger upon considering them, or the pallid worms that tickled her feet like great wet tongues, but the day might come. The day might come soon.

He'd given her clothes and food, after the second day. If he was neglectful, water was rarely a problem down there, although this was often thickened with dirt. You got used to that, too. Just like you got used to your own waste being in the same room.

Thankfully there were no rats. That might have changed things.

A few times, he had left the trap door open, and she had flailed like a maniac at the walls, screaming in frustration every time she slipped.

She heard him laugh but did not see the masked face. She never knew how long he lingered, listening to her struggles. Once, he left the trap door open all night. She could see the stars through the canopy of fir trees, a clear velvety sky tinged blue in contrast with the bristly black arboreal frame. This sight might have been beautiful, in other circumstances. She flinched at every snap and swish of foliage, at the passage of living creatures in the forest floor above.

She did not move all night.

Neither, it seemed, had he.

Or more likely, he'd never been there.

With the pink light of dawn revealing the deep green swaying above her, the bone mask peered over the lip of the trap door. There was no way to tell if he was smiling. There was a suggestion of a tongue flapping behind the splintered, ingrained teeth in the jaws, as if he meant to lick the false face he presented to her.

'That's good,' he said. 'That's more like it. You're getting the idea.'

He slammed shut the door. She only sat there, in the rank dark, chin on her knees, and waited for his return.

It was all she could do.

While he made his way back down the slope, a text message came in. He frowned at it; it was an automated message, which alerted him to the use of certain debit and credit cards.

It showed a receipt for a return ticket to Romania.

This stopped him in his tracks.

'Ah,' was all he said.

# 39

Becky's computer pinged; opening up the messaging app, she saw Bernard's face. He looked as if he was in the cockpit of a plane, tightly packed among shelves packed with computers, monitors and electrical equipment. His afro was interrupted by a headset with a microphone.

'Hey, Becky.'

'Hey yourself. What's going on? Are you broadcasting from a cupboard?'

'Ah, this is kind of my own personal museum. Look at this one – a BBC B Micro, classic of the genre, this.' He lifted up an ancient beige computer unit with red and black keys.

'Maybe some other time,' Becky said quickly.

'Ah. Sorry.' He grinned and slid the computer back onto its shelf. 'Hobbies, you know? I can't shut up about them, at times. Hey, how's things going with the dig in Spain?'

'The dig? You make it sound like fun. A treasure hunt.'

'I guess it is, in a way.'

'They're carrying out tests. Once they find out what they need to know, I'll have been proved right. And that's another link in the chain. How about you – did you turn up anything for me about the Romania case?'

'There was another name – a political assassination, apparently. A family with connections to the Stasi in eastern Germany, and the KGB. Some of them lost their heads. Seems a bit murkier than some lust murder, though.'

Becky sat forward. 'What was the name?'

'Rosie's guy isn't sure, but he said it's something like Arkanescu.' Becky made him spell it out. 'There's very little about it online anywhere. That's the only link. In the entire internet.'

'You couldn't find anything?'

'Not a bit. Dark net, or regular net. Now that in itself is suspicious.'

'Arkanescu. A political assassination, was this?'

'Yeah, so they believe. It could be more like kneecappings between gangsters, these things. It dates from roughly the same time as the Kranczr case, within a couple of years, anyway. But I didn't turn up anything else – even with the help from our contact in the Dupin Collective. Not quite what you're hoping, I know, but... I got a link to somewhere which might have information about it.' Bernard pressed a key, and a static image flashed up. 'A public records office. Doubles as a public library. Like... a place people take books out.'

'Quaint,' Becky muttered.

'Has microfiche, records, old editions of newspapers. Apparently they are going to start a programme of digitisation in the next two or three years.'

'But nothing's online yet.' Becky noted the address; on her phone, she was already searching for the nearest airport, and the next available air tickets.

'Nope. It's all analogue, for now. If anyone has extra details about the Kranczr family, or this Arkanescu mob, it'll be there. Now, you could maybe look into paying someone to check it for you, but...'

'It's all right. I think I'll go myself. My time's my own.'

'Okay. But there's one other thing I wanted to talk to you about.' He bit his lip; Becky wondered if he was going to ask her on a date. 'There's security issues, here.'

'What do you mean? You've set up firewalls, haven't you?'

'I have, but... so did Rupert. The same ones I've got. And he found Rupert.'

'We'll have to do something different, then, Bernard. Landlines? We could go analogue. Difficult to trace.'

'I'm not so much worried about me, Becky. I'm going to get moving soon and keep moving. He can't get all of us, can he? Not at one time, anyway. It's you I'm thinking about. He could trace you. I'd be surprised if he hadn't already. You must be his priority.'

Becky smiled. 'Yeah, I meant to talk to you about that. Find a landline or a phone booth, and we'll go through it. And hey... anyone ever told you that you look like Barack Obama's hipster brother?'

Bernard scratched the back of his neck, squirming with embarrassment. 'Aw, we haven't got time for flirting,' he mumbled, and cut the connection.

# 40

The public records building was squat, functional, and almost certainly Soviet era in origin. It was also a public library as well as a records repository, and had only one member of staff, a tiny little woman whose face resembled that of Louis Walsh.

Becky had tried to learn some key phrases in Romanian on the plane, but it had taken on the tones of homework at 9 p.m. on a Sunday night; too much to bother with, with no stomach for a fight with the promise of sleep. She wrote some key phrases down, utterly failing to memorise them. She dozed on the flight – sheer exhaustion overcoming her usual misgivings about unconsciousness in transit.

It took her a while to smooth out the mid-air incident when she saw the killer, in full robes, stood in the aisle beside her seat; when she jerked awake, kneeing her tray seat hard and spraying the remnants of a glass of cola everywhere, she realised that she was in fact confronted with a stewardess who'd been trying to cover her with a blanket.

Once on the ground, in the middle of the night, she spent the rest of the night trying to shut out the thundering jets and sweeping lights which quivered the curtains of her airport hotel.

The next morning, after a taxi ride with a driver whose natural thick black eyelashes she envied on a level that bordered on bigotry, she entered a squat building spiked with barbed wire.

It was more command bunker than library. Parts of it were shuttered, and she feared that it had closed for good sometime since the last update on its modest, poorly-constructed webpage. The cladding on the surrounding apartment blocks was the colour of toast, but radiated no warmth. Becky was reminded of post-war tenements she'd passed on one weekend she'd spent in Glasgow, half of them boarded up and praying for a wrecking ball.

Fortunately, the place was open and comfortably lit, and the linoleum floors were buffed to a high sheen. Becky was reminded of a school on the first day of a new term, and the mix of feelings that sight engendered.

The little Louis Walsh woman had been reading what looked like the latest Dan Brown paperback, and was at first startled to see Becky, then delighted. She began some small talk, and it took Becky a long time to calm the woman down and explain in what she hoped wasn't a stage Dracula accent that she did not speak Romanian.

The woman's English was no better than Becky's Romanian, but she understood what Becky was looking for when she presented the phrase written down in block capitals, carefully copied from the online translator. *I am trying to research my family tree; I need to see some microfiche files from 1990.*

They still existed, of course, as they did in libraries everywhere. The lady knew precisely where they were kept; canvas was moved, disturbed dust caused them both to sneeze, and finally some beige cases were unearthed, edged with clear brown plastic. Inside were the files, all neatly stored. The woman pointed to a big grey machine with a dark screen in one corner, hidden at the back of neat, thick rows of bookcases. 'Waiting here all this time,' Becky said, smirking. 'Looks like my luck's in.'

Only one other person came into the library, a stooped old man in a beige anorak who raised a hand in greeting towards the front desk without looking up, and then selected one of the day's newspapers from a rack.

The microfiche was easy to use, and similar to the ancient files she'd delved into from time to time in her own paper's archives. The screen whirred as the ancient cooling fan clicked into gear. Text swam into view, pulled into and out of focus by a lever on the right, while with her left hand Becky manipulated the microfiche, moving the image round the screen with the concentration of a bombardier on an attack run.

She started her search a few days before the bodies were found, just to be sure there wasn't any error or discrepancy with the dates.

The Louis Walsh lady fussed round Becky for a while, trying to get her own family name out of her. Becky toyed with saying 'Nastase' or 'Draculea', these being the only other Romanian surnames she could call to mind, leaving aside Ceaușescu.

Her instinct was for caution, but on a sudden whim, she decided to tell the librarian the name she was looking for.

The woman frowned for a moment, then her face fell, and Becky knew, at that very instant, she was on the right track. Her host made some frantic gestures at the screen, then actually tried to cover Becky's eyes.

'It's okay,' Becky said. 'Arkanescu, popular name.' She turned over the printed sheet. '*I know there was a murder*,' read one of her pre-written phrases.

The woman looked as if she might cross herself; instead she pursed her lips, placed a hand on Becky's shoulder, and moved off towards her desk on the other side of the bookcases.

Becky let silence settle again. She was aware of the slanted roof, the grey light which intruded through the skylight, and particularly the large, echoey spaces in between the rows of bookcases.

She turned back to the microfiche, moving through the days, amazed at how archaic the fashions and hairstyles were back in those days, a rough period she was just old enough to remember. What she knew from what Bernard had turned up for her was that the Arkanescu family had disappeared in early June 1990, after Ceauşescu's regime fell. It seemed that the bodies had vanished, turning up dumped in a mass grave near – Becky had guessed it – a historic site which had featured a Neolithic settlement, complete with caves, bones, sharpened flint heads and other basic tools.

That tip had been sourced from a translated website run by a ghoul based in Budapest, embedded deep in the dark web, who boasted a striking array of crime scene photographs dating back as far as photography itself.

In contrast, the official files Rupert had dug up on the Europol computer had been sketchy at best, lacking in detail or images, with no sign of the name Arkanescu anywhere.

Becky had tracked down the town where the Arkanescus had been abducted, and taken a leap of faith. Rather than focusing on time, Becky looked at location; this was the most easterly case with a similar MO which fit the pattern that Bernard, and Rupert before him, had been able to find.

She fed in a fresh film, carefully lining up the precious celluloid links, dating from the second day after the family vanished, one day before the bodies were found.

A voice like striking a match on bare rock said: 'You will not find much about the Arkanescu family in that file.'

Becky hadn't heard the man approach; she thrust the chair backwards, the casters squeaking, and leapt to her feet.

An older man in a beige anorak held up a hand, amused more than surprised. 'I'm sorry,' he said, in excellent English. 'I didn't mean to frighten you.'

'What do you want?'

'I was talking to Hana. She likes to talk.' He wheezed a smoker's laugh and stifled a smoker's cough. He had stark white hair and sparse stubble poking through his cheeks. 'She said you were looking for the Arkanescu family.'

'Yes. They used to live here. Did you know them?'

He chuckled. 'I knew of them. They led very charmed lives. Until someone took them away.'

'What do you mean?'

'They were connected to the secret police. Through the son, Nikolai. They wanted for very little, but some of their friends, neighbours and even family sometimes disappeared. That was how things were. This did not happen so long ago.'

'What do you think happened to the Arkanescus?'

'Everyone knows what happened to them. They knew too much; they were made to pay the price for being part of the secret police, after Ceauşescu went up against the wall. That was why they were made an example of. Butchered,' he said. The old man took a particular relish in this, grinning broadly, displaying incongruously white dentures.

'Where were the bodies found?'

'Near the caves. The site had been closed off – signs said this was for archaeological work to take place. But there was no archaeological work. Police believe whoever did it had set up the killing ground well in advance. That's how I knew it was planned by the killers; it was no accident, no random killing, as many people believe.'

'You said killers – more than one?'

'Of course. There had to be. The father was a strong man; there were two other strong boys in their twenties... one man couldn't have handled all three of them, plus the mother and the girl.' His grin faded. 'I knew someone who found some of the bodies, someone who worked in the history department on the dig. They never recovered. Life is never the same, after you see something like that.'

'Some of the bodies? Not all of them?'

'That is correct. The younger girl's body was found months later, in the woods. The older boy, Nico, was found a day or so later, miles away. Or what was left of him.'

Becky nodded, scribbling notes down.

'Well,' the old man said at length, bowing politely, 'I hope I've been of some help. Anything else you'd like to know?'

'Just one thing. How did you know the family was connected? To the secret police?'

'The boy was *in* the secret police. Nico. He served in the army. They say he travelled to Russia, to train with the KGB. Someone said he was with the Stasi, in Berlin. When he came back, people stayed out of his way. He was wrong, anyone could see it. Not a nice boy. I knew of him, through family. People who went to school with him. A bully, even as a child. The other children lived in terror of him. Even those in his gang. He carried this on into his adult life. This is why they made such a mess of him. They only identified him by his uniform. No one knows why the younger girl was taken away, though. Perhaps it is better not to know.'

'It is,' Becky said. 'Better by far. Thank you.'

The man bowed again and moved off, his soft shoes making the barest squeak on the glassy lake of linoleum. He waved to Hana, the woman behind the counter, then took the exit onto the street.

Becky turned back to the microfiche; she had a compact camera to hand, which she had meant to use to snap images of the local news reports of the case, but the old man had been a stroke of luck.

Then the file ran out, unexpectedly, just on the day that the bodies were found. She frowned, scrolling back and forth, then she removed the microfiche and compared it to the one she'd accessed earlier.

It was shorter. Some frames had been snipped out, cleanly and evenly.

She turned to the next microfiche; it was the correct size, but the date was two weeks later. The one after that was in sequence, then the one after that.

There could be no doubt. Someone had taken the microfiche of the newspapers which covered the crucial dates. Other frames had been directly excised.

Becky frowned. She skirted the rows of books, heading back to the librarian's counter. On the way, something in the play of the light across the smooth flooring changed, and she noticed four curved trails heading across the linoleum, shiny and stark as a slug's pathway in the morning. These corresponded to the wheels of the desk unit which contained the clunking microfiche machine.

Already knowing the answer, heart pounding, she gesticulated towards the librarian. She flicked through a phrasebook, and managed to say, gesturing towards the microfiche machine: 'Someone else? Here?'

The woman nodded.

'Today?' Becky asked.

Again, she nodded.

'Here? Now?'

Hana nodded again and pointed across to the stolid rows of bookshelves. 'Here,' she said, nodding vigorously. 'Now.'

# 41

Becky took the long way round, not wishing to alarm the woman, or tip off anyone hiding among the shelves that something was wrong. She skirted the end of the far wall, edging past the children's section. A poster of a grinning tiger, poring over an open book, crept past her shoulder.

She pulled out the pepper spray, took a deep breath, and approached the rows.

The stacks were at least ten feet tall, edging towards the roof. They had been laid out by a madman, surely, edging out into some areas, cutting off others. If shown from above, the closest geometric shape the layout would have corresponded to was a swastika. It was somewhere that left alcoves and corners, the type of place a person could settle down to read, undisturbed... or perhaps to lie in wait for someone to blunder round a corner.

There were also the tops of the shelves to consider – tall enough and broad enough for a man to lie down on, his weight easily borne by the books below. This was a place she knew she should not go to.

But he was in there.

She filled her lungs, keeping her head and back straight. 'Bastard,' she bellowed, in a borrowed voice. 'I'm talking to *you*. You in here? Fancy a catch-up?'

Perhaps this would have been the perfect moment for a timid old man to appear, or a crooked old lady with a shopping trolley, knock-kneed and confused, raising their Romanian copy of Jilly Cooper or Jackie Collins. But only silence answered.

And then, the tiniest creak.

Becky took deep breaths and forced her legs to move. The blood was roaring hard enough in her ears to blot out other sounds. She picked one of the stacks and stuck her head round. No one there; it was the western section, ancient Louis L'amours, seemingly dozens of copies of *Lonesome Dove*, gunfighters drawing on each other, fierce Native Americans with feathers and warpaint.

Alert for any movement, she visualised what she would do. Get very close, pepper-spray his eyes, poke them out if need be... then he would be at her leisure. Her mercy. She did not consider that he might have a gun. It did not seem to be his style.

Becky tiptoed round another corner, an intersection of science fiction, marked by a sign with a rocket ship, and crime, signified by a row of identical, glum-looking skulls. She peered through the gaps between the stacked shelves, sometimes crouching low, alert to anything that might have moved in opposition to the natural parallax view of the books as they scrolled past.

The key thing was not to get trapped; to keep a line of escape clear. If he should appear between her and this route, so much the better.

She padded as silently as she could, and even considered removing her boots before she remembered she might need them to kick with. She visualised it; springing on her heels, scissoring her best foot forward, toe-first, into his throat. It could be moments away, seeing his face at last.

It happened very quickly. With a wild shriek, one of the bookstacks shifted behind her.

Becky jumped a full foot in the air like a spooked cat. One stack of books swung round behind her, cutting her path off. There was only one way out, indeed; a left-hand turn, away from a corner of Romance and Adult sections closing off the path ahead.

Then she heard him breathing – fast, excited breaths.

She could *see* him. He was directly to the left, clearly visible through a gap between the books and the shelf above.

She looked into his eyes – the eyes she knew so well, thick and black irises, bulging wide.

The eyes disappeared briefly, as he slipped on the bone mask. Then the face swept away like a flicked page, and his heavy footsteps thudded down the row of books towards the final corner.

Coming for her.

# 42

Becky turned towards the stack of books blocking her way. She threw her weight behind it, but it budged only a little.

Then he appeared. He wore a plaid shirt and jeans. The bone mask was there, the patchwork skull of a stag or a bison, shorn of horns, the nude jaw and mean little teeth yellowed with age. And then those same eyes, and the same long, curved knife in his hands. He was a giant, now, as tall and as broad as he had been sparse and lean as a younger man.

He paused a moment to take her in, then grunted, before he charged.

All the training, all Becky's strength, every blow she'd struck at heavy bags, sparring partners and even real people – it all melted away. She didn't take a deep breath from low in her diaphragm; she did not crouch in a defence stance; she did not bounce on her heels, ready for combat. She screamed, a desperate, feral squawk. She dropped the pepper spray.

Becky scrambled up the stack of books like a monkey, featherlight. Adrenaline gave her wings, took her up in its hands.

He leapt for her, sweeping the blade down with one huge, swinging blow.

She glanced back a moment before she reached the summit of the bookstack, one foot trailing over the edge. The outer edge of the uppermost bookshelf burst open as if by a gunshot; a book spine flailed in a shredded flap of cloth and hardboard; Becky felt the tip of the heavy blade glance off her boot. But then she was above him, scrambling over the roof of the bookstack, clods of stirred dust clogging her nostrils.

Then the ground shifted, alarmingly.

He shoved at the stack before she was over the top and dropping down the other side, and it leaned crazily as she landed on the floor.

She felt the sliced edged of her boot digging into her skin. She wondered if the blade had gone right through; if she was leaving footprints of blood as she ran along the rows of sci-fi books. The streaming rocket tail on the sign was a jaunty insult.

Hana was nowhere to be seen; there was no one behind the counter. She was alone with him in the main room.

She ran round the empty corridor and burst through the door. Outside it was the way out – but somehow, he was ahead of her, running towards her from a different entrance, yelling. He must have taken another way, to get between her and the main exit.

His guttural voice filled every molecule in the empty air, reverberating through her body to the marrow.

He was between her and the front door. His blade traced silvery arcs in his pistoning arm as he sprinted towards her.

She ran, a flight straight out of a nightmare. There was a door ahead and to the left, and she jerked at the handle. It was unlocked; she ran through it into a dark blue corridor lit by small, dim windows set high on the walls. A storage cupboard was to her right, the handle of a mop jutting out of a crack in the door, preventing it from closing. On instinct, Becky snatched the handle as she ran towards two other doors.

He jerked open the door behind her. His breathing, muffled by the mask, was still slow and steady. Through the thunder of their feet she could hear that he was gaining on her; *he was faster than her*. She was braced for the kiss of the steel through the back of her neck, or between her shoulder blades. Once, Becky felt a sharp sweep that tugged almost playfully at her trailing hair.

Then she gripped a door handle and pushed through a door to the right.

She was in a tiny office, with space only for a desk and some filing cabinets; she slammed the door shut and tipped one over, blocking the doorway just as it was pushed open from the other side.

The door thudded once, twice, only a sliver of space between the jamb and the open edge. Becky jammed the second filing cabinet against the first.

The door jerked once more, meeting yet more solid resistance; then the person on the other side backed off.

The world settled back on its axis. Becky became aware of her hands, shaking in a near-comical palsy. At the windows behind her, a faint breeze stirred some venetian blinds badly in need of a dusting.

In the sliver of space at the crack of the door appeared a single shark-black eye, marooned in the dirty yellow of old bone like a filthy china cup. The pupil seemed freakishly large, reflecting the light in brilliant silver points, giving them an almost feral cast.

His voice was shaky with the effort of running, but clear, and loud.

'Little bitch, where will you run to next? Where can you go now?'

Becky kicked out at the filing cabinet; the eye snatched away before the door could slam shut on it. It pushed open again, a little further this time. The eye reappeared, thinned out in mirth.

'Ah, the day is coming near, when we can be together. I look forward to it. It won't just be a day. It will be days, weeks, months… a lifetime of suffering. So much of it that you might love me by the end. Or perhaps we should just have a morning? Like your mother, brother, father and sister? Little suckling pigs, fresh for the kill, ready for the *roast*.' He bellowed this last word. 'Of course, that day would be a lifetime for you. All you have left. My little pet. When shall we play?'

'Sooner than you think.' She allowed her jaw to sag, forced one long, slow breath, despite her quivering nerves and galloping heart. 'I'm looking forward to it as much as you.'

'Are you really? You look frightened and weak to me, little pet. Sweet little dog. You imagined perhaps we might dance together? That we would fight? *You?*' He laughed. 'There is only one dance left to us. By the time I'm finished with you, you might beg. You did before? Remember? Remember begging?'

Becky said nothing. She moved round to the other side of the desk and pulled the cord on the venetian blinds. They covered a window criss-crossed with reinforced glass. Again, she was reminded in a flash of the Glasgow trip, off-licences glimpsed through a taxi window. There was grilling outside, and she knew an awful sinking feeling, the realisation that these walls would continue to shift and close in on her until there wasn't even space to breathe.

At the corner of the grilling behind the window, she noted that one of the boltholes was empty. A gust of wind clanged the grille against the window-frame, then snatched it back again; it gave away several inches of space, maybe more. Hope flared.

'We can talk about your father, Becky, can we not? I'd like to talk about him. Imagine having such a coward for a daddy. No wonder he died as he did. He must have welcomed the knife. I wouldn't blame you for that. No one would. He was the biggest pig of all, Becky. You should not blame yourself.'

Becky came back round the front of the desk, and spat at that gleaming, gleeful eye.

As if from a nightmare, a hand took its place, with a blade at the end of it, slicing the air in quick, hard strokes. Becky felt the air scatter from its path, and she cringed back.

'You remember this knife? Don't you? Remember what we did with it? I'll see the scar again. I'll kiss it better for you. We'll talk about that day. We'll relive it again and again. I have so much to tell you. So much.'

The knife retreated. Becky's bag was gone, lost in the maelstrom of the library, and all her weapons with it. But she had another.

She snatched up the mop, and darted the handle through the gap. She knew the satisfaction of a grunt of pain, saw the single eye squeeze shut. Then she ran round the desk, tore open the reinforced window and leapt on the sill, kicking hard at the grille penning her in.

It burst open on the second kick, swinging free, tethered only by the elderly bolts on the right-hand side. Becky was through in a single bound, keeping her feet together for the ground-floor drop onto a grassy area.

Becky sprinted round the other side of the library, teeth gritted. This time. This time. No mistakes.

The front door of the library was still swinging when she got there.

In the near distance, out of sight, a car started and roared away.

Spots of liquid glowed on the shiny linoleum of the corridor, and she glanced down at her foot, the floor of her stomach dropping like a conjuror's cabinet.

It was blood. Hers.

The knife had split her boot and sock, and nicked the hard edge of her heel – deep, but not into the bone. She was not aware of pain, but knew it was coming. She limped into the place where the random order of the bookshelves turned to outright chaos.

A treacherous relief flooded her system and laid a calming hand on her shoulder. He was gone, surely gone.

The woman behind the counter burst through the door. If she had resembled Louis Walsh before, now she was his demonic double from another direction, shrieking, jabbing her finger.

'It wasn't me,' Becky said. When the woman drew closer, her voice growing more shrill, Becky cut her losses and left. In the distance, she could hear police sirens.

She limped past the toast-textured tenement blocks as best she could, in mortal terror again now that she was in the open. If she had been watched on the way in, traced somehow... perhaps he had been tracing her progress all along. Bernard hadn't been cautious enough, it seemed. Or she hadn't been paranoid enough.

This was where the trail led – the trail he'd unwittingly left, leaving a path by omission in Rupert's files, the blank places where he'd excised his past from databases drawing an arrow, pointing towards this town, the place where the line halted at its easternmost point of his crimes.

Her hire car was untouched. She allowed her paranoia a check of the back seat and the boot, even underneath, lest he should be clinging to the superstructure, before she drove back to her room in the centre of town.

There, she bit at the hard skin beside her thumbnail.

She had no choice now. It was time.

Becky took out an older phone, the screen battle-scarred, and dialled a number.

While the phone rang out, Becky tried to picture the size and shape of the man in the mask, the length of the limbs, how lean he had seemed. She'd never forget the eyes, of course.

Finally, Bernard picked up. 'Becky? How did it go?'

'He's here, Bernard. He almost got the drop on me.'

'Jesus! How?'

'I don't know. It could be a total coincidence, but I reckon he's tracking me. You were bang on the money.'

'You all right? He hurt you?'

'Not so much. I let him get away, Bernard. I let him get away.'

'What are you going to do now?'

'I'll get out of here. Just the same as he will...'

### Him

The screen of his phone lit up in the passenger's seat beside him, a sudden blue flare like a laser beam. He snatched it up and parsed the information there in moments. It was a signal, pinned to the centre of a map, a red arrow pulsing.

Excitement flooded him. 'Here and now,' he said to himself softly. 'Little bitch, this is where it ends.'

He used the phone as a sat-nav; it wasn't far. He started the car in the backstreets where he'd parked near the library, and edged out into traffic.

He was there in moments. He drove past the building twice, instantly taking in the front door, the lack of a concierge. He gained glimpses of the other side of the block as he drove round, again and again. There was one wall that edged onto a back yard, hidden behind some trees. Nice and quiet, well-hidden.

The app was very detailed. The flashing light on the phone told him which room she was in.

Taking care that no one watched him, he parked up, then padded over to the wall. His long arms reached the very top, and he scrambled over nimbly enough, though no one was around to hear him grunt, or to see him clutch his lower back as he steadied himself at the top.

A quick check of the phone; she was one floor up. A wall separated out the back yard, where the rubbish was dumped.

Pulling his hat low over his brow and raising his hood, he heaved himself onto the narrow edge of red brick wall, perpendicular to the hotel, and padded over the narrow top, as sure-footed as a cat.

What a foolish place to stay, he thought wryly, checking the phone one last time. When it came right down to it, she was just another idiot.

*I might have to do her quickly*, he thought, regretfully, as he pushed at the smudged glass of a bathroom window.

Inside, he had to fight to keep his breathing steady, so great was his excitement. He knew she was just behind a door at the end of the corridor. He crept as slowly as possible, paying little attention to the spyhole. Even if she was watching him approach – a black-edged nightmare crawling through the fish-eye aperture – she had only seconds to react.

He booted the door open, and was surprised when it offered little resistance, sending him off-balance as he lurched into the room.

There was just a bed, a sink, and an open doorway into an empty bathroom. No sign of the bitch.

He frowned, glancing round the room. The only other piece of furniture was a cheap writing desk. On it was a phone, brand new. Its screen brightened suddenly.

And then the muzzle flashes erupted all around him.

He blinked, holding his hands up.

It was the flash of cameras, from every direction, seemingly from every corner of the room.

A voice came from the phone.

'Hi, dickhead. It's me, Becky. I'm not home right now, but you are. It is you, isn't it? Say hello to the viewers at home. I know your name now. It's Nico, isn't it? Or is that just what your family called you? We'll have that catch-up I promised you, Nico. Very, very soon. I guarantee it.'

But by this point, the phone was speaking to an empty room.

## 43

'Disappointing,' Bernard said. He was on one of the secure phone lines; Becky had decided never to use video messaging again.

'It could have been better,' Becky said, uneasily, the phone cradled at her shoulder. She was making an adjustment to the whiteboard in her kitchen, now. She'd cleared a space in the middle and written a name. His name. 'Nothing wrong with the quality, we just didn't catch enough of him. I can't even be sure if it is him, I guess. I'd know for sure it was him if we had his eyes. But it's a lot better than nothing.'

'A question… are you sure it is our guy?'

'What do you mean?'

Bernard sighed. 'I mean, have you considered… it's a copycat? Or someone related to the original killer? I mean he must be old, you know, if it's the same guy. But for an older person he moves quick enough. And he got over the wall and through the window…'

'He could be in his fifties. That's not so old, and definitely not infirm. You ever seen a Tom Cruise movie?'

'Just saying. Keeping an open mind.'

'I doubt it's someone else.'

'What makes you so sure?'

'If there was a team, they'd surely have got me by now. Besides – we got information on where he's from. He came to intercept me. That proves it. We hit pay dirt. It's him. We've got a name.'

On her computer screen was their guy, from multiple angles. He hadn't hung around to dismantle any of the equipment. Unfortunately, he had got lucky – his eyes were obscured by a low hood he kept on all the way through.

He hadn't smashed the phone or taken it with him – something he must surely have cursed himself for, later.

Becky stared into the long, straight jawline, the cruel little mouth, the tip of a long, thin nose. *You panicked, didn't you? You ran out of there. And you'll be scared now. Maybe a bit desperate. If there's a time for you to make a mistake, this is it.*

Becky had been back home for a day. Though she tried to dampen down her elation, she was exultant at having caught him out. She'd used the second of the phones which she'd connected to Rupert – the back-up she hadn't smashed after he was killed. Bernard's eyes had lit up when she'd mentioned its existence.

The trap had been his idea – a simple relay, cameras set up in rooms, motion sensors and flashes.

It meant she'd had to rent out two rooms in Romania, with the compromised phone left in its own room along with the camera equipment Meanwhile, she'd got Bernard to book her a room separately, keeping her true location off-grid as far as possible.

They'd assumed that their guy had accessed Rupert's records, and was tracking Becky's spare phone – and from there, maybe a host of other things. As he had already made contact with Becky, there was every possibility that he would track the outstanding phone and pinpoint its location if it was used.

The assumption held good for when he had tried to kill her in the library. Eager, but still frighteningly controlled in his approach, he'd put it all together in seconds, from almost the moment she'd used the compromised phone... and he had walked straight into the trap.

As to how he'd got into the room, no one was quite sure – he must have scaled a back wall, but it was improbably high and narrow, requiring the dexterity of a cat and the strength of a gorilla to get to the top in the first place. And surely there would have been witnesses along the back court of the hotel.

But there he was, on the screen.

Well, part of him, anyway. He wore a hooded top pulled low, and a dark green combat jacket over the top, with boots, dark trousers and the collars of same plaid shirt he'd worn at the library visible. Dressed for a secret mission. What had those jacket pockets contained? Knives, rope, tape? The only thing which gave Becky pause; there was no mask in this scene. Perhaps it was too risky to take into the open. It would have meant taking a backpack, and it seemed that he wanted to get his business over with quickly after missing his target at the library.

She allowed herself the satisfaction of marking his face. It made him more real, more present; a solid shape, no longer an idea.

She had avoided thinking too hard about her initial reaction to his physical presence in the library. Here, at last, had been the situation she'd trained for. The confrontation she craved.

And she'd run.

Becky knew the coping mechanisms, what she should say to herself. *You were shocked. Survival instincts are there for a reason. It was an unusual situation. It's not every day you are confronted by the killer of your family. The man who now, undoubtedly, doesn't see you as a project or a plaything. A man who knows he must kill you to stay out of jail. Or the grave.*

But the reality was, she had missed her chance.

Bernard's voice shocked her. 'You reckon he's about sixty, then?'

'Late fifties, early sixties. Look at the lines by the mouth. The neck, just at the open collar. That's not a young man, for my money.'

'Could be a heavy smoker.'

'Yeah, or a burn victim. But I'd guess that's a man well into middle age, for sure.'

The image wasn't perfect, but it was enough – the chin, the jawline, the height predicted to a degree of certainty; just under six foot. Less than she'd supposed. And the boots, of course. Size fourteen. Same as before.

If only they'd got his eyes.

'Not a bad job though, hey?' Bernard said, with a hopeful Antipodean rise at the end of the sentence.

'Not bad at all, Bernard. Good work. Thank you.'

'S'nothing. See you.' And he hung up.

A minute or two later, one of the phones vibrated on her desk, jolting her. Becky was growing weary, ground down by too much travel and not enough sleep, and it took her a while to find which phone had received a message.

It was her work-a-day phone, and the message was from Aaron.

While the cat's away…

She rang the number; it diverted straight to answerphone.

Pulse, racing, Becky pulled on her coat and lifted her keys.

# 44

Bright light was an act of treachery in the basement bar. Its ancient stone steps and the greenish tinge of moss and algae were better suited to the bottom of the sea, or a fish tank. People could and probably had ended up with broken necks, slipping down those stairs.

*I'll probably die in a basement*, Becky thought, as she pushed open the pitted door.

The place was quiet, bleachy-fresh and just opened for the day. Apart from Aaron, the only other people inside were a bunch of students, some of them almost certainly too young to drink, who had begun a long afternoon with pitchers of toxic-looking lager and baskets of fries.

The pub was called The Cat's Cradle and was famous for hosting live music. Becky supposed that this was still a thing young people did nowadays, though she was a good five years away from her days of following live music. Even then, it had been mostly covers bands in the pubs, kids from conservatoires making beer money. Where had all the young hairy bastards gone?

She had come here in her Before and After days. In the former, The Cat's Cradle was somewhere to get wrecked, to damage her hearing and possibly even meet people she knew; a place you could depend upon to collect livid bruising and black eyes, borne proudly, if there was a crush at the front.

But in the latter days, the After days, her attendance had been a dare – a bet with herself that she could go to a gig, stand at the back, and watch a live show without anything alcoholic passing her lips. Aaron had accompanied her on many of these trips; slow, steady, and yes, dull Aaron, who might have resembled an accountant when he was still in his teens. He'd shown up to one gig in a short-sleeved shirt, and explained that he had done this to himself because places like The Cat's Cradle could get sweaty when there was a big crowd in.

There he was, with a tall pilsner glass in front of him, the rim and the insides still foamy, sat near the stage. He didn't look up. The gloom seemed to magnify his greasy pallor.

This was a new kind of shock for Becky, in a life not exactly bereft of them. In the past four years, Aaron had been a constant. She'd realised that there was nothing between them in terms of attraction, but they had come to depend on each other. Whenever things threatened to tip one over, the other had stepped in; but Aaron was the stronger, the one who always attended the meetings, the one who never stumbled. He was part of the firmament, the nice guy who would end up getting the girl at some point in his life. Whenever Becky wobbled or worse, Aaron was there.

But now something awful had happened. She felt a stab of guilt and shame, knowing that she'd neglected him; and then a hard belt of anger. How *dare* he, she thought. Here and now, in the middle of everything else; how bloody *dare* he?

She chose her opening lines carefully. 'I never had you figured as a cry for help-type person, Aaron.'

He nodded, numbly. 'Me neither. But there it is.'

As she sat down opposite him, she noticed the stubble at his cheek, and then she picked out that scent favoured by truly pathetic males; old sweat and deodorant.

She kept her voice neutral. 'How much have you had?'

'A couple.'

'How many since you came off the wagon?'

'Hard to say. Loads.' There was an impish cast to his features, a sour sarcasm that made her want to slap it off him. This wasn't safe, solid Aaron. This was someone she didn't recognise. The look did not suit him. 'How about you? You had a few of late?'

'None whatsoever. And I've needed one, I'll tell you that.' She planted her elbows on the table and leaned forward. '*What happened?*'

Aaron shrugged shoulders which seemed to have sagged in the middle like an old bed. 'Lots of things. Work. Some girl who pulled the ripcord after a month or two. All the classics. Then there was you.'

'What about me?' she asked, levelly.

'I was daft. I thought I could look after you. I got the impression you were trying to catch the guy who killed your folks. The way you were speaking... I was sure you were heading for trouble. Something awful. I couldn't have that happen to you. I wanted to make sure you were okay. I wanted to protect you. And you just... took off.'

She couldn't help it. She giggled. 'Protect me? Like Batman?'

His sour smirk dissolved into his usual smile, dimpling his cheeks. 'I was thinking more like Superman, to your Lois Lane. But yeah. I was worried. All that stuff in the papers... It was wrong. I know it. But I was worried. And I couldn't find you. There it is.'

'It's done. Forget it. Come on. We're going for a coffee. We can get absolutely wired on caffeine and biscuits. Off our nut on cake. Like we used to. Much better than beer. What is that you're drinking? Super lager?'

He swilled an inch or so of beer at the bottom of the glass. 'They had it on offer. I think they brew it themselves. They call it Acid Reflux.'

'Then we'd better grab a big creamy latte. Somewhere else. Come on. I'm buying.'

'We okay then?' He slurred a little. He'd been drinking for days, she realised. There was even a scratch along the side of his neck, and what looked like a bruise on his cheek, settled into the faded yellow of old age.

'We're always okay, Aaron. So long as you're okay, we're okay.' She laid a firm hand on his shoulder and waited until he looked up at her. 'You're meant to be the strong one, remember? You're meant to be sitting on this side of the table, and I'm meant to be there. That's the deal. That's how it works. That's how *we* work.'

He nodded and shoved the glass aside. 'If we get a creamy latte, can I have half a Flake on top?'

'You can have the whole thing. Come on.'

They both blinked into the light. Aaron held onto the bannister. 'Something so wrong about coming out of a pub in daylight. Always said so.'

'Don't worry – you can creep out of the coffee house under cover of darkness.'

One of Becky's phones tugged at her elbow, an insistent burr.

It was Labelle. 'Becky – can you speak?'

'Of course, fire away.'

'There's been some developments in Spain.'

She gestured to Aaron; for a moment she thought he was going to slink back downstairs into the bar, but he waited, giving her some space. 'How many bodies?' she asked.

'Four. We've linked them to the case of the missing family in Spain. It was thought to be a mob hit.'

'It's our guy though, isn't it? He's been using the place as a burial ground.'

'We're keeping an open mind.'

'Oh, bollocks. Come on. Admit it. I've been right, all along. I tried to tell you there was a link between my case and the others.'

'It was ruled out before. Forensic evidence…'

'Can be faked, falsified, and even excised from official reports. You can't account for these gaps. But I can – you've been hacked, by the killer. I'd say you should start combing your files. I will give you all the help you need.'

But not his name, Becky thought. *That's for later.*
*That's for me.*

# 45

Becky saw Devin McCance displaying signs of clear stress, and found it difficult to be in the same room as him. That was the difference between McCance and her, she supposed – he wouldn't have felt that tiny twinge of sympathy.

McCance ran his hands through his blond-tipped scalp. It seemed to be thicker than before. She wasn't sure if 'leonine' suited him as a description – 'tarantula' would be better – but he was almost certainly the type of person who clicked on hair restoration adverts on the internet.

He said: 'I don't believe this... you're paying Becky to write a fuckin' novel? Out of our own budget? She quit, Jack.'

Across the table, Jack Tullington folded his hands and sat back. He was dressed in a charcoal grey suit – new, by the looks of it – and despite his bulk he appeared dapper and composed. He was somehow more intimidating without the hat, but McCance did his best to belly-barge with him.

'This is completely ridiculous. And I'll tell you something else, Jack, on the record – it's favouritism.'

Rose, the Human Resources drone who chaired the previous meeting, didn't respond to this, but scribbled notes at speed.

Jack Tullington arched an eyebrow. 'Care to explain what you mean?'

'Absolutely. We know that you're some sort of surrogate stepfather to this character.' McCance jabbed a thumb in Becky's direction. 'That explains the cushty deal she's got. It's got a name, Jack, and that name is nepotism. And that's before we get to... what are we saying? Publishing deals? TV tie-ins? Is this a joke?'

'It's not a joke, Devin. It happens to be good business. We print extracts, we distribute it, we get the digital sales. Her book would be a bestseller. Even if they never catch the guy who did it. And we can even sell advance rights to other papers.'

'Much for? A tenner?'

'It won't be nothing. It's as close to money in the bank as we can get, these days. Becky's already turned down offers from major publishers. Isn't that right?'

'That's correct,' Becky said. 'I've been hard at work on the book during my sabbatical. I didn't intend for the splashes in *The Salvo* – I apologise for that. It's the nature of the beast. I got scooped. For what it's worth, it's helped me. It kept the story in the headlines.'

McCance's nostrils flared. 'So that's the idea. You catch your parents' killer, while we pay you for it? Nice work. But it's still nepotism. I want nothing to do with it. It's not passing through my news desk, or my staff'

'You don't have a choice,' Jack Tullington said, gravely.
'How's that?'
'You won't be running the news desk. You won't be running anything. For a while, at least.'

McCance sat back and took a deep breath, marinating in the inference. 'You're sacking me,' he stated.

'Absolutely not,' Jack said brightly, leaning forward. 'You're being placed on paid leave, pending some inquiries.'

McCance chewed this over for a moment, then laughed. 'Okay. No problem. Listen Jack, I think I'll start my gardening leave now, if you don't mind.'

'I was hoping you would,' Tullington said, flatly.

'You'll be hearing from the union. Or maybe I'll go straight to my solicitor.'

'That's entirely up to you.'

McCance drew Becky a look of such clear contempt that she wondered if he might conclude by sticking his tongue out or brandishing two fingers. He closed the door quietly behind him. After a few cursory remarks, Rose from HR concluded the meeting.

'Seems a bit harsh, Jack,' Becky said quietly, when they were alone.

'Och, he's a dickhead,' Jack said, sipping at a glass of water and loosening his tie. 'He's had it coming. Showing some bad signs. Turning into a cliché. I hear tell he's been spending time in the powder room on nights out.'

Becky raised an eyebrow. 'On the toot? You must be paying him too much, Jack.'

'Much more than we're currently paying Shazia – a perfect replacement. She's straight as a die, honest, fair, and doesn't wobble.'

'Doesn't sound like any journalist I've heard of.'

Jack grunted. 'We heading out for a coffee? I'm clear the rest of the day.'

'Actually, I've got plans. But there was something I wanted to talk to you about.'

Jack cocked his ear, as if expecting Becky to scratch behind it. 'Okay.'

'First. You were good pals with Mum and Dad, right? We know that.'

Jack's expression didn't change. 'Go on.'

'You didn't know about any problems they had? In their marriage? Nothing Dad told you about?'

'How do you mean?'

'Were they ever in any trouble? Threatening to split up? Any bad fall-outs?'

He looked shocked. 'Nothing. Absolutely nothing. He'd have told me. I mean, they had ups and downs – every married couple does. Jesus Christ, if I had a tenner for every time I fell out with Mel… But nothing bad. Not that I knew of, anyway. What kind of thing do you mean?'

'Did he worry she'd been unfaithful?'

Jack snorted. 'Cards on the table, love – before she gave in and married your dad… your mother was in big demand. Every man had a wee fancy for her. And there were a few people who wondered why she ended up with your dad. Well – folk who didn't know him, at any rate. She was beautiful. Like you.' He smiled kindly. 'And he was a wee barrel of a guy. Everyone thought he played rugby – that seemed to annoy him more than being told he was too short. Folk thought they didn't *look* right together. But as for any idea that she would be unfaithful… hand on heart?

No. Never. She was devoted to him, and he was to her. And to their kids, of course.'

'Okay.' Becky tapped her notepad. 'There's something else I had to ask. Why were you having me followed?'

'What?' If he was acting, he was first in the queue for a BAFTA. Jack looked as if he'd been punched.

'Why did you hire someone to tail me? You know – that private detective in Spain. What's the story with that?'

'I don't... Becky, I have no idea what you're talking about.'

'However much you're paying him – I'd ask for a discount. He fell for some pre-school anti-surveillance tricks. I'd send him on a course before he heads back out on the road again, if I was you. He should be okay to get back into it within a couple of weeks. Although he might have a limp.'

'Becky, I have no idea what you're saying.'

'Don't *lie*!' she roared, slamming her hands down on the desk. 'He *told* me, Jack. He had your name. He spilled his guts out. You hired him! To follow me!'

Jack raised a hand the size and consistency of a sledgehammer, but it wavered, and in his watery eyes was the expression of an old, old man.

'Becky... I swear to you... I didn't hire anyone to follow you.'

'Who did then, Jack? Under your name? Who did?'

She slammed the door shut on his stammering.

# 46

Him

The trap door opened, flooding that filthy space with light. Out in the world, it was a sunny day, but the sun's rays blinded her.

The girl yelped in fright, covering her eyes.

'Hey there!' he cried, jauntily, his voice muffled by the mask. 'I've got some homework for you. Got some lines to practise. Do it, and you can have some food. Won't that be nice?'

Her

Becky settled down in Fullerton's armchair. She liked that it wasn't too soft. It placed a firm hand on the small of her back. It was a hard but fair governess rather than a soppy aunt.

She wondered if it had been designed that way. She wouldn't put it past Fullerton.

'Sorry I've not been around for a bit,' she said, settling back in the chair. 'I've been a bit busy.'

Fullerton, stationed at the other end of the room, rubbed his whiskers. 'I noticed that.'

'You must be one of those weirdos who still read the papers.'

'If you want to talk about newspapers... that could mean a whole new block of therapy.'

'I guess. Do you offer ECT?'

Fullerton began his spiel. 'Okay Becky. I want you to stare at the blank space on the wall...'

He flicked a switch on a projector, and a black and white spiral appeared on the dim white wall directly opposite her. It was a more up-to-date version of his old disc. Becky's mind reached for things to compare to the concentric circles as her brain struggled to process the shape, in alternating black and white. Perhaps it was the rings inside a tree; a coiled worm; or simply an unending vortex, twisting in on itself to infinity.

*Cheap trick*, she thought, as her breathing slowed and a dense, pleasant fugue settled round the back of her neck and shoulders. *But sometimes they work the best.*

'Now, Becky, I want you to relax, breathe deeply. In through your nose, out through your mouth.' His voice changed register – higher, reedier, slightly raspier. She thought of it as his Barney Rubble voice, though perhaps there was a hint of Rod Stewart in there. It was the voice of a kindly uncle who could make the whole house explode with laughter.

'Your eyes feel very heavy. You need a nap – you can't hold on any longer. You need to let go, and let them close, gradually. We're going to count backwards from twenty... nineteen... your eyelids are so heavy... eighteen... that means Peak Freans, nibble sweet, tout suite. Because we knows beans means Heinz, strong means lion... seventeen... dream for bream, fishies for me, warm green sea...'

Becky tried to remember his nonsense patter every time she emerged from one of Fullerton's sessions – to see if there was a set rhythm and meter to it, if there was something in the cadence of the vowels and consonants that lulled her into the trance. Each time, she struggled to recall exactly what he said.

'So we come to the forest, Becky. You're in the forest, and you're entirely safe. You're invisible, and invulnerable. You're locked tight in a beam of light, no one gets in, no one gets out, nothing can harm you. You're breathing slowly, easily, calm. You're listening to the sounds of the night. You hear owls hooting. But it's not a lonely sound; it's a fluffy white sound. Little mice play in the branches – you can hear them scurrying, but the owl leaves them alone to play. There's a high, clear moon. It's peaceful, Becky. It could be a painting. Above the trees you can see blue as well as black, that deep blue of a clear night. There's a crooked tree. You remember the crooked tree, don't you? Then you come to a clearing. There are people in the clearing. Who's there, Becky? Who's in the clearing?'

An almost imperceptible frown angled Becky's flesh where her fine eyebrows met.

'You're warm, cosy and calm, Becky. You can see them, but they can't see you – they can never see you or speak to you. You can see what's happening, calmly, dispassionately, clearly. Who's there, Becky? Who's in the clearing?'

Her voice might have come from the bottom of the ocean. 'Mum's there. She's not... she's not wearing anything.'

'Who else, Becky?'

'Clara and Howie. None of us are wearing anything. We're outside and we're cold. He's tied us to the rocks. We're all crying. There's a big fire in the middle of the rocks, so we can see each other.'

'Where's your dad, Becky?'

'I can't see him but I know he's there. I heard him shouting. Was sure he was dead, but now he's crying.'

'Who else is there, Becky? Who can you see?'

The frown deepened. 'The man is there.'

'What man? What is he wearing?'

'He has on a white gown. Like a priest. He has on this...' Her breath hitched in her throat. 'Mask. He has on a mask. It's made out of bone. It's like a cow's skull. It's held together with wire or thread. I can see little bits of his face through it... he's got these big black eyes. He's laughing at us.'

'And who else?'

'Nobody.'

'Look hard, Becky. Are you sure there isn't someone else?'

'No. Nobody else. Just us.'

'And your dad isn't with the man?'

'No. Dad got hurt. We heard him cry.'

'Did you ever see them together, Becky? The man and your dad?'

'Yes. They were fighting.'

'Can you hear your dad now? While the man is in the forest with you?'

Becky didn't say anything. Her lips moved, but no sound came out. She was there, in the forest. The sounds. The bite of the rope. Shivering.

'Becky? Can you hear him? Your dad?'

'Not any more.'

'Look at the mask, Becky.'

'No.'

'It's absolutely fine, Becky. We're going to go deeper. Now you're deeply asleep, and you're invisible, totally invulnerable, nothing can get in, nothing can harm you, no weapon in the world can reach you. Look at the mask. Look at it calmly. You're cool, dispassionate. You're looking at the mask. Are you seeing it?'

She could. There were the bulging eyes, the tongue flicking over the lips, just visible inside the long jawbone with the weird teeth.

'Do you recognise those eyes? Do you recognise that face?'

'No.' She said it again, almost a shout. 'No!'

'Does it have a beard? A little bit like me? My beard?'

'No.'

'Is it your dad's face? Is your dad's face in there? Can we be sure, Becky? Can we ever be sure?'

'No.' But the face had changed. Tufty, jowly cheeks appeared beneath the wired-up parts of the bone mask; it was as if a spider was trapped in there, thrashing blindly. The eyes weren't so large or freakish any more, but still black, like her father's, aglow with unholy mirth.

'Can we be sure, Becky? Is it Dad? Dad may be mad and it all seems so sad but aren't you glad the truth is had?'

'No.' In her mind's eye, the flesh and the beard hair withdrew, and the eyes she remembered returned. And also the voice. Calm and cold, rough-edged.

Fullerton allowed a pause. Then: 'What about the other man?'

'There's no other man.'

'There is. There is another man, isn't there? You've seen him. He's the one who hurt your dad, while the other man hurt you and Clara. There's no other explanation.'

'Dad tried to fight but the other man was too strong. The other man hurt him and said he'd kill him if we tried to get away. "I'll slit his belly," he said. "You'll see what's inside him."'

Becky's voice mimicked the other, in the croak of a child trying to scare a friend after lights out.

'But is there another man, Becky? You see the other man. He's not too tall, is he? He's a white man and he has the other mask on. The other mask, Becky. The skeleton mask. The one the police thought the first man wore, the one they thought he bought it from a shop. That's what they told you at first, wasn't it? The mask, the other mask, the other man. Two men. Two peas in a pod. There must be two because twins wins and blends in and there's a pair in the square with two dice in the air.'

'No.'

'You see him, don't you? The other man. You know there's two – not one, no fun in one, the sun's gone with one but with two it shines through and the truth comes from you. Two. You see the other man, don't you? The one who helped? You see him, don't you? Does he look like your dad?'

'I see him,' Becky said quietly.

'What do you see?'

'He has a beard. Under the mask. Or a moustache, I think. It might be a moustache. He's...' her brow cleared. 'He's a bit like you. He's quite short, stocky. He has a belly just like my dad. He's wearing my dad's jeans, and a pair of boots.'

'What else do you see?'

'He has... on top of his head... a hat.'

'A hat?'

'Yes... a cowboy hat. He takes the mask off...' Becky's breath hitched in her throat. She licked her lips, swallowed, and continued. 'I recognise him. I know him. I know who he is.'

'Who is he, Becky?' Fullerton said. 'Who do you see under the mask? Who is the second man?'

'It's... Yosemite Sam.'

'Who?'

'Yosemite Sam. The rootinest, tootinest, shootinest varmint in the old west. Pow-pow-pow-pow!' Becky aimed twin guns at the floor. Then she opened her eyes, rested her head on the back of the seat, and smiled. Her eyes were clear and her voice lucid. 'Now would you like to explain what that was all about?'

Fullerton flinched, and raised a hand as if to ward her off. 'Becky, we're in the middle of therapy. I haven't brought you out of the trance yet. It can be dangerous if you don't let me bring you back gradually.'

'I haven't gone anywhere, Dr Fullerton. I'm not sure I ever did. Hypnotherapy was quite relaxing to start with. Bit like a foot massage – it was okay, but I'm not sure I'd ask for it on a spa day. Like peach ice cream, you know? It's fine and all, but you really want choc ice. You know? Choc ice twice as nice, sugar and spice, sage advice... what a crock of shite.'

Fullerton recovered his poise. 'We were making progress.'

'Someone's making progress – that much I know. But who? Why are you introducing these new elements into what happened? "Is my dad behind the mask?" Of course he isn't, you berk! My dad got his legs broken. And what's with this second man you keep gibbering about? There was no second man. I know there was no second man. There was one man – one bastard. He beat my dad to a pulp. That was after he threatened to kill us, and to be fair he was as good as his word. He tied my dad up to make him watch. Then he… well, he died. I saw my dad die. I saw them all die.'

'There is a theory that there were two men.'

Becky snapped her fingers. 'A theory! Great! Let's hear your theories. What do your theories have to do with my mental health? Or your practice?'

'I am trying to help. You said you wanted to go back, to go over all the details. All the possibilities. You said that yourself.'

'I want to go over everything in case there's something I missed – something subtle I can't remember. But the nuts and bolts of it, the blood and the screaming, who did what to whom – that, I remember very well.'

'Becky, this is lifelong trauma. I'm trying to help you process it.'

'You're a goddamn liar, is what you are. Are you writing a paper on me? Something to present to the BPS?' She gestured at the diploma on the wall over his shoulder. 'Something to make your name with? To claim you cracked a famous murder case?'

'No. Becky, calm down. Please.'

'I want answers – what is it you want with me? Why are you trying to implant false memories into my mind?'

'I'm not. Please stay calm.'

'You've had this planned for months. "We don't fully understand what happened, Becky." "It's all a bit formless, Becky – some things in the case don't add up". You've been sending me down false paths. You've been grooming me. Why?'

'That's not true.' He stood up, his face blank. 'Not for months. Just this one session.' He started forward.

Becky leapt from her seat. 'Not one more step, or I'll break your neck. I swear to god, lift your hands, and I'll end you.'

Fullerton paused. Then a curious thing happened. A mask was removed; a professional edifice crudely ruptured. His face twisted, appeared to implode. His shoulders sagged, as if a pin had been pulled in his spine, and he collapsed to the floor. He hunched over on his front, elbows on the floor, utterly supplicant.

For a bizarre moment, she wondered if someone had shot him – had a bullet come through the curtains? But nothing had hit Fullerton. No solid objects, anyway. He was safe, invisible and impregnable in his gloomy office.

He sobbed, his face in his hands. He tried to say something.

Becky sank to her haunches, bringing her face level with his. His veneer was gone; tears ran down his cheeks into his beard. Even breath seemed to torture him. It was as if he was being strangled.

Finally, Dr Fullerton managed to say it.

'He's got my daughter.'

# 47

Becky had taken a good stretch at the age of 16 – she was only a little taller now than she had been then. So it didn't make much sense that her Aunt Cecilia's garden should seem so small, so compact, as she headed along the path towards the bungalow door. Since she'd moved out aged 18 for university, she'd only stayed there for the odd Christmas, and even that had been an ordeal; two introverts, both of whom wished Becky was somewhere else.

The old girl had kept the place in good order, the window boxes and potted plants an orderly splash of colour on the paving slabs. Even the smallest cactus in any flat Becky had stayed in tended towards riotous assembly in short order; Becky marvelled at the patience required to maintain discipline in a full garden.

Cecilia was in similarly good order. She would never take to fat, and she had sorted out her hair, cut shorter and cropped high, with tawny highlights in among the grey. Her clothes seemed more stylish, too, a cashmere sweater clinging to her ultra-slim frame, a skirt trailing toward her ankles.

*She's dressed up for me*, Becky realised.

They didn't hug, or even shake hands.

'You're looking well,' Cecilia said. 'Got a touch of the sun? You been away?'

Becky smiled. Here was the type of passive-aggressive inquiry she remembered. 'A bit. You've seen the papers, I guess?'

'I could hardly miss them,' Cecilia sniffed.

A conservatory had been built into the sprawling garden. They took tea there, on prim wooden furniture. Everything was small, dainty, breakable. This was a place where a child could not be allowed to run free.

The small talk ran out soon enough. 'You ever been a big letter writer, Cecilia?'

'Whatever do you mean by that?'

'Just what I asked.'

'Not really. I used to send letters to your mum now and again. She was the big letter writer in the family. Forever scratching away in notebooks, too. I guess that's where you got it from, in fact.'

'I remember. She always used to leave poems in birthday cards. She could knock out some verses in two minutes flat. And she loved dirty limericks.'

'Ha! That's true.' A smile struggled to break free on Cecilia's face. 'She sent me some crackers.'

'That's kind of why I'm here. I never asked before. But you're the only person who can have them.'

'What?'

'Mum's papers. Her journals. The novel she tried to write when she was in her twenties, the one dad used to tease her about. And her letters.'

'That stuff… it'll be buried somewhere in the loft, or in the shed in the garden.'

Becky gestured towards her own clothes; a band T-shirt which had run to the same texture as greasepaint on an evil clown's brow, and elderly but much-loved jeans frayed at the hems. 'I'm dressed for digging. Let's go find them, Cecilia.'

'God knows where they are, Becky. Is this why you're here? To tear my house apart?' Cecilia glanced at her watch.

'You don't have any appointments, Cecilia. That's why I asked you to clear your diary today. Come on.'

'Why do you want to do this now? I don't understand.'

'Cecilia, those documents belong to me,' Becky said quietly.

Her aunt's eyes hardened. 'I think you may find that possession is nine-tenths of the law.'

'If you don't give me my mum's papers, you'll have a court summons to answer within the next thirty working days.'

Cecilia's face took on the lineaments of amusement, but this did not soften her features, which were far removed from mirth. 'Threatening, now. That's very like you. That's the girl I remember, all right.'

'It's not a threat, Cecilia. It's a guarantee. I want to see her papers.'

'Give me a week, then. I can't just disrupt my home life to please you and your whims.'

'Now, Cecilia. I want them today. Not tomorrow, not next week. Right now.'

'They'll do you no good. No good at all,' her aunt said quietly.

'I'll be the judge of that. Cecilia, I don't know what you think I'll find, or what it's going to do to me. Maybe digging it up will hurt *you*, not me. Maybe that's what frightens you the most. I don't know. But I have to see those papers. It's important. There are some things I have to get straight in my head.'

'You're trying to catch him, aren't you? The man.' Cecilia sipped at her tea. 'Jack Tullington came around. He told me.'

'Is that right? When was this?'

'On the anniversary. He came with flowers. He always does. He's a good man.'

'Yes. Very smart man, too.' Something struck her. 'Did you give him Mum's papers?'

'No. Of course not. He didn't ask to see them, either. If I didn't give them to you, I'm hardly going to hand them over to him, am I?'

'True.' Becky drummed her fingers. 'I'll say this for you – you're consistent. Come on, let's go. It's fun clearing out garages and attics and sheds. Bagsy your old *Bunty* annuals?'

## 48

Him

He listened to the coffee machine bubble and spit, impatient for the liquid to collect. A ghost shifted in the reflection on the glass pot.

He spun round, and there she was. His wan daughter, her dyed black hair casting her face in a sickly light.

'I didn't know you were here,' he said.

'I didn't know you were home,' she replied, yawning and stretching. 'You look guilty. What have you been up to at your conference?'

He smiled. 'Why aren't you at school?'

'Study leave.'

She still wore a nightshirt, a grubby cotton garment with a goggle-eyed cartoon character on the front. It barely reached the top of her spindly legs. 'That's too short. And you've had it for years. Didn't your mother get you some nice pyjamas?'

'I thought those were from Father Christmas. When did you become interested in what I wear to bed?'

He grunted and poured a coffee. 'It's midday, and you aren't studying.'

'I take a while to get into my stride. I'm a night owl. Like you.' She crossed to the fridge. 'Actually I was thinking of taking a walk in the woods. Get some air in me.' She nodded towards a plastic box, filled with apples and cheese sandwiches. 'I take it you're going on a hike, too? You've got a big appetite. It's like you've got enough for two, there.'

'I was considering it.'

'Maybe I'll come along with you.'

'If I don't cramp your style.'

She smiled. 'Look at your shoulders! They go all bunched up when I suggest we do something together. Like a little squirrel. It's all right. I know you've got your little routines. Your training routes. You're a creature of habit. I understand. I won't get in your way.'

He closed the lid on the lunchbox, pressing down the edges with a smart crack. 'Now you sound like your mother.'

Her

'God's sake, Cecilia. This is the cleanest basement I've ever seen.'

No dripping water or dangling bulbs, here; the light had a shade, glass blades that fanned out like an outstretched hand. Cecilia's basement was a place of stacked boxes which had never known the rough hand of a house move, or the chill effect of damp. Everything was uniform, as tight and well tucked as a hotel bedspread. No bric-a-brac, nothing that hadn't been carefully stored and tended well. If there was dust, then it was well hidden.

Ditto the spiders.

'It's called cleanliness,' Cecilia sniffed. 'People used to take pride in it. Your grandmother was a stickler. She used to lift the carpets and scrub the floorboards.'

'That must have been a big laugh. Unnecessary, much?'

'Well... she was a little bit mad, in fairness.'

'Cleaning up is one thing... but this is the first basement I've gone into and not sneezed. You could carry out surgery in here. Anyway – what do you mean, "people used to take pride in it"? I run a tight ship at my flat,' Becky added, a trifle defensively.

'I'm sure. Just like your old room, upstairs.'

'Point conceded. Okay. Where do we start?'

Cecilia gave a sad smile. 'There's no need to search. I know where it is. It's in the chest. Here's the key.'

It looked like a pirate's key, and it fitted what looked like a pirate's chest. The lock clicked open, smartly.

'I'll leave you to it,' Cecilia said. To Becky's surprise, she turned on her heels and left, but the door to the staircase remained ajar.

Although there was no chill in the air down here, Becky shivered. She felt the hairs prickle on her neck at that gap, and the view of carpeted stairs which issued no protest at the light touch of Cecilia's footsteps.

She remembered the library.

She closed the door quietly, then knelt down by the chest.

The papers inside were piled high, but folded neatly, and had clearly been gone through in some detail. Unfortunately, Cecilia's fastidiousness stopped short of a proper filing system; they were in no particular order. Becky passed ancient bank statements over in her hands, MOT invoices for cars she remembered. Even the smallest material connection to the dead, the most superficial link between consumerism and family life, caused melancholy to bloom in her breast.

She shuddered when photos appeared – strictly analogue, a long way away from the selfies age, many of them misfires. Her mother's hairstyles ranged from the Sheena Easton cropping mistake of the early eighties to full perm horror, then back to her graceful bangs into the early nineties.

Her father's rotund cheerfulness was a constant all the way through, barely changing. There was Howie, going from a quiet, watchful baby to a reserved little boy, clutching his teddies tight. There was one photo which caused Becky a physical pain in her chest – Howie, Christmas morning, with a shiny robot from a movie or a TV show, borne aloft like a football captain with a trophy, beaming. He had been so happy he had actually cried when he unwrapped it.

She drew a feather-light finger over that face.

'Howie,' she said, barely a whisper.

And then came Clara, still in those heavy metal branded shirts, trying to impress some boy out of shot. And young Becky was there of course, looking washed out. She remembered painful stomach cramps around this time, and a general listlessness in the following days. Thin. Wan. Unkissed. Still a little girl in the same way you saw that Clara wasn't.

The branding of the high street chemist stencilled on the back of the photos bore commentary written in Becky's mother's own hand. Dates, occasions. The odd sarky line, her own trademark. One image of Howie, sobbing, face contorted and his lip pooched out far enough to admit a landing helicopter, was captioned 'season's greetings'.

Becky traced the thin indentation of the pen strokes with her finger.

Soon she got to the letters. These were bound with string, the paper all the same delicate lilac shade. There were piles of them; mostly in her mother's hand, some in her father's. Love letters. Dated before any of their children arrived, before they were married. Tender. Erotic. Embarrassing beyond description. 'You are my sun and my ocean,' her father had written, in fat, thick letters which blundered through the blue lines of his notepaper, in an indecent hurry to spill across the page.

Then her mother, nearer the mark, curt: 'I'm writing this in bed with my legs propped up, and wishing you were between them.'

The decorated their letters – hearts that flew away to form distant flocks, murmurations of kisses, half-moon faces tipping jaunty winks. Then caricatures, her father's far better than her mother's; Grandma Bessie, wielding a two-headed battleaxe, and then – achingly accurate – Cecilia, in a long black cloak, scythe in hand.

Then the other letters appeared. There were no words crossed out, no parts underlined. There was a faint scent to them, a hint of something you rarely saw or smelled any more, Kouros or Aramis. Maybe something sweeter – a scent a teenager would buy for themselves.

After a time, Cecilia knocked gently. She passed a steaming mug of tea to Becky. 'Did you find what you were looking for?'

'Yes,' Becky said. She made no effort to hide the fact she'd been crying.

'There are some things which it's maybe best not to know. Do you understand why I didn't want you to have them? Your mother was writing to another man. I know it's hard for you to take, but there it is. Do you see why I wanted to protect you from this?'

'You had no right to keep them from me,' Becky said.

'I had every right!' Cecilia's voice swelled, bouncing off every surface. 'You know how hard it was, seeing those letters, reading that stuff, after having that happen to her? It's as if it wasn't enough that she was killed. I had to have her shamed, as well. Her memory sullied. As if it wasn't enough that she was murdered! My sister!'

Becky allowed silence to return, then said, 'I understand why you did it. But you're mistaken.'

Cecilia frowned. 'Say again?'

'You're worried about these? The letters from the French boy? The ones addressed to the American girl? Dad must have roared laughing at them.'

'I don't think so. In fact, I think he would have been enraged. Your mother was... beautiful. There's no doubting it. She was modest with it, but men adored her. I accepted it; I was never jealous. That wasn't something I ever wanted for myself, and it wasn't something I wanted to deny her, either. It's pointless feeling bad about something you can't change. I was proud of her, in a funny way. But I think these letters tell you something. Had your dad found out... something horrible might have happened between them. I thank god he died in ignorance.'

'He knew all about them, Cecilia. The whole thing was a joke. I got what I came for.' Becky waved invoices at her, plus a stack of printouts from an ancient dot matrix printer, the perforated edges running ragged in places. 'The letters confirmed what I already knew, beyond a doubt. It's the business stuff I was here for. I need to take it all away.'

'Well, they are all yours, after all.'

'They are. I'll take some of the letters… Hey, French letters. I just got that!' Becky giggled. 'Anyway, I'll leave the others, but I'll be back for them, in time. Once this is all cleared up. And I promise to explain everything.' Becky even kissed her goodbye, though she stopped short of skipping up the flagstones or patting the waving fronds and lolling tongues of the plants.

Something in the contact with her loved ones had energised her. It had been sad, the blow of seeing their faces had been painful, but as time crept on there was something life-affirming in it, too. If she hadn't exactly high-fived their ghosts, she felt a little closer to them, a little more supported. It was only at those times when she felt the presence of them, as opposed to their terrible absence, that she realised how much support she needed in life. That she still walked on unsteady legs, like a new-born foal.

There were three names to work with, now, from the legal paperwork. Partners in her father's house-building business. One was LaFleur, and the other was Tullington. All connected to a plot of land in France.

The place they'd gone on holiday. The place they died.

The third name was Nico Arkanescu. The one she was looking for. She felt sure of it.

He was the 'who'. But she'd never thought there was a 'why', until now. A reason beyond the unreasoning lust of a madman.

There were no paparazzo waiting for Becky as she returned to her flat. The checks she carried out were routine, now – a quick glance at the security cameras, to make sure they were working; a thorough check of the stairwells, to be sure no one lurked in dark places; then a check of cameras and sensors, video footage she'd recorded herself while she was out. There was nothing; all clear.

Not long after she'd had a cup of tea and began composing an email to Bernard on her secure computer, a wave of tiredness stole over her. The travelling, the stress, had finally caught up with her. She barely finished the mug of tea, leaving it lying on the kitchen counter. With light still showing through her pale blue curtains, Becky pulled on a top and snatched up her silky pyjama bottoms – a mismatched pair, but they combined to make her most comfortable jim-jams – and threw back the covers. She stumbled comically while trying to put her legs into the pyjama bottoms; she wrestled with them on the bedspread, head spinning. She wasn't even aware of putting her head on the pillow before she was spark out.

Then came the familiar dream, the familiar setting.

She lay back in bed in the dark blue of the night. A pale moon slit the scene through her fine curtains, washing the white walls with silver.

The door clicked open and then he was there, padding softly into the room. He had on his mask, of course, with the glittering black eyes beneath. The white gown he wore was an ethereal presence in the moonlight, an illustration of a ghost in a child's book. He stood at his customary position at the bottom of the bed, breathing softly, hands held loosely by his sides, the knife glinting in one of them.

Staring. Hardly moving.

Becky's breath was shrill in her throat. She tried to speak in the gluey fashion of dreams. 'Nuh, nuh, nuh. Nuh!'

Her heart was out of control, a prize mare in full flight, her limbs twitching. She tried to sit up. She could not move, frozen. Awareness began to flood in. She wanted it to be over, to be awake, for the knife under her mattress to be in her hand, to begin the performance of the traumatised stagger towards the kitchen sink for a glass of water.

He was positioned a little further back than usual, so that Becky could see his feet. His footwear was obscured; he was wearing plastic coverlets over the top of them, of the type she'd seen the forensic officers wearing at her family's graveside.

That's when she knew she was fully awake. And that he was standing at the foot of her bed, for real.

# 49

For a whole minute or more, there was nothing but his breathing, and hers. She opened her mouth to shriek but couldn't do it. She might as well have been underwater, chained to the bottom. Her head pulsed, with a slightly sour taste in the back of her throat, like an awful vodka hangover.

The moonlight and inky shadows enhanced the eerie effulgence of his white gown; his eyes caught twin points of light like the surface of an oil slick. They seemed to dance as they took in her wide-eyed fear.

She could hardly move her hands beneath the covers. Drugged, surely, she thought. Even the effect of her pulse was muffled. A dull throb radiating out from her chest was the only confirmation that her body had gone into stress overload.

All she could do was snatch thin, reedy breaths, fluttering her nostrils like the gills of a fish.

With a supreme effort, neck cords straining, she lifted her head. 'Nuh... No,' she croaked.

He started forward, with the fluid grace of nightmares. His hand reached out, and the tip of one finger traced the path of a tear down her cheek, tickling the corner of her mouth.

'Please,' he rasped, 'don't try to talk. You'll need your strength. We have the whole night to get through.'

He sidled round to the edge of Becky's quilt and felt underneath it, round the edges of the mattress. All too soon, his fingers found the handle. He brought the blade up into the light; she could tell from the changed cast of his eyes that he was grinning.

'Is this a present? For me?' He stretched forward, the tip of the machete tapping Becky's nose. 'We'll put this to good use. I wonder if you imagined using it on me? Cutting my throat?' He traced a deathly soft line under Becky's chin with the tip of the blade, barely touching her skin. 'Or perhaps putting it through my heart?' The blade lowered. He used it to draw the quilt back over her shoulders, and then her chest. Finally, he cast it to the floor.

Becky felt the sudden chill of exposure across her arms and lower legs; her knees were bent slightly, but no more than that. She was utterly helpless.

*I'm going to die here. There'll be no fight. No payback. Only this grim conclusion.*

*They'll never find my body. I won't be buried alongside my family.*

He laid the machete down on the bedside table, then snatched up the mug Becky had left there. He sniffed at the cup, then disappeared. She heard the ludicrously prosaic sound of someone washing up in the kitchen. She strained with everything she had to lift her hand and grasp the knife handle that lay inches from her head, but it was no use. One more piece of torture. When he returned to the room she exhaled hoarsely and gave in.

He chuckled, deeply, and waggled a finger at her. 'You've been a very clever girl, setting all those cameras up. It might even have saved you, if I wasn't a clever boy.' He crouched down beside her. The bone mask filled her whole field of vision, the eyes unblinking.

'The relay with the phone was clever, too. Someone helped you do that, I think. Another hacker, probably. I'll get to him, soon. It'll be your fault, when I do – just like the last one. Except I won't be quick, this time. I'll take days to finish him. He'll plead with me to end it. Take a moment to think about that.'

She tried to spit. There wasn't enough moisture in her mouth, not enough power in her lips.

'Though you must be insane to think I would make the same mistake twice. Especially when you insist on coming back here. You may be clever, and you may know some clever people. But no one's as clever as me. Isn't that right?'

He straightened up, took a deep breath, and gazed at her body. She felt totally exposed, although she still wore her night clothes. 'And haven't you grown,' he said. The lust apparent in the low register of his voice stirred Becky's first feelings of despair, a level beneath panic and fear. 'Yes… you filled out very well. Very well indeed. But I need to know more than this. I want to see right inside you. As deep as you go. It will be a pleasure to see your bones shine. I want to hold your heart in my hand while it still quivers. Like a little sparrow.' His formed a fluttering bird shape with his hands, then leaned closer, chuckling.

With a thrill of hope, Becky saw his head was perfectly placed for a knee to the temple; even a blow at half-force would put him out, perhaps for good, bone mask or not. She would have the supreme satisfaction of seeing his eyes roll up in that mask, even if she faded and died here in the aftermath.

But she did not even have half-force; she did not have a fraction of what she needed. Her leg quivered uselessly as she arched it a slight angle – then sagged, exhausted. It was worse than having the knife close to hand.

'Bastard,' she wheezed, stumbling over the hard consonants.

He chuckled. 'I got your dose just right. I have an eye for girls' weight. They might make a chemist of me, yet. Or a dressmaker.'

The tea, of course. He'd been in the flat. He'd done something to the tea bags – which meant he knew that she took a cup later in the day than she should. He'd also tampered with her camera, the computer feeds – and most likely the security cameras dotted around the building. She remembered someone – either Rupert or Bernard – telling her how easy it was to loop old footage through camera systems to make it look as if nothing had happened. All you had to do was match up the numbers.

*He might have been here for days.*

'Turn round, my darling,' he said, voice hitched low in his throat. 'Let me see...'

He gripped her right shoulder and buttock, turning her onto her side. She whimpered, uselessly.

'You know what I want. There. That's it. Oh.' His voice quivered with excitement, now, as his hands caressed her shoulder in a long, slow slalom down to the small of her back, finishing just above her buttock. Becky could not turn her head to see it, but she knew he was tracing his fingers along the length of the scar. It tingled at the touch. She had just enough strength to grit her teeth.

'That's it. Where I marked you. Know that whatever happens to you, I'm going to keep this part. I'll cut it out, preserve it, and keep it safe. Like a flower pressed in a book. It will live forever. That's one part of you that will escape the earth. And the worms.'

He allowed her to slump back onto the pillow, head lolling. His breathing became harsh, the eyes darting over her body with some urgency.

'Now we begin,' he said. 'Now we're together.'

Then he took up the knife. If she had one wish, it would be that she could scream, just once.

That was when one of the phones ranked on top of her dresser rang.

The sound of Micky Mouse whistling in *Steamboat Willie* caused the man in the mask to flinch in surprise.

The phone's lockscreen flashed as the handset jolted into life, jostling its stablemates.

The police phone.

He crossed over to the dresser and peered at the handset. 'Interesting,' he whispered.

Becky's voice hitched and caught once, twice. With one more huge effort, lightning pulsed across her visual field as she said, in a voice like grinding metal: 'You're... fucked.'

He crossed over to the net curtains and peered out.

The phone rang off. Then the intercom buzzed, long and hard. Then it buzzed again. A voice sounded at the speaker.

'Becky?'

It was Labelle. Labelle was at her door.

'Becky, are you in there? Is everything all right? We need to talk to you.'

'Little bitch. Lucky little bitch.' His shoulders quivered with rage, his fist tightened on the knife handle, and she thought: now he must stab me. He has to.

But he didn't. He turned to a holdall he had left on the floor, unzipped it, and stuffed in her machete. Then he threw the quilt back over her, before turning his back and removing the mask, giving her a view of white hair with patches of black. He pulled a beanie hat over his head, then threw the mask, the knife and then her teacup into the holdall. Without looking back, he whispered, 'Until next time. It will be very soon. I'll get you. You can't hide forever.'

'Neither can you,' she breathed.

He vanished into her front room. He snatched something off the kitchen counter – teabags? – then she heard the balcony door slide open. The wind howled.

The intercom buzzed again. 'Becky? We're coming up. We're going to come in.'

A short farce ensued as the door crashed, heaved and buckled. Becky had barely moved, only managing to turn her head to the side.

Labelle and Marcus thundered along the corridor before finally finding the room; light flooded the scene. Becky could only half-close her eyes against the glare.

'Holy shit,' Marcus said, his face pale. 'I think she's dead.'

Labelle was aghast. 'Becky – are you all right? There was a report of a prowler in your street. We were in town. Becky, can you hear me?'

Labelle lifted Becky and her head sagged at an awkward angle, the replaced quilt sagging off one shoulder. She croaked, 'He was here. The balcony!'

Marcus sprinted for the corridor. The wind howled again as the balcony door slid open.

Marcus returned, shaking his head. 'Nothing. And if there was someone out there – he must have been Batman to get over the roof, or land on the ground.'

Becky's head leaned against Labelle's shoulder. The detective smoothed back her hair, tenderly. 'Becky, what's wrong? What's the matter with you?'

Marcus snorted. 'It's obvious, isn't it? She's drunk. Let her sober up. We'll give her the news in the morning.'

'Shut your mouth,' Labelle barked. 'And get out of this room. She's not decent. I'll get her clothes on and we'll take her somewhere safe.'

# 50

Becky tried to sit up straight. She was in a cosy but functional little room. It was warm and sunny beyond the window, but a chill clung to her that no amount of heat or layers of clothing could remove, as if she'd been for a long swim. She took sips of warm tea, her hands shivering.

Inspector Hanlon, Labelle and Marcus faced her across a table. They'd spared her the harsh lighting of the interview rooms, but Becky's eyes and head still hurt.

'Tell me this, though,' she said. 'I was right about the burial site in Spain, wasn't I?'

Hanlon leaned forward. 'Yes, you were right. But we don't know that there is any link between that case and yours.'

Becky glared at him. 'You know I'm right. You know the man who killed my family is the same man who abducted and murdered other families across Europe. Who knows how far he's travelled; how much he's done?'

'As I said,' Hanlon continued calmly, 'we're looking into everything.'

'And what about the gaps in the database? The evidence removed from your files? I'm guessing they simply don't exist in paper form.'

Marcus frowned. 'How do you know about this?'

'Newsflash – I'm a journalist. I did some digging. My job, in other words.'

'And does "digging" mean "hacking"?'

'Oh, take a wild guess, hotshot. Christ's sake, I've done your job for you, and you still just sit there chewing your own face! What's the *matter* with you? Don't you want to catch this fucker?'

'We'll come back to that,' Labelle said, placatingly. 'I promise, we're doubling back on every case file, checking everyone who's accessed it over the years.'

'You'll find nothing,' Becky said. 'But with the gaps, you can triangulate. You can at least look at when and how he managed to remove your records.'

'He's a policeman, you're saying?' Hanlon asked. His tone was neutral.

'Not necessarily, though if I was to put a bet on it, that's where my money goes. If he is a policeman, he's not a bobby on the beat, or even a detective. He's most likely in admin, maybe IT, a computer expert. If he's not, then he's working with someone who is.'

'We'll check every angle,' Marcus said. 'Be sure of it.'

'I wish I was.'

Labelle said: 'Regarding your prowler, someone called to say they'd seen a man lingering on the stairwell of the building, shortly before the stairhead lights were cut off. No firm description – a tall man dressed in black, is as much as we were able to get.'

'CCTV?'

'Nothing,' said Labelle. 'Not in the building, and nothing in the streets nearby. It shows the lights going off in the stairwells, the timestamp is pristine. No sign of anyone coming into the building after you arrived until we appeared.'

'And you'll find the same on my computer, minutes before it cuts out. It's as if he wasn't there. He's extremely clever. He managed to hack into my security system, and the building's.'

Marcus took a deep breath. 'There was also no evidence so far of anyone being in your room. The only thing to note was that your balcony was unlocked.'

Becky sighed. 'From memory, there's a drainpipe which he could climb down to the flat below, which was empty… in fact, that's more than likely where he was hiding all along. He's still agile. I can say that for a certainty.'

Marcus nodded. 'We checked that. There's no sign anyone's been there since a letting agent arrived to check over the place two weeks ago. No electricity usage, nothing.'

'Okay. Maybe he bypassed the flat, and just dropped down onto the grass… in fact, that's possibly what he did. He's shown some skills in getting into and out of difficult places. He probably dropped onto the patch of grass in the garden, then vaulted the wall. Difficult, but he could have done it. It's a plausible solution.'

'It could be that.' Marcus' mouth slanted. He couldn't help himself. 'Or it could be that he was Spider-Man.'

'Look, I know how it must look to you. But I can assure you he was there.'

'You suffer from night terrors, don't you?' Marcus asked. 'This is from statements you gave recently on the anniversary of the killings. You see figures coming into your room, dark shadows. Is it possible...?'

'No, it's not possible.'

Labelle coughed, and her eyes met Hanlon's for a second. 'Becky... can we ask about your drinking? You seemed very confused at the flat.'

'I told you why that was. And I didn't call you – someone else did. To report a prowler.'

'The person who called didn't give their details,' Marcus said.

'Well, it wasn't me, was it?' she spluttered. Then she realised what he had said. 'You don't believe me. You think I called for help, but I didn't need it.'

'No one's said that.'

'You don't have to.' Becky got to her feet and winced as a bolt of pain shot through her. She needed a bath; to sink up to her neck in it. This was a comedown from the drugs he had used. She entertained a slight fear it might never wear off. 'Do you think I'm making all this up? A cry for attention, maybe?'

Labelle got up but held back from patting Becky on the arm. 'No one's said any of these things. We have to ask questions because we want to catch this man. We believe someone was in your house. We believe you. Okay?'

'The bollocks you do.'

'*I* believe you.'

'Then why don't you do what I say? Check the information trail. If he's not behind it, someone close to him is. Someone who's part of his group – the same group Edwin Galbraith was in.'

'He checked out,' Marcus replied. 'We've looked, very closely – there's no trail whatsoever. Edwin Galbraith isn't linked to any crimes. He may have had some strange interests, and his wife backs this up, but he was not a criminal. He was depressive, if you must know. His medical records show a history of treatment.'

'And why do you suppose he's not linked to any crimes? Why do you suppose all reference to him has been deleted off the dark web? It wouldn't surprise me if his suicide was staged.'

'Listen to yourself,' Marcus said, not unreasonably. 'Everything you're looking at seems to tie in to this man you're hunting. Everything, in your view. You've uncovered this big web of lies and deceit which no other police officer has. In thirty years, all these inquiries, all these police officers… thousands of hours, millions of pounds… somehow, you think it's all connected to you. Then you claim the guy has been in your house, but there's no sign of a break-in.'

'What about the library in Romania?'

'No one saw anything. According to the librarian, you pushed over some library racks and went crazy.'

'That's nonsense, absolute nonsense… the lady was there, the librarian. She *saw* the guy come in. She must have a description… There was another man there, too. He speaks good English. Ask them.'

'We did. They saw nothing.'

'And the guy that broke into my hotel room?'

'A burglar. A flat was broken into across the road, a couple of hours later. There's been a spate of break-ins in the past year or so in that area. Pretty standard.'

'What about the face on the photo?'

'It's indistinct. What we can see doesn't match anything on our files... facial recognition turned up a blank.'

'I don't believe this. Fullerton's daughter – Christ, you've got to give me that.'

Labelle cleared her throat. 'She got in touch.'

'Your arse, she did!' Becky spluttered. 'Did you actually speak to her?'

'Yes,' Labelle said, quietly. 'There was a misunderstanding. On several levels. She played a trick on her father; walked out after he wouldn't give her money for a gap year.'

'A cry for help,' Marcus said.

'She ran off with a boyfriend,' Labelle continued. 'She left cryptic messages about being "taken away". You misunderstood what Fullerton said. He misunderstood what she meant by her note. Nothing more. There's no kidnapping. We've *spoken* to her.'

'I can't understand it. I don't believe you've been taken in by this. Knowing what you know. I just don't believe it.'

Marcus leaned forward. 'No, you don't, do you? As far as you're concerned, it doesn't add up, unless it relates to you. And that's the problem. Only you can see this big conspiracy. Maybe you should start believing what you see and hear instead? The hard evidence, in other words.'

'Don't say another word to me.'

He sighed. 'Becky, I don't doubt you've done amazing things. You've struck on something – on your own initiative, you've found a burial site. You've turned up a link which we are now taking seriously. As far as catching your guy goes, the one good piece of intelligence you've given us relates to the standing stones, and stone circles. That does seem to match up. There's something in there that we can work with. There are links between the cases, we're starting to believe that now. It may bring us closer to the killer. And I accept, there is something odd about the missing data on our computer systems. But you've got to be objective about the rest...'

'How objective do I need to be? He was in my room! He's attacked me twice! Oh, bollocks to it. This is a waste of fucking time.' She turned to Hanlon. 'You agreeing with this?'

Hanlon folded his hands and sighed heavily. Becky stood up before he could speak and headed for the door.

'Wait a second,' Marcus snarled. 'Wait and listen. Listen to my point of view. There's possibly a link between the cases. Possibly. But all the same, you're making a lot of leaps of logic.'

'Are you even paying attention to what I say?'

'Yes,' he snapped, 'in great detail. And every instinct is telling me you know more than you are telling us. I want you to tell me something new – something I can use. Why don't you tell us how you found all this stuff out? What is *your* link? What's the source? Are you withholding something? For your book, perhaps? Or is there another reason?'

'Everything I know about this guy, I've already told you. It's up to you to chase it. You're the police, not me.'

Marcus checked himself; he bit at the side of his mouth in frustration. *Something went wrong in the weaning there,* Becky thought.

'We're doing everything we can, Becky,' Labelle said.

'Good. Please keep me informed.'

'Wait,' Hanlon said. 'Before you go – do you have somewhere to stay? We'll be carrying out tests on your flat – you can't go back. Not tonight, anyway. You'll also be given police protection for the time being.'

'I'm not sure,' Becky said. 'And protection won't be necessary. He'll assume I'll be under police guard, for the time being. I'm probably about as safe as I can be, for now. I'll see myself out.'

She felt the phone shiver in her pocket – the clean one she'd kept hidden in her car. Only Bernard had the number. She called him back as she sat in the car.

'Becky? Everything all right? I couldn't get through. I was worried.'

'Everything's okay, Bernard. I guess. Listen, before you start, I need you to find somewhere safe to stay. I've been as careful as I can be, but all my data might have been compromised… everything. And he's looking for you. Same way he was looking for Rupert. He's a hacker, I think, and a good one – maybe as good as you guys, or better. Either that, or he knows a hacker. He knew Rupert was poking around some files that related to him and tracked him down from that. He might have access to better equipment, better systems. Government grade. You're in danger. So's Rosie. Jesus…' She pinched the bridge of her nose, and shivered. 'And it's all my fault.'

'Wait, it's okay. It's all right. I've got him.'

'Say again?'

'I've got him. It took a while. I fed in the name you gave me… Nico Arkanescu? I ran a fuzzy search. It's like what we use to crack passwords. Instead of swapping letters for numbers or other characters, I messed around with different spellings. It looks at English variants, French variants... really, really clever software. This guy I know in Belgium wrote it.'

'Skip that. You said you'd got him? Who is he?'

'Nicholas Arthur. That's the name he's using now. And get this. He's a consultant, a freelancer, but he works at Interpol. He lives in Brussels. Born in Bucharest. Changed his name. That much is on file, buried very deep. A paper scan that was made recently from old records. He maybe doesn't know about that, so he couldn't remove it. But there's nothing else, I've checked – no sign of his birthdate, birth certificate, nothing. That's weird. It looks like he's probably physically removed the rest. You thinking what I'm thinking?'

Her hands shook as she scribbled down a note. 'Yes. I think I am.'

'You going to tell the police?'

The pen wriggled out of Becky's fingers and rolled into the footwell of her car. She clenched her fist. 'Not yet.'

# 51

The man at the front desk seemed too young for his suit, as well as his job. The collars reached up high into his chin like a pair of encircling hands.

'Do you have an appointment?'

'I don't – I'm happy to wait.' Becky had dressed up for the occasion, and she allowed what she hoped was a dazzling smile to break over her face.

Poor boy; he actually blushed. 'It's very unusual for us to take visitors here – it is not a working police station where you can just walk in.'

'It is a police station, though, isn't it? I have some vital information about an investigation.'

'Which one?'

'The inquiry which is ongoing at the dig site in Spain. Plus the Becky Morgan probe.'

The young man's fingers didn't skip a beat on the keyboard. He accessed something, frowned, then looked up at Becky.

'That's right. I'm Becky Morgan.' She smiled again.

'Why don't you take a seat? I'll see if Mr Arthur is busy.'

'That'd be fine.'

Each exit was watched; if not by Rosie Banning and Bernard by the main doors, then by two private investigators she had hired. No one knew what Mr Nicolas Arthur looked like – no pictures of him existed anywhere on the net, and there was certainly nothing on the Europol site – but anyone leaving in a hurry would be noticed, and every detail recorded. Tracking him and having him arrested from there would be an easy matter. ('Unless the bugger invented teleportation,' Bernard had added.)

After a while the young man turned to Becky. 'Mr Arthur is free at the moment,' he said, pleasantly. 'He'll be happy to see you now. Hold on and I'll provide you with a guest pass.'

Becky was squeezing a rubber ball in her right hand; she switched it to her left, smiled again, and took the pass while the young man on reception buzzed her through.

She was perfectly calm as she followed the lift to the third floor, as directed, and was prepared for someone ambushing her on the first and second floors. No one appeared; nor did the lift plunge near the top, a scenario which she had envisaged as being unlikely but not impossible.

The foyer was bright, well-lit and thickly carpeted; even the security door seemed warm and inviting. 'Information Technology', said the sign.

Becky waved her pass in front of a sensor, and the door clicked open.

She strode through the corridor, scanning every face she passed. One tall, broad man in a plaid shirt was pouring coffee at a machine set up on a counter. He turned to flirt with a girl who stood alongside him, and his shy grin, as much as his pudgy face and blond beard, told Becky he wasn't the one she was looking for.

Third door on the right was his office; a silver sign proclaimed the name. Before she could knock, the door opened, and Mr Nicolas Arthur appeared.

His face registered shock. 'Oh. It's you.'

'Yes.' She took a second or two to recover. 'And you are?'

'Nicolas Arthur.' He extended a hand; Becky took it. 'Won't you come in?'

He offered her a seat at his desk. The office was tidy, almost obsessively so. The glass in a set of broad internal windows allowed only the merest silhouettes to pass along the corridor outside. Along with the sparse furniture, it reminded Becky of a Japanese dojo. Robes, steaming cups of tea and gorgeous, servile women would have completed the picture.

'Well, this is unexpected,' Nicolas Arthur said, sitting opposite Becky at the desk. 'What can we do for you?'

It wasn't him, of course. How could it have been? If Nicolas Arthur wasn't the brother of the boy on reception, then he could easily have been his classmate. Finding that policemen were getting younger and younger was an old canard, but thinking that the IT guy was young was a new one on Becky. He was thick around the face, but it looked like puppy fat rather than good living, as if his flesh was taking a while to settle into its surroundings. He was about an inch shorter than Becky, thick round the chest and shoulders, and a pair of thin-rimmed spectacles clung to his nose. The accent was thick, and difficult to place – Polish, perhaps – but it wasn't the voice she knew.

In a prominent position on the desk – perhaps a little too prominent – was a picture of Nicholas with a pretty blonde girl with a gap in her teeth. A compact desktop computer and monitor were the only other things on the desk – no folderol, no notepads, no coffee rings. His hands, folded on the desk in front of him, were tiny, pink and babyish. It simply wasn't him.

She hadn't actually prepared for this eventuality. 'I just wanted to give you some information about the missing data in the investigation.'

'Oh!' He leaned forwards. 'That's causing us quite a headache.'

'Yes... I believe you were hacked.'

He paused. 'I'm not authorised to give you any information, of course, but... yes, it'd be safe to say we've been accessed.'

'I have a tip from an anonymous source that your personal data has been hacked.'

'Mine?'

'Yes. Nothing serious, just your personal profile. Apparently you are from Bucharest?'

He laughed. 'Something I am asked a lot. I was born there, but my family moved after Ceaușescu died. I've lived in Germany most of my life. The accent is odd, I know.'

'Nicolas Arthur is your real name?'

'No, my real name is Angelo Ianescu. My mother changed it when we moved abroad. Wanted to sound English, would you believe. Thought it would open doors for her.' He shook his head, laughing.

'And it also says you were born in 1954?'

'Really?' He turned to the computer. 'Where?'

'It's buried in an old version of the main site. Not cached, I might add; it must have been dumped during a redesign.'

'I wasn't born in 1954,' he chuckled. 'I was born in 1984. For all our firewalls and passwords and encryption, there is no defence against a typo.'

'You've been working here a while?'

'Ten years. Long enough to get laugh lines,' he deadpanned. Becky smiled, unable to help herself.

'I found it odd that there's no mention of you anywhere.'

'Well, there's a reason for that,' he said, becoming serious. 'IT is important to police investigations, I don't need to tell you that. Our department and others across the service are becoming more and more like undercover operations. We're under attack by hackers all the time – we've got to be alert and stay on top of the game. We've got people placed with various networks, of course, but we have to make sure we don't get broken into. In your case, it looks like we were unsuccessful.'

'Could the breach have come from inside here?'

Arthur drummed his fingers on the desk. 'We can't rule that out. But we do know that the breaches pre-date our move to this office, and there appears to have been nothing in the past ten years. Our old offices were just round the block. It was so much easier to hack information then – if you knew what you were doing. There is another explanation, one that's quite embarrassing for us, if true.'

'Go on.'

'Carelessness. A lot of the data in your case files was scanned or re-typed manually from handwritten reports, or placed on old computer discs which became corrupt over time. It has happened before, and the trail of missing files does follow a recognisable pattern. Documents are misplaced, or filed in the wrong place, or records are not properly digitised. There are crimes committed every day; it's a big task to feed everything into a computer system from incidents which happened decades ago. But,' he added, raising a hand, 'your case was particularly high profile and it has always had active elements. So we would never rule out something fishy going on.'

'I see.'

It wasn't him; it couldn't be. She only had to look at his face. The realisation was taking its time to sink in. 'Well, I thought I was bringing you some more information.'

'And, I'm guessing, you came to see the guy in charge, too. Would that be right?' He was still pleasant and open, still smiling. 'I'm also guessing you're investigating in your own right. Well, let me say – I don't blame you at all. I would, if it was me. But I want you to know that this isn't just a matter of showing up for a job, for me. People are absolutely appalled by what happened to you, *appalled*. There are decent people out there, and decent people in this building, too. We're desperate to help you find this guy. And we will.'

'Thank you,' she said, in a voice close to a croak.

When he saw her to the door, she almost expected him to hug her, but he only shook her hand and passed a business card. 'Please don't hesitate to call me if there's anything you need. As you can see, where you're concerned, you don't need an appointment.'

Twenty minutes later, she was having coffee with Bernard and Rosie Banning.

'Not him,' she said simply.

'Definitely?' Rosie arched an eyebrow. 'Could it possibly have been him? Height, voice, anything that matches at all? You were drugged, the last time you met.'

'No, it's not him. He was young, pudgy. Quite sweet.'

'How about the profile we dug out?' Bernard mumbled, midway through a forkful of three bean salad. 'What about his age, the name? It all ties in with the guy you're looking for.'

'He explained that – the date of birth is a typo, apparently. And they don't show faces or data on the website. Security issues. Strange that they should for so many of his colleagues. Loads of them have official Facebook and Twitter accounts, explaining exactly what they do.'

Rosie's eyes narrowed. 'What are you saying?'

'He was telling me an absolute pack of lies,' Becky said. 'Isn't it obvious?'

## 52

Becky was just in time. She'd already seen a van go down the driveway and took advantage of the open gate to walk up to the door. The house was two storeys, bulky and sprawling, dumped in the middle of suspiciously trim lawns. The curtains on the lower level were drawn back from the windows to show a house cleared of furniture, floorboards bare, walls magnolia. Becky imagined she could smell paint.

A small woman emerged from the front door, blonde and in her fifties but extremely fit-looking with high, severe cheekbones. Becky supposed she wore casual clothes, but they still looked expensive; the jeans alone looked very high-end. She was followed by a young man carrying a pile of box files, the uppermost balanced beneath a fashionably stubbled chin. 'Just in the back of my car with those,' the woman said, unlocking a Land Rover parked on the driveway for him. Then she saw Becky, and she frowned.

'Yes? Can I help you?'

'My name is Becky Morgan. I'm here to talk about your husband.'

The frown deepened. 'I recognise you from somewhere, don't I?'

'I was with your husband shortly before he died.'

Realisation smoothed the frown on her face. 'I know you, now. Becky Morgan. That's your name. They identified you, you know. From the CCTV with my husband. Then there were more stories. That business with your family. I've been reading lots about you.' Mrs Galbraith's tone was neutral.

The young man with the pile of box files glanced uneasily at Becky as he struggled to release them one by one into the boot of the Range Rover. She moved to give him a hand, instinctively.

'No, don't bother,' the woman said, raising a hand. 'Stay exactly where you are. You're a reporter, yes?'

'I work for a newspaper, yes.'

'Then you can turn round and leave my property, please, or I'll call the police.'

'I'm not here on a story.'

'I don't care why you're here. Get out.'

'I want to talk to you about the day he died.'

The woman sighed, and her neck muscles tensed; she was gym-strong, toned thanks to a lifestyle of spin classes and pilates, but the lines on her neck gave away her age. *Now what does that remind me of?*

'There's nothing you have to say to me about the day he died, I can assure you.'

'There is. The inquest verdict was suicide, wasn't it?'

'You know very well what the verdict was.'

'I don't believe Edwin Galbraith committed suicide.'

The woman took a step closer. Becky suppressed a desire to put some distance between her and Mrs Galbraith. Her face was very close to Becky's, and two grey eyes peered into hers. 'And just how do you think he died?'

'I think he was murdered. By the same person who killed my family.'

The man with the box files called out; Angelica Galbraith dismissed him with a wave and he disappeared back into the house. 'I read about your family,' she said, at length. 'Dreadful business. I can't imagine having to go through something like that.'

'It's all relative. I can't imagine having to go through what you did, either.'

'Finding him... hasn't been good for me,' Mrs Galbraith said. 'Not that it was a violent scene, of course. Exhaust pipe through the window. Classic, really. He looked as if he was fast asleep. I'm only glad our children weren't home. So how do you think someone managed to kill Eddie?'

'Your husband was mixed up in something horrible. He was the weak link, and he was about to be exposed. So he had to go.'

'I've read all about you,' Mrs Galbraith said, brisk and businesslike as a school headmistress. 'It seems you're writing a book about your experiences, aren't you? Your search for the killer.'

'I'm not really writing a book. You may be mixing me up with a colleague. But I do want to find the man who did it. I am almost sure your husband was killed. Maybe to order; maybe because he knew too much. There were drugs in his system, weren't there? A cocktail of opiates, something to sap him of energy, to knock him out for a while.'

'Yes. He took something to make his passing... comfortable. Hardly a method chosen by a psychopathic killer, is it?'

'He might have been drugged. The killer's clever, Mrs Galbraith. And he's always well prepared. He's got all the cards. But he's starting to play them badly, and he's getting worried. Your husband was murdered. I aim to prove it, in time.'

'And my husband associated with a killer, did he?'

'Yes. He was mixed up in a bad business. I'm sure of it.' Becky took a half-step forward. It gave her no satisfaction when Mrs Galbraith flinched. 'And you know he was, don't you? You found something. Or suspected something. What wife wouldn't?'

Angelica Galbraith glanced down towards the paving stones, plucked free of weeds and altogether too bright for a well-trodden pathway. They'd been cleaned. 'Come inside,' she said.

There was a kettle and some cups left in the kitchen, a room roughly the same size as Becky's entire flat. Mrs Galbraith offered to make tea. Becky chose to have a glass of water.

The man in the plaid shirt passed by the doorway, boxes braced on his shoulders. 'Is that your son?' Becky asked Mrs Galbraith.

The woman ignored this. 'So. You were saying?'

'You found something. About your husband.'

'It wasn't something I found,' Mrs Galbraith said. 'It was something that was missing.'

'Like what?'

'Not a physical thing… just a lack of something. Files had been deleted on our desktop computer. He had them encrypted. I never pried into those, believe it or not, but I was always curious.'

'If he killed himself, I guess it could be possible he deleted something he didn't want you to see before he did it,' Becky suggested.

'That crossed my mind. Then it turned out that my computer had been tampered with, too. I got my son to look into it – he works in computer technology. He showed that someone had accessed the computer while I was out, at roughly the same time as the desktop computer was last accessed.'

'What would they have been looking for?'

'I don't know. It was odd, though. Eddie didn't even know where I kept my machine, that's the thing. And the locks on the balcony door stick a little now, where they hadn't before. It's possible someone broke in.'

'Did you have any suspicions about your husband?' Becky said gently. 'I'm sorry to ask. I need to know. If there's anything, anything at all… it could help find the man who killed him.'

'Nothing concrete,' Mrs Galbraith said. 'Just suspicions. The things you get suspicious about, but don't follow up on. Times that didn't add up; when he was working late, apparently, except I called his office and he wasn't in. I suspected an affair. What do you think he was mixed up in?'

'I'm not sure. Is there anything at all in his personal papers that can help? Did he have any interests or join any clubs?'

Galbraith shook her head. Then she brightened. 'He was into classical music – that's about all I can think of. I don't like it. Too dull. Our house sounded like a dentist's waiting room at the best of times. I like rock n' roll stars, myself. Bad boys.' Her smile was brittle. 'But classical was his passion. He was forever going to shows and recitals. Concert halls, orchestras.'

Several beats passed. 'Did he have any concerts lined up?'

'As a matter of fact, he did. He got tickets through for a show of some kind.'

'Do you still have them?'

'Right over here in the drawer. Found it wedged in between the bills. You'd think he'd hidden it.'

She crossed over to a drawer set underneath the slate-coloured kitchen worktop, and brought out an envelope. Inside was a ticket, black embossed cardboard with golden lettering. It looked like it had been hand-crafted, not printed and torn off. 'Here it is. Ticket for one. Doesn't mention a venue, though.'

*Command performance*, said the golden lettering.

*January Orchestra.*

No venue, and barring some filigree round the scalloped bordering, there was nothing save for an odd cruciform symbol in the bottom left hand corner.

# 53

She was a tall girl with glorious glossy black hair that induced an alien kick of jealousy in Becky. She had a delicate nose, full lips, coffee-coloured eyes and an almost maddeningly perfect complexion.

*She's still got some growing to do. She'll get lovelier still. She's a real credit to him.*

Still clad in her school uniform, the girl had gone into a newsagent's to buy a magazine; outside, she'd said goodbye to some friends – among them two or three spotty, scampering males who jabbed and elbowed each other, so far out of her league it was tragic. The girl perched on the seat in a bus shelter and idly watched their performances. The front cover of her magazine was completely dominated by a brutal close-up of a glossy, ebony face, a study in feline cool. Becky didn't recognise the model, but she clearly needed no introduction to readers.

The expression on the model's face and on the girl's above were curiously matched. Becky started the car and crept down the street, pulling up alongside her. The teenager squinted, an unconsciously hard expression in which she most clearly resembled her father, as Becky rolled down the window.

'Hey, Lisa.'

'Becky?'

'You heading home? Get in, I'm on the way. I'll take you.'

Lisa slid her long frame into the passenger seat with some difficulty, having to adjust the seat to allow her legs.

'Sorry,' Becky said, 'usually that seat's just for my bag and pints of milk I pick up at the shop. Is your dad home today?'

'I think so,' she said. The girl seemed ill-at-ease next to her, but then she always had, after she'd grown old enough to be told what happed to Auntie Becky.

It was a short journey from the town centre into the village, set in the midst of farmers' fields and tussles of forest. It was a quiet little town with whitewashed brickwork and even one or two thatched roofs, a place that warmed your heart despite its clear tweeness. Sullen stacks of smoke climbed from chimneys, even in these warmer days, and Becky recalled with a shudder a very bleary night or two in The Cherry Blossom pub a decade or so ago.

Was she still barred? In a town like this, that might extend over several generations.

'Have you had much luck with the case?' Lisa asked.

'Bits and pieces. There's a link between what happened with my family and one or two others.'

'I read about that in the paper. I hope you catch him.'

'I'll catch him.' Becky felt the hairs on the back of her neck stir. To say it aloud was a bold act. She had rarely articulated it before. The very statement dared admit to her rising hope.

He was out in the garden in their compact, but sturdy bungalow, pulling weeds out of the flower beds running along one side of the front garden. He wore a bell-bottomed polo shirt which had probably been old when Becky was young, and a pair of fag-burned trousers turned up above some flakey golf shoes of a similar vintage. She heard him grunt as she pulled up behind him. He frowned at the car, taking a while to recognise the faces behind the windscreen.

He wiped his hands on his trousers as he greeted them. 'Becky. This is a wee surprise.'

'I was just bobbing around. Thought I'd come in to say hello. You free for a chat?'

She was ushered into a kitchen dinette area. The Formica-topped tables and red benches, installed around 1989, had an American diner feel to them. They were of an age to be paroled from the 'naff' zone and cross over into 'kitsch'.

Becky accepted an offer of a cup of tea, and was relieved when Lisa, changed into Lycra, headed out for a run.

'Mel not home?' she asked, as Jack Tullington slid into the seat opposite her. Perhaps it was the lack of the large overcoat and hat he usually wore, but the man seemed somewhat reduced, as if his shoulders had accordioned in towards his neck. He'd always looked old to Becky, but never less than sturdy.

'Mel? She's off to her mother's. She's been gone a couple of days. The old dear doesn't keep so well. Getting on a bit.'

'Sorry to hear that.' Becky nodded out of the window, where Lisa's head could be seen bobbing past above the fence outside, at a keen twelve miles per hour. 'You know, that's the first time I've seen Lisa in years. She in her senior year at school, now?'

'Just about. Be at uni soon. Time flies, eh?'

'She's going to be a real beauty. Six-footer already, hey?'

'The height comes from her mother's side, you won't be shocked to discover.' He chuckled, but his body language was wrong, hunched, defensive. Maybe it was because he was out of context; perhaps it was because he was missing his hat. Grey curls straggled round his balding head, fringing his ears like bent spokes on a bicycle. 'Now – since we parted on such bad terms last time, why don't you tell me why you're here?'

She took a deep breath. 'I wanted to apologise. When I accused you of having me followed. I know it wasn't you.'

He relaxed a little. 'It was a tad harsh. But I forgive you, lassie. Want to tell me who *did* have you followed?'

'Your brother, of course. It was a real breakthrough in the case.'

'My brother? Angus?'

'That's right. The guy who made all the property deals. The guy who was putting together the package for the property through in France. Along with the French connection, LaFleur.'

Jack's eyes narrowed. 'What property through in France?'

'Oh, come on. Don't play dumb with me, Jack.'

'Angus had his fingers in a few pies, both before and after he left the police, I won't deny it. But we haven't been close for a long time.'

'No, I gather you fell out round about when my family died.' She sipped her tea, studying him closely.

'We're brothers. Brothers sometimes fight. Angus is a strange guy.'

'Strange guy is right. Two terms in prison – one for fraud, one for assault and battery. That's ignoring all the minor things on his record. Not bad for a former copper, even if he was bent. I wonder if he was a good source for you – all that Glasgow gangster stuff you made your name on, back in the day.'

'It was all a long time ago,' Jack said. 'He was a daft boy, but he learned his lesson. He made good.'

'He did – it seems he moved on from crime to property development. It's not too great a leap of the imagination, to be fair. I can think of a few estate agents I'd have in the stocks, if not prison.'

Jack sighed. His chest and shoulders seemed to inflate to their usual elephantine frame. 'Becky, love, I'll do anything for you. I *swore* I'd do anything for you. And I'll make good on that until the day I die. But so help me god, don't insult me and my family in my own fucking house.' His shoulders sagged, then, just a little. 'What is your point?'

'My point is that your brother involved my father in an investment scheme over some property in and around Europe. It seems that the deal wasn't quite on the level – shady enough for my dad to want to pull out. He was worried it amounted to little more than a Ponzi scheme. But before he decided to withdraw the money, he checked the area out for himself, by taking a little holiday there. He brought his family out with him. The idea was to check out possible locations for a new hotel – a side project he had, supposedly without your Angus' knowledge. A fact-finding mission, and a family holiday, rolled into one. And on that very holiday, they were all slaughtered. Except me.'

'And you're saying the two things are linked? The investment and the murders?'

'Only circumstantially, I thought. And then I checked out other property links connected with your brother. One in particular got my interest. A housing development on a flood plain, in clear breach of planning regulations. Bogland. Your brother managed to get it through council planners – but one of the investors got cold feet. Guess what happened?'

'Do tell.'

'He and his family vanished. Not a trace of them. Their house was quite close to some ancient standing stones. There's even a tumulus nearby. Pre-Roman. Fascinating stuff. I think it's been on a BBC4 documentary.'

'Are you suggesting that... my brother, Angus... is the man who killed your family?'

'Not at all. I'm saying that the guy he hired to do it killed my family. And a few others, too.'

Jack laughed, shaking his head. 'What reason could Angus have for killing your family?'

'Money, obviously. Staying out of jail, for another. My dad was committed to the deal before he went on holiday, but not in writing. He had made it known to his solicitor and various accountants that he was thinking of pulling out of the main funding deal – even stated openly that he thought there was some fraud involved, that he might be being ripped off. After he died, Angus found another gullible partner and it all went through. Angus got all the money. Just like he got the cash for the houses on the flood plains.'

'This is ridiculous, Becky. It's fantasy world stuff, this. Your parents and your brother and sister weren't assassinated – they were murdered by a lunatic. Totally different thing, surely.'

'Not for the guy I'm looking for. It's what he did for a living, as well as a hobby, when he came to the west. I think he mingled business and pleasure for a good few years.'

'The guy you're looking for, you say. He's a copper, you say. No, wait, he's a contract killer. What's he going to be next, a taxi driver? An airline pilot? A fucking deep-sea diver? How about an astronaut? I've got it – the killer is Mr Ben!'

'Now you're insulting *me,* Jack.'

'This sounds like madness, Becky. You reckon this guy, this international serial killer and now contract hitman, breaks into your flat...'

'How do you know about that?' Becky asked, sharply.

'The same way you know about things – I'm a journalist. I talked to some sources. You know what they said to me? "The Morgan lass is cracking up. Wild goose chases. Seeing devils everywhere."'

'Well, the next time you see your source, ask them how this crackpot managed to turn up evidence that was practically under their nose, and found those missing bodies. Ask them to explain that.' She got up.

'Becky, what are you going to do now? Because if you're going after Angus...'

'Is he going to snuff me out? Tell him not to worry – his man is on the case to finish what he started. I've passed what I know about Angus onto the police. I happen to know they arrested him three hours ago.'

Jack blinked.

'So, if you're in any way connected to any of his property deals, now might be the time to worry. I guess time will tell, won't it? Because I really need to know, so you may as well tell me: how much did you know, Jack? Were you involved in those deals?'

'I swear to god, barring the odd piece of chat, I didn't know about any business deals or set-ups. I'm no businessman. I wasn't interested in Angus' work out of uniform. In the early days, he was good for a tip, but little else. Your dad was interested in business, though. We all grew up together. He and Angus met up at the odd social event or wedding. Angus had some propositions, and your dad followed them up. He made money on a few of them. Money that's now in your pocket, I should add.'

'I think my dad saw the light. The letters I picked up prove it. He was going to turn Angus in. I think that's what did for him. Everything else, all the other details from the day... it was all in the execution. The perfect cover for what was really going on – who would suspect a thrill killer was actually a hitman? You'd never even consider it.'

'Becky, I'm going to ask you to leave, now. I just...' He raked his fingers over his thin-thatched scalp and trailed them down his cheeks. 'I'm always going to be here if you need help. I promised. Remember that.'

'So long as I have a doubt, I won't ask for your help. And I have a doubt, all right.' She stared at him, intensely; his eyes darted, but he did not completely look away. 'You'll get a phone call from the police, soon, I think. Just routine. But they'll ask you some questions. You might find it all a bit awkward. Good luck, Jack.'

# 54

He came out of the gym with a gaggle of female friends. Becky supposed he had more fat than all the women put together. Without glasses, his cheeks were flushed rosy pink. Some of the women hugged him before they dispersed into their cars.

'I suppose he's quite attractive,' Rosie Banning said, from the passenger seat. 'In that Harry Potterish type way.'

'I have to admit, I was thinking that. You'd have a nice cuddle on the couch on a Friday night, some wine and crisps, watch *Graham Norton*. I'd see him right.'

'Doesn't half have a lot of women round him,' Bernard said. He had opted to take the back seat of the tiny rented Fiat, and his knees practically cradled his chin. 'Don't reckon he's struggling for female company.'

'That's true,' Rosie said. 'So – gay, then?'

'Definitely gay. That'd be just my luck.'

He got into his Peugeot, put on his glasses and pulled out into traffic before Becky started the Fiat and followed him.

He was early for his appointment, having reached a handsome glass-fronted building in an industrial unit on the outskirts of the city. His cheeks were still a little flushed; he fretted over them in the mirror of his sun visor before getting out.

'Vain,' Bernard said. 'You should write that down in your notes, Rosie. "He was a very vain man..."'

'He's an actor,' Rosie said. 'It's a whole new level of vain, if you're an actor. In fact, I'll write *that* line down. That's not bad at all.' She did, too, pinging the band off a leopard-skin-sleeved notebook and scribbling a quick note.

'What now?' Bernard asked.

Becky settled back in her seat. 'Wait for him to come out. He won't be long.'

She was right; he appeared at the front door less than forty minutes later. He had a plastic cup of vending machine coffee in his hand; steam curled up from it despite the bright sunshine.

'Here we go.' Becky sprung out of the car. She didn't wait for the other two to follow her.

His eyes registered the dull, gonging shock of someone who's been caught in the act, but he quickly recovered, and smiled broadly. He switched his coffee to the other hand, and even attempted a handshake. 'Miss Morgan, isn't it?'

'That's right.' She shook his hand and smiled. 'I'm Miss Morgan. And you're not Mr Arthur.'

He frowned slightly. 'Say again, please?'

'Don't waste my time. That building's where your agent works. She's quite a good one, too. What's your next role? Got something big lined up?'

'Um, I'm actually late for a meeting, Miss Morgan. If you don't mind…'

'You're not going anywhere without me. Not before you've talked about what you were doing at Interpol, pretending to be someone else, just for my benefit.'

'I'm here on a case, in fact. Now, excuse me.'

She gripped his wrist. 'You? On a case? You don't go out on a case. You're the guy from IT. If you are who you say you are, you're a desk jockey. But I know you're not who you say you are. You're an actor – stage work, no TV just yet. Though it seems you're up for anything if the right offer comes up. Such as impersonating a policeman.'

'Get your hands off me. Or I'll call the police.'

Becky withdrew her hand. 'Hey, *I'm* going to call the police. They can decide if you've broken any laws or not. But first we're going to talk about your last commission. You'll tell me everything you know.'


As it turned out, it wasn't much. The four of them repaired to a coffee shop round the corner. Bernard sat in front of the man, whose name – his stage name, at any rate – was Willem Durning. Bernard glowered at him, gangly arms folded across his chest.

'Would you mind not doing that?' Willem asked him, a slight tremor in his voice. 'It's very intimidating.'

'I'll do more than intimidate you,' Bernard said, in a growl which crumbled like a stock cube on the last word. Rosie Banning hid a smile behind her hand.

'It's fine, Bernard' Becky said, raising a hand. 'Go and grab us all a Danish pastry or something. Willem isn't going anywhere. Are you, Willem?'

'I'll be leaving this place as soon as I've finished the coffee. I promised you a talk over coffee, and nothing more. Otherwise it's kidnapping.'

'We're in a coffee shop,' Becky said. 'How can it be kidnapping? We're just sitting here, calmly and quietly.'

'Just make sure you tell us all you know,' Bernard muttered to him, from the side of his mouth. His coffee repeated on him in a high-pitched belch as he stood up. He placed a hand to his mouth and whispered, 'Pardon'.

'Sorry for bringing the muscle in,' Becky said – shooting a glance at Rosie as she smiled, again, 'we couldn't be sure if you'd get rough or not.'

'I'll be as honest as I can – I had no firm contact with the man who hired me. He arranged everything through my agent. It was a strange deal, but the money he offered was far too good to turn down, for any of us.'

'How much?' Rosie asked. She raised her eyebrows when he told her. 'Not sure I blame you.'

'Your agent – she had a contact telephone number? An email address?'

Willem shook his head. 'No. No traceable contact details. She told me all about it – it was all a bit cloak and dagger. Initial contact by phone, no number left. It tickled her, actually – the money was left in a safety deposit box in an old storage warehouse. I guess it tickled me, too. It was so intriguing. I might as well tell you, he made us sign non-disclosure agreements, which I am now breaking.'

'I wouldn't worry about that,' Becky said. 'How about your lines – how did they come about?'

'Again, he gave me a script, urged me to learn most of the responses. Most of it was deflection. He set me up with a pass and had briefed his staff that I was in to carry out some IT work on his behalf.'

Becky drew a line under her pad. 'Well, thanks for your help. I might as well tell you, you'll be hearing from the police soon, as will your agent. I'd keep your fee in the bank, for now – it might well end up getting seized. Impersonating a police officer is a crime, as I'm sure you know.'

'I think you'll find my IT qualifications are in order, Miss Morgan,' he said.

'Yeah. That fits, I grant you. Actors have to work, at your level. Guess it beats working in a cinema. There's just that whole false name thing though, isn't there?'

A pallor had long since whitewashed Willem's gym-rosy complexion. 'This man... Mr Arthur... what has he done?'

'He's a murderer, Willem. He's murdered lots of people. Including my family.'

'Him? He's the one? The one they're looking for?'

'Yep, absolutely no doubt about it. He's a serial killer, a pervert, a contract killer... or a pleasing blend of them all. And he might well kill you. He doesn't like loose ends.'

Willem said nothing; he finished his coffee, and stood up, just as Bernard returned with a tray full of Danishes.

'Where are you going?' Bernard growled.

'Out.'

'... But I got you a Danish?' He looked at Becky uncertainly.

'Work on your technique,' Willem said, patting him on the shoulder. 'Either that, or you've been miscast. You're no tough guy, my friend.'

Once he'd gone, Rosie clapped her hands. 'We've got him, surely. We've got a name, and a job – the lot.'

'We don't have anything,' Becky said simply. 'We've got no evidence. He's been quite careful to remove it, over a period of years. You probably still couldn't trace him. False names, god knows what other identities. We've only got a theory. Even when I let Labelle and Marcus know about this, you can bet there'll be a cover story of some kind to back it up. They'll reckon I'm insane. They already do, in fact. Even when I've given them some evidence. He's careful. We need to catch him with his pants down, so to speak. Nothing will stick.'

'He's not going to start killing again, surely,' Rosie said. 'Those days are over.'

'Apart from Rupert,' Bernard said, through a mouthful of pastry.

'Who's Rupert?'

'Rupert is… one of Bernard's colleagues,' Becky said. 'He died.'

'I should bloody say he did,' Bernard said cheerfully. 'Here, I'll show you.' He brought out a smartphone.

'Don't show her that,' Becky said, clutching his wrist.

Rosie frowned. 'This Rupert, who died. You mean, our guy killed him? This was recently?'

'Yes.'

'How?'

'Chopped his head off,' Bernard said. 'Live, on air. Right in front of Becky. Used his mask and everything.'

Rosie looked shocked. 'And you didn't think to tell me? What have the police done about this?'

'Nothing,' Becky said quietly. 'It's been palmed off as some kind of drug turf war.'

'But... you saw it? This happened where, online? Bernard's got footage? What more proof do you need?'

'I didn't record it. He did – and it's been edited and overdubbed to look like some kind of drugs execution. Our guy must have made Rupert read out another script. Then he cut in the actual execution, pardon the expression, minus the mask details, before posting it online.'

Rosie clutched her throat. 'Someone's dead? Because of what we're doing? And this guy's out there, on the loose?'

'Rosie, there's nothing we can do about that, now. The police know about it, trust me. Again, there's no reason for them to link it to my case. They don't believe me.'

'Why didn't you tell *me*? Someone got fucking *executed* on camera, on your behalf, and you didn't think to say?'

'What difference would it have made?'

Rosie stabbed a finger at her. 'You're withholding things. From everyone. What else do you know that you aren't sharing with us?'

'Relax. I'm going to tell you everything. And I'll tell you how we're going to catch him. Red-handed.'

# 55

Becky leaned her head against the train window. The vibrations soothed her – even the jolts were like being rocked by a harsh mother.

'Remember when you thought travel was glamorous?' she asked, fuzzily.

'Don't sleep on us now,' Rosie said. She'd been perked up by a nice lunch, but her fires still smouldered. 'You were going to explain everything.'

Becky straightened up. 'Okay. We'll go right from the start. Rupert used some contacts in Russia to dig some stuff out – the stuff our guy couldn't get rid of by hand.

'The guy we're looking for is called Nicolai Arkanescu, AKA the Black Angel. There's your book title. Bernard? Exhibit A.'

Bernard fiddled with a tablet computer. He showed Rosie a fuzzy black and white image of a young man no older than 20 in a military cap. The image had been blown up and had lost definition as a result. The face had a long, square jaw and his eyes were shaded by a deep, dark brow.

'He was born in Bucharest in 1954. He served in the army for a while, then was recruited by the Romanian secret police. He disappeared for a number of years, possibly to the Soviet Union. We suspect this was for a spot of higher education. Exhibit B, Bernard. Now, brace yourself.'

The next image was in black and white, of hog-tied bodies. They were missing their heads; the blood looked oily in the flashbulb's sudden flare.

'He gained a reputation for carrying out political assassinations. His calling card was to remove the victims' heads. He was encouraged in this; there's some suggestion he was deployed across the former Eastern bloc to carry these out. He was an instrument of terror, often used for rogue elements within official circles. The line between police and criminality was blurred. He seemed to have been feared even *within* official circles. His record shows he was a known sexual sadist and rapist, who had taken to torturing his victims before killing them. This was passed off as a brutal tactic to extract information, but it tied in with his natural inclinations. A busman's holiday, you could say.

'The assassinations stopped sometime in the early eighties – and that's when Nicolai Arkanescu and his family were shot and burned, along with their house. Exhibit C, Bernard.'

Next came an indistinct colour image, a blackened shell of a room. Rosie had to squint to see the bones.

'I take it he didn't really die?'

'That's the theory. The long-standing rumour was that Arkanescu killed his own family after a birthday party and left a surrogate body behind. Faked his own death; probably he'd annoyed the wrong person higher up, or was fearful of someone taking revenge for his handiwork. He used this cover to defect, years before the Berlin Wall came down and Ceauşescu was shot. There were some tell-tale signs at the scene – the heads were removed, that's the big giveaway. He is known to have hated his family. He was a bullied child, with few friends at school. There are some suggestions he was abused, perhaps by his father.'

'This is quite a leap,' Rosie said.

'I agree. Sounds speculative. Until we look at the pattern of murders which started in the west, round about the eighties. We have a map of the ones we know; these include my family, the Spanish family, the family in Orkney, one in Ireland, one in Sweden, three in Germany. And now, the Gursky case in Russia. Some of these were officially solved and people were jailed, but they show a pattern that fits with what Arkanescu did in Romania in his killer kindergarten days. Torture, humiliation, death by stabbing or cut throat, or decapitation. There was also a family home torched, as was the case with the Sloan family in Orkney, with the husband made to look as if he'd done it then killed himself. The western cases were all linked to organised crime or dirty politics – because he had been hired by the gangsters involved to kill them.'

'And he went from there to somehow working with the police?'

'He did. In Germany first of all. He even solved one of his own cases, while he worked as a detective in

Dusseldorf – pinned it on another maniac, beautifully. He has an eye for opportunity – he also studied computer science back when computers still had punch cards, and set up early databases. He was commended for it.

'He moved with the times, too; at Interpol he was one of the go-to guys for IT, a father figure for the young ones, something of a legend. Then he went off-grid; then he reappeared as Nicholas Arthur, brand new building, brand new colleagues, sat in an office by himself, in a lower-level job, with no one any the wiser that the guy sat at the desk isn't actually him. His time is his own – he's wealthy enough by now to be able to set up a sock-puppet worker connected to the entire European police network, giving him all the access he could ever need to cover up what he's done. Meanwhile, he can travel round Europe, doing whatever the hell he likes.'

'So this let him cover his tracks,' Rosie said. 'Hence all the missing evidence, case files. He made it all disappear, switched some evidence round, and he answered to no one. There's nothing linking him physically with these crimes.'

'Correct. And who knows what else he messed with? He must surely have corrupted physical evidence as well as digital records. DNA samples might have gone missing or got switched... once you convert hard science to data, or once you can access archive samples and you know where they're kept, the rest is easy. He might even be thinking ahead to future court cases. If evidence is corrupted or tampered with, it's inadmissible. Perhaps he had an even larger plan, something we can't see yet. We can only guess.'

'So he just toured Europe, for a spot of rape and murder?'

'Yes. At first. But then it gets even murkier. In several cases, it seems that the families were targeted deliberately. He put his earlier skills to good use – he worked as an assassin. The Black Angel was the name he went by, according to some information he allowed to lie on file at Interpol. I reckon he was proud of that. It seems that he mingled business and pleasure, eventually. Soon it wasn't just his targets who were being killed – it was their families, too. He has a thing for families.

'In lots of cases – the Irish family; the family in Orkney; the Spanish family, and now the Gurskys – they were connected with organised crime. Rivals ordered the hit. This allowed the Black Angel – our guy, Arkanescu – to carry on doing what he enjoyed doing, and get paid well for it. The fact that these were gangland hits also helped muddy the waters. Police were more interested in the paymasters, not necessarily the assassin. When he moved into the 1990s, he was doing lots of these killings for fun, and his professional services weren't required. But he still carried out the odd hit. Including my family.'

Rosie's jaw dropped. 'You're kidding.'

'Nope. You had it right – you and the Dupin Collective. Through a family connection my dad got mixed up with the wrong person – the brother of his best friend – a former copper called Angus Tullington. An unhappy accident, you could say. Tullington a bent copper, resigned from the force with a bad reputation, then went into property – or organised crime, as many of us call it. My dad got involved in a deal Angus Tullington set up in the South of France, but the whole thing was crooked. Dirty money, tax dodges, money-laundering, and some very nasty people who wouldn't want to draw the attention of the police. My dad got cold feet and wanted out – and was considering going to the police. He also saw some other land that he liked and was considering buying it. So he mixed business with pleasure. He took us all on holiday to check it out. Term-time holiday too, I might add. And that's when Arkanescu carried out his contract on us, twenty years ago.'

'Except you got away.'

'That's right. I was a loose end. And usually he snaps those off. But for some reason, he didn't get involved. Until I did.'

'He likes toying with you. He is a sadist, after all.'

'That's true. He did say as much, to be fair.'

'You've spoken to him? Since Bernard's friend was killed?'

'More than once. He's tried to kill me twice. He's been trailing me, as surely as I've been trailing him.'

Rosie snapped: 'More bloody revelations! You might have told me!'

'I warned you when you got involved in the first place – this is a very dangerous thing you're doing. I also warned you he might come after you. You told me I was being paranoid. I said you were in this of your own free will and could get out of it any time. That's still the case. Is there any part of that you don't understand?'

Rosie was silent a moment. She gazed out of the window at the blurred countryside. 'So where are we going now?'

'We're going to a little gathering of like-minded souls.'

'The January men,' Bernard said, rattling his tongue over the consonants.

'The January *Orchestra*, actually,' Becky said.

'The sex group you found out about,' Rosie said. 'The one Edwin Galbraith was involved with.'

'He was indeed. Among other groups. He was in the Billy Goats Gruff online forum, which quite enjoys doing things to young girls dressed in school uniforms, often while they're tied up. January was something else. What, we're not quite sure. There's one reference we've been able to find. Tied to a stone circle, in northern Italy.'

'Two women got butchered there,' Bernard said. 'The most recent case.' He flashed another image up; Rosie shielded it with her hand, and turned away, sickened.

'The police were interested in the details and wondered if it was linked to my family's case, but, surprise surprise, some of the evidence gathered didn't fit. The big giveaway, as ever, is that the data on this case is sketchy; files removed, evidence missing, testimony expunged. It's all very familiar. But this involved a lot of people, not just one. This had the look of a mass ritual. Our guy's involved with the January Orchestra. He is probably paid to set it up; he's an administrator by nature, so it fits. It's a better, more discreet way of keeping his hand in, without having contact with gangsters.'

'It's a sex ring?'

'Sex and murder. The ultimate elite group for sex killers. High end dining, as they say in the Sunday supplements.'

'First we had gangsters and hitmen... Now we've got elites carrying out murder? Too far, this,' Rosie said.

'Oh, it happens,' Becky said. 'You've worked the crime desk. You know about swingers, doggers, rapists, abusers. Incest, ritual murder... stuff done by the proper, one-percenter weirdos. Speak to social workers and family lawyers – they'll open your eyes, if they still need opening. They'll tell you what goes on, and how often, in every part of the country. Then think about child sex rings, dirty politicians, bent coppers, you name it. Think about all the opportunities of the internet. If you can think about something depraved, you can bet it'll be online. It happens. They're out there, we all know it. It's happening somewhere, right now. And people co-operate with it. They enjoy it. And they cover it up.'

'Why do they do it, man?' Bernard said. 'Too risky, surely? Nowadays, with surveillance culture, DNA, forensics, technology… it's hard to get away with this stuff, now.'

'Maybe that's the juice, for them. The power. The secrecy. And it helps to have a man on the inside, covering for you. It's probably made our guy extremely rich, the connections he has. As for the rest of the January Orchestra… maybe it just works as an elaborate set of bribes, an old boys' club you wouldn't keep the old school tie for. Maybe it's like the Masons, or the little clubs you get in the blue-chip universities. Shagging pigs' heads, funny handshakes, that sort of behaviour. That sort of tribalism. Once you take a vow in these kinds of societies, you're stuck with them. And if you're a powerful person, you can expect a leg-up from people into the same stuff in the authorities. Or a rolled-up trouser leg, at least. Power creates perversion.'

'What about Edwin Galbraith?' Rosie asked.

'It seems Edwin Galbraith was too high-profile to be allowed to live. He was news – too much of a risk. I'm almost certain our guy snuffed him. But his wife was kind enough to pass something on to me.' Becky held up the January Orchestra concert bill.

Rosie studied it. 'I don't see any details. What does it all mean?'

'Took a while to crack it. Bernard figured it out.'

Bernard saluted, then pointed to a line of embossed figures on the bill, difficult to see unless the card was slanted a certain way, catching the light. 'These numbers are co-ordinates. I spotted the latitude/longitude line of figures straight away. But that latitude reference is more than 90 degrees – so it's nonsense. When I tried fuzzy logic, the nearest I could get was the middle of the ocean.'

Rosie folded her arms. 'So the theory was nonsense.'

'Not quite,' Becky said. 'There was something else I noticed when I went over the paper with a microscope. Hold it up to the light again, Bernard.'

The ticket was made of thick, expensive-looking creamy paper. Rosie studied it for a while, then pointed to the top left-hand corner. 'There's a watermark. A cross?'

'Yes. A cross. But these guys don't seem like the church-going type.' Becky turned it upside down. 'Now it's a headless cross.'

'Devil worship,' Bernard said, with a wicked gleam in his eyes. 'Everything's inverted.'

'That being the case, we spun the co-ordinates round, fed them in again. And we found… what Exhibit are we up to, Bernard?'

'E,' Bernard said, and showed a picture of a set of menhir, lodged into the earth. They were coloured by a weird shade of lichen, more yellow than green, like a late summer sunset.

'Standing stones,' Rosie said. 'In France. But further north, in the Grand Massif. Where we're going, in other words.'

'That's right. Standing stones is what he likes. I know from experience. Maybe it's a ritual thing, some evil practice that pre-dates him. Maybe it's something personal. Maybe January is an ancient club. Linked to druidic sacrifice; I don't know. But we do know that there's going to be a meeting of the club. And he'll most likely be there. I also think he might be holding a teenage girl hostage, maybe for use in the ritual – the daughter of my therapist.'

'Seriously?'

'Seriously. He somehow tracked me down and tried to get my therapist to implant false memories while he was trying to hypnotise me. I'm not that great a hypnosis subject. I knew it was bullshit from the start. I knew what he was doing... I just didn't know why.'

Rosie turned the ticket the right way up. 'This looks like a date – 6$^{th}$ January?'

Bernard grinned. His lips didn't seem to know what to do when he gave a full, unguarded grin, twitching across his teeth. 'So, turn the date into numbers, spin it round, and...?'

'Oh six, oh one... that becomes oh one, oh six... that's 1$^{st}$ June. That's next week.'

'Exactly right. So whatever January, and our friend Mr Arkanescu – or Mr Arthur, as he's now known – have in store, we can steal a few yards, set up a shitload of surveillance, and catch them all.'

'For god's sake, Becky... I know how badly you want this guy, but... why not tell the police?'

'He is the police,' Becky said, curtly. 'I admit, there's nothing to tie him to our case. And they've done little or nothing with the rest of the information I've given them.

Plus, he can make it all disappear if he really wants to. And – bearing in mind he's wired right into the system – if he gets wind of an operation, he'll get spooked, and they'll crash the whole thing, emergency pull-out. This,' she said, raising the ticket, 'will just go back to being gobbledegook, a sheet of paper which only proves I'm paranoid, and nothing will happen at the standing stones, there will be no reference to January anywhere, and I'll look like even more of a lunatic than I already do. No, we'll have to catch them red-handed. This is a chance; we have to take it. On the day, I'll live-stream it right to the police. Bernard's going to set this up. That's where we're going now.'

'It all sounds good,' Rosie said. 'But I'm not quite buying what you're saying with the police. Have you actually named him to the police? Raised your suspicions?'

'No. There's no point. He'll come out clean. Arkanescu is just a name that pops up here and there – there's nothing linking an individual named in paper files thirty-odd years ago to the individual we're looking for now. We probably don't even know the name he goes by now. I'll look like a loon. Nicolas Arthur, the guy we met answering to that name, will only be able to say that he was hired for a job, with nothing connecting him to previous crimes – and you can bet that he's going to resign very soon, or maybe even mysteriously disappear. And from there I'll have to admit I hacked their system, into the bargain – which could put me in jail for a long time. We still can't put the finger on exactly who he is. We don't know his current name. We don't know where he lives.'

'But... why don't you tell them anyway? What have you got to lose?'

'Cos she wants to catch him.' Bernard grinned. 'And kill him. Don't you?'

'Can't do that if he's in jail,' Rosie said. 'Makes sense. But it doesn't make sense putting ourselves in danger.'

'We'll set up the surveillance and get evidence. Then we nail him. I don't want him dead. I want him in jail. But it's up to us. Rosie – think of your book. Bernard – think of Rupert.'

They pondered this a while as the train roared on.

# 56

Despite the date, and the green leaves, it was a soggy day. The path through the woodland left their boots clogged with muck. The route was old and overgrown in places. Since they'd parked up their hire car, they didn't see another soul. It wasn't that cold, but they wrapped up warmly.

'Looks like someone's been through here recently,' Becky said, pointing out a part where the bracken had been chopped down, to allow passage.

'With a machete,' Bernard added. 'Or a chainsaw.'

It took an hour to walk through the woods towards the standing stones site. They stood in the shadow of these sullen blocks, frozen blobs of rock that stood eight feet high in some sections. 'It's a stone henge that was surrounded by a wooden henge,' Becky said, 'a place of ancient sacrifice. Lots of people used to gather here.'

Rosie pointed out a long, flat slab of rock. 'I'm guessing that's where the sacrifices were done.'

'That's where they did it. And that's where they'll do it next Saturday.'

'Where they *think* they'll do it,' Bernard said, resolutely. 'There's no way we'll let that happen again.'

Becky smiled wryly. 'Thanks, big guy.'

'I'm just surprised your dad didn't stop it.'

Becky's face fell.

'Bernard!' Rosie spluttered, aghast.

'Just saying. He should have fought. It annoys me.'

'He did fight,' Becky said, coolly.

'Not hard enough, though. Did he fight when he watched that guy do that to you? His daughter? It would drive anyone mad.' Bernard's shoulders wriggled. 'He should have been like a wild animal.'

'My dad wasn't a wild animal. He was a clever, thinking man. He did all he could for us.' Becky felt her pulse throb in her temples.

'Just saying what I'd do. Situation like that.'

'Let's hope you never find out what you'd do. Situation like that.'

Rosie stepped between them. 'We take your point, Bernard. Maybe set up the equipment, now?'

Bernard mumbled, then shouldered canvas bags filled with equipment.

Rosie said, 'What's the script with this stuff, then? Cameras? How will you keep them charged?'

'Long-life batteries,' Bernard called out from the trees. 'And the cameras are set off by motion. Pretty standard stuff on nature documentaries. Bird watchers use them all the time. Or nosey neighbours. It's all linked back to a central computer – mine. We can get a stream of any camera content when the motion sensors are tripped. I've got half a dozen trained on the stone circle. Anyone comes round here in the next fortnight that stands taller than a metre and a half, we'll see them in glorious Technicolor, high definition. Or night vision. Or any setting we like. On Saturday night, we can livestream it to the police.'

Bernard's resistance of any offers of help spoke more of distrust of anyone handling his toys than any gentlemanly impulses to spare them an extra load. He had the bulk of the work to do, fastening tiny cameras to the trees and bushes round the perimeter of the circle, and a few along the path to the woods. He clambered up high in some cases, a surprisingly nimble creature once liberated from solid ground.

'What a fucking gangler,' Rosie muttered. She looked Becky in the eyes. 'And what an insensitive prick. No wonder he spends his life in front of a computer in a basement. Are you all right?'

Becky shrugged. 'I'd be more annoyed if I thought he meant it maliciously. Some people mean to upset you. He clearly doesn't. He's awkward, not nasty. And he's been key in finding our guy.'

'If you're right about this... my god. You're going to be a hero.'

'We're a team now,' Becky said, shortly. 'Priority one – we take a prime twat off the streets. We all get to go home. And you get a book out of it.'

'I'll be sure to sign you a copy,' Rosie said.

Bernard dropped to his haunches from a tree, then straightened up. Rain beaded his 'fro and ran down his face, and he wiped his hands on the side of his trousers.

'We're nearly ready to get it all tested out.' He made his way back to a holdall, then pulled out a laptop. Heading for the shade of a tree, he hunched down against it, frowning in the bluish glare of the screen.

'One thing you didn't explain,' Rosie said to Becky. 'The love letters; the mystery French guy.'

Becky laughed. 'Le herring rouge. Leif was writing to my sister. They'd set up a rendezvous – for the day after we all got killed. That was suspicious. Obviously the letters he was writing to my mother was even more suspicious. But there's an answer to that. My mother knew all about the pen-pals' business. She was writing to see what Leif was like, without steaming in and making inquiries. But my mother being my mother, she posed as a love rival. He wrote back to my mother. My mother replied. She knew what he was doing. It got a bit flirty. It must have tickled him, having two women chasing after him. He had no idea. The idea was to surprise the young man, on the day, with both of his pen-pals at once.'

'So your mother was having an affair? With Leif?'

Becky laughed harder. 'Of course not. My father knew about it. He even wrote some of the letters – or he dictated them. I remember them doing it, one Friday night, while Clara was out. It was a joke, something they did for a laugh. Some documents I found at my aunt's even showed that my father thought about going into business with Leif's father, once he found out who he was. Or rather, what farmland he had for sale. Leif's father wasn't connected to the initial French deal, the one that got my father killed, for a few miles across the valley. My father saw the farmland was being sold off and he wanted to buy some off him. They even arranged to meet up. They knew Clara was writing to a French boy, so they checked him out. They checked out where he lived. They liked the place. My dad had been looking to build some gîtes and let them out as holiday homes.

'The pen-pals' thing led to the property deal – not the other way round. It wasn't connected to the property package put together by Jack Tullington's brother, the one which got my family killed. Entirely separate thing, though it looks too much of a coincidence to be true at first glance.'

'Leif's letter-writing habit has caused a lot of confusion.'

'That's right. In hindsight, though. It must have been a grand old joke for everyone concerned at the time. Maybe it turned my mother on; who knows? Maybe that added to it. She was like that, my mother. I wouldn't call her a flirt, but she was playful. She had a funny bone. So did my dad. He liked that side to her. That's why they got married, I guess. I remember them roaring about things in French accents and referencing someone called Lucky Pierre. Someone to look out for, like a policeman. They made up crazy double entendres to put in the letters. I heard them do this, while Clara was out. I didn't get the significance of "Lucky Pierre", either, for years. It must have been a gift for the real killer, examining all the official evidence later. A nice smokescreen. Was the mystery killer Lucky Pierre? An excellent piece of luck. It skewed the investigation for years. There are still people out there who think Leif did it, or his father.'

Rosie frowned. 'What's a Lucky Pierre?'

'I'll tell you later. How's it looking, Bernard?'

'All tickety boo,' Bernard said. 'All up and running.' Shielding the screen from the rain, he turned the laptop round and showed them a rough map of the woods, with the paths and the stone circle mapped in rough white blobs. The cameras were marked in orange smudges, flashing at various intersecting points.

'We'll get the video when the cameras are tripped, and this map here is where we'll see various people tracking through the sensors.'

'We're doing this remote control, yeah?' Rosie asked.

'Sure,' Bernard said. 'We'll be far away from here when the bad guys show up. Wouldn't want to be stuck out here at night, would you?'

'That's my thinking too. It's getting late, now. I reckon we should wrap this up for today.'

'Just before we go, I need to do a couple of tests. Either of you fancy going back to the path? You should trip a few of the sensors, so I can double-check it's all working.'

'Sure,' Becky said, and turned to go.

'Wait – I'll come with you,' Rosie said.

They started back down the broken, haphazard trail of stones; ferns and bracken snagging their trousers. 'What are you going to do when you see him in handcuffs?' Rosie asked.

'Not sure. Mainly I'll be happy it's over.'

'What if it isn't over? I mean, what if it just ends up you and him?'

'Let's hope it doesn't come to that.'

Rosie stopped. 'Look me in the eye and say that.'

Becky looked her in the eye, at least. 'Hey – if he appears in front of us right now, he's got a fight on his hands.'

'Oh, I know it. I've first-hand experience of your karate skills, remember, Daniel-San.'

'Don't worry. I'm not looking for a fight. Believe it. I'm going to hand him to the police. I'm not going to gamble my life for the sake of some comic book showdown. Besides – what are you expecting? He'd be a fool to show up here, now.'

One of Becky's phones burred in her pocket. It was Bernard.

'Hey, Bernard – I have to hand it to you, I can't spot where you hid your cameras. I take it they're working okay? How do we look, fatter or thinner? In fact, don't answer that.'

'Get back here,' Bernard said, almost in a whisper.

'Eh?'

'Get back here, now. Get off that path.'

'What for?'

Rosie caught the alarm on Becky's face, and reflected it back at her.

All round them, sodden, sagging trees flailed in the wind.

'There are people coming. They've already set off some of the perimeter cameras.'

'What kind of people?'

'They're coming!'

'Who?'

But she knew who. She heard it whispered in the slow dripping in the trees, saw it in the branches' indifferent shrug beneath the weight of the water; felt it in her galloping heart.

'They're moving fast,' Bernard babbled. 'They look like they know where they're going. They're heading *right for you*. Get back to the stone circle, quick!'

# 57

Bernard was nowhere to be seen when they reached the stone circle.

'Where is he?' Rosie clutched at her head. 'Is he fucking in on it?'

'I don't know.'

'It all seemed too good to be true. I should have known. This smelled like a trap, but I ignored it. I thought you knew what you were doing!'

'Keep your voice down,' Becky hissed. She scanned the menhirs and the flat slab of rock. *Perfectly set up*, she thought grimly. *For us.* 'Look out for Bernard.'

Suddenly he appeared through a place where the treeline grew thick, his skin slick with rain. Panic was evident in his eyes, the set of his shoulders, the way his fingers squirmed into the corner of his mouth. 'Over here,' he hissed.

He shielded the laptop from the rain, despite the tree cover. In the pitiless grey half-light, the falling rain glittered like spears.

'The sensors were tripped off, all over. Look.' He clicked open a window, and spooled back footage from a camera.

A figure dressed in black rushed past.

'What was that?' Rosie whispered. 'Was that a mask?'

'There's another two, look. One's got some sort of animal head on.'

Rosie clamped a hand to her mouth, eyes bulging. 'We've got to get out of here – now. We're going to be fucking slaughtered! This was a trap! We walked straight into it!'

'Calm down,' Becky said. 'Let's think it through. Where are they?'

'Look at the map,' Bernard croaked. He indicated the simple white and black graphic, with the stone circle in the middle. Orange dots which indicated cameras blinked – in every direction. Too many to count at a glance.

The moving dots flashed and drew nearer.

'They're all round us,' Rosie whimpered. 'We're cut off.'

'There must be a way of keeping track of them,' Becky said. 'Don't panic. We can surely get through the woods without running into them. Keep the computer on. Which way?'

Bernard blinked rapidly. He seemed to have shrunk, head bowed. 'I... I don't...'

'Bernard – think. Show us a path. Look at this row of dots – let's head through the middle. It'll take them a while to converge.'

'That's through the woods, Becky. It's choked thick, there's no path.'

'Then it'll give us a chance, for god's sake. At the very least, we can hide. Which direction?'

'Through there.' He indicated the treeline he'd just emerged from.

'We're going to die out here,' Rosie moaned. 'What happened with your family, it's going to happen again. It's going to happen to us. Who are these freaks?'

Becky turned to follow Rosie's gaze; too quick for her to make out any detail, a dark figure ducked away into a thicket of bushes, leaving the branches twitching.

Rosie simply fled into the woods. Bernard followed her, the computer cast aside.

For one treacherous moment, it occurred to Becky to leave them, to head off on her own; the better to split up, to get away, to survive. Then she tore after them. 'Wait! We've got to keep a straight line!'

Rosie was already gone; Bernard was directly ahead, tearing away a branch that snagged in his hair.

'Remember the map, for god's sake,' Becky cried. 'Stick together. Don't split up!'

It was too late; Bernard accelerated into a clearing and was gone.

Rosie screamed, somewhere in the forest, then stopped abruptly; a magpie took fright with a bubbly *chough* and fluttered away overhead. Then there was a sudden, terrible silence.

Becky leapt over a fallen tree draped with moss like a stole over a queen's shoulders, then crouched down low behind it.

To the right, the branches were beginning to settle after Bernard's passage. The rain continued to come down, drenching the trees in a gentler patter.

'Piggee!' someone cried, startling her. 'Where are you, Piggee?' The voice broke up into laughter, high, shrieking, gleeful.

Several voices answered, as if in a pack howl.

'Piggee!' someone yelled. A woman's voice. 'Here, Piggee! We're coming for you!'

'No no no no,' Rosie moaned close by. 'No no, please, oh god, please.'

Then a long, loud, terrifying shriek sliced across the forest. It was cut short after a second or two. Then Becky heard loud, sustained laughter. Men's voices.

*Rosie's attack alarm. Dear god, please help her.*

Becky bit her lip and crouched lower. The fallen tree might have come down years ago, its trunk over-run by other vegetation. A crop of weird red and white polka-dotted fungi grew inches away from Becky's hands.

She breathed via her diaphragm, making herself as small as she dared, hoping to make as little noise as possible.

They've been here before, she thought, with growing nausea. Been here and done it already, maybe. Either way, they know every inch of this place.

She heard some thrashing to her left, close by. She cocked an ear, straining for sound.

That was when she spotted something glinting in the foggy light, something in the crook of a branch – a camera lens. Not one that Bernard had planted.

*They were here before us. They had exactly the same idea. They're watching me now!*

Then two gloved hands slammed down on the tree bark, six inches from Becky's head. A face appeared above them. It was covered in a black leather fetish mask which stretched over the entire head, with a zipper for a mouth. Spikes jutted out of the top of the head in flexible leather fronds; two eyes seemed to bubble out of the eyeholes, glassy with mirth.

'There you are, Piggee!' the figure shrieked, the German accent horribly muffled.

Becky sprang to her feet and planted two punches on either side of the head, quick as blinking, her knuckles smacking hard against the mask. The man – clad in a black top and trousers – pitched onto his side, braced against the fallen tree, hands upraised.

Becky pummelled his ribs while he cowered, a good dozen punches, then snapped his head hard to one side with a last, tremendous right cross which detonated where his ear should have been.

He rolled off the tree, completely limp, and fell out of sight.

Becky leapt back over the fallen trunk and ran, but another ghoul was already blocking her path. This one had the face of a startled rabbit, with rotten yellow teeth as incisors and marbled cat fur for a face, criss-crossed with chicken wire.

'Stay, Piggee. Stay there,' said this one. London accent, this time.

Becky didn't bother to fight; she swerved, returned to the overgrown path, then ran roughly in the direction Bernard had taken. From the map, she knew a clearing should appear; from there, she had a path to the road. That could lead to where she'd left the hire car, driven off a pine-needle strewn path and hidden from sight.

Provided they hadn't found that, it gave her a chance, just the slimmest chance—

Half a dozen other figures broke cover, all around her, all clad in black trousers and long-sleeved tops, and all wearing masks of some kind. One man wore a black rubber mask fashioned like a pig's or a boar's, with steel tusks and a motorbike chain through the nose. The chain was held by a woman in a featureless porcelain mask, framed with blonde hair. The chain rattled as the man in the pig mask dragged on it, and the woman struggled to hold him in check.

Becky ran blindly, branches tearing at her. One whipped her cheek, keen as a slap, but the sting barely registered. She had to make that clearing; there were signs Bernard had come through before her.

A shrieking silver skull mask surged into view, sprung from a clump of ferns, teeth angled into rising arrowheads on a chromium plated surface. As he reached for her, Becky used her momentum to launch a flying kick which crashed into the man's chest with a terrific impact that jolted her all the way up to her hip. The chromium head whipped forward, and the shoulders folded in on themselves as if on a hinge.

Becky leapt over his flailing legs as he landed on his back, and carried on. Someone else took her by the shoulder and tried to lock an arm round her throat. She didn't see the face, or even hear a voice; all she knew was muffled breathing and the press of hard, ridged plastic against her cheek.

Then her shoulders rolled; she took the arm, planted her feet, and threw the figure behind her full on the deck with a serpentine convulsion of her shoulder blades. She heard a plastic mask splinter against rock; then she was running again.

The clearing was near; she fancied she could see the road. She was past the last line of trees, skinning the heel of her hand as she forced herself through a tight gap in the bark. Perhaps Bernard had made it; he might even be waiting with her by the car. From there...

The clearing was tight, an oval space perhaps thirty feet long, the grass short.

In the middle of it, dressed in black, quite calm, hands at his sides, stance relaxed, stood the man she was looking for.

The bone mask was intact. There were the large dark eyes, just as she remembered them.

'Hello Becky,' he said, in that familiar, rough-hewn voice. 'Together at last. Come to me. Do what you've always wanted to.' He made a gesture with his hands spread. It was not an aggressive motion; rather, he signalled as if she might run to him, as a child to her father.

She closed on him, but not to embrace. The stun gun was out of her jacket in an instant; she fired while she still ran. The twin needles sparked at his black clad chest, and he staggered – but did not fall.

He plucked the twin prongs from his chest and hurled them away.

He rapped at his chest; he had a bulletproof vest on.

Stupid. Her chance was gone.

Momentarily shocked, she tossed the gun, then sprinted at him. Defence was the foundation stone of her training, but she had plenty of attack in her – had even envisaged exactly this moment.

She tried the flying kick again, but he was ready for it; he slapped her foot away and then blocked the elbow smash she followed it with, the motion of his flexed arm mirroring hers.

He kicked at her left foot just as she braced it to shift her weight, and almost sent her sprawling. A hand clamped round her upper left arm, hard enough for his nails to break the skin; then a tremendous punch from his free hand jackhammered just below her ribcage, blasting the breath out of her and pitching her onto her backside.

Shrieks and howls of glee sounded from the trees behind her.

In a split second, Becky catapulted back to her feet, her blood cooling rapidly. He stood back to allow her to get up, then she attacked him again, darting punches at every available point of his body with incredible speed. It became nightmarish; she could not land a clear blow. Time and again her fists found his elbows, his forearms too thick and bony to hurt.

She surged close to drive a knee into his groin and at last he grappled with her, awkwardly. One hand ensnared her hair and forced her head back, and she screamed in pain and frustration. She gripped the mask. It was an old thing, and the bones felt seamed, as if they'd turned to stone over time.

Her fingers crab-walked across the pitted face towards his eyes, but by that time he had kneed her in one kidney, and her body curled inward, involuntarily, as she gasped for breath.

Then a whistling punch numbed her cheekbone and tugged comet tails across her field of vision. As the world sparkled and undulated like swift water and the other side of her head nestled in cool boggy earth, the faces in the trees started forward, a nightmare jewellery box of leather, metal, plastic, bone. Some were formed into faces, some fashioned into animals; others were merely twisted in their design, a free hand granted to a lunatic.

Becky clutched a fistful of gungy earth, a divot disturbed by their stampeding combat; as she drew back to lob it between the deep wells of Arkanescu's eyes, something sparked into life in his hands.

Her body jolted clear of the earth, then landed hard. She wasn't sure if she had screamed, or the whole forest had. Her hands and thighs twitched in an obscene jitterbug.

Becky smelled burning, and twin pillars of smoke tapered into the air from the twin prongs that jutted from her breast. Her vision blurred, but she could make out the trail of wires leading from the darts to the stun gun in his hands. Her own stun gun. The one she'd left behind in Romania.

'Fine toys you have,' he rumbled, tossing the weapon away. 'You know, I'd never thought to use these things until I met you? You give me ideas, Becky.'

Something else glittered in his hands as he started forward.

Before she could speak, he crouched beside her and triggered the pepper spray into her eyes. Then, at last, she screamed.

Hands gripped her, from every direction, and held her fast.

## 58

The sun sank, drowning the rain in the horizon. A clear night emerged, with starlight and a startling full moon. The air was alive with shrieking birds and not a few bats.

Torches were lit round the perimeter, illuminating the obscene faces.

Becky, Rosie and Bernard were fully clothed and tied upright to three separate menhirs. Their arms and legs were firmly lashed and thick, new hemp looped round their bellies and under their armpits. Their circulation was cut off and reattached, tingling Becky's limbs as she struggled against her bonds.

*The first rule of escapology; wriggle room.* She had none.

Her vision was still blurry, but had largely cleared from the stinging blast that had blinded her for more than two hours. A man with a goat's head mask had come along eventually, the absurd features tilted at an odd angle as he scrutinised her. He actually sniffed at her face, the hairs at the nose stirring.

'I think I have a hanky in my pocket, if you need it,' she croaked. 'You sound a bit bunged up.'

'Not as bunged up as you're going to be,' the man with the goat's head had said, in a musical Aberdonian burr.

'Fuck yourself, Jimmy.'

The goat's head pondered her in silence for a second, and then he slapped her hard across the face. The pain in her cheek sparked back into flame along with the pistol crack impact. She did not have enough saliva left to spit at him.

'I'll be last on you,' the goat declared, its glassy yellow eyes catching the torchlight. 'I asked specifically. When you're completely broken, when you've been used in every way it's possible to be used, when you've already begged for death, I'll be last. Think about it.'

When white robes replaced the black clothes they had all worn for the capture, Becky supposed it was showtime.

Masked faces lined up round the stone circle, and then the January Orchestra's concert began.

It was a vocal performance, a hellish choir dominated by a bass drone enunciated by the muffling effect of the masks. It rose and fell in languid waves, the key changes setting Becky's teeth on edge. It had a strange beauty to it, ranging from a soprano at her highest possible setting to the burr of a wartime bomber, but it wasn't a tune Becky would have listened to long under ordinary circumstances.

None of the three captives had spoken much since they were tied up. To be fair to Bernard, he had put up a fight, arms and legs thrashing like a spider trapped in a glass, but he was quickly subdued and lashed to the stone. Rosie had simply collapsed, sobbing and pleading, and was led almost gently to her berth.

Arkanescu, who had never removed the bone mask, cupped Rosie's chin and stroked her hair as they tied her up, talking too low for Becky to hear.

While being dragged to the menhirs and being tied up, Becky hadn't fought, having been unable to see who to fight. She conserved her energy and took stock of her injuries; nothing broken, though she'd been briefly worried he had smashed her cheekbone. Lumps and bruises were the worst she'd suffered. For now.

As the chorus droned on, Bernard's posture had devolved into alarming insectoid-like twitches, so far as his bonds would allow, his whole head jerking back and forth. His mouth undulated like a caterpillar flailing at the outer edge of a leaf.

'Can't they stop that fucking noise?' Rosie moaned. Her face had grown paler as the evening wore on; it complemented the moonlight. Her eyeliner had dried into cracked black veining down her cheeks, and no one had come along to lick them clean. 'How long are they going to keep singing? Stop it!'

'Rosie, try and stay calm,' Becky said.

'Stay calm? They're going to rip us apart! No one will find us.'

'I'm thinking.'

'Yeah, you've got a plan, haven't you? Like you planned to bring us here and catch him. *Catch him!* What a joke. It was a trap. All along. That bitch Galbraith set you up. And you fell for it! Maybe if you'd told me about what you were planning before roping me into it, I might have realised that!'

'I didn't know who to trust,' Becky said. 'That included you and Bernard. I was leaking information all over the place. I had to keep some stuff quiet.' Her head sagged. She felt dizzy, as well as exhausted. Despite the fatigue, her body rattled and quivered, her nervous system on autopilot. It was a futile gesture, like the tremors of an old dog a day or two away from his final trip to the vet's. Doubt and guilt added to the horror, the certain knowledge that while she might always have been damned, the other two had surely followed this path thanks to her.

She scanned the trees, slowly and deliberately, trying to ignore the keening monsters. There was nothing. No one else.

'It's your fault, you stupid bitch!' Rosie roared, finding her voice at last. 'You wanted to collar him yourself. You wanted revenge. Well, go on then – there he is! Make a fucking citizen's arrest!' She arched her head back against the unforgiving stone, and screamed, high and loud. 'Help! Help us! Help! Somebody please help us! Please!'

Bernard started whimpering, a high counterpoint to the constant, oscillating drone of the chorus.

Clad in white, glaring at them from beneath the bone mask, Arkanescu appeared in the middle of the clearing. The mask was etched against the moonlight like a clutched, spectral fist.

He raised his hands and gestured. The droning fell to a whisper. Then he came forward and stood before the three prisoners spread-eagled on the face of the stones.

'Welcome to the rest of your lives,' he said, and bowed, mockingly.

Then the bone mask nodded to the left and right.

The man with the goat's head and the chromium skull-face with the arrowhead set of teeth lumbered forward.

Becky took no consolation in the sight of the latter limping heavily.

They stood either side of Rosie. She grew hysterical, bucking like an animal.

'Don't take me... take her, she's the one that's after you!' she wailed, indicating Becky.

Rosie's bonds were cut, and she was dragged towards the long, flat stone. The blood plummeted out of Becky's face, as if a plug had been pulled. While this was happening, Arkanescu gazed into her eyes, ignoring Rosie.

'I have access to thousands of pounds, and my uncle is a trader in the City of London,' Rosie gibbered. 'He has access to potentially millions of pounds. Anything you want. Property. Fake passports. You can disappear.'

They forced her face down onto the slab, pulling her arms out and holding her tight. Rosie's chin rested awkwardly on the surface, but it was no great effort for the two men to restrain her. She had not yet begun to fight.

The goat's head figure stroked her hair. Becky saw a tremor in his gloved hands as the fingers combed through Rosie's shiny black locks.

Bernard emitted a light, whistling sound, then uttered a stream of nonsense syllables, barely pausing for breath. It took a second or two for Becky to realise he was praying.

Arkanescu strode forward.

'I'll fuck every one of you,' Rosie wheezed. 'I'll do anything you like, as many times as you like. I'll do it for days on end.' She indicated Becky, eyes bulged in desperation. 'That bitch knows everything. She's got data hidden away all over the place. She's got about twenty phones, half a dozen computers. I can tell you the passwords. I know where everything is. And Bernard – he's been tracing you online. He's a hacker. I know more. A lot more. I can get you access to everything he knows. He knows people in Russia.'

'Child,' Arkanescu said, gently. 'There's no need for you to worry. That's all taken care of.'

'Please don't hurt me.' It was a little girl's voice.

'You won't suffer. You're the lucky one.'

Arkanescu tenderly parted her hair at the back of her neck, uncovering a plaster-of-Paris strip of skin. Then he tilted her chin slightly with his left hand.

She was frantic. 'I'll be yours for life. For life. I'll never leave you. Anything you want, you can have. I'll stay with you.'

Rosie's words died – she died – as he swiped downward with the machete he had concealed underneath his robe.

Metal clashed with stone in a shrill impact. Becky flinched; the obscene audience sighed collectively, the singing abruptly halted.

Rosie's face registered shock, eyes wide, mouth dropped open, and an eruption of blood seemed to coalesce with her slick black hair as the blow all but severed her head. The wide-eyed shock remained rigid on her face as Arkanescu twisted and tugged with a brutal, practised motion like a vet birthing a lamb. He raised Rosie's head high, a trophy, the black hair trailing, cascading and seemingly taking root on the sacrificial altar, slick and bright in the moonlight. Her blood only blushed into full colour as it soaked Arkanescu's gown.

The chants from the audience became frantic; some of the penitents shuddered, and one or two threw themselves to the grass, a black pastiche of evangelical fervour.

Arkanescu threw the head high and far, the hair streaming out as it turned end over end; and as it came down among the throng they fought for it in a terrible facsimile of a scrum for a bridal bouquet.

The goat's head and the chromium skull face tore at the clothes on Rosie's body with indecent haste. Other figures loped forward. One tore off a chequerboard-patterned mask and lapped at the blood drenching the stone where Rosie's body had lain seconds before.

Bernard retched, noisily, and began to sob.

Arkanescu wiped the blade on a clear spot on his sodden robe; he nodded again, and a large group surrounded Bernard.

They cut him loose. He did not fight; she heard his clothes tear. Someone started howling, high and loud, the cry of no living creature Becky had ever heard.

'Leave him alive,' Arkanescu said, with calm authority. 'Hear me. Spare him his life – but only his life.'

Bernard was borne across to another flat stone, already naked. A phalanx of dark figures closed round him like a fist. That was when he screamed, reaching an uncanny pitch until a hand clamped over his mouth.

Arkanescu approached, the machete hanging low in his right hand. Ignoring the Rorschach patterning of Rosie's blood – surely still warm – this was exactly how Becky had first seen him. He was flanked by the man with the chained pig's head, and his female keeper.

'You look nervous, Becky,' the woman said, in a high, excited voice. 'There's no need to be nervous.' She began to giggle.

Somehow, Becky found a response. 'Nice to see you again, Mrs Galbraith. I do like your outfit. This man is the chap who helped you with your boxes, is he?'

The man in the pig mask grunted, and actually pawed the ground with his foot. Mrs Galbraith tightened her grip on the chain looped through the chromium tusks.

'It is nice to see you, too. Not too uncomfortable, I hope?' Galbraith asked.

They cut Becky free, and she sagged to the ground, crying out in pain as her joints, her very blood, complained.

The masked figures did not manhandle her.

Arkanescu was composed. He gestured towards her with the knife. 'We can end it now, if you wish. This is my one and only offer.'

'Fuck yourself.'

'That's good. I'll take that as a rejection. Not because you think you can still win. Because you're a coward. You want to run. Like you ran before. You think you still can?'

Becky said nothing. The pig man gripped her by the arm and pulled her upright. Angelica Galbraith placed a thin, sharp blade at her throat.

She whispered in Becky's ear: 'Give me an excuse.'

'Let's walk a while,' Arkanescu said. He led the way, back turned, totally unconcerned.

*Perhaps he realises that I can't summon the energy to kick him. That I don't have the fight in me to shake these two off.*

The pig mask's chain clanked at Becky's ear; the man underneath it was breathing hard.

The four of them wandered through the stones. Becky ignored Bernard's terrible sobbing; the riot of bare skin that cascaded over him on the flat stone. One man was already astride him, nude except for a wolf's head mask thrown back in ecstasy.

Bernard screeched something that might have been her name; she might even have seen his eyes, thrown wide in fear and agony. She squeezed her own eyes shut until they were out of the stone circle.

'What you got in store for me?' she asked. 'Wicker man? Maybe burn me at the stake?' She regretted having said it, immediately.

'No – a proposition,' said Arkanescu. 'An opportunity to live and thrive.'

'You offering me a job?'

'Not exactly. I want you to be by my side. I want to finish what I started. I want you, whole, complete. Unbroken.'

'Great. When do I start?'

'You'll say yes, of course.' The yellowed head swung round to face her. 'Who wouldn't? But I want you to consider the options. I want you to understand what's about to happen. You will be completely under my control. Any resistance you might have will be broken, and broken utterly. Even as you consciously process this – even as you resist it, again and again, for months, maybe even years – you must understand that you will break. You will know this phenomenon. Stockholm Syndrome, some people call it. I call it simply obedience. I will be everything you desire in a husband, because you will obey unquestioningly. No matter what I do to you, you'll love me. You'll adore me. You'll worship me. It is inevitable. Your life will be mine to do with as I please. And you'll thank me for every moment of it.'

Becky said nothing. They followed a path through the trees, only dimly lit by the moon and the faint embers of the torches encircling the standing stones.

'Please, let me have her. Let me have her now,' the pig-headed man gibbered.

'In a moment. First, though, Becky has to do something for me.' He produced a long, double-edged knife, and turned the handle towards her. 'In a few moments we'll go back to Bernard. You'll put him out of his misery. You won't use this knife to fight. You won't try to get away. It's too late for that. You remember how this goes. Don't you?'

## 59

Then

'Here's what we will do,' the man in the mask told Becky. 'I will give you the knife. And you will use it on your father.'

She must have refused, because he became rougher then, propelling her forward. Her dad was not dead, she saw, but he appeared drunk, lying in the long grass, legs bent at crazy angles after their fight. His eyes had a twinkle to them; it was only when she got closer that she saw they were tears. The knife was heavy in her hands; she dropped it once, and the blade sank deep into the ground. The man retrieved it and folded it in her hands.

'Stab him, Becky. Do it, attack him. It's our only chance!' her mother cried.

This seemed to anger the man in the mask. Tearing off her bonds, he hurled Becky's mother to the ground, fending off her thrashing limbs as if subduing a kitten. Then he simply sat on her head. Her hands and legs thrashed; her screams were muffled, and presently, it was done.

The man waited a minute or two, then rose, sighed and yawned, finally scratching his chin beneath the mask. He didn't say anything to Becky – just nodded towards her father.

'It's okay, sweetie,' her father croaked, in the voice of a man double his age. 'It's okay. You can do it. We're not going to make it. I just want you to know that I love you. That's all we have left. That's all there is to think about.'

'Do it,' the man said at her back, urgently. 'Enough talk. Do it, and I'll let you live. That's the choice. Don't, and you die.'

'Becky, it's okay. It's okay. You can do it.' Her father nodded and swallowed. Tears threaded through his beard and dripped off his chin.

Becky punched the knife through his doughy belly. She had little strength but the blade was sharp.

He had held his head high, brave, even proud – until the moment the blade sliced through, and he screamed and thrashed. His blood covered her in a raw, metallic shower.

That was when she dropped the knife and ran.

Laughter followed her. Laughter, and footsteps. She ran blind.

He came close to her once, then very close, a second time, as the foliage tore at her, with a million crucifixion nails puncturing her bare feet.

When she dared to look back, there he was, within grabbing distance, forcing his way through the branches, the mask somehow still in place. Huge, dark eyes glaring at her. Intent. Horribly focused.

Then he stumbled. She got lucky.

He cursed her as he lurched to his feet.

And Becky ran for her life.

## 60

Now

'You won't struggle,' the man in the mask insisted. 'You won't fight. You'll kill your friend the same way I killed the squaw. Right through the neck. Take his head. You try to resist, you die. If you're lucky, you'll pass before I allow the others to violate you.'

'Whatever you say,' Becky mumbled. Her shoulders drooped.

'Cheer up, girl,' Arkanescu said. 'Your friend will thank you. Look at him.' The long blade tapped Becky on the shoulder, then indicated what she didn't want to look at.

She glanced at the stone where Bernard had been laid. A riot of flesh covered him. He wailed miserably.

'Who wants to survive that? It would be a kindness. You've wished for death many times, Becky. You know that feeling.'

Becky said and did nothing, utterly mute.

'You can live, Becky,' the man in the mask insisted. 'Unharmed, from now on. You can come with me, and live.

You can come home. I'll be a father to you, if you prefer, not a husband. You see the truth in this, don't you?'

The pig-headed man said, 'You promised us we'd have her. I'm not leaving here without having her.'

'You'll shut up,' Arkanescu said, in an even tone.

Then their attention was diverted. Another figure stepped into the clearing, one with a fox's head mask. This figure was dressed in a brown overcoat and grey jeans.

Galbraith addressed this newcomer. 'Aren't you on watch?'

'That's not the man we left on guard!' roared Arkanescu.

'Who the fuck is it then?' Galbraith cried in alarm.

'Insurance, bitch,' Becky snarled.

The new figure raised the long barrel of a shotgun.

'Shoot him!' Becky screamed. 'Finish it! Do it!'

The man with the fox head hesitated; that half-second was enough.

The pig-headed man grabbed Becky and locked an arm round her throat, a knife pressing into the flesh beneath her chin. He held her in front of him as a shield, while Galbraith leapt aside. Arkanescu turned and ran.

The figure in the fox mask shouldered the rifle, tracked the fleeing figure of Arkanescu, and pulled the trigger.

In her panic, Galbraith dodged the wrong way. In the thunderclap of the shotgun blast, she was hurled off her feet and onto her back, legs failing comically. The leather of her costume was shredded and smoking at the neck. Her mask had been blown off her head. Her lower jaw had gone with it, and her eyes were glassy.

The man in the fox mask cracked the breach, spitting out spent shells. He groped in a pocket for more.

The pig-headed man took his chance; he hooked a foot round Becky's shins, shoved her onto her face, and moved to intercept the man in the fox mask while he reloaded.

Becky sprung upwards on the heels of her hands, in a fluid deadfall that absorbed any notion of impact; then she leapt fully off the ground, scissoring her legs at the hips, her right foot whistling round in a high, wide arc.

The contact was perfect. The chain in the pig-man's nose rattled; his head snapped sideways, and he crashed to the earth without a sound.

Leif tore off the fox mask. His hands shook as he tried to feed red cartridges into the barrel. Like the burner phones, like the relay set up in the Romanian hotel room, Becky had put in a safety net; she had asked him to trail them in the woods. A doubt had nagged at her over the set-up; she had urged Leif to watch over them. He had been suspicious of her, and while she was tied up she had been sure he had simply decided not to come.

'Come on,' he hissed. 'This is our chance. The police are on their way.'

'Where the fuck were you?' she screamed.

'I was late... I didn't expect to arrive and find this happening now! I'm sorry!'

'We have to get Bernard.'

'Bernard's finished. So are we if we don't get out of here, now!'

Some of the throng surrounding Bernard had heard the shot and saw the commotion; some instantly fled into the trees, but several ran forward, the goat-headed man who had licked her face at the forefront. He passed a twelve-inch butcher knife from hand to hand as he approached, braced to attack.

Becky grabbed the knife the pig-headed man had dropped and turned to face him. She had the satisfaction of seeing him hesitate, then change his stance, this time to flee. Becky threw the knife from the shoulder, like a dart; it found purchase dead centre in his mask, just above the eyes – though not deep enough to seriously damage him. A flustered, pudgy face with a reddish beard emerged as he tugged the goat mask off, the knife still jutting from it. A single red trickle travelled down his forehead, dripping off the bulbous nose.

'Come on,' Becky bellowed at him, her blood high. 'I'm still here. You said you were going to do me last. Is that right? *You?*'

But he was joined by more figures, sprinting towards them. Weapons glinted in their hands.

Leif gripped her by the arm, as the hideous faces closed in. 'There are dozens of them. We go now – or I'm leaving you here.'

Then the helicopter's blades rose above the hubbub. White light bleached the scene, stopping the horde in their tracks.

Some did not even bother to gather their clothes. As they scattered into the forest, Bernard rolled off the flat stone, stark naked. He lay on his back, knees and elbows at weird angles, unmoving.

The trees parted again. Uniformed police surged into the clearing, some with guns, some with dogs. The woods were alive again.

'Drop the gun, Leif!'

He did as he was bid. Both raised their hands.

They made her and Leif kneel apart from the rest, even as Leif explained he was the one who had called them and it became apparent he was with Becky. Becky submitted to the handcuffs, even as she saw the masks knocked off the heads of the ones who'd surrendered. There were no familiar faces among them; these were mostly middle-aged men, bald, chubby, and startled.

She strained to see Bernard, but her view was cut off by a black line of French officers.

Eventually she saw a familiar face; Labelle.

'Becky!'

She tried to rise to her feet, even as a firm hand from the arresting officer tried to force her back down. 'He's still out there,' she gasped. 'He got out into the woods.'

'We'll get them.' Labelle placed a hand on her shoulder. 'We'll get them all.' Then Labelle hugged her, tight. 'I thought we had lost you. How did you know they would be here?'

'I lucked out. We thought this would be a possible venue for them in the next few weeks. Turned out, they were tracking us.'

'You're safe now, Becky.' Those bright blue eyes melted a little, just for a moment. 'And he will not escape these woods, I promise you.'

'Thank god. Thank god,' Becky said, the adrenaline beginning to wear off. 'They killed Rosie Banning. They took her body, they did something... I don't know...'

'Rest up,' Labelle said. She spoke to the arresting officer in French almost too quick to follow.

'Come on,' she said to Becky. 'I'm going to take you somewhere safe.'

'How about Leif?'

'Did you fire that shotgun?' Labelle asked him, nodding towards Galbraith's body.

Leif nodded, dumbly.

'Then we'll have to process you. Separately, of course. Becky is coming with me.'

'Just a minute.' Becky twisted, and tore through the phalanx of police. One arm caught her by the elbow, and pain flared where she hadn't noticed it before.

'Let her through,' Labelle told the officer.

When Becky reached him, Bernard was wrapped in police jackets. He shivered in the cool night; one eye was swollen shut, and he didn't seem to see Becky, until she took his hand.

'However this ends up, I'll be here for you,' she said. 'Got it? I won't let you suffer alone.'

Bernard nodded, slowly.

'Becky.' Labelle's hand was gentle on her shoulder. 'Let's get out of here.'

The detective led her away from that place.

# 61

The overhanging branches were frantic with flashing blue light as Labelle gunned the car through. There were a number of checkpoints; stern faces gaped at Becky as the policewoman handed over her ID.

'Where are we going?' Becky said, as the car sped up.

'Safe house.'

The forest soon fell away as they turned onto the main route.

Becky's hire car rolled past them, forlorn and alone in its needle-carpeted parking space.

Becky could only allow her shoulders and lower jaw to sag so far before her body reminded her of the previous few hours. The pain from the punch in the side of the face was particularly intense, but apart from chips in her incisors where they'd clashed together, nothing seemed too serious. Muscles and joints bridled at their cruel and unusual treatment, and however bad she felt at the moment, she knew it would be worse in the morning.

She turned slightly in her seat, and that's when another red letter for the senses arrived from her chest, where the stun gun's twin prongs had punched into her.

'Ugh, that's just nasty,' she said, reaching into her top and tentatively touching the fresh scabs.

'You all right? What did he do?'

'Ah, it's nothing.' Becky grunted, then tugged out a long, curved wire from beneath her clothes. 'I hated this bra, anyway.' She sniggered; and that's when it overtook her. Soon she was bent double, sobbing, body wracked, hands tearing across her scalp.

A hand touched the small of her back, gently.

'Take it easy,' Labelle whispered. 'My god. What you've been through, Becky Morgan.'

'He took another one,' Becky said, her palms placed over her eyes. 'I watched him kill Rosie. That poor lass. She thought she was onto another scoop. I never told her the full truth about what was happening until it was too late... She might never have come if I'd told her everything.'

'Whatever happened to that girl was down to an evil bastard – not you,' Labelle said. 'You had nothing to do with it.'

'And Bernard... what'll happen to him?'

'We'll take care of him.'

'They absolutely obliterated him... tore him apart like jackals. God, he must wish he was dead. *I* almost wish he was.'

'He'll be looked after. He's safe now, that's the main thing.'

Labelle took an exit down a narrow road; the canopy of trees returned. Becky caught sight of her face, the distortion of it clear in the smudged light reflected off the glass.

'This safe house doesn't seem very far,' Becky said.

'It's not. It's one of several the French police use out here. Mainly for witness protection, or people working undercover.'

'Where's Marcus?'

'You're about to meet him.'

'Is Hanlon here?'

'Not yet. He's on his way from the UK.'

Becky listened to the engine labouring as the car climbed a hill. 'You know... I'm not ready to sit an exam, but I've done a little bit of homework on police procedure. And I reckon you're being a bit naughty.'

Labelle frowned hard in the dashboard lights, concentrating on the road as it became uneven on the slope. 'I'm one of the senior investigating officers on this case, and my priority is to get you where it's safe. No one knows who else is hiding out in that forest – they may decide to try and take a shot at you. I can't risk that happening.'

'You didn't process me at the scene. Forensics should be going over my entire body with tape and tweezers as we speak, but no – nothing. And you didn't offer me any medical assistance, despite the fact I've practically just walked out of a blender. That's not regular practice.'

Labelle exhaled slowly. 'The entire scene is a warzone until we round everyone up, as far as possible. It'll take days to gather all the evidence, maybe weeks. There'll be a doctor at hand when you arrive at the safe house. We'll process you from there.'

'It also begs the very good question of how you managed to be here, in the first place.'

'We were following you, Becky,' Labelle said. 'We knew where you'd gone and came after you. Once Leif put in the call for help, we were on-site quickly.'

The safe house hovered into view soon enough, a single-storey family home which stood in complete incongruence to the forest. No lights shone outside, though the white walls took on an eerie effulgence in the moonlight.

It might have been a magical cottage to some, but to Becky, lonely cabins in the woods had all the wrong associations.

'Wait here.' Labelle stopped the car right outside, and unclipped her seatbelt, switching the engine off before re-triggering the headlights.

The faint light of a mobile phone blinked on in a hallway through a frosted window in the building; then the door opened.

Marcus stepped outside, shielding his eyes from the headlights before intercepting Labelle. Becky opened the door a little to listen to them speak.

'What are you doing?' he hissed. 'And what's she doing here?'

'You said you wanted to talk to her first.'

'Yeah, but down at the station. With everyone else!'

'It's safer here for her.'

'Balls it is. Where's Hanlon?'

'Hanlon's on his way.' Labelle gestured at Becky.

She got out, wincing as she placed her foot on the ground. The high kick on the pig-headed man had looked spectacular and felt good at the time, but she'd sprained her foot upon connection with his face.

She stumbled. Marcus started forward to help her, but Becky held up a hand.

'I'm fine.'

'Go back in the car,' he insisted. 'We're heading back to the scene – lots of people will want to talk to you.'

'No,' Labelle said. 'I've got seniority, and I'm saying she stays here.'

'Can one of you please make a decision? I'm very tired,' Becky said, hoarsely.

Labelle and Marcus began to argue – so quickly, and so ferociously, that Becky wondered if they were lovers. Then some movement caught her eye in the car.

The bone mask contemplated her coolly from the back seat.

Air escaped from Becky's lungs, as if from a puncture, and she sank onto one knee. Impossible; she'd even *looked* in the back of the car, paranoid to the last, before getting in.

Neither Labelle nor Marcus noticed until the man in the mask opened the door, got out, raised a pistol, and fired.

## 62

Marcus' mouth jerked for the last time. It seemed to spit in reverse, a red plume erupting from the back of his head. He fell without a sound. His blood was lurid, almost luminous, in the headlights from the car.

Labelle had a gun in her hand, too. She pointed it right at her. 'Don't move, Becky.'

Becky did, all the same – backing away slightly towards the woods as Arkanescu closed in on her.

'I knew it. I knew it was too good to be true.'

'And yet you went along with it,' Labelle said. 'Silly mare.' The detective giggled – and even through the rising terror Becky felt a faint tugging at her consciousness, as if nagged in the depths of a dream by a sound from the real world.

Arkanescu spoke, the barrel of his pistol levelled right at Becky's head. 'She said "don't move". So stay where you are. That's it. Good girl. Now – do you want the big surprise or the little surprise?'

Becky had worked up plenty of spit this time. She aimed for his eyes but fell short.

Arkanescu snorted. 'Well, after that, I'd say we should start with the little surprise.' His laughter was like stones grinding down a drain. 'Who knows how she'll react to the big one?'

'I must say, I resent being belittled in this way,' Labelle huffed. She reached up with her free hand and picked at her eyes. Presently, she took her hand away, blinking, then presented her open palm to Becky.

The contact lenses were still startlingly blue in her hand, even without their common framing.

'What the fuck?' Becky screeched.

In a clear English accent, Labelle said: 'Is that all you've got to say to your superior sibling, sister of mine?'

# 63

Becky found herself bargaining with it, babbling, 'No. You've got the same eyes as her, but... you don't look like her. So that isn't true. That can't be true.'

'But I cut my own face up, Becky. You remember that part, surely?' Labelle – or Clara – gestured down either cheek with the barrel of her gun. 'Plastic surgery took care of it – the best money could buy, in fact. The passing time and hair dye did the rest. There's some scarring, but not as bad as it might have been. Looks like I've got bad skin, rather than scars. I think they made a good job of it. Although I do miss my lovely natural hair colour. Like yours, in fact. That's one thing I envy about you.'

'He switched bodies, didn't he? Placed someone who looked like you at the scene. He'd carved her face up, too. Planned it all out.'

'Yep. Our mutual friend already had a girl stored away in the forest, alive. He's *always* got a spare or two. She was a good match. And he killed her right before he broke into our happy little chalet for the night. Then he swapped her body – and her head, for that matter – for mine.'

On this last two words, Clara laughed hysterically.

'Clara, he killed our family! *Shoot* him.'

'He slaughtered some piggies,' Clara said. 'Was there ever a pair of bastards more deserving of the knife as our pathetic parents? Then there's that little shit of a brother. Wouldn't have amounted to anything. Abysmal. The runt of the litter. Waste of time and space. God, do you remember how pathetically he died? Pfft. Like a slow puncture. Like a fucking fart.'

'You know this isn't right… for god's sake Clara, I don't know how much you've been helping him, but you have to stop him, now!'

'She won't,' Arkanescu said – again, in an entirely different voice. 'Don't waste your time. She is more than a daughter to me, more than a lover, more than a partner. She's mine. Aren't you, my clever girl?' Arkanescu's hand tickled Clara's chin, and she simpered, a ghastly parody of affection. 'She'd no more shoot me than I'd shoot myself.'

'Interesting, though,' Becky said. 'That night at my flat. What was that all about? She interrupted you, old boy, didn't she? It did seem odd, her and Marcus just showing up like that, rather than uniformed police. And you were surprised. Was it a set-up to make sure I didn't suspect her… or did she do it without your knowledge? Or…' Becky's voice became that of a sour primary school child. 'Was Clara jealous? Was that it? Was she trying to stop you – but still making sure you got away?'

Clara laughed. 'You and your stories, Becky. Someone called the police. Marcus and I were in town, liaising with

Hanlon. It was luck that we heard the report come in, knew the location, and got there in time. We were lucky.'

Becky arched an eyebrow at the bone mask. 'I would watch her, if I was you. Not totally trustworthy, is she? I should know, if you don't.'

'Let's not waste any more time,' Arkanescu said.

'So what now?' Becky said. 'We play happy families? Go on holiday?'

'Yes,' Arkanescu said. 'In fact, we're going to go back to the place we first met. We'll find that crooked tree. We'll spend some time there.'

Becky gaped for a moment. Then sniggered.

Clara and Arkanescu shared a glance, uncertain.

'Crooked tree? The one near the standing stones? Bent enough for a person to lie on? Is that right?'

'That's right. You remember, Becky.'

'No... I don't quite recall.'

'You do,' Arkanescu insisted. 'The crooked tree. Where your family died. You know the place. What happened there.'

'No, you don't understand. I don't recall, because it doesn't exist. I made the crooked tree up. Just a little detail, to see if you were paying attention. Something for you to focus on, to use in your therapy sessions. And it was a guiding light for me, too. So that any time you mentioned the crooked tree, I would know what was real and what wasn't. It was a safety net. In the end, it's trapped you. I take it you had a false beard?'

Arkanescu chuckled. 'Silly me.'

'That's right. Silly you. You can take the mask off now, Dr Fullerton.'

And he did.

# 64

Dr Fullerton grinned.

Even as he laid the bone mask on the ground, the lineaments of the figure seemed to contract, away from the giant he'd become. With the fake beard and hairpiece removed, the lower half of his face resolved itself into part of the image she'd seen on her camera shots from Romania.

'You were clever with it, I suppose,' Becky sneered. 'Hiding your tracks – literally, I mean.'

He raised one boot. 'Size fourteen. Platform heels; padded inside. To throw the police off the scent. And to give me a few more inches in height, too. You could say I was forensically aware. You know what they say. Once a copper, always a copper.'

'I'll say this for you – you've got one hell of a CV since you left the Stasi. IT, psychotherapy... You're a real renaissance man.'

Fullerton grinned. 'Isn't it brilliant? God bless a free education system. I had an interest in the field given my studies back in Mother Russia. The Stasi were keen on psychological techniques. I had a complete education.' Fullerton affected a mock Eurasian accent at this last part.

'I got it wrong,' Becky said. 'I knew you, from the top of your head to your toes. I always knew I would recognise you instantly – I'd catch your scent. I'd bark like a dog if you got within ten miles of me. I knew... but you were right there in front of me, all that time.'

'Yep, actually, you knew nothing,' Fullerton said. 'You said you were a terrible patient – I say you were superb. I planted all kinds of things in your head – while you were awake, not while you were under. I suggested to you that I was a giant, a monster. Taller than I am. Then I kept suggesting that Dr Fullerton was only a tiny little fella. But I was only little old me, all along. Not quite a short arse, as I'd suggested to you many times, but six foot isn't so tall these days, I guess. A happy medium, you could say.'

The edges of reality seemed to flicker and warp; Becky no longer trusted her own eyes. Fullerton might have been a black hole, sucking in the light. 'You couldn't have got away with this on your own.'

'That's right – I had plenty of help along the way. There's a lot of people like me out there, Becky. Everything's possible. And as you and your buddies found out, before I offed most of them, I've got lots of connections, all over the place. Including my girlfriend, right here, in the police, at the top of the cold case team looking for me. Give us a twirl, Clara.'

And she did, mock-coquettishly.

'I went by lots of names, but Arkanescu was the one I couldn't quite let go of. I even carried it into my old job with the police. Over time I scrubbed it. Of course, I led you towards that identity, once I knew you were trying to hack into the police system. I rubbed pieces out here and there, and left crumbs in their place – traces towards the real me. Just enough to get you interested, not enough to blow my cover unless you knew where to look. It's so easy to move identities once you're in with the bricks at the police. If you know the right guy, you can create anything for yourself, move anywhere. I even created a fake IT specialist at Interpol. All to throw you off what should have been obvious. That I was grooming you and setting you up. From the very start.'

'And what about the party tonight? All those people who got arrested? What about them?'

'That's taken care of a problem. I've enjoyed the January Orchestra over the years. It's given me a lot of pleasure. They're like-minded souls. But it was time to tie up some loose ends. Firstly, your annoying little buddies; then January itself. So thanks for that.'

'You're dreaming. You'll never get out of here – every single one of them will rat you out.'

Fullerton shrugged. 'They can't rat anyone out – they don't know me. Never have. Never seen my face. There isn't a trace of me anywhere. If the police are lucky they'll find some other fake IDs I left dotted around. Ones I know for a fact you didn't find. Cul-de-sacs, blind corners. Dead men's shoes. Meanwhile, they all go to jail, and most likely never get out. But... let's talk about you.' He nodded towards Clara.

Becky did not resist as her sister placed her hands behind her back and snapped the handcuffs over her wrists.

'Oh, I always had plans for you, Becky. Always.' His fingers ran along the length of her jaw, tilting her head. 'I know what you're thinking. "Stockholm Syndrome. I'll never join him." But you will. There are so many ways I can convince you. Like I did with lovely Clara. I've got so many great secrets to share, so many adventures for us all to have. A family at last.'

Becky's throat clicked twice, and Clara had to strain to hear her. 'He'll kill you,' Becky croaked. 'You're not useful any more. I'm your replacement. He doesn't need you. You know too much. For god's sake, shoot him, get this finished.'

Clara stroked her hair; Becky tried to twist away. 'Silly girl,' Clara said. 'You silly, sweet girl. You can't see it, can you? You can't see how beautiful it's going to be.'

'You can't be fucking serious.'

'You know...' Clara's eyes misted over. 'The first time I saw your face on that afternoon, I thought I'd lose control. I was freaking out, seeing you again. I was so sure you'd recognise me. Recognise *something*. We'd gone over the scenario so many times, but even so...'

'Let's go,' Fullerton said. He shoved Becky, keeping the gun on her.

'How did you get in the car?' she asked.

'The magic of the movies.'

'You were in the boot. You must have been. Then you got through into the back seat.'

'Don't worry yourself about that. I'm surprised you didn't twig what was happening, though. A police car was the only possible way I was getting out of those woods without being seen. Now, enough of the chat.' Fullerton clapped his hands.

That sound was followed by a gunshot.

# 65

Fullerton gasped and jerked forward onto his face.

Behind him, Marcus, eyes bulging above a ruined face still trailing blood, his former smirk obliterated, lurched to his feet. There was no sign of a lower jaw, and what must have been his tongue lolled wetly.

Clara turned the gun towards him.

Becky yelled: 'Hey! Sis!'

As Clara turned, Becky leapt forward, head-butting her full on the nose.

Clara fell away with a single, high squeak. She landed flat on her back, spread-eagled, blood streaming from her nose, eyes rolled back in her head.

Becky saw the gun in Marcus' hands waver as she crouched, back turned, her cuffed hands scrabbling for purchase in Clara's coat pocket. Then she remembered the stun gun, spitting uselessly at Fullerton's chest. She screamed, 'Marcus, finish him off – he's got a bulletproof vest!'

It was already too late; another gunshot convulsed the air, and this time Marcus stumbled backward, hitting the side wall of the cottage then sliding down it, trailing a long crimson curtain down the whitewashed brick.

From the ground, Fullerton fired again, destroying what was left of Marcus' face. Then he got to his feet and fired twice more at the prone body.

As the gunshots faded, Fullerton winced, rubbing the small of his back. 'That's not the first time it's happened to me... Come to think of it, counting your Taser, it's not the first time it's happened to me *tonight*. I'll never get used to it. Now come on. Into the boot with you, Becky.'

She stood up; Clara's gun was in one hand, still behind her back. Fullerton's brow wrinkled sardonically then he raised the gun at Becky's head.

'Please,' he said. 'Unless you know some spectacular gun stunts with your hands tied behind your back, and I'm talking Sammy Davis Junior levels of talent, don't bother.'

Becky dropped the gun, then let him approach two more steps.

She kicked out at his knee. He mostly stopped it with his shin, but there was good, satisfying purchase. He stumbled, and she jerked a shoulder, smacking it into the side of his face. Again, this had only a cursory effect, but he was off-balance enough to merit trying something more spectacular.

Becky planted a knee in his groin, then another somewhere around his ribs; as he fell forwards, she hitch-kicked him full in the face. He cried out and tried to turn with the momentum of the blow. As she wound up to crash another kick into his head, he had spun on the heel of his hand and hooked a leg round her calf.

Becky was pulled onto her face, with no means of breaking the fall. Then he was on his feet, and at her.

She turned her head from most of the punches as he screamed in a diabolical temper, flailing at her uncontrollably, but not all of them. Her arms and back were pummelled; one ear exploded, a couple of her back teeth splintered; then another punch smacked her cheek, on the same spot he'd hit her earlier.

She tasted dirt and blood.

A kick into the meat of her thigh deadened her leg. Then she was airborne, lifted cleanly and easily off the ground. She was raised above his head, then hurled downwards. She expected his knee to interrupt her spinal column, but only the ground met her. She had no chance of breaking the fall while still in handcuffs.

The earth stole her breath, shuddering her to the core.

She was aware of Clara stumbling to her feet, hand pressed to her face.

'Tell them the bitch stole your gun and went crazy,' he hissed, lifting her pistol from the ground. 'Knocked you unconscious, stole your gun, shot Marcus. Similar calibres; you couldn't do that by yourself. It makes sense.'

Clara nodded numbly. Then she saw Becky and ran forward. She managed one kick into Becky's ribs before he stopped her.

'Time for that later, my darling. Time enough.' He slapped her across the back, checking her. 'Let's not waste our chance. We can make it look like she escaped and vanished. All evidence will show she attacked you.'

Clara nodded, blood trickling between her fingertips.

'Good. And now,' he wheezed, turning to Becky, 'as I said before we were interrupted... let's get in the car.'

He left no room for doubt, or manoeuvre. She was hogtied as well as handcuffed, a rope from the back of the car looping round the cuffs and forcing her legs back. Her joints stung.

For a brief moment she wondered if he would cripple her, as he had crippled her father all those years ago.

As if reading her mind, he pondered hamstringing her, his long knife poised against the meat of her thighs. 'Shall I? Shall I?' he exhorted himself. 'Hmm.'

Then he reconsidered; with one last look at her sister's face, ruined once more and oozing blood, Becky was thrown in the boot.

He grinned at her, face framed by the edges of the boot. 'Make yourself comfortable.'

There was a movement in the trees behind him. Then someone yelled, in English: 'Hold it right there!'

Hanlon. Other voices joined him, speaking in French.

Fullerton's face fell, and he lurched away. Clara cried out and raised the gun; there was a single crack, and Becky saw her leg jerked away as if on a string, pitching her onto her face.

The boot slammed shut. Gunfire crackled; someone screamed, a young man.

'She's in the boot! Hold your fire!' Hanlon cried.

The engine started; the car roared away.

# 66

*Wriggle room.* Becky had very little. But tucked tight in her hand was the ring of keys she'd taken from Clara's pockets.

Gently, ignoring the rocking of the car, she groped for the key which felt the right size, then transferred it to her other hand. She could move the other hand just enough, wrists strained fit to tear in half, to scrabble the key against the lock.

Sweat soaked her face and stung her eyes, though she had no light whatsoever to see with. Music pounded through the vehicle, indeterminate at first. Then she picked out the haunting drear of steel guitar and realised he had tuned the radio to a country station.

'Just one more indignity,' she muttered to herself.

Hope flared as the key slithered into the lock. One turn and she was free… But it would not turn. It was the wrong key, after all.

Becky rededicated herself, extricating the key and trying again with another, every physical and mental agony intensified. She had compartmentalised the pain, already thinking through to the next stage. Figuring out how to move the back seat of the car from inside the boot. This was surely how he had managed to get out of the boot and into the back of the car in the first place. His hypnosis might have distorted Becky's perceptions, but they had not made him invisible, and the boot was the only way he could have stayed out of sight, escaped from the forest and then crept into the car.

So there had to be a way. Something he had studied and practised. A mechanism to exploit, or a knack a regular user would have.

*Look for opportunities, no matter how small.*

Meanwhile, Becky's hands searched for another key – a smaller one, one she'd automatically discounted before. She'd try them all if she had to, systematically.

Then the car slowed down. She picked out a faint whining sound. It grew louder as the car slowed.

A siren. And the roar of a motorcycle.

The country and western was stilled a moment after the car stopped, and in her cramped pocket she imagined the chilly blue lights flailing over the entire scene. She wondered how Fullerton's bloodied face would look in the officer's torchlight. She kept quiet, continuing to fight at the keys, relishing the opportunity of an unmoving foundation beneath her for a moment.

'Sir – can you show me your paperwork, please?' The French police officer sounded young.

'Sure,' Fullerton said, amiably. Then came two gunshots, jolting her.

The front door of the car opened; she heard Fullerton pacing outside, cursing. Something slid across the road;

then came the sound of a bike being wheeled away, then the crunch of undergrowth.

Fullerton got back in the car and they sped off, faster than before. The steel guitar resumed.

Becky fed the key into the lock. It turned smartly; the cuffs separated. Hope surged.

Next she tugged at her wristwatch. Part of the strap came away, revealing a spring-loaded hatch which she prised apart with ragged fingernails. Inside was a blade, no larger than that found in a pencil sharpener, but keener yet.

*You don't know about all my toys.*

The rope coiled round her legs was cut thoroughly quickly and cleanly, and she howled against the gag in silent agony as her legs cramped up, suddenly freed.

Next, her hands searched the edges of the chair facing onto the boot, looking for a way in. She found it almost immediately, a long slit in the lining which allowed access to the gauzy stuffing inside, wrapped round the metal superstructure. Her fingers found the lever quickly.

No sense in making it complicated, Becky thought, grimly. She pulled the switch and felt the seat shift forwards.

She gave herself a few moments to allow circulation to re-inflate her burning veins. She braced herself for sudden light, and action. Then she hammered the seat forward with the flat of her hand.

Becky saw his eyes flare in the mirror. Then she was upon him, a rat sprung from a trap.

She smashed an elbow into the corner of the jaw, spinning his head nearly 180 degrees and cracking the window opposite. Not sure if he was unconscious or not, she snapped a punch at him with her other hand, flattening his nose with an eggshell crackle.

The car veered across the road, splintering a barrier; their headlights sliced the lanes to the left, into the path of an oncoming car.

Becky gripped the wheel; shocked faces were lit up by the headlights as the other vehicle swerved out of their path just in time.

Fullerton's hand hooked into her hair and pulled her head back as she tried to clamber over the seat and force her foot onto the brake. No handbrake; it was one of the newer models, an automatic mechanism.

His free hand grasped for her throat but she twisted her head away, then drove the heel of her free hand into his right eye socket with a quick, sharp snap of her wrist.

He screamed above the steel guitar, but kept hold of her hair, jerking her back. She went with the momentum, sagging, using the extra space this generated to bring both her legs round the front seat and into the driver's compartment.

Her head touched the passenger door. Then she hooked her legs round his neck.

Becky flexed her hips, and his roaring and yelling ceased instantly; the hand entangled in her hair went limp.

Becky struggled to a sitting position and saw with horror that the car was continuing on its path across the opposite side of the road, veering at a less severe angle. Another crash barrier was skittled; the car glanced off a tree, and Becky and Fullerton were hurled together in a mockery of an embrace.

Then the dark, moon-dappled lake filled the windscreen. Becky finally reached the middle pedal, but it was too late. They fell, bodies levitating briefly from the seats.

Then, with a roar, the car was gulped down into black water.

# 67

The car angled down, engine gurgling to a stop, headlights illuminating a steep descent into about ten feet of water. Weeds waved as the car reached the bottom, sudden and green amid a puff of startled mud as all four tyres anchored in the silt.

Water surged in through the cracked windscreen, gushing over Fullerton's face as he lay against the door, unconscious. Becky took a breath, felt the water reach her shoulders, her chin, her nose.

The pressure had to equalise, she thought, trying to control her panic.

When the water's cold fingers reached her eyes she pulled the door handle.

The black tide was like a bomb going off, encompassing everything. Becky panicked for a moment, head striking the roof of the car as the remaining air was stolen and replaced with frigid water. Her fingers found the edge of the door and she pulled herself out, bubbles tumbling from her mouth.

She kicked hard, mindful of the sodden miserable drag of her jeans and her boots and jacket. Becky struck out, crossing the beam of light as, incredibly, the headlights persisted.

Her feet found the roof of the car; she tensed her thighs, then launched herself upwards.

Her head broke the surface, and she screamed into the darkness.

The headlights were an ominous twin glow on the surface, as if an immense creature encircled her from below. Becky dragged her damp hair off her face, took two or three gasps, then dived down, heading for the glow.

Visibility was poor, the lights her only guide. This time the drag of clothes and boots helped; her fingers found the door frame, and she could just about make out the face, the blank eyes, swaying in the water as she took hold of his shoulder.

He would not budge; seatbelt, of course. She reached in, finding the mechanism by instinct. Becky's lungs burned as she tugged the limp body free, braced her feet on the car bonnet and windscreen, and leapfrogged up towards the surface.

Her face only just cleared the water, and she gasped, almost losing her hold on the dead weight below. Then she kicked towards the sandy bank, where the tyre tracks still glistened in the muck, trailing down towards the water.

It grew shallow very quickly, and she heaved the body out.

The face was blank, the eyes sightless, the neck and jawbone twisted at an uncanny angle like a toy treated poorly by a truculent child.

Becky took a deep breath and pinched the ruined nose. Then her lips locked with his.

# 68

They found clothes for her – way too big, old jeans roll-necked above heavy boots, a pullover several sizes too big that might have been better employed as a continental quilt. Becky wondered who they'd belonged to; why the police had kept them.

She still shivered in Hanlon's car, despite the dry clothes and the coffee in her hands. She'd been given painkillers which had soothed all but the dull aches. She dared not look at herself in the car mirror just yet.

'I want to thank you for saving my bacon,' she said.

Hanlon drew his hands down his face. Becky saw that he had badly-bitten nails, almost painful to look at. 'You can thank Marcus for that. He suspected something. He told me she'd been behaving erratically. Not calling things in. Too willing to go off-message. Said she'd been shooting you down in private, disregarding what he thought was good intelligence. He suspected she was involved. He was *listening* to you.'

'He was a good copper. An arsehole, mind you. But a good copper.' It was hard to believe she'd watched him die; one more jolt. 'What's going to happen to her?'

Hanlon sipped his coffee. 'She's been charged with... just about everything. I'm betting she'll claim all kinds of things. I suspect an insanity plea is coming. Maybe justifiably, I don't know.'

'She's sane, all right. Sick, but sane. I don't want to... I can't even think about that at the moment.'

Hanlon cleared his throat. 'If I was you, I'd take a long holiday, Becky. Far, far away. I wouldn't think about anything. You got him. Be satisfied with that. It's over.' He laid a hand on her shoulder. She wanted to sag against it. 'It's *over.*'

*No, it isn't. Not quite.*


His daughter had committed the sin of wearing dark glasses so as to appear inconspicuous. She was tall, slim and gothic, so the effect was more akin to painting a target on her back. Becky watched her moving through the mall, waiting until she bid farewell to a similarly attired boy her own age before making her move.

'Zoe?'

The girl turned. Becky could see the frown crease her brow above the glasses. 'Who are you?'

'I'm Becky Morgan. I'm the one your father tried to kill. I'm the one whose family he slaughtered. I'm the one whose sister he kidnapped.'

The girl turned, alarmed, and fished in her jacket for a phone.

Becky held up her hands. 'I just want to talk. We're out in public. There's probably a video camera on us, right now. I'd have to be crazy to do anything to you.'

'Crazy is right.'

'Look. There's a girl out there. This one.' Becky showed her an image on her phone; a smiling girl with long, fine curly hair. 'She's the daughter of a Russian businessman who went missing along with his family recently. I've a feeling she might still be alive. This is something your dad likes to do. Your dad's movements match up with hers. She might not be the only one. He kept lots of girls, over the years. He held some back. He kept some of them alive, after he'd killed their families. He likes to play a long game. He spends years torturing them, brainwashing them. My sister was one. He did it to me, too, in his way, over a lot of years.'

'I've told the police everything I know.'

'I know what you told the police. But I have to know if you're telling the truth. Where does he keep them?'

'Leave me alone. There's an officer within two minutes of here, and you'll get arrested.'

'I don't think you've told them everything,' Becky said. 'You're his daughter; you must know some of his little secrets. You must have a suspicion.'

'Why don't you go and ask my mother?'

'Your mother's unwell. She genuinely didn't know a thing. Maybe you think you'll be blamed. But you won't. You can't be. You can tell me, and I'll fix it. I'm not with the police. I don't have to follow any rules. I'll say I figured something out. They'll believe me. I figured everything else out. I've been trying to find him for most of my life; I'll make it sound plausible. I know they tore the house apart, but he wasn't stupid enough to leave any traces where he lived. I think he might have kept his prisoners close by. It makes sense for him to do that. Do you have any idea?'

The girl took off her dark glasses. Her eyes were clear, but unfocused. Becky wondered if she'd been drinking. 'You got a pen and paper? I never told you this. We never spoke. Got it?'

Becky nodded eagerly. 'Please. Anything.'

'There's a place he goes to in the woods. There's something up there. My boyfriend tracked him one day with his drone. For a laugh, you know. Actually, I wondered if he was having an affair.' She smiled at that. 'He disappeared into the trees, and we lost him. It's about a mile and a half down the road from the house...'

Becky pulled up in a lay-by. It was disconcerting to emerge from the cool interior of an air-conditioned car into tinder-dry, hard-baked summer air.

She checked the map saved to her phone, tightened the laces on her boots, and set off up the path.

The steeper it got, the more confident she became. Wasn't this just like him? she thought. This was the middle of nowhere, not part of a walking trail marked on any map – and yet, what a risk he had taken.

That was if what the girl had told her was true, of course.

The wooded area where his daughter and her boyfriend had lost track of him with the drone wasn't too dense – she could see through the trees to more open, hilly country, where the sunlight overlaid the emerald with gold. But in here, among the woods, it was dark.

Here, among the standing stones. Less than six miles from his front door.

Becky's eye was drawn to the right spot before she'd consciously processed it. She stood at a line of bushes which were at odds with the summer verdant forest round her – bare branches, hawthorns, nettles.

When she came forward for a closer look, the ground became hard, and hollow.

There was a trap door under her feet, right in the forest floor.

She wondered idly if he'd booby-trapped it; a parting gift, to be sure. Maybe a crossbow bolt between the eyes, or perhaps a funhouse lever that would throw her onto sharpened stakes. One last laugh.

But underneath the trapdoor there was a bricked-up space, the walls slimy with earth and moisture. Flies butted her face, and a stench of human waste caused her to flinch.

Something moved in the filth down below, something large. Becky thought it was a badger, or something larger still – maybe a wild boar, given this part of the world. She saw filthy, clotted hair and muck. It was only when her eye picked out hands and ragged cloth over a bare ankle that Becky realised she was looking at a person.

'Hello?'

Two eyes widened amid a mud-encrusted face.

'I've come to rescue you. You're safe. The man is gone. He can't harm you any more.'

Becky dropped down a rope; the figure beneath scrambled up it, terrifyingly fast. She seized Becky's hand, but before Becky could take hold of her, the girl found her feet, and sprinted away from her, wailing at an unbearably high volume. She sprinted down the path, parting ferns and ignoring the snapping nettles.

Becky ran after her, gaining quickly. The girl sprinted into the forest, glancing back occasionally, eyes bulging in sheer fright and panic.

'It's okay,' Becky said. 'You're safe, I promise. You're safe.'

The girl burst into the sunshine into the open hillside. The sudden, strong afternoon light shocked her. Then she sank to the floor.

Becky approached slowly, hands raised. She felt an ancient panic rise in her throat, seeping out of her chest. 'I promise... I promise, I'm here to help. I'm going to make sure they take care of you. Oh, you poor lass.'

'No!' the girl wailed, hands flailing, as Becky approached. 'No! Leave me alone! Don't touch me! Don't touch me!'

# 69

'Your uniform doesn't fit you,' said one of the patients. He had a cheek; he was wearing an ancient set of star-spangled pyjamas. The man was being escorted out of the toilet by another nurse as Becky passed them. The nurse who was accompanying the patient, a beautifully clear-skinned girl with dark red hair, merely wrinkled the corner of her mouth and shook her head at the man.

'You're a charmer to the last, Richard. Come on.'

Becky smiled understandingly and moved on down the corridor.

Entry to the high dependency unit was strictly controlled, and getting access to a pass was a risky business. Bernard had had to work hard to clone one, then mock up a fake ID that might pass muster. But he was good at what he did.

Becky had to give her spiel to the ward sister, a tiny Scottish woman with eyes like bore holes in a glacier. Despite facing near-feral levels of suspicion, her paperwork and pass checked out. As did her story about studying terribly difficult patients.

'What was the name of your supervisor?' the ward sister asked, as Becky was taken down to room sixteen. 'A couple of the girls in here studied at Brackley College. You should say hello.'

'Fotheringham,' Becky replied, over her shoulder. 'That was his name. Bit of a lech. Good nurse, though. You know how it is.'

The ward sister did.

He was guarded, of course. The policeman was young, but seemingly hewn from a mountainside, with a chin that would have struck sparks against metal. He checked her credentials for a long time, then double-checked it against the visitors' list, but said absolutely nothing to her before nodding her inside.

In the room, he was braced at an angle, a ventilator and heart rate monitor keeping a steady beat by the bedside.

He noticed her, right away. She saw it in his eyes.

'Don't get up,' Becky said, pulling up a chair.

He inclined his head, almost gracefully. There were still staples in his jaw, and his eyelid was closed up tight, as if it had been welded shut. Ugly yellow bruises signposted where surgery had taken place.

Becky tested the springiness of his pale blue mattress with her hand. 'Well, that looks comfortable. I wouldn't mind getting some of that in my house. Maybe you could move in with me? Wouldn't that be something?'

He said nothing, sniffing slightly.

'I won't take up too much of your time. Just to let you know that I'm around, and, if I need to, I can just slip into your room, any time of day or night. You don't even need to be awake. Just think of it. Your eyes open up – you can still open both your eyes, right? – and there I'll be. Like your own guardian angel.'

Becky watched his chest rise and fall in time with the ventilator.

'I'm glad I've had the chance to speak to you. I dunno how doped up they're keeping you. Not too much, I imagine, with all that nerve damage. But I know you'll want to thank me for keeping you alive. I always wanted you alive, you know. No one believed me when I told them, but it's true. This is the best of all possible worlds. And you're only alive because people were kind. Those people we nearly crashed into, when we went into the lake. They acted so quickly to get help. The air ambulance was there in minutes. You might have just slipped away. Wouldn't that have been a fucking tragedy?

'But now, I get to watch you... existing. Any time I like. I can even check on your progress remotely. That guy I was with... the one you might remember from the forest? Bernard? He's going to keep an especially close eye on you. It's almost like he bears a grudge or something.'

No response. Just the rise and fall of his chest, deep and regular controlled breathing.

'The slightest change in your condition, and I'll drop everything to come here. But let's hope there are no emergencies, and you live the rest of your life in peace and quiet, right here. They're taking good care of you, I see. Arse wiped, pits washed... even a shave, I see. How the other half lives! Your every need catered for. Well, not *every* need, obviously.'

His heart rate had begun to climb. A new colour kicked in on the monitor, moving from green to yellow.

'In a way it's a shame your neck had to break. I had wanted to disable you, but not quite so severely as that. Knee ligaments split, maybe the loss of an arm or two, something like that. But *paralysed*... What a drag! And I'll never hear you speak again, either. Pity. Maybe you could get one of those blinking systems in place with the nurses? I hear they can train people to do that. It'll take a good while, but then, spare time's not exactly your biggest problem, is it?'

She got up and drew nearer. The eyes followed her.

'Don't be alarmed. I'm not here to snuff you. I brought you something. It'll remind you of the good times, and maybe bring you some comfort. You take care, Dr Fullerton. I've got an appointment with a family member now. You rest easy. You'll need your strength, for the long, long years ahead. I wish you good fortune and a long life. I really do.'

She placed the mask over his head, gently, almost tenderly. She glared into the glassy black eyes until the heart monitor pinged into the red, triggering an alarm.

The other nurses burst in, joined by the policeman. There was no mask on Fullerton's head by then, of course.

'I'm not sure what happened,' Becky said, backing off to allow the others to take over. 'I think he saw me and it upset him.'

'We've got him,' the ward sister said. 'It's happened before. I need you to get Dr Penrose – he's on the ward.'

Becky nodded, and slipped out the door.

# 70

Jack Tullington's head parted the roses. His hat snagged on them, tilting at a weird angle before he snatched it off his head, swearing.

Becky smiled from her doorway, folding her arms. 'How did you know I was a flowers girl?'

'I didn't. In fact, I thought you were the polar opposite of a flowers girl. It just seemed like the most uninspired way to make an abject apology.'

'Mission accomplished.' Becky took the bouquet from his hands. 'Though you've nothing to apologise for. Angus coughed. To everything. He said you'd nothing to do with it. Hey, there's some brotherly love, at least.'

'Yeah. At least.'

'Take your hat off, Jack, for goodness' sake. You're like an undertaker out there.'

'I wanted to see how you're doing, truth be told,' Jack said, once they were sat down.

'I'm fine.' Becky winced as she sat down. 'I did my back in kicking some clown in the head, mind you. Started playing up days after I did it. Is this what happens to men when they get over 40, Jack? With your beer bellies and all?'

'I wouldn't know,' Jack said, gazing into the middle distance, until she laughed, properly.

'Thanks for coming to the memorial.'

'Least I could do,' he said, quietly.

'How about Cecilia? I didn't see her there.'

'You know what? Cecilia's had enough. She sold up and went to New Zealand. Clara still being alive, and knowing what she'd done... Cecilia just turned the cards in. She's got a friend out there. Someone she writes to, would you believe. Gone to see out her days on the other side of the world. I'm not sure I blame her, either.'

'No. Jesus.' He scratched his chin. 'Incidentally... Job's waiting for you, whenever you want to come back to it. Though I wouldn't grudge you a shot at publishing a book in your own way. We didn't sign a contract, after all.'

'We didn't, but we had an agreement. That's good enough for me, Jack. Joint byline, though. Me and Rosie Banning.'

He nodded. 'Always the goody two shoes of the family, weren't you? Speaking of which...'

'Oh, her.' Becky brightened up. 'We've started corresponding.'

'You're joking.'

'Nope.' Becky crossed to a kitchen drawer and pulled out some loose handwritten sheets. 'I can't see her yet, Jack. Maybe I never will. Maybe, in my head, she's better off dead. She's been in touch, though, a lot. I've written back, too. It's been lovely. You'd think nothing had happened. It's her. She is in there, somewhere.'

He glanced at one letter, shaking his head. 'Cookery shows? High teas? Is this some kind of sisterly code language?'

'Nope. It seems she's a killer in the kitchen. So to speak. She runs a class. The other girls in her block must be delighted. If this decade has taught us anything, it's that you can't underestimate the social clout of good baking.'

'After she gets sentenced, she might look back on those times with fondness, I guess.' Jack's grin faltered when he saw that Becky's face was stricken. 'Sorry. It's fucked up. Everything is fucked up. What else can I say?'

'Not a lot.'

'So what's next for you?'

'A tattoo, I'm thinking. A long one.' She indicated her back, just to the right of her spine. 'Been considering it for a while. I was thinking a big snake, or a dragon, but that seems trite.'

'How about a really long, thin butterfly?'

Becky snorted. 'Actually, I was thinking "Harley Davidson", in big 1970s bubble lettering, angled to the right.' She drained the last of her coffee. 'I'll be back at my desk in a couple of weeks, Jack. Maybe make it three. In the meantime, the police don't need me, and I'm going to take off somewhere hot, and try not to think for a little while.'

'Not a bad idea. Not going alone, I hope?'

'I'm not sure who I'll take,' Becky said.

There were other letters in the drawer besides Clara's, in a different hand, written in French. Ones she had not wanted Jack Tullington to see.

Then the buzzer sounded. Becky answered the intercom.

Aaron Stilwell's face filled the video screen. He grinned, mock-earnest, and winked. Becky buzzed the door, and let him in.

'You've got company, I see,' Jack said, replacing his hat. 'I'll head off, kiddo. Hey – that your boyfriend? He looks pale.'

'No, not a boyfriend. Not really.'

'Oh.' Jack stood up straight. 'One of *those* sorts of set-ups, is it?'

'One of what sort of set-ups?'

'Spot of shopping? Long lunches? Tiny little dogs? Incredibly mean-spirited comments and gossip?'

'Ah. No. How quaint of you. No, he's not one of *those*, as you put it. At least, I don't think so.'

'Just a mate, then?'

'Something like that. Maybe a bit more.'

'Like what?'

She smiled. 'Family.'


Forever


'Oof, I can feel that on my solar panel,' Becky's father said.

'You should have worn a sun hat,' her mother replied. 'Like everyone else.'

'Ah, the Red Spot of Jupiter's a good look, anyway.' Becky's father patted the top of his head. He worried too much; a little more scalp was showing through the top of his head, but not too much. It was more of a 50p than a chimp's arse.

They were on their way to the lake. The cloud had burned away, now, and the breeze had stilled. It was more like high summer than spring, and their father was uncomfortable in the rising heat. But it still seemed like a perfect day to Becky. The heat haze blurring grass where the ground ran high lent the day a blissful air of unreality. Oneiric, she knew, was the word.

'I should have brought my drawing paper,' she said. 'I want to sketch this.'

'Or, you could simply take a picture,' Clara simpered. 'Like normal people.'

The setting was perfect, the lake – more of a glorified pond, really – smooth and untroubled. The boat, though, was less impressive.

'Will we all fit on that?' their mother asked, glancing at the rowing boat. The paint had flaked off in patches, looking more like battle scars rather than normal wear and tear, the old wood showing through like knuckles on a clenched fist.

Howie was delighted by the craft, though, as was his father.

'Make 'em walk the plank!' the boy yelled, tearing towards the boat.

'To the sharks!' answered his father.

Once they were inside and steadied, they criss-crossed the lake. The water was lazy in the slow heat and pocked with thousands of insects, barely rising to a ripple with each slap of the paddles.

They sang high and loud, for the first crossing. 'Row, row, row your boat...'

Even Clara joined in, out of the side of her mouth, though she rolled her eyes at their father's astonishingly good natural tenor.

By the second crossing they were tired and sweaty, and brought the boat back to the jetty through unsteady navigation by Becky.

Howie helped to tie the rope, and after a picnic, their father took them deeper into the forest.

'There's a stone circle round here,' their father said. 'From thousands of years ago.'

'Did cavemen make it?' Howie asked.

'Kind of.'

'It's a place where they held sacrifices,' Clara said. 'They kill little boys out here.'

'Yes,' Becky said, 'and mouthy older sisters, too. They tie them up, then they put gags in their mouth to stop them speaking. Then they take a knife…'

'*Becky…*' her mother said, frowning over the tops of her sunglasses.

'Do they?' Howie asked. 'Cool!'

They found it soon enough. As their mother and father sat in the shade, the children chased each other round the stones. Howie leapt on top of one of the flattened slabs, declaring himself king. The girls fought to prise him off, tickling him when they finally did so.

Their laughter rose high and sweet into the air, rich with the promise of the summer to come; in the shade, their parents drew closer and smiled, their mother leaning into their father's shoulder. He kissed the top of her head, and held her tight, and they watched their children play. Together, they might have been the only people in the world.

# Acknowledgements

Special thanks to Hannah and the team at Aria for giving me a chance, to Vicky for spreading the word, and to Sue for the last-gasp goal-line clearances. Also thanks to anyone who put up with the typing and gave me advice in the writing of this book, including Marty. There are loads of writing buddies who have been brilliant to me over the years, including Liz, Brendan, Hereward and many more – too many to list in fact!

And most of all, thanks always to my wife Claire for all her help and support.

# About P.R. Black

Author and journalist P.R. BLACK lives in Yorkshire, although he was born and brought up in Glasgow.

When he's not driving his wife and two children to distraction with all the typing, he enjoys hillwalking, fresh air and the natural world, and can often be found asking the way to the nearest pub in the Lake District.

His short stories have been published in several books including the Daily Telegraph's Ghost Stories and the Northern Crime One anthology. His Glasgow detective, Inspector Lomond, is appearing in Ellery Queen's Mystery Magazine.

He took the runner-up spot in the 2014 Bloody Scotland crime-writing competition with "Ghostie Men". His work has also been performed on stage in London by Liars' League.

He has also been shortlisted for the Red Cross International Prize, the William Hazlitt essay prize and the Bridport Prize.

# Hello from Aria

We hope you enjoyed this book! Let us know, we'd love to hear from you.

We are Aria, a dynamic digital-first fiction imprint from award-winning independent publishers Head of Zeus. At heart, we're avid readers committed to publishing exactly the kind of books we love to read – from romance and sagas to crime, thrillers and historical adventures. Visit us online and discover a community of like-minded fiction fans!

We're also on the look out for tomorrow's superstar authors. So, if you're a budding writer looking for a publisher, we'd love to hear from you. You can submit your book online at ariafiction.com/we-want-read-your-book

You can find us at:
Email: aria@headofzeus.com
Website: www.ariafiction.com
Submissions: www.ariafiction.com/we-want-read-your-book
Facebook: @ariafiction
Twitter: @Aria_Fiction
Instagram: @ariafiction

Printed in Great Britain
by Amazon